"The universe exists for man to discover himself."
1994 Oil Painting by Phillipe

Tall Tales, Half-Truths, and Big Fat Lies!

Tall Tales, Half-Truths, and Big Fat Lies!

Re'al "Bull" Oney, L.L.C.

iUniverse, Inc.
New York Lincoln Shanghai

Tall Tales, Half-Truths, and Big Fat Lies!

iUniverse books may be ordered through booksellers or by contacting:

iUniverse
2021 Pine Lake Road, Suite 100
Lincoln, NE 68512
www.iuniverse.com
1-800-Authors (1-800-288-4677)

ISBN-13: 978-0-595-38155-5 (pbk)
ISBN-13: 978-0-595-82655-1 (cloth)
ISBN-13: 978-0-595-82523-3 (ebk)
ISBN-10: 0-595-38155-3 (pbk)
ISBN-10: 0-595-82655-5 (cloth)
ISBN-10: 0-595-82523-0 (ebk)

Printed in the United States of America

PREFACE

The sky was now quickly filling with billowing, suffocating sulfuric acid-rain clouds, which had been blown apart by the sky-high explosions of all of the volcanoes puking their insides out. Mars was a feeble old girl who was dancing her last waltz. The heavens were pitch black, with orange bursts of scattered light plumes that looked as though the devil had awakened in his angriest moment. He was right on time…

"Dr. Dargod Toasts Wife Tara"
Good-bye

(In the Beginning...)

Dargod smiled at her, handed her the drink and then leaned over to caress his wife Tara. They realized their time on planet Mars, as they knew it, was nearly over. Each toasted the other for the last time, as they slowly sipped their bitter nectar from slender decanters, for their love was a bond so strong that neither wanted to say good-bye, nor leave their beloved Mars.

They sat quietly together upon their balcony holding each other closely, allowing the nectar to work its venomous Coup de Grace, a sad farewell. The venomous nectar would put them under, each into a deathlike state; a motionless state, from which their demise could only be reversed, when someday, someone else, could be knowledgeable enough to inject into them the prescribed contents from the vile of antitoxin that was placed nearby.

Extracted venom, taken from a known deadly vertebrate, was used in part of this miraculous mixture, which would reduce their heart beats into minute, silent impulses, capable of keeping their blood from freezing, and not decomposing, while also allowing their hearts to be at an almost complete state of rest.

If the planet burned, it all was for naught. If no one returned to Mars, it was for naught. But Dr.Dargod was relying on his calculations of preparedness that Mars would freeze, not burn.

Those were his verbal commands given to this family; those were his written instructions that became our family's promise. Dargod's words of wisdom, and the wisdom of all Martian life, which our father had diligently recorded, and then arranged so that it would be repeatedly spoken from headpieces that would play over and over again. We, his children would lay asleep, deep into a hypnotic-type state of learning. It was the knowledge of the entire universe and the summation of all Martian intellect that filled our brains.

Mother succumbed first from the AloevectorP23 ingestion, as her small body offered a sigh and she closed her eyes and advanced into deep comatose sleep quickly. He checked her pulse, and it was getting feeble. At that moment, he was pleased to see her leave so softly, but the ache within him overwhelmed his heart. "Oh, if she could have only persevered and have seen our children go safely at last," he moaned.

Just then began the deafening drum roll roar of all three untested rocket ships blasting off with bright blue flames mixed with a tremendous turbulence of smoke, and then leaping into the dark billowing clouds. Each was lost to view, one after the other upon its own course of destination, and resounding into a rhythmic burst of enormous energy.

Father knew that his own flesh had escaped upon one of the ships that he helped build in the few months prior. These three ships' successes were the only and the last efforts to offer Martian life's reprieve upon another planet. Dr. Dargod's plan for our destination's planet was Orbital Unit M3AU, Earth.

The other sister ships were sent out on different charted routes in a plan to save our dying civilization known as Martians.

We were the travelers aboard this ship to Earth, forenamed Dargod's Nova; daughter Marietta, son-in-law Josef and I their only son, Jamison. My sister Marietta was with child, brought to light only the week before, but kept quiet since it may have prevented our departure.

The other selected travelers were picked by a lottery and were also young adults from throughout the planet. Those selected were of the highest intellectual degree and came from the finest institutions. We were all aboard our ships and asleep, each now zooming into space.

Dargod was now the last truly living Martian. He picked up Tara and placed her in their coffin that was placed deep within our dwelling, inside his lab. Then he finished his drink and crawled inside beside her and sealed the door. Dargod then awaited the deep sleep. Soon the chill would engulf them and they would exist no more. Dargod had been the Grand Governor and had supervised all of the launch preparations, and now he was done.

Mars's surface was turning into layers of volcanic dust with a center developing into burning, hot molten iron. Volcanoes, unlike anyone had seen, had burst through the crust and then bled our planet dry. The oceans had all dried; the air was descending with less than two percent oxygen, insufficient for mortal life. This entire catastrophe was a result of normal galactic aging of an old planet, heated by the biggest star, but accelerated by foolish men. Life had quickly and systematically surrendered its vitals to a predestined destructive happenstance.

Dargod's life flashed within his mind as he lay beside his lovely wife. He envisioned his boyhood, his young adult and manhood, and the first wonderful meeting of Tara, his soul mate. He sneered as he recalled man's last catastrophe. The explosion, which was just one of several blunders by overzealous, greedy conglomerates that cared nothing for the other Martian people, but pursued a venture only to fill their own purses. Mars had always recovered somewhat from mishaps, but was always left scarred after the fact.

The last major blunder however, which was the industrial invention of radiant-infused, embedded power, also was employed to thrust some of Mars's travel ships. The fuel and hydrogen mixtures, which had always propelled the space ships to transverse the universe at great speeds, had been inflamed with the radiant-fusion treatment, after only a few experiments for successfully increasing the ship's power plant. But then suddenly, there resulted a massive blowout at one industrial plant with its excessive use of the radiant mixtures; that explosion had also choked out all hopeful chances for life's recovery on Mars.

Dargod regretfully recalled that last massive chain-reaction explosion, which engulfed our whole planet and beyond. The effects caused a body to burn when they were outside their abode. Incurable, severely painful sores formed upon most every exposed limb.

We Dargods then remained deep inside our father's cellar lab, where he had previously stored all of his experiments. Those experiments were always protected by huge air filter systems to prevent germ contaminations. But those lab filters began to fail, because the outside environment was so thick with choking volcanic dusts and extreme summer heat.

Death's sleep had quickly become better than life. Father had applied to each of us his own scientific repellent cure. It was the clear liquids squeezed from our own Martian desert flowering medicine plant, called Aloetta. Its affects were amazing, but due to the environmental changes, the outside plants all withered, and died. Only Father's lab specimens remained alive; just long enough to withdraw sufficient liquids to perform Father's life saving tasks.

The rich industrialists had sported their own shielding, protective suits, which they had pre-designed and arranged for, in case of emergencies like this. They knew catastrophe could exist with their meddling. Very few chemical suits existed however; just enough to protect only the greedy themselves, before the oxygenless gases left them also, helplessly suffocating. A doctor's prescription wasn't necessary. Every medicine that could take a life was readily available to all. Suicide was constant, as life was not wanted here. Hell, itself, could have offered a better retirement.

The same greedy, industrialist scourge had hastened to build a recovery life-ship-station. They spent all their wealth, which they hoped would have provided them safe haven far beyond the mess they themselves had forced upon Mars and our people. After all, they couldn't take it with them, could they?

As fate would have it, the devil got his due. The four rocket ships that they first designed were seriously flawed, and only one ship was converted quickly enough to be used for them all. Instruments that they thought unnecessary, some for navigation, some for warning of malfunctions, were taken out to allow extra room. This was their fatal mistake.

As they all crowded onto the one life-ship, the summer winds that blew hard, delayed the launch by weeks. When they all had decided to escape, regardless of the conditions, the planned exit exploded upon the launch pad and cremated the filthy bastards.

"Ha, ha, ha," Dargod exclaimed out loud inside the dome, but to no available ear but his own.

He recalled how at the last the good unselfish Martian people bonded together to hurriedly revamp the remaining three rockets that were left behind, poised for takeoff. They all decided that they must send only a select few into space. They must let future planetarians know of their existence, their learnings, their beliefs, and their mistakes. At the last, these ships were their only hope. These three ships and we passengers represented a hope for an after-life away from Mars for someone. It was all for one and one for all as everyone combined.

Dr. Dargod's expertise was summoned, as he was the Governor Elect, and most noted scientist. He worked to exhaustion redesigning and inventing. In less than three month's time all was completed. As luck would have it, the winter season began and quelled the winds.

A lottery was then performed by our people to withdraw only three individuals' names to be placed aboard the three remaining revamped, but untested, vessels. My father, Dr.Dargod was one name revealed in the drawings. He and my mother Tara quickly decided that Marietta, Josef, and I their son Jamison, must take this trip instead, for it would be many years of unconscious flight, a flight no older being should resort, father demanded; but it was their unselfish ways that made the decision to remain and let us live.

Father had explained to us all before we had left him that we must leave everything behind, except our wisdom, and make new life rebound upon the previously, but lightly-explored planet, called Earth. It was a sickening thought we three shared, but Father convinced us it was his and Mother's only real chance to go on with their lives, at a later time. For our also loving them, we had to obey.

No one really knew if life existed there anymore, it would just be our father's educated guess, but in centuries past, the returning rocket explorations proved that once there was sufficient oxygen there, which would support life. Surprisingly, there were others with human-like characteristics, but they were believed to be dull in the mind.

What other creatures inhabited the Earth's planet was an unknown. But those Martians that had lived there reported that those hairy-like inhabitants were combative and uncivilized to peaceful existence. It would be for each one of us to help them progress as quickly as they could learn. This was also embedded within the recordings.

Mars was an old planet, for which time had quickly run out for all of its inhabitants. And, no matter what man had done to disrupt the balances of the environmental equations, the last event, the bursting of the atmospheric bubble, was the worst. That fierce explosion disintegrated the invisible shield that protected the planet and its inhabitants from the deadly ultra violet rays and excessive heat. The mishap accelerated the whole equation to where everyone could then see exactly what those terrible people had done to us all. They had issued a death warrant with no last minute reprieve.

Dargod eased back into his position next to Tara, found her soft hand and he too succumbed to the juices of the serpent and began his suspended state of being. Life existed on Mars no more, as the planet absorbed its last inhabitants, groaned several more centuries, and then quietly gave up its own life to morbid cold nothingness.

"The Long Voyage"

The Long Voyage
(Chapter two)

Space is an odyssey unlike anything mortal man can imagine. The nova begins all planetary life. A star is born of a womb that is millions of light years deep, perpetuated by crystal gases and swirls of matter that collect upon each other to form new occupants in a huge family of neighborhoods. Each component relies upon the other's magnetic body to push, to shove, and repel, eventually settling into an orbit that suits their contents.

My father had prepared our ship with all the known essentials of knowledge. Ten discs, compiled from the total Martian knowledge that were placed in metal vacuum-sealed enclosures. Each was to be opened, or not to be opened, when their destination was achieved, or failed. The discs' equivalent knowledge could be heard over frequency modulators within our sleeping vault capsules, and continually being repeated to us.

Our father also explained that if in fact Mars offered a life's reprieve to him and Mother, and somehow allowed him to complete another ship, he would seek us on planet Earth. He wrote his promises down and they too were sealed. All this he preplanned to be the guidelines to life on Earth, as they were on Mars; rules that one must follow which were the basic truths of life itself. He called them the "Ten Commitments of Life".

There was no calculated time guarantee as to how long our trip and our state of being comatose could possibly last. If it worked as desired, it could be for eternity. Only time would tell, as Father had made many replacement capsules, and stored them aboard our ships. It would be trial and error, sufficient only if they work properly.

The potion had worked exquisitely upon Father's lab specimens, we knew. On the day of travel, Dr. Dargod had placed his own prize pet species aboard.

He called it a Unicorn; however he hadn't included his mate. Curly was a very small four-legged animal that sported a protruding appendage that resembled a horn between his eyes, but was really an extended tuft of hair.

So it was that our deeply narcotic-induced family of Dargod traveled through a preprogrammed space route in a vessel named Nova. Our bodies were chilled to nearly freezing by exterior airs that were vented into our small onboard capsules.

An onboard computer named "Saturn" piloted Nova. Nova's voyage had been charted by using multi-galactic maps of all that was then known of a vast universe. We Martians were a brilliant people, who for thousands of years lived beyond our planet; always venturing to explore whatever our vast universe could offer.

This flight to Earth had been evaluated by many of our scientists who had been upon Earth and returned many times, for hundreds of years. They all resolved that this place called Earth was one of the most forgiving; a comparable planet that met our Martian lifestyle, if in fact, the atmosphere could be penetrated.

Earth rotated on its axis frequently providing seasons and was the closest of the many known planets to journey. Other planets offered more, but the planet Earth was relatively new…only five billion years old. Martians had only used Earth as a refueling port of call. It was now remembered only as a ghostly monument to lost explorers, since the great disturbance.

Only within the last decade had ships been developed that could exceed the speeds necessary to enter into the now deeper atmosphere of the Earth. Centuries long ago, scientists had once placed our own Mars's inhabitants upon Earth to explore its wealth. But a strange phenomenon occurred while they occupied there that created a thick impenetrable, atmospheric barrier. Several large catastrophic meteorites collided with the Earth, all at one time. The sky went dark with debris that spewed high into the atmosphere, shading the planet. Now hidden from the sun, the temperature held below freezing, as the whole Earth chilled.

The inhabitants were all believed to have died, as communications became impossible. But no one knew for sure. It was highly speculative that life could have sustained on Earth, until many centuries later, when Dr.Dargod himself, glassed the planet and observed the clearing of the atmosphere, and the swirling of dark cumulus clouds, which probably meant a water, hydrogen, and nitrogen content. These were the essentials for life; he was inspired. Our scientist father began to devise a plan to understand Earth's composition.

All previous space exploration vehicles, and each small exploratory party aboard them, had lost radio contact. No rescue ships were launched thereafter, at a time in Martian science where ships could not begin to penetrate such an atmosphere. This layered web shrouded the planet like a fierce protective encasement. Earth became known as "the graveyard". It was too prohibitive to fly there. It became much safer and easier to fly to other known planets to take aboard and replenish the stocks of oxygen, hydrogen, and water that were also abundant on other planets, which were not protected by impenetrable atmospheres. Earth was then left to quietly simmer for a thousand years, or so. Ships flew by, but never visited. Still, they sometimes wondered.

Our life ship, Dargod Nova, was uniquely powered by a powerful H2AO2 solar seeking, energy-collector engine, using its self-replenishing hydrogen fuel cells, which virtually meant that the ship could be set in perpetual motion, using inertia in a vacuum forever and a day. In time of needed thrust, the hydrogen burning rocket's engine could launch the missile at speeds in excess of a quarter-speed of light within a vacuum. But the friction of the atmospheric conditions entering Earth had to be precise; otherwise the ship would be repelled out of orbital configuration, or drawn into Earth's gravity field at a pace so fast it would burn up; either case was destructive. The pilots had to be awake to initiate the adjustment speeds. No Martian had ever piloted so fast a bullet through an atmosphere so dense, as that of Earth's. It would be a first, or last, for our family of Dargods.

Our trip's length was calculated to be approximately sixteen light years, however the time to recover from the comatose state was unknown, as it was experimental with all the space travelers. The ships cruised through the vacuum, piloted by computers, and if the computers malfunctioned, it was the end.

As Josef and Marietta lay beside each other for months, and then years in a deep sleep, they could not have known that Marietta was giving birth to her child. And since the womb is a fantastic machine, it continued to nurture the unborn fetus, until its miraculous birth one day through the canal. At the last moments of delivery, the child entered his orbital world, filled with the serum from the continuing lifeline's umbilical cord attached to his mother. The newborn baby lay between her legs, for an unknown time, under her garment, also in a comatose state of life, just as she.

The journey was a good one, relatively speaking. We voyagers did not witness the sparks from under the panel upon takeoff, where a loosely connected wire shorted out, and the onboard timer clock faltered, allowing time to pass without a record.

Almost three decades of Martian time lapsed. The time was nearing for our family to awaken. But the ship slipped past each additional orbit of the earth for incalculable times, until the friction of the Earth's atmosphere finally warmed the ship's hull. The friction's warmth brought a noticeable change to our metabolism. We began to arouse, one by one. Day by day, life flowed more quickly through our veins, as our heartbeats normalized. Surprisingly, it was the Unicorn that awoke first and in a hostile, feverish state of hunger, it began kicking inside his cage.

Like an alarm clock, we mortals awoke, but with the thought that we had never been asleep. Josef unlocked his capsule, walked gingerly, almost floating, over to the Unicorn and fed him his due. Turning around, he systematically unlocked us.

Marietta began more slowly to arouse and had not awakened. I myself felt that moment of instability, as I experienced my first taste of weightlessness. That was marvelous!

Our horrors were soon met, when an infant's bawl broke the deafening silence of space. Marietta squirmed to the affects of child bearing and showed dried bloodstain at her lower section. She troubled with regaining her senses and we thought she had suffered a hemorrhage while coming through space's pressures. A ruptured vessel was something we were not prepared to address. That, to our surprise, was not the fact.

Marietta eventually came back to conscious life. She opened her eyes and saw her baby boy being held and wrapped in swaddling clothes by Josef. I was now an uncle!

Upon examination of Marietta, Josef saw that the birth happening had occurred, possibly many, many years prior, but the boy had not grown and remained an infant

The child had done everything on his own. The umbilical cord had dried and had already disengaged. He was a frail looking man-child, but with his features no one could have mistaken him, but to have been the son of Josef and Marietta. They decided to name him Josef Dargod, for the first son always carried the name of his father on Mars. The groom, however, always received his married name from that of his new bride's parents.

Big Josef immediately took heed to the charts and written instructions, but we all seemed somehow qualified to take over the ship. We had been unknowingly schooled, for who knows how long, in every facet of controlling the ship.

Nova was ours to command, or destroy. There was no returning to…to where, I thought? I had become misplaced with amnesia.

When Marietta discovered the clock's malfunction, and Josef repaired it, our new world's start up time was now the beginning of our time, and also the birth date given to little Josef, who we now called Jesus, to avoid confusion

Because Marietta's mammary glands had long ago returned to non-pregnancy state, and carried no milk, Jesus received his meal of dehydrated food, which had to be dissolved by microstar ray and rehydrated. We found a small tube of no apparent purpose to deliver the substance to the always-awaiting mouth, of the perpetually crying baby. It quickly became very close inside the ship's cockpit.

It wasn't for the lack of fear that drove us to quickly chart our entry into Earth's atmosphere. We were definitely afraid of the unknown ahead. It was the strong, pungent smell of the baby's fecal remains that drove our initiatives to dodge them as they came floating, suspended without gravity, from out of nowhere to smack us in the face…yucky! No plan had been prearranged for that. We became very desperately brave to find relief. We were in Earth's gravitational pull, so we were in the planned area of entry. We had to move and move quickly.

The calculations were made so that we slowed the ship's speed for entry. Secured in our flight seats, the now reprogrammed computers spit out the orders to the hydrogen engine to perform on command. We felt the violent shaking of the ship's distress, as it fought off corrections made by friction and wind. I found myself strangely seeking supernatural help.

We were all stressed, I thought. We each silently prayed for various reasons. I was hoping that my own calculations were accurate. We knew not where that thought to pray came from, but it was an event that was to become never-ending. We all later discussed this strange inner desire to ask for His guidance, as if it were expected.

The entry into our new world's atmosphere was an event that only the few had seen for many centuries from this angle. It was indescribably beautiful. It brought us all first thoughts of…Mars…Mars? Oh, so long ago, but lingering vividly in our minds, as yesterday.

Our instruments delighted us with the high outside readings of oxygen, hydrogen, and nitrogen; we could exist here! We circled many times to view the beauty and discover the seasonal patterns. Our choice would have to be made as a final destination, so we entered the lower atmosphere to take a closer look. Our streamlined ship became more maneuverable now, below the upper limits.

We took control of the ship by deactivating the computer's hold upon the controls. It flew like a graceful bird, for its design was a long established feature that provided a safe haven in space. We were able to further decrease our speed as we continued to circle our new home's circumference, searching for our final resting place.

It became apparent that the season of sun was much more hospitable to our way of living…I then wondered what our way of living was? I did not remember.

Taken from the maps of a past traveler's expertise, certain formations were deemed better to land upon; each were chosen for the rigid support of the ship's entire weight. As we glided lower and lower, the enormous pulling weight of gravity became severe for Marietta and her child. It drew upon her strength to move. For unknown reasons, we men were able to transverse without too much difficulty. Poor dizzy Marietta became very ill and just verily managed to hold onto Jesus.

Josef had located a point on the map, marked with a cross that was represented as a perfect landing point, as we were nearing the new warmth of the seasons. We all quickly decided to proceed there as we hurriedly strapped ourselves into our launching chairs again, while Marietta held onto Jesus. Those feelings again came upon us as a prayer thought, directed to an unknown spirit from inside us.

Initiating the landing procedure required two people at the controls. The hydrogen engine groaned as we completely inverted to slide backward onto the Earth's surface. This procedure took several hours, as we hung in the atmosphere, while slowly decreasing our generated speed. This Earth's rotation was much faster than we planned and the time to descend began in the daylight, but was finished in the dark hours. Our ship's bright flames lighted up the heavens about us, but we could not see anything.

Just before we established contact with the surface, the ship hovered for some time above the ground, while again we reduced the engine's deceleration slowly. With a thump, we made a landing. We had arrived!

Mt. Sinai
"Hi, Neighbor!"
PWK

Our New World
(Chapter 3)

The landing was completed and we again took measurements of the outside air content. The readings were very high in sulfur content this time. This deflated our hopes immeasurably. We had to wait until light to see exactly where we had come to rest. To our amazement, it didn't get light for quite some time. Tests concurred that even with the sulfur content it was technically safe to exit the ship in respirator gear, so I volunteered. We all knew if this was our new world's environment, our lives were short-lived, as we hadn't enough usable oxygen to last more than a week. So, I decided to take hope in Dargod's calculations that this was suitable for our living and eliminated wearing the complete body suit.

It was still necessary to dawn the air breathing apparatus' shell headgear, which consisted of a clear spherical bubble worn only about the head and chest, which filtered possible contaminated air with its two tanks. Whoever stepped from this ship had to immediately worry about contacting foreign substances and disease. For those purposes there was a decontamination wash tent thrown outside that I had to erect to shower in, after exploration. I waited to do that, for if and when, I returned.

I checked the communication pack and I could be heard on the intercom. Josef asked me if I was ready to begin and I answered, "I am!" I was ready. Josef handed me the laser repeller weapon for protection, and a laser signaler, which was used to measure depths and heights, or if directed towards an intruder's eyes, it would render that assailant blind. I hoped no demon could overcome the two, or I was then defenseless.

The hatch opened to a dim light and I was dismayed to see the new planet's appearance. Hugh walls surrounded the entire ship and it appeared that we were inside a huge dead volcano. I relayed that message back to the ship.... "Yes, that's exactly what we did…land inside an inactive volcanic mountain, which justifies the high sulfuric content also…, hummmm? Why do you suppose the maker of that map designated a landing zone here?" I questioned.

"I don't know," Josef replied.

I struggled under the new gravitational pull, trying to ascend the walls that surrounded us. I saw a stream of bright light flowing through a large hole in the cavern's wall and made my way up there. It showed so brightly, I was blinded. As I neared the opening I could see a bright, metal object that protruded abruptly out. Its mirror image reflected upon the ship, with a ghostly affect. It was the remnant of one of our past ships that had long ago landed here, I reasoned. I could not get to it.

I peered over the crest of the opening and witnessed my first sunrise upon Earth. It was the same sun that brightened the day on Mars. "That's where we came from!" I shouted. My mind was restoring! I was happy, then suddenly saddened, as I remembered our hastened departure, and leaving my parents behind. Somehow, I then believed that I would return to them one day.

I climbed through the opening and down the mountain's slope and eventually lost contact with the ship. It took two sunrises to complete going down, as I slept cold and uncomfortably upon rocks. When I finally left the rocky terrain and stepped onto a level ground base, I scooped up some soil into my pack for later examination. I looked up from where I had come, and wondered if Marietta was capable of that treacherous descending. The ship was completely hidden to any curious eye. I now understood why this place was chosen as a landing point. This land was fertile in many places, fit for much life. I continued to search for life and similarities to our life on Mars.

As I walked along, I came upon grasses and bushes. There were trees with figs and dates, just as those that once flourished upon Mars. There were white clouds in the sky and they certainly reminded me of Mars. "Thank you, oh, Dargod," I summoned in my thoughts. "Thank you for your knowledge and for providing us with a safe haven." I looked to the heavens and thought I might see our planet, but could not.

I was intrigued to see trees that we on Mars called pallam trees, growing on this planet. Maybe some Martian long ago had planted them here. They certainly grew well. The sun was very warm here, and I became thirsty, not only for a drink, but to continue on surveying our new world and home.

Suddenly, I noticed a long moving stream of objects along a distant ridge, moving, oh so slowly toward me; I then hid in bushes. It must be the people of this Earth coming towards me, who were to be my new neighbors, I thought to myself. They rode upon a funny looking beastly conveyance that was a large, long necked beast with humps on its back.

They all circled the pallam trees and set up tents, just like the wash tent that I had back at the ship. I eased into position and watched as the dark skinned beings gathered around a liquid place in the ground, bent down and began to drink of its contents. There was water on Earth, too! It was just as Dargod had spoken. He was certainly the master of knowledge.

I listened to them speak their language and thought that I understood some of their tongue. Could this be? I ventured even closer and listened further. My heart was pounding with joy. Though these people were light years away from Mars, they possessed almost the same tongue language that we had learned in our lesser institutions on Mars. Imagine that? It seemed as though they now spoke about themselves and it was in an archaic mode of time, for they spoke of the quickness of their travel and the prominence of the Pharaoh…Pharaoh? I once had read about such Pharaoh people in our history volumes, which lived on Mars thousands of years ago.

I was beginning to now understand that this planet was not as progressed as Mars had been…maybe this is good I thought, very well for us. "Thank you, Dargod," I whispered to myself. It was as though Dargod was always with me, wherever I went.

I had been on Earth only three sunrises, and I had already found that this soil was like Mars's, only with different dimensions. The inhabitants here were nearly the same. But, were they friendly? Except for my very light skin, which was now feeling pain from the sun's rays and turning very red, we both walked upright and wore clothing. Except, of course, for the big, air purifier dome on my head…Hummm. Was I to let them view my presence? I waited.

I stepped out from the bushes and tried to summon this lone man who had come to the water. He stood up, mouth agape; his eyes stretched wide open, and to my surprise he screamed something vile and grotesque. When he drew a large curved sword from his side and bellowed at me, the others arrived. But quickly they fled to their mounts and left the man alone. He once again shook his sword into the air to thwart me, but when I advanced to greet him, he dropped his shiny weapon and ran away screaming. He ran to his mount, leaped high onto its back and lit out hurriedly across the plain at full lope. He could really ride that thing! I quickly regressed into the bushes.

Why was he afraid and why had he run so haphazardly? I started to scratch my head, when I felt the dome…. that's it! He probably thought that I was a man from outer space…. ha, I am! I bet he spreads a lot of horror tales. There will be no crowds to gather around this water hole.

Another herd of transported beings arrived, but this time they were upon a burrada, as if on Mars, before they all became extinct. My heart fluttered to see such a sight! Surely the people that I was witnessing were the predecessors left here when our scientists explored here. They surely must have survived! I decided not to seek them out until there was more daylight upon the land.

I watched them from the bushes as they soon set about putting up their tents, just as the sun left the sky. They seemed peaceful and soon retired to their tents. I found comfort in the contour of the soft soil and just lay on my backside looking into the night. The stars shone brightly overhead, and the beauty of space, from where I just had traveled, was never so far away, I thought. I found a date fruit upon the ground beside me and took a small bite of its flesh to my tongue. It was sweet, so I ate of the fruit and I was very delighted to find many more.

The sun again arose on the fourth day, and I knew that I had slept soundly. To my surprise, the whole group had all left silently. I ventured near the water, and found its taste was very pleasantly cool and good. We could survive here, I then knew, as I filled my liquid container full.

I then was startled by a goath, which was not with the band of Earthlings, but untethered and roaming free. It was another animal from Mars and was a nannete with a kid suckling. Her milk flowed, squirting freely, as the kid pushed and butted the bag. She was full. I thought that this was the answer to little Jesus' hunger. I coaxed the animal to me by holding out dates that I gathered lying about. She came to me, eating all. I took a strap from my waist and placed it around her neck, and I lead her. The kid followed. I never knew a goath could smell so good! It was like home to me.

I began my trek back up the mountain with great news of this new world and home. On the eve of the seventh day, I entered the crevice in the wall and descended into the cavernous pit. Dargod's Nova sparkled, lit up by the bright sun's rays that were beaming down upon its brilliant surface…it was blinding and I could not look upon it.

Josef met me with a hug at the ship's door, which was now wide open, and had been so opened since the day after I had departed. Josef's air quality tests had improved substantially after the volcanic dust settled back to the floor of the volcano after the disruption of our landing. Marietta was much better too, but her child Jesus barely clung to life. Jesus was desperately ill, with the slightest sound of weak whimpers coming from his mouth. We fed him the goath milk from the tube, but we were certain that he would expire. It was in desperate hope that we all descended to our knees and summoned Dargod's knowledge together in a deep mind's thought, so that his knowledge might guide us and give us wisdom and strength. It now seemed so natural to pray for Dargod's help.

It worked. Into our minds came the thoughts of the stored capsules of AloevectorP23, that if we put into his body, ever so lightly, hoping that it would defray the certainty of death, at least until the nourishment of the goath milk could strengthen his body. He ingested the potion mixture with milk and soon became still. He looked dead.

I then told Josef and Marietta about all the bounty of our new world that I had found, and the people's likenesses to our own Martian people, just outside this mountain. They were anxious to see it all. But without Jesus, it meant nothing now.

Not knowing how well the goath's milk would nourish the baby, we then decided to gather our essentials, readying to leave this shelter. I told them of the hot sun's rays and the dress of the people that I saw gathered at the water. We had only similar clothes in our bedding, so we put on the wraps of night-time about us. The cloths of bathing, we tied about our heads. We prepared Jesus in a pack and placed him upon Josef's back. The mother goath with kid and Dargod's unicorn were left to graze the grasses outside on the mountain. The goath had given her best to us. And I knew my father's prize unicorn would find nourishment. The nannete seemed very friendly towards him. We left suspecting a new flock might develop someday there.

The descent was quicker than before, because I knew the avenue well. We entered upon the flat land on the same day, and moved towards the water and the pallam trees. We camped there on the eve and enjoyed the fruits and cool water there.

In the middle of the nighttime, a band of weary souls rode into camp upon their burrada and quietly set up their camp. Among the group, were women who ventured to the water to fill their jugs. I heard them call the water place an oasis. I could hear and understand their tongue, as they sometimes giggled at their senseless sayings.

They paid little attention to our presence and went about their business. I ventured into their midst and was asked from what tribe had I descended? I did not understand, "what tribe?" They were very beautifully featured people with dark, silky hair and eyes that shone dark as the night.

"My name is Jamison Dargod," I explained in a graceful whirl of my fingertips and arms. I had seen this done in the camp before.

"Then you are of the Dargod tribe," one said, as if it was a common tribe. "I should have known by your beautiful light skin."

"It's a long way to Bethlehem," another said.

"Where are your stock and steeds?" another questioned.

"We are without stock or steed. We have traveled on foot from a great distance," I told them.

"It must have been the thieves!" shouted one who knew; for he had had all of his possessions taken by the murderous scavengers recently along the path.

"Oh it's a shame," a lady sighed. "And you have a girl with you, I see."

"Yes, she is my sister, Marietta, with her husband, Josef."

A tall man came forward from a tent to inquire of our will. I told him that we were lost and searched for someone who could assist our ill baby.

"Oh!" The ladies all ran to Marietta's side to see. They stepped back aghast, all looking very concerned. When they saw the very pale skin of the baby they declared it was dead. They surrounded Marietta and smothered her with sorrowful hugs and gestures.

"He is not dead!" Marietta blurted to them. "He is only in a deep sleep, until we find a physician to assist."

They couldn't have understood and thought that this mother was refusing to give in to the realities of death. This baby's pale skin wasn't the look of a living being, Dargod or not, they thought.

They summoned their eldest woman to see him. For she was the most experienced of all, with twenty grown children afoot. She stared at Jesus and felt of his arms. She placed her head near his heart and could hear no beat. He had passed, she also thought.

She tried to take up the child in her arms, but Marietta would not allow her to do so, and held Jesus to her bosom, which was small and without milk. They could see her problem. The women gathered together talking, and in a moment's flurry they dispersed, only to return with their own belongings to offer up as gifts for the sadness of Marietta. The clothes were spun of old frame, but brightly painted. The warmth of kindness has no barriers in space, I thought.

Marietta could feel the kindness from their hearts. She grasped their outreaching hands in a show of gratitude. Kindness and generosity were two virtues that were not very plentiful upon Mars when we had left, but seemed to flourish here upon Earth. My sister accepted them gracefully.

The gentlemen all came to offer up a burro, its Earthly name that we called the burrada on Mars, and a skin of water. The women presented a blanket for Marietta to sit upon. Josef at first declined, but looking at Marietta, accepted them and a hug was exchanged. It was different than our Martian way. Then the eldest man spoke some wise words to us when we humbly offered our thanks.

He said, "If ever a needy person crosses your path, remember this day, and give this kindness to him."

They all said, "Ah men."

I suspected it was an agreement gesture.

Had we really come to such a wonderful place? We had nothing to give this world but our own knowledge. However, we stood helpless here to show them our advanced technologies, having no real resources to promote them on this planet. We would therefore have to live the lives of the present Earthlings, and be thankful just to be alive.

The man then offered Josef the lead rope and said it was a donkey from his herd of steeds, and that Marietta must not be forced to walk the hot desert sands on foot. They gave us all sandals of their time; a light, loose fitting piece that allowed the Earth's dirt and sands to enter. They mused at our soled shoes, saying that only a rich king had such a shoe to wear, but a king did not walk upon the desert, he was carried. Our feet would not last a mile, he said. The kindness overflowed, for they were good and kind people.

The men again offered to help bury the little baby, but big Josef declined, pointing to Marietta who was shaking her head no. They would not understand our science and we could not tell them outright. So we took on extra liquid and prepared to travel.

We received directions for the path towards Bethlehem, the only destination we knew.

"You will have nothing to declare, so you will have to get work," one man inserted. We were confused by his words. We hugged them each and every one, which also must have been their custom when departing, then headed towards the sun.

The Earth's sun was unforgiving, as we journeyed out into the unknown. We had spans of washout on Mars, just as the Earth had its desert. We had felt the burn of the sun upon our skin for a link's time, when Josef spotted a rare Martian aloetta medicine plant growing up right in front of us. He quickly broke open its long leaves and smeared its clear sticky contents upon the baby and upon our bare bodies. Its soothing relief was instant and we could not believe our fortune. We were astonished how much bigger aloetta grew here on Earth than on Mars. We could now travel safely in the sun and comfortably upon the desert. We thanked Dargod!

At the eve, we placed our tent upon the highest ridge. Around its perimeter we placed a repelling powder that kept all crawlers and fliers at bay. Mars had those little humming mistoes, too! Had they mistakenly transplanted the pests here, also? They were called mistoes because they often would buzz around your head while you were trying to sleep at night, so when you pulled your cover over your head for protection, your feet and toes were often exposed to be bitten…thus mistoes.

As we sat about eating our meal, we discussed the many beastly beings that we saw here, which also walked upon Mars but carried different names on Earth. We saw many different birdos in the heavens, and slithers and zards scampering upon the sands. We decided that we must stop the comparisons, for it saddened us all. All these same beasts upon Mars had become extinct, and though not to forget our Mars, we decided we must talk of our new home only. It was difficult, but we soon managed our thoughts more closely, as best we could.

At the rising of the sun, we continued. We ventured upon some travelers who were also traveling by burro to Bethlehem. They told us that they were displeased to pay Caesar's taxes and cursed him in words I did not understand.

"One day, one fine day," the man said, "our Lord will send us the Deliverer, who will lead us from this bondage. He will be known as the 'Chosen One', he will lead us out!" he proudly exclaimed.

His wife said, "Until then, my husband, you will pay your taxes for each of the poorly chosen words you speak," as she laughed at him.

Taxes? Caesar? Should we venture into this Bethlehem? We were but pass-ersby looking only to make a home in a new world. We did not want bondage.

Soon others joined our little caravan, until we all became a large troop trudging the sands in the same direction. The blowing sand bit into our skin, as a stingerding on Mars would do. Oh, I must not think of home, I told myself, if even only about bad things. Then, we saw in the distance the build-ings of a town. We entered and were met by men dressed in shiny battle gear.

"The Roman soldiers," it was whispered.

They were anciently equipped, compared to my laser. Bethlehem was a tra-ditional town that resembled the towns in the books of ancient Mars. Surely this was not the best of the advancements in architecture? Unfortunately, I overheard one say they were pleased with the improvements made about the city. I knew that I could offer up many improvements, but only if their technology grew ten fold; right now there was none at all which was useful to me. I feared the lack of their knowledge would cast us as wizards of the mystic, a shameful contriving person on Mars. I thought too much again.

Josef, Marietta, my nephew baby, and I continued past the taxman at his table to search for a physician who could help us. We searched everywhere throughout the city and asked to no avail. No one understood whom we wanted. It was nearing the eve, so I went into a sheltered place to find room to sleep, as the nights were very cold.

The clerksman, who was named Barabbas, told me that there were just two rooms left. The price to stay overnight there, he told me, was five denar each. I asked what that denar was and he scowled at me, and told me that no beggars were welcomed there. I just realized that here on Earth, in this very town, money was used and we had none.

"What are we to do, sir, with a woman and child?"

He then showed remorse and directed me to his own beast barn. He told me that we could use the straw there for the night. He peered deep into my eyes and asked me if I was a thief?

"If you take anything from my barn, the only man who grants you kindness," he said, "Caesar will punish you ten fold!"

I assured him we were with neither vile, nor guilty thoughts and thanked him.

We found the barn to be smelly and dirty and set about placing new straw upon the floor. I set a beast's feed trough near a solid wall and hoped the draft would be nil. Josef unlatched his pack and sat it gently down. The baby, to everyone's extreme surprise and happiness, screamed out in hunger. He had survived! The first words out of our mouths were, "Thank you, Dargod, he is alive!" We hugged him and looked to feed him.

A goath beast stood before us laden with milk. But being warned by the clerksman not to take anything, I went back into the clerksman's inn and told him that the child had come to and we needed milk, since Marietta could not supply him. He offered up the goath beast's milk and gave me a container to collect the liquid. He sent his wife to assist.

As midwives were their custom, Lydia, the clerksman's wife, went to Marietta who had now lain upon the new hay with the baby in her arms. He looked a very frail newborn, but his voice was strong enough to startle the beasts. Lydia became startled also. She then noticed a fresh newborn-looking baby with the umbilical cord totally absorbed, and the mother without the passing of blood and specimen. Knowing that this was the case, she knew this could not be!

Josef drained the gotten milk into a container. Lydia offered up a goath skinned nippled bag when she saw that Marietta was narrow in the bosom. Lydia went back to the building and returned with one of the nipple bags of her own child, and also her curious husband. They had evidently discussed the unusual birth of no bloody placenta. The baby was so small and new looking that surely there would be blood.

We each sat in the last light of the eve and held little Jesus. He had over-come the worst and was feverish only to the nipple of milk. He nurtured well; now he would live!

"Thank you, Dargod!" we all exclaimed.

The clerksman's questions were non-stop. Finally, Josef told him of our truthful adventure from another planet called Mars.

"We are not of this Earth, but we have traveled from afar, from within the heavens."

The clerksman Barabbas immediately stood up and dismissed this truth. He said it was unworthy to say untruths and he became very angry. He then insisted this whole thing to be an untrue hoax to gain free shelter, so he began to rant and rave. He was about to send us into the night, baby and all, when I directed him out into the open. I then pointed to the heavens and fired off the laser shooter's-signaler, high into the night's sky. The burst of energy lit up the entire sky and the essence hung airborne for many minutes. It lit up Beth-lehem like no other time in their lives.

The clerksman fell to his knees upon the ground, his eyes shown wonder and horror. His bent body hugged my feet in forgiveness. Then he jumped up and went running back into his building screaming. He summoned anyone who he could to tell of this extraordinary event he had witnessed. He was a real believer now!

Many viewed the laser shooter's essence near and far. Many people gath-ered around, as a crowd of excited travelers appeared and surrounded the beast barn. Into the night, the clerksman told everyone of this story. The story spread quickly, with each story passed on more fantastic than the last. People viewed little Josef as the "Chosen One", they said. The laser shooter's burst of energy had become a stationary star that hung over Bethlehem pointing the way.

Lydia closed the door to the beast barn and Marietta and her child slept upon the straw. Josef and I sat outside and watched the people come and go.

Someone then said loudly, "The day has come, our Savior has been born!" I could not believe what my ears were telling me. I looked at Josef and him at me.

He laughed saying, "Ha, who are we to say this is not the truth? But, thank Dargod for this day."

We were warm in our hearts that little Josef returned to health. He would be the first born of our own Dargod Earth family. And I, Jamison, was his uncle. We both happily leaned against the barn and sheltered from the cold, until the morning's sun arose to warm our bones again.

At the dawning, little Josef continued to bawl loudly, as Josef retrieved more milk to feed him. Lydia came to the barn and offered up bread that she herself had baked.

On that day, we shared with Lydia and her husband Barabbas, our wealth of knowledge brought from Mars, but they did not have the aptitude to understand any of this phenomena and it was all for naught. They listened in awe, as if it were holy.

Barabbas left to serve up food and drinks in his inn tavern, for he had many friends and guests there. He would bring a few men to view Josef, then leave. We discovered that being the businessman that he was, he already was charging travelers to see Jesus. Lydia was ashamed and disturbed. We were just grateful for them allowing us to stay in his beast barn. His stories became severely altered, until we could not recognize one of the happenings of which he spoke so loudly.

In the middle of the next day, came several men of importance. They had traveled far to see the child of another universe. To our surprise, they brought many gifts and placed them before Marietta's feet. They kissed her feet, then washed and applied scented oils to them, and little Josef's, too.

"And what is the name of the 'Chosen One'?" one asked. "How shall we call him?"

"We call him Jesus," I told them. "His father is Josef."

"Are you relatives of a great leader, once of the Dargod tribe of Nazareth? Could he be of your blood?"

"I do not know, for we are travelers from afar, too," I added.

The men left many valuable gifts of monies, of gold, and oils for little Jesus. Soon others came and did the same. There were silks and yarns, beads and bracelets. There were chests filled with coins. Jesus was wealthy. All this was so they could find favor with this child who they perceived to be the "Chosen One". There was no end to the people bearing gifts. There was no end to the tales told either. Barabbas had spread the word like the sands that blew across the desert fields.

We were offered up four camels, the beasts with two humps, to bear the offerings. The camels were heavily burdened with their loads when we left. We had decided that we must go to this town of Nazareth to find the Dargod family.

We did not travel alone, as there were followers who could not get enough of the sight of the "New Born King", they told us. We thanked Dargod for placing us in such a generous position. Marietta was treated like a queen. Ladies began to cook for her and one even nursed Jesus on her own breast. She herself was with child, but her large bosoms were heavy and fat, and the rich milk dripped freely from her brown nipples. It was heard that this birth was of a virgin with no placenta; our "Virgin Queen," someone implied.

The travel to Nazareth was long and uneventful. Jesus handled it well. He suckled at will and gained weight with each serving of the milk. We now had a whole herd of goath beasts. We were blessed.

On the sixth day of travel, we entered into Nazareth. The taxman was there with the Roman soldiers. He gazed upon our load and asked what tribe we were from. I told him Dargod.

"You may pass without due," he told us.

It was good to feel important for nothing we had accomplished. We again all thanked Dargod's name. He had provided well for us all. It seemed that wherever we were, Dargod was watching over us.

No one could identify with the family name of Dargod in the settlement we stayed. But the buildings were of new clay and seemed to be built much higher and stronger than in Bethlehem. There was a running spring that provided an abundance of water. There were gardens of pallam trees with fruits and dates.

We found a dwelling to purchase that fitted our needs. The people that had followed us from Bethlehem bartered the sale with its owner, until it was ours. This place had tall, protective surrounding walls and a big gate. We paid with the coins of the offering. This building was a large one and also addressed the main street, so as to offer a storefront, with living quarters behind. It was sat-isfactory. Baby Jesus needed a stable home, not a stable.

Within a few weeks new visitors rarely came, because of the high fence that secured the property. After searching the entire business ventures available to us, Josef decided that without the use of tools that we had become accustomed to on Mars, and the technologies, the only job we were capable of doing really well here was carpentry.

The first step would be to find wood to use and metal to make our own tools. Josef would draw from patterns he remembered from Mars. I could not get those kinds of Mars' thoughts from my brain, possibly never completely. Everything we built was learned knowledge from Mars, everything.

In three weeks time, Josef had built several chairs and a very nice large table. He was as proud as I had ever seen him. He would take his son and hold him closely as he pounded and sawed, just to let Jesus observe the skills of his carpentry work. Josef placed a sign facing out towards the main street on which he had hand carved the words "Dargod Carpentry". We had found teak wood that was sold in the big market, as well as iron that was hammered flat by human hands, but manipulated still by the use of a forge. All these were ancient ways upon Mars, yet foreign and new to our own Martian techniques and uses.

Our ideas soon overshadowed our skills and we searched for a blacksmith to assist us in developing the metal. His name was Joshua, a young man with many talents from Jericho. His strong arms were full and hard and he was able to bend the metal into beautiful fasteners, latches, and made nails that we invented. He also knew how to carpenter and mason. He was a kind man and took favor from little Jesus, who frequently reached for his strong arms to hold him. For it was not a man's manner to take care of watching a child, but Marietta was now some sort of royalty, which amused her as much as it did me. I remained respectful in her presence, though she was just my sibling.

The business grew without my input. I began to teach to those who would listen and found a coin or two after each session for my payment. I moved into my own quarters and began my lectures on many sciences and behaviors, all on a daily basis. My audiences grew large and I had to teach outside in the big garden to facilitate the need. I had become known and called a "scholar of knowledge" and became summoned into the governor's service, eventually to become his "wise problem solver"…I was enjoying this life.

When the notice arrived for me that Caesar summoned me to Rome, I was in disbelief and refused the summons. I was then forcibly taken up immediately upon a cart, and whisked into the desert by twenty soldiers. I was escorted to the sea. I had not the time to alert Marietta of my leaving, so I was sure they thought that I had met my demise.

I traveled for three months aboard a boat, commanded by a Roman Governor named Zealous Aquaintus, a loud and obnoxious scoundrel. I kept my distance long. For it was he who had taken the credit for my teachings and now he too was called to Caesar to answer questions. He needed my knowledge to answer. He was a cheat. He offered money to me to assist him. I had no choice but to concur. His lieutenant stood by me upon the deck and we talked every eve. He was an honest man.

Caesar was a scrawny little stature of a man, who when he walked, reminded me of the cock-birdo on Mars. But he commanded this world, and Caesar's word was the law. Working beside Aquaintus, I advised Caesar of many things, all of which I had true knowledge; each idea and suggestion was gainful to Caesar. But when I fell ill from drinking unclean water from a well, and could not be summoned for questioning by Caesar, Aquaintus spoke up on his own to Caesar about certain advisements of which he knew nothing. He was an aggressive fool who sought reward and advancement.

Aquaintus's head was quickly lifted, when he caused a catastrophe in Caesar's finances and was responsible for the loss of many soldiers with an ill-planned assault upon a neighboring band of dissenters. I was pleased to learn of Aquaintus's plight; henceforth, I alone became Caesar's personal advisor.

During the daylight, I enjoyed the power of a Governor and had servants placed to my pleasure. When the doors closed to my home at night, all the servants came to eat beside me. I sent their poor families many of my bountiful foodstuffs and silver cutlery, for I felt it was very wrong for one man to have so much, when others about him starved. I became very close with my entire household. They were, after all, my new family.

My time went well. I received a return notice four years later from Josef and Marietta that I had sent explaining why I had disappeared. Their reply was disturbing, as they said the people were starving and starting to plan revolt against the new Governor. He had over-taxed heavily and retained the monies for his own coffers, in the great name of Caesar.

I advised Caesar to call for an audit of his tax monies and alerted him to the discrepancies of certain revenues that he received. Soon, the Governor's head too was lifted, because Caesar's word was law!

I was pleased, until Caesar, himself, became irrationally bent on collecting taxes and heads. I became unsure of just how he felt about me. He once told me that a review of my palace showed that he had paid me very handsomely, maybe too well. The food that I consumed there, he suggested, was that of a small army. Ha!

I brought a young scholar forth into our special sessions, whose parent was of the Senate, and to whom I had personally tutored to take on as my assistant. His name was Pontius Pilot. He was an honest man with a fair heart. When I suddenly felt it necessary to tour Caesar's kingdom, I placed Pontius in my stead, and summoned a ship to the Mediterranean. I never was summoned to return, and Pontius had fulfilled my hopes.

Four months later, I found myself near a mountain identified as Sinai. It was the place of our landing years ago. I wondered of the ship's nature. I found myself dismissing my aides and sending them back to Caesar with a message that all was not well amidst his subordinates, because of the lasting starvation of his people in the land of Judea.

I found a beast and rode it into the desert towards the mountain. I had returned as an inhabitant of great wealth, and along the way I received much respect. But the people around the oasis found contempt in their voices for me. I knew they were bearing the burden of my gained wealth. When I drank the water from the oasis, it brought about a strange feeling into my soul of remembrance of Mars, and a sudden thought that maybe all was not lost. Maybe I only had to manipulate the radio frequencies to talk back to my parents. This was my motivation, as I left my steed upon the grasses and ascended high onto the rocky volcano. A long day of reestablishing my breathing wind slowed my way. I had become fat. I set up camp alone on a pile of rocks and absorbed the cold night air.

The sun reflected brightly, as I identified the hole in the wall. I was at last nearing the view of our ship. To my amazement and delight, several wild looking, one horned goaths, pranced about the opening, but scurried away when I reached the hilt. I stepped through the opening, and behold, there was our ship!

The glare of the ship's luster was still blinding and heat from its reflection could actually be felt on my skin from its path of light. I moved into the shade and speculated. The inside walls of the volcano had deteriorated, thus allowing many cinder rocks to fall free to accumulate about the ship's perimeter.

It was as though I was coming home, so I hurried down the rocks. I suffered injury to my knees and backside when suddenly I tumbled. And when I slid continuously, I arrived at the bottom with a thud.

I collected myself and regained my senses. I questioned my knowledge to remember the sequence of events that would open the big door. Had all that time in this dark pit exhausted the power aboard? Without delay, I proceeded to push the pad with the sequenced board of numbers that unlocked the ship's door.

In a moment, and without hesitation, the big door lifted. There was still adequate power on board. It wasn't until I was inside, that I recognized the factor of the sun's rays shining through the entry hole in the volcano. The sun's rays shining through the hole were more than sufficient to maintain the power supply. My father, Dr. Dargod, had perceived this in his quest of knowledge, I'm certain.

I went directly to the ship's console and turned on the communication antennae. The directional was rotating already, so I delivered the prescribed message.

"This is Mars's Dargod Nova from Earth, to Dr. Dargod on Mars, do you receive?" I repeated the message several times. I felt empty inside when there was no reply. I left the controls operating and slumped down upon the Captain's seat. There was an official looking note written by Josef, and the words addressed to our new world that he had proclaimed this land for Dr. Dargod, and the sovereign world of Mars. An attached Martian emblem's flag embossed it. I held it close, dreaming daydreams from the past, but fell asleep listening to the static of the radio.

The ship smelled fetid inside. I searched and I found several soiled swaddling garments that were still there under the console. I supposed they had been accidentally dropped there. I threw them outside and cranked open the ventilators. It was then that I saw that the rocks piled up against the ship's fins could ultimately damage them, if they collected much longer. That would have to be a future thought also, I envisioned. I certainly couldn't remove all that rock without help. What could I do?

Then it occurred to me that if I started the engine, it could blast the rocks clear, if I did it right. Besides, it would be like restoring the existence to a lifeless ship. I turned on the reactors and initiated the rotator sleeve. The sudden burst of energy was deafening, as I stupidly in haste forgot to close the ventilators and the big door. Now I was sweeping up cinder dust for hours and wondering if I had damaged any instruments. But it had surely cleaned up from under the ship. Billows of dust arose high above the ridge and the fire from the engine lit up the dark sky. The people at the oasis would certainly be concerned that Sinai, the old dead volcano, had come back to life.

I tested the virtues of the ship and knew that she was able to ascend, if I were so inclined. I found a huge reserve of AloevectorP23, but took only sixty capsules for my future use, if needed. There were many, many, more capsules inside that big chest. I then wondered just how long had my father speculated on the drug's use, or had he mass-produced the venom expecting many Martian users. Each capsule had life's sustaining properties. They would have provided many useful alternatives, if a catastrophe should merit their use. I waited until light, and closed up our ship. I thanked Dargod that it still was maintained; for I was now absolutely certain that this volcano was in his big plan. However, my beast had wondered off its tether and was gone, so I was afoot.

I found a large moving caravan; their beasts of burden were laden with trade goods going to the east. The entourage was headed across the desert from the oasis and I was able to barter for a camel. I headed out alone towards Nazareth for the first time in nearly twenty years. In Bethlehem, I began to hear the shouts of scorn for the Caesar and at the same time stories of the "Chosen One" of Nazareth. Could this be? I wondered.

Many poor beggars greeted my entrance into Nazareth. I pitched coins away to them, which cleared my path. There, on the main street still stood Josef's shop, and Josef was standing with a man of business. I waited for him, but he did not recognize me. I lowered my camel, ventured closer, and listened to their conversation.

It seemed that Jesus was about in the hills somewhere, speaking of love and peace towards all mankind and had not finished doing his father's work, the man accused.

"But he is," spoke Josef. "I have your order done."

I ventured to the side entrance and saw Marietta. She was comfortably seated on a lounge and enjoying the harp.

"I didn't know you played," I spoke.

She looked hard, and then ran to me with a hug. "It's been so long, it's been so long, my brother!" She hugged me the Martian way. The long embrace brought tears to both our eyes.

"You haven't aged one bit," I said. The same was returned.

"Maybe it's the potion," she inserted. "During my awful sickness, Josef administered just one capsule, and I immediately became well again. I think its potency had begun to wear off, so now I know how it feels to need restoration from the capsules when the time comes. I became aged, and feeling slow and very weak."

Marietta summoned me to the inside for liquids as we waited for Josef's entrance. We sat gazing into each other's eyes and tried to read each other's history, since I had abruptly departed.

"How is Jesus?"

"He is a grown man and does his own will. I'm afraid one day he will not return. He travels sometimes far away and does not return for weeks. He will be pleased to know of his uncle's return. He has asked us many times if you were returning."

I learned that he too was considered a scholar, as I had been. For quite some time, many people who were his elder had come to him for advice.

"Josef tried to teach him the carpentry works, but his mind was set distant before he was born that he had great things to do, he once told me. He was born a child, but with an adult's views," Marietta continued. "I get afraid when he speaks out against the Governor, and Caesar, that there might be reprisals. The Governor only sends warnings by word of mouth. Jesus is just listening today, near the great river. He often listens to a man called John the Baptist who speaks there, and tries to cleanse the people's thoughts and soothe their worries."

I could not wait to embrace him, for he was but a child of five, or so, when I left.

Josef came into the room and halted his thoughts when he saw this stranger speaking to his wife.

"Pardon me, sir, who are you?" he spoke to my turned back.

"Only another man, who loves your wife as much as you do," I jested. When I turned around I saw an angry face turn into smiles, as Josef rushed to embrace me. He too held me tightly, and I him.

Then we talked of the last decade and how this Earth had been good to us. We continued after dinner and into the night. We both learned much. When I told them that I had been back to the ship, they were saddened. For Josef had vowed never to mention the ship, for he feared knowing of its demise would destroy all their hope of ever returning. I told them I had started the engine and Dargod Nova was as good as before. Josef then was very pleased.

"This Earth is a good planet also and will be just as prosperous as Mars," I told them.

This brought confusion as to his loyalties, he told me. He was accepting his place here on Earth.

When Jesus did not return for six days, Marietta mourned her fears, so I left to search for him. I could not locate his place and asked many, who all said that they knew him well. I began to understand the people's wrath, as Roman soldiers dragged me to prison for seeking his whereabouts.

"I have done nothing wrong, but to ask a simple question," I told the Governor at trial time.

He looked queerly at me and asked if he knew me. I told him that I had once stood with him upon the deck of Caesar's ship, headed to Rome. Fear came to his eyes, when I told him I was of the Council; a position high above his own.

"Release this man you fools!" he screamed. "What would you do with me?" he asked.

"I will notify Caesar of the incompetence of his Governor, it will be his decision," I boldly stated. "But as for me, I will forgive you."

I knew that I could afford to be generous, for I suspected Caesar himself, may have put me in prison for my long absence. I had not contacted him for almost a year.

I began again to search for Jesus. But this time I fell into the hands of thieves near Bethlehem. One loud thief kicked me hard, but when I saw his face, I thought I recognized him. He kicked me again, this time in the head and my world spun into the dark. They stole all my belongings, and then tossed me into some bushes. I was left there bleeding upon the desert sand to expire. But, I awoke momentarily, and found myself lying under an aloetta plant. With all my strength that I could muster, having lost much blood, I managed to peel open a large aloetta leaf and spread its miraculous medicine about my wounds, before I passed out again.

Days lying in the hot desert sun should kill any man on its own. I awoke again, a very weak and scarred man, but I was alive. I had lain bleeding out in the sun, only in a loincloth, but the aloetta had protected my skin and healed my wounds beyond belief. I struggled to the upright and found a stick to lean upon. I began to walk toward an oasis that was very familiar to my memory.

I found shelter among the pallam trees and spent many days mending my body. It was the time of year that no fruit grew, so I was very hungry. Aloetta was not a plant that you should taste, for it was bitter. I could not catch a zard, or a deadly cobra that lifted his ugly head up and hissed my presence. I became desperate and slept near the water. Possibly a birdo, or rodent would venture into my grasp, for I was getting weaker.

But one eve a small group of men walked silently into my presence around the water. My body was filthy and had browned; my hair was uncombed. I appeared as a beggar. No words were spoken.

When he appeared, I felt warmth about him, as he lifted me up from the sand. He helped me to a seat upon the bank and washed the dirt from my face. He washed my wounds and began to brush my hair. I did not know this man, yet he found it in himself to help this beggar-looking man. He broke off a piece of his own bread, closed his eyes and said, "Dargod, find a blessing for this man and heal him."

He then gave me the bread and said, "Take this, my uncle, for you have found me."

I stared in disbelief, for longer than I remember. I, who searched for him, in turn had been found.

"Thank you, Dargod," I spoke.

He embraced me and went directly to his bag and withdrew some clothing for me. I sat there in amazement, as a newborn studies the faces above him in a crib. We shared soft talk, and then slept for the night.

The morning brought life and we struggled to make conversation, until I mentioned the ship. His eyes widened and he said,"So it was you who fired the ship. I was fearful that it might have been an intruder of lesser qualities. I received word that the volcano had erupted and feared the ship was lost. I venture there now to view it."

"It is as new," I told him.

"Then there is no need for my travel there, for the eyes who witness a trespasser are sure to follow. We shall return to Nazareth together. My mother weeps sometimes if I stay away too long, and that burdens me." We left the oasis.

The cold of the desert can bring angry thoughts to man's mind. My shivers were mounting and I longed for more clothing, but there was none to be gotten. We had traveled to Nazareth together, but I somehow felt distant to this man that I knew only as a small boy. He had worldly knowledge, though he had not left the plains. The repeated soundings of my father's word, had of course, I reasoned, found his infantile ear and remained in thought. He probably grew to think it came from his own father's mouth. But it was mine.

I felt that we could never have the close relationship we once shared as before because he was in a world of his own and I was now just an intruder. I was sorry for these feelings, but it was a certainty.

Marietta and Josef were excited to see their son and they held him tightly and praised Dargod for his safe return to them. They wondered about my well being. I told them of my plight with the thieves, and how Jesus had found me. There was much celebration that eve, but Jesus kept his joy in reserve. Marietta played her harp and we all sang joyful songs.

At the light Jesus was gone without saying his thoughts, so we knew not where he had gone. We could only wonder of him, for he was a grown man and had to pursue only his will.

The stout captain's announcement that then blurted loudly at the entrance to Josef's main gate was a message dictated for my return to Rome. Caesar summoned me once more. I hoped it wasn't to behead me, but the soldiers' escort meant that it was urgent. I bid farewell to my sister and her husband, not knowing if, or when, I'd ever see their faces again.

We headed out of Nazareth in a large caravan. The proceedings brought onlookers. I was dealt a passing moment of this man standing along the road with his hands held up wide to the heavens saying, "Go back to Caesar and tell him his children are hungry and angry!" It was Jesus!

I felt the cold dagger that his words intended. The soldiers dispersed the crowd and we continued. I knew not if Jesus saw me.

The travel was quickened by the new season's winds, and storms threatened our ship's structure. But in less than three months I was in the council court of Caesar, awaiting his presence. The chamber door swung open, and to my surprise, Caesar greeted me with the utmost pleasantries.

He welcomed me to sit beside him and to inform him of the news of his holdings. He was not pleased to learn why the people of Israel complained so, for the total coins he gained from there, were collected in a dismal amount, he told me. They did not fill his awaiting coffers.

"The people are taxed to their hilt, they can not, and will not withstand more,"I reported. "They are hungry and plead for mercy of the burden of their heavy taxes. Such a relief would guarantee their alliance to Caesar and when times become more tolerable they will gladly give up their fair share. They would praise your name."

"Jamison," he told me, "you have softened too much while living in my pleasure. Israel needs a stronger hand to punish those who don't obey. For that reason, I am replacing the Governor with Pontius Pilot. I feel he has the wisdom and the will to succeed with my orders," he advised.

"Pontius Pilot!" I blurted, "My own student? He is a man of respect and I am certain he will be observant to the Israelite's needs. Good! When will he supersede the Governor?" I asked.

"He is already there. He landed with your returning ship. Did you not see him?"

"No, I did not."

I went to work in Caesar's council and my time was steadily consumed, until I felt the need for another assistant. I selected a student and tutored him in a new class called "Caesarism"...my own version of, "how to tolerate an ignorant boss!"

Months became years. The words of the unrest still came out of Israel, but fell on deaf ears.

When the word came of the crucifixion of Jesus, I felt the sadness of a father and the madness of a tormented bull. I immediately went to Caesar. He said he knew of the matter.

"The man put to the cross was a rebellious nuisance, they tell me; nothing to scowl about."

He said that Jesus' own people had chosen his death over a convicted murderer named Barabbas.

I was alarmed. Barabbas had become a thief and murderer? My feelings then turned toward my sister and I worried.

"He was my nephew!" I proclaimed. "Why wasn't I told?"

"Who knew?" Caesar asked. "Who would have thought a servant of Caesar had a nephew that would be rebellious?"

I became furious.

I left his sight and went to scream in a dungeonous lower room. The first Martian to be born on Earth became the first to die! I wept for some time. I became complacent and worked for many months, only when the direct call from Caesar summoned me.

I was sitting in council, when a note passed to me from an unknown, alarmed my senses. It read, "Jesus is alive!" I searched from whom it may have come, but there was no evidence; no one.

My hours in conference were spent in discomfort and distress. I could not concentrate. We adjourned with little accomplished.

I left the council hall and was confronted by a man who beckoned me to a corner. He was the messenger.

"I have come from Bethlehem, sent by the carpenter Dargod of Nazareth. At your will, he wants you to come to the ship. He said that you would understand."

I directed the messenger to go to my palace and wait. I went to my study and penned a note to my assistant that I was called away for a death in my family; the only excuse to be accepted by Caesar for long stays. I immediately set sail with the messenger.

Again, I found the shore of the Palestinian plains and headed upon my camel to Bethlehem. I rewarded the messenger and he returned to his place. I traveled with great anticipation and had thoughts of how one could survive a crucifixion.

I stayed at the oasis in the eve. Many travelers had stopped there and all seemed disturbed that the Romans were going to slaughter them all. They fled their city dwellings into the desert to hide, for Roman armies traveled in great numbers and their wide path would be death and slavery. I slept lightly.

Before the sun shown, I was off towards Sinai. I grazed the beast and ran up onto the rocks. At one high elevation, I turned back to search my eyes across the desert plain to look for followers. Barely visible was a huge fire from the direction of the small town of Ababasi. The Roman army, I thought, was advancing.

The volcano's wall was nearing, as I made my way to the opening. I entered not knowing what I would find. The ship was standing and the big door was open. I climbed the ramp and went inside. I startled Josef and he rose up with his fists. A sigh of relief came upon him and he descended to his pilot's seat. I looked to the travel capsules and saw Jesus' body, sleep-like inside of one.

"Where is Marietta?" I questioned immediately.

"She did not come."

I learned that she had stayed at the business in Nazareth after Jesus was put to the cross. I then learned the plight of my nephew, as Josef immediately began telling me the whole story.

Jesus had been having large followers in his meetings in rebellion of Caesar. He was taken captive to the prison and questioned by the Governor Pontius Pilot, who asked him where did his loyalties lie, with Caesar or his Dargod? His answer, "Dargod," placed him in prison for treason. On the celebration day of Caesar, when a life's reprieve is offered to just one death sentenced prisoner, the Jews selected a thief named Barabbas in Jesus' stead, thus placing the death responsibility of Jesus onto the Jews. On the executioner's death date, Jesus was made to bear a cross along his path to crucifixion for which Josef had devised this plan.

Josef offered Jesus a gourd of water containing one AloevectorP23 capsule, and a very slight amount of a serpent's venom, when Jesus passed the chosen place. This elixir eventually placed Jesus into the exact state of being of unconscious, which he experienced while absorbing his mother's umbilical cord, during his birth-flight to Earth.

"I then was made to bear his cross while he drank. I don't know how he lasted as long as he did. But, I am certain though that he felt little pain into his last conscious hour. Thank Dargod for that," he sighed. "Poor Marietta stayed by his side until the end, pleading with the soldiers to spare her son, but they ignored her. She herself did not know of my plan, as I was uncertain if I could ever save him. I went to the tomb where Jesus lay, and one soldier knew me. He allowed me to apply aloetta juices to his body. While I was there, I could not feel any life signs coming from his body, and I feared he did die. But my mind told me this was good and one day Jesus would awaken. In the night, I took Jesus from the tomb with the help of the friendly guard and placed him on a camel, and brought him here. I have not returned to Nazareth since, hoping for your arrival. That was six months ago and my mind worries for Marietta. But I dare not leave the side of my son."

I consented to stay with Jesus and praised Josef for his wisdom. Josef lingered about his son's body, anxious to witness some sort of life, but that didn't come in his presence. We agreed that I would stay until either Jesus' body regained life, or decomposition began, which would mean permanent death. He left and I remained the guard.

On the hour, I peered into the capsule for signs of life, but I detected nothing. I noticed that the time registered upon our ship's clock was 00033, which also was the year of Jesus' recorded death. Three months passed and there was no change, but that was good. It also meant that one-day Jesus would arise.

One day I fired up the engine to test its functions. The volcano's rocks had not fallen as before, but I needed something to occupy my mind, as I felt so alone. When the engine was accelerated, the vibrations from the engine's blast summoned me to quickly shut it down before we lifted off. The rocks, the dust, and the enormous fire flames were sure to excite the people that could look upon Sinai. Again they would not tread here for fear of eruption. I had found some satisfaction and certainly self-proclaimed amusement. But not only was my amusement kindled; I was certain that I saw a slight stir in Jesus, just as the rocket became alive and it too stretched its frame to yawn briefly.

Three days later, without advanced movements, Jesus sat up with eyes still closed in an unconscious state of being. His face drew up into a hideous contortion as he spoke out, "Oh, Dargod, oh, Dargod, why hast thou forsaken me?" And then, he lay back down. I jumped to his side and noticed that he breathed. I felt his chest rise and fall and I felt the strong beat of his heart.

"Oh, thank you, Dargod!" I exclaimed. For I knew my nephew had not succumbed to death's vile defeat, but would live his life on Earth again. Jesus was not then ready to reenter that day's life and remained asleep for over ten days more. I grew impatient to tell Josef, but I could not possibly contact him.

On the morning of the tenth day, Jesus sat up again and recognized his uncle. We embraced. His immediate thoughts were of his mother, and he longed for her gentle touch.

"She mourned so before my plight on the cross that I could not bear living any more, while seeing her painfully so. I looked upon her and caught up all of her pain, but I could not dry her eyes."

My nephew was incoherent at times and it was some time until he regained his rationale. But we talked and I explained that he must not go back into that society for they would surely condemn him again. He must stay within the ship's security and I would go to his parents and delight them with the news of their son's life. I was anxious to tell them.

"This is the ship of my birth, is it not?" he spoke. "I will renew my time with Dargod and review his 'Ten Commitments to Life'. There's something I need to know. Go to my mother and tell her that her son longs for her, but neither she nor Josef should seek me, until I am prepared to present myself at my timing before my followers. That day won't be long," he spoke. "Now go and tell them all that I have arisen," he ordered me.

I felt sternness in his command and I am sure his mind had a plan. I left the ship and traveled to Bethlehem, where I paid a willing soul to deliver my over-due notice to Caesar that I, his lowly servant, had died, while drowning at sea. Now Jesus and I both would be living remote lives.

I found Marietta about her woman's work in her house and she froze to my presence.

"He sends you all his love," I told her. She then collapsed to the floor and sobbed loudly. I went to hold her and comforted her. Josef, who was aroused by her whimpering, came into the room with a questioning face.

"He has risen and is regaining his strength and wisdom at the ship," I informed him.

"Praise Dargod!" he screamed.

But they both were dismayed to learn that he did not want them to come to him then, but await his return, as that was his order.

"He is a changed person like I never have known," I told them. "He had a determined look about his face and his words are commands. I don't know what has caused this change. But I tell you he is committed to his way. He asked that we tell his followers to spread the news that he has arisen."

The news spread quickly within the month that Jesus had risen. His followers now mentioned as his disciples, offered open prayers to Dargod's Jesus in the public town's market places. People had seen him and when he briefly spoke, he told them that his Father had called him to ascend to his side, and he would be leaving this world to prepare a place for all who believed in the good and righteous ways of his teachings of Dargod. One day he would return to gather up his followers and take them to his heavenly Father's house where there were many mansions. This was his promise.

Two years had passed when Jesus finally walked into his father and mother's home. He had decided to stop ministering to the people who granted his death so easily, and pursue other avenues. He had taken up residence with one of his follower's sisters, and had become committed to her by vow, and lived in Damascus, and then Tyre for the rest of his life. He chose not to renew his life by AloevectorP23, which only was suitable to the blood of a Martian. He became a father of ten, a grandfather of fifty and it continued for six hundred years.

He remarried twenty times and I was there to celebrate each, until the potion finally wore off. To his dying day, he believed in the "Ten Commitments to Life", and often renewed everyone's faith by his acts of teaching his many relatives, who in turn, continue to spread the word today. I could not let him pass alone, so at the time of his leaving; I injected him with the potion and carried him back to his birth ship. I was very tired also, so I too, absorbed the potion by capsule and fell into a resting, rejuvenating state of being beside my nephew…time passed on by.

The New Age
(Chapter 4)

It was 0001130, because that was the clock's view. It was our time, not Mars's. I had awakened into a new age, in a new time on Earth, inside a renewed physical body. It was a glorious feeling. But this time it was Mars's time and not the Earth's. I don't know why we didn't think of this before. It was suddenly stuck in my mind as I aroused from the sleep. The Earth's rotations were faster than that upon Mars, so I would have had to calculate the difference. It would be easy to make adjustments, I thought, but that would have to be done at some other time. Now I was more ambitious. The clock on the dash was our time; our Dargod family's own time, for no one else relied upon this instrument. I hoped it was accurate.

The ship was absent of my nephew, but Josef and Marietta now occupied their previous capsules. Apparently my nephew had awakened first and brought them to this life ship, and had changed his desires about renewed life. It was deja vu. It was the new beginning, where I had awakened once before.

I found a note written in my nephew's hand that read, "The clock read 0001075 when I awoke. You did not possess renewed life signs yet, so I went to find Josef and Marietta. They were in a tomb and I had to bring them here in a state of death. I do not know when they expired, but I am sure that one day they too will recover, since I injected them with the potion.

"For science sake, they had not decomposed and were wrapped in aloetta leaves when I found them. They had many children and relatives buried beside them. Therefore, I have siblings and I am grateful for that. Their other relatives, who I don't know however, were decomposed; some had turned into dust. I don't understand their relationships to my parents, except they had the name of Dargod in the city tombs where I found my parents.

"I will monitor you all from time to time. You will find the outside world is very different. People have pleased me by actually going to war to fight for my Father's beliefs. There have been several sustained crusades, they call them, but I feel all is not over.

"The Earth's knowledge is expanding and there seems to still be a need for my teachings in places I must go. This means I must venture to the east with renewed energies, where a tyrannical Emperor named Genghis Khan rules. I will return when this terrible tyrant's land becomes Christian-like. That's the new term for the followers of my Father's words…I like it. Oh yes, thank you, my dear uncle, for maintaining the chain and retrieving this poor soul from death…Your nephew, Jesus."

I could not wait to peer from the hole in the wall of the volcano. What would I witness after all this time? With renewed strength, I penned a note to Jesus that I would go to the north and seek knowledge from there. I too wrote that I would return at times.

This time, I thought, I would prepare for the unplanned. I possessed many coins, as the last time I was ignorant of money and was perceived as a beggar. I planned to make a better entrance into this new world than the last. I also took a laser weapon, in case thieves presented themselves for my valuables. The weapon needed testing. When I get outside I will test it, I thought to myself.

I bid farewell to my sister and her husband lying in state and sealed the big door. I then traveled to the hilt with renewed strength. When I gazed upon the new old world, it had not even changed. There were rocks and desert as before. The sight of the clear blue sky was invigorating though, as I came down from Sinai, again as a young man.

The scene at the oasis was little changed. Ah, yes, the liquid was still cool to the lips, as I tasted its pleasures. I made haste to the north, though my thoughts were south towards Nazareth. I found that my clothing was suitable but not in style with the togs being worn by many. I would escape the thought of being a beggar, I imagined.

Alone, I took out my laser from my waist and pointed it at a distant rock. The trigger's squeeze, then lightning burst beam brought the rock to intense heat instantly and it exploded into dust. It was working well I thought. I was now ready to dedicate my travel to the unknown as a new person, and I quickened my step headed north. After I had walked for an hour, I turned west and realized how nice it would be to sail the distance without the blisters that were forming upon my feet. An aloetta plant which I discovered and used soon soothed my sore feet, but eventually I sought the shoreline of the Mediterranean Sea and a ship's passage to the northern lands.

I found a merchant ship sailing in that direction, which I learned from the ship's captain, was the new Byzantine Empire. I enquired of its inhabitants and found them to be a different people, whose spoken language was other than the ones I knew. I would be lost there, I thought. I must press on to a place that would be receptive of my own ways, and spoke my tongue, or something I could learn quickly. I had learned many languages, some better than others, but there were so many dialects that I just eventually adapted to the tongue I learned from the environment I was presently living. Or I remained silent.

While I was waiting out some horrible rains, I met a traveler one day named Marco Polo. He had sailed east from Italy looking for trade routes to the Empire of the Great Khan and after a mighty long voyage had returned successfully. I asked him if he ever had heard of, or had seen a man called Jesus. He actually said that he had met him! He said that Jesus had confronted the Great Khan and was being detained there on a friendly basis. The Great Khan presented him to his people as a great man of knowledge and peace; imagine my delight. The rains stopped, and I think I could have swum to Sicily faster than the boat I was transported upon.

On the isle of Sicily, I rode upon a sponge boat that was taking its load to Sardinia. From there I shipped with another merchant that was returning to Corsica. I stayed for several weeks and enjoyed exquisite cuisine and wines of the hill country. I almost stayed, but I was determined to locate the western shores of the Mediterranean, so I walked for months upon the whole island to the northwest shore and waited for passage. The long hike made my body stronger, and my light skin had become very dark from the sun.

I began to realize very quickly that it was very difficult to return from an absence of my previous life. I somehow took on the characteristics, both in tongue, and mannerisms from the people with whom I had begun to associate, or I lived with, and it happened more than once. Sometimes, I just fit right in without adapting to changes, sometimes not. This new world had many different peoples and I was beginning to think I was the outcast.

Even though the body physically was restored, my mind was lagging. Events that I should have been aware of were new to me, and I was looked upon sometimes as a naive person. I made excuses about my long travel absences about the world, which prohibited ready knowledge. That was my offered pawn of ignorance to questioning minds.

Almost six months had passed. At the next port of call I boarded a German vessel that was headed to the port of Barcelona. This was a very pleasant trip for I enjoyed the happy fat Germans who drank what they called a lager, always in great quantities; every single night they would get completely under the spirit's hold and they often passed out prone upon the deck, mostly after much song and dance. This occurred every night! Their women walked the deck late at night very lonely, for their men were wasting away in their cabins asleep, and I found much comfort in the large bosomed women who said, "Yah, das ist gut, not?"

Barcelona was the most beautiful port that I had ever seen upon Earth. I explored her beauty and found many foreigners, including myself, visiting the senoritas that danced and twirled to the Spanish guitars out in the streets. The music was festive and joyful. The spirits of wine flowed in tall slim glasses. I had lost all my headings by this time in my life as a young fool; my best judgment, my long memory, education and good moral character.

One day, while I walked a back street near a sidewalk cantina, a guitar and trumpet band played loudly, drawing much attention, including mine. A lovely dancing senorita twirled and stomped her feet, while also clicking on her castanets; a tiny instrument held in her fingers. Her eyes flashed black as the night and her hair was shiny-black, silky-looking and it was propped up high upon her head, with what looked like a fan entwined into her hair. She smiled and twirled, and twirled and smiled, until while watching her moves, I became dizzy and very infatuated and moved towards her like a moth to the bright flame. I was seated too far back in the crowd for my own desires.

I wanted more, so I moved closer and finally I sat down at an empty table for which there were few available near the front. She suddenly stopped in front of my table, but continued the gyrations of her body. Then, like a slithering, striking serpent, she came to my place and ran her soft hand across my cheek, which dazed me so, that I catapulted backwards from my chair onto the street. My drink's porcelain mug actually turned upside down upon my head, and then shattered onto the floor to everyone's loud gleeful laughter. I must have really looked the fool, for I heard her sweet voice loudly speak, "Ponerse* de pie, leventarse machacho grande!" I think she called me big boy.

She was a lady who enjoyed teasing men into her alluring den of beauty, and she easily had made a fool of me. She extended her hand with a glorious smile and I longingly reached for her touch, but she then pushed me back to the ground with her foot and stood there with one foot on my chest, like a conqueror with a trophy kill. I was totally humiliated. She looked down onto me and finished her song and dance right there. I lay there befuddled, but still looking up at her in a deep lusty, burning love, as she accepted the loud applause and laughter of the crowd upon her finish.

She then left me dazed and disheveled, lying on the ground. Her perfume's wonderful fragrance was a fainting memento, as she went from my view. I guess it was worth the torment and laughter, for with all of her magnificent beauty, she had chosen me, I thought. I slowly picked myself up, as people laughed and pointed my way.

I picked up my chair, and then slid quickly into it, but my heart had not recovered from the vacancy it felt by her leaving. I had never fallen in love so hard, so quickly. Then the crowd of men stepped aside, as the woman returned with a cool fresh drink for me, and asked to sit at my table. Heaven, I thought, surely had arrived!

"Como te llamas, senor?" She spoke with her beautiful red lips; her flashing eyes never leaving mine. Her softly spoken, flowing words were in a tone of voice that sounded like a Spanish princess might.

"Me llamo, Jamison," I choked out. "No hablo espanol. My Spanish isn't very good, I'm afraid," I tried to tell her.

"Well, Jaam-i-son, I speak Ingles un poco…I a-pol-o-gize, for using you…in my song, but everybody here knew…which, what, that…I did you to ex' cite zee crowd. I a pol o gize," she insisted.

It was my first seduction and I was enjoying it. Two hours later, I found myself very drunk, still intoxicated by her beauty and suddenly once again lying on my backside upon the ground; but this time there was no "a-pol-o-gy drink". We had ventured into an alleyway looking for a secluded room, which she said was hers. I was quickly knocked down, beaten up, and then robbed at knifepoint by three sleazy-looking hombres of everything I had on me.

All my money and papers were stolen, just like the thieves of the desert. But this time they also took my laser and I immediately became very worried what they might do with its excessive force. They knew not what tremendous power they now possessed.

It did not take long to find out where they had gone. Within the hour, I sobered up some when everyone was running away screaming from a deafening blast that took the whole roof off of the cantina. It could only be my laser's power acceleration, I judged. I ran to the still-burning and much flattened cantina building and found the three men who had beaten and robbed me lying dead. They were all blown apart by the enormous blast.

There too, lay the mangled body of the beautiful dancing senorita that I had fallen for by their sides. The laser was undamaged, and lay still clutched in her hand, which meant that she was in with them, and she had probably picked up the laser, and then accidentally pulled the trigger. I could see all around me that many buildings were also blown apart, maybe twenty or so. I hoped my ignorance of allowing my urges to overcome my judgment hadn't caused more awful deaths than these; I was not so sure.

My money bag was still in the grasp of the other hand, blown several meters away. Soon people started returning towards me, so I left as quickly as I could with all my previously stolen possessions.

I soon began to feel the pain that was inflicted by the beating. I found a park bench amidst all the mass confusion and the screaming, and wished I had the potion. In my bag had been many capsules of AloevectorP23. When I searched, miraculously they were still there. The thieves probably knew nothing about drugs, or they might have sampled them unknowingly. Good, I was relieved now and finally decided this was not the right time. The time for them would be in time of complete disaster. I could not just use them at my leisure. I had to have purpose.

After a while, I found myself again at another cantina, kilometers away from the other, and there I found comfort just sitting, and nursing my pain with the spirits of the grape. A huge man came into the cantina and placed his tall pith hat upon the table next to mine, the bill of which was embellished with fancy braided gold. He was a man with a slight limp and a glass piece in his eye. His long mustache was the twist of an Italian man. He certainly was a spectacle to behold.

After a few minutes, and after quaffing several glasses of vintage liquid, he stretched back in his chair and leaned over to talk, unsolicited by me.

"Terrible thing, I say, wasn't it?" The image of an Italian quickly diminished, and I wondered no more of his origin.

"What's that?" I replied.

"The great explosions down the road, man, did you not hear of it?" he inquired.

"Oh, no, tell me."

"It is believed a falling meteor fell from the sky and hit the place…kaboosh!" he waved his arms.

He scooted his chair next to mine and then began telling me the scene, but didn't stop there but lent his whole life's story. He spoke all about his travels around the world. He had been everywhere, and spouted out the continents, one by one, in his own order; each had its own story attached. I was bored to the hilt, but I was sore and too tired to leave, until he mentioned the Sinai Mountain.

"What happened at the Sinai?" I blurted in.

"I say, the ol' girl erupted upon my exploration's ascension to the top on that very day I had found a hole in her wall. I thought I was a goner, by jiggers!"

"When was this?" I asked. I was very curious as to how close he had come to his biggest discovery.

"I don't quite remember exactly, maybe ten years ago, but I made it to an oasis and hurried off into the desert. Her rumble was deafening."

"Ha!" I laughed.

"Sir?" He felt I was rude.

"I'm sorry; I imagine there was much fire and smoke that would scare anyone."

"And a rumble, sir, that shook the very ground beneath my feet. It was colossal!"

It was I, you stupid oaf, I thought. It was the Nova blowing her tube. Ha!

He continued to tell me of his many adventures. Somewhere, I learned that his name was Benjamin of Tudela. He had explored Egypt, Assyria, Persia, and Middle Asia. These were all the known travels of the time. But now, he stated, was the greatest adventure of all before him and that he was now ready to begin as soon as transportation was gained.

"Africa!" he exclaimed. "The Dark Continent," he mysteriously sounded out. "The marrow of some of the most incredible and horrifying stories ever to be told," he explained.

The horror stories he told were of everything from voodoo, to pygmies with human heads dried upon their sticks. There were diamonds, as large as your fist, and chunks of bright gold lying openly upon the hillsides, all to be gathered by one's own hands. His quest was of two fold, ultimate fame, and outrageous fortune; he wanted both! For he loudly proclaimed to all, that he was the "Benjamin of Tudela!"

But I thought to myself, "I am Jamison of Mars!" I wished I could have revealed it. I bet that would top all of his biggest adventures…but?

He had planned to leave from here to Tangiers. There, he would solicit a guide and the local natives to burden all the property onto the Congo Rivers.

"Every waterway that flows is called a Congo River," he explained. "Since they all eventually flow deep inside the continent, few rivers have been named because very few explorers have ever returned while trying to explore there, or just trying to map them all. Never returned, never returned," he repeated. "Isn't that exciting?"

He assured me that he would succeed. I became so intrigued by his words that I wrangled an invitation from him, and I immediately accepted.

"It might be nice for once to have an intelligent being beside me to talk to, instead of a herdsman blurting babble," he told me. I was in, but how deep would it get?

He immediately went about telling me more and some stories raised the hairs upon my neck.

"When we get to the river we will pick up a very young man who has found a route, but needs financial and moral support. That's where I will need you the most, as a lookout of sorts," he spoke. The young man was a missionary's child, I learned.

He continued to tell me of the hippopotamus of three tons and thirty foot long crocodilians. There were reports by native guides that survived those beasts, that they had devoured not only the entire crew of a boat, but the boat itself. And when the victims were tossed from their dugouts into the raging river, meat-eating fish swarmed them and took their flesh off to the bone, in a boiling, fierce feeding frenzy. Only the skeletons were left in seconds. His eyes were flared with excitement.

I felt myself reaching for my laser and embracing its comfort in my mind. For no Earthling man, nor beast, could withstand the enormous power of her extended ray.

"Her ray, her, I thought?" I will give her a name. I will call her North Star after the brightest, twinkling red star in the heavens that I thought surely must be Mars. She was my security here on Earth.

Within a week, I found myself aboard a sleek ship reviewing maps that Ben had purchased from travelers abroad. All were incomplete. Some were torn or burned. But one had blood spots on it. That made it all the more intriguing. Our imaginations of riches and treasures without measure lit the fires that drove a man to pilot other men to their maximum. Ben was the epitome of pilots.

In one month we embraced the sandy shores of Tangiers. Beggars, thieves, and women of the night, asking only a "favor" of us, met us at the gang plank. But Benjamin was a terror on his own, bent on a mission, without any hindrances or delays. He blew past their outstretched hands without notice, until he found a white-suited, short man who wore a crumpled up, sweat-stained, white hat that looked very round upon his fat head.

He was our guide, and the boss man here. His whip cracked and everyone fled. After hollering gibberish to a group of seated resident natives, they all sprang up to gather Ben's packs and my own. Impressive, I thought.

"Excellent fellow, isn't he?" Ben chimed.

Ben had sent word ahead of his demands from Barcelona through this local, who wished to accompany this safari into the heart of the wealthiest continent on Earth.

Without delay, we set our course due south. Into the bush we walked towards who knows whatever lived in there? The sun was very hot, but the canopy of the trees offered relief. I was unprepared for the mistoes from Mars that buzzed my head every step I took, and often bit my bare spots. I needed different attire.

My wish was soon granted, as we came from the tall trees into the streets of Barootse. We not only put on pith helmets, but also fine woven netting about our heads. Tan shirts were issued and soft boots with high tops. I was handed a rifle. Ha, a devise that shot lead from powder. So ancient! I had never really seen one before, but the history books of Mars told of them. My laser could confront an army of these, I thought. It was amusing. This technology was the newest of battle inventions, Ben had told me. Ben brought the rifle to its raised position. A spark flickered when he pulled the trigger and it sounded. Billowing smoke that erupted to no end made me cough excessively.

"A very colossal piece," Ben hollered.

I longed so to have him witness the massive energy of my North Star. She would certainly raise his eyebrows, I thought. Maybe someday I'll have the opportunity to amaze him.

From Barootse we again entered the canopy of the tall trees. This time I became aware of the jungle, as multitudes of colorful birds squawked while many monkeys jumped from tree to tree. They were following our caravan of bearers. Occasionally a large snake would rear up in our path and the head bearer would slice it in two with his big machete. He chopped our way through tangled vines and bushes. Then suddenly I saw it. It was an Orcadian; the flower of Mars. That proved that Martians had been here long before these humans, much longer. When the bearer whacked its beautiful stem, I drew it to my nostril and inhaled the sweet smell of Mars's past. I remembered Mars as it was before the disaster.

"Let's keep moving!" shouted Ben to me.

I held the flower to my breast and then placed it on my helmet as a prize. But there were many along the way and I imagined that my people had surely congregated here. We pressed on.

On the eve, we camped and sat about the fires that encircled our entire camp. It was the flame, I learned, which protected us from the real dangers of the night. Loud roars erupted from the darkness, breaking the silence. Some roars close to camp sometimes caused a panic with the natives. Some bearers in camp bore the scars of an attack of a lion or panther. Some had relatives in the belly of one.

The lion's foot is soft upon the forest's floor of the jungle, just as the panther was black as the night. But their eyes showed up brightly in the light of our fires from a long distance. If one were spotted, a drummer would start beating a loud pounding, which scared off the intruder…hopefully.

A quick breakfast of mush and a mixture of sugar cane tea, and we were walking.

The day's travel continued to be hampered by the tropical growth that sometimes was alive. One of the bearers had a twenty-foot long snake drop from a tree upon him and it tried to squeeze him to death. His screaming brought the whole caravan to his rescue, as the bearers pounced upon the big snake and withdrew the victim from the serpent's deadly clutch. It had wrapped at least six times around his skinny body. Ben said that the serpent could have swallowed him whole. The birds and monkeys began their loud chatter as they seemingly approved of the removal of their dreaded predator python enemy of the trees.

The bearers all cheered as the lead bearer whacked its head off with his machete and tied him on a carry pole, still squirming. Later, after we had almost set camp up on a site, they brought that serpent into camp and began chopping him into pieces. To my disgust, they fought for the remains. Their stomachs pooched after downing the snake's raw flesh.

"This is good," said the fat man. "I don't have to feed them tonight, ha!"

BEN
FAT MAN
JAIME
PWK

On the sixth day, we began smelling the muddy water of a river and the native bearers were more careful of their step. The deadly cobra lay motionless in the river valley and they were as plentiful here as in India, Ben told us.

We ventured two more days along the river's path, until we entered a grassy opening with a large hut. Several dugout canoes capable of hauling twenty people each, sat on the bank ready for us. I wondered then if the stories of monstrous crocodiles devouring twenty people at a time, and their boats too, were really true. They were really gigantic.

"Oh, Youuuwhooo!" a shrill call erupted from the fat man. Then a short, but very trim, white man came from the large hut's entrance to greet us.

"Strapping young fellow, isn't he?" whispered Ben. "He reminds me of myself as a boy."

His name was Jaime Ferrer, the young man who wanted to continue with us into the Congo. Jaime was a very young man, probably in his late teens, I guessed. I learned that he had traveled extensively his whole life with his missionary parents, until their deaths a year and six months before, he told us. They were captured and then butchered and eaten by cannibal pygmies. The fire of hatred for the little people was in his voice.

He called Catalonia his birthplace, but England as his home. He would try to complete his parents' explorations of western Africa and then return.

Ben and Jaime spent the eve by candlelight looking at maps and planning. I sat on a log by the fire swatting at mistoes, and watching the fat man sweat. He could only speak of the riches that he expected, and his greed, I feared, was his only nature. I did not feel comfortable speaking around the man, nor did I have trust in him.

There comes a time in one's life, or lives in my case, that one must make some very important decisions. This upcoming event was now my decision; were we to venture into this jungle of death, for unproven riches? What we were about to partake upon was a trip into the "almost unknown". Almost, was the key word, for we already knew death had many doors at its entrances to the Congo that were deep inside this jungle.

In the early light of morning, ten of the natives were paid off, and they quickly left in one of the wooden dugouts to return to their homes. Twenty others were encouraged by the guide to continue on, with their chance for pay and to kill a few pygmies who had every once in a while slipped into their villages and had taken their children or relatives. When that wasn't enough, the fat man promised to pay them double. They looked at each other, but only ten decided to remain with us. We then left two dugouts behind.

The bellowing roar that sounded around the first big bend caused panic to our natives. Jaime fired a shot into the air and twenty enormous hippos scampered into the water and submerged. Only one enormous male surfaced and snorted loudly, blasting water from his nostrils, as his big eyes were trained upon us when we let the current carry us past him without much movement.

"So this is a hippopotamus?" I whispered to Ben. Ben was silent.

They were called potties on Mars before they became extinct. How eerily queer, I thought. I was reliving prehistoric Mars, I imagined. How wonderful!

The oarsmen then steadily churned the water and we made very good time. By noon we had seen many crocodiles, but none as large as reported. When I mentioned this to Jaime, he advised me to just be alert for there were many more in some areas.

"It depends on the food supply," he told me. "Where we are headed, we could be considered their main dish!"

"Oh, jeez!" the fat man hollered. "Ouch, ouch, ouch, what did I do?"

Quick, uncertain words came from our now squirming fat guide. He had dangled his hand to feel the cool river water flowing past the dugout when a fish came to him and nipped the end of his fingertip completely off. He bled profusely and his horror-filled eyes stared at the bloody stump.

"Don't let the blood get into the water!" Jaime screamed. "Or we'll have them jumping into our boat! Wrap that up quickly," Jaime ordered.

Now that was really something, because there were no fish like those where I came from, I thought. Jaime wrapped the fat man's finger with his own neck scarf to stop the flow of blood. The fat man then hunkered down inside the craft and didn't look up for some time.

The day ended near a steep waterfall. From here we had to lower the boats over the falls. But for tonight, we just turned the boats over and sheltered under them. We all lay down upon the rocks with bed rolls near the running water's eddy, and we didn't dare start any fires. The rocks were slippery with green algae, but the natives quickly gathered up forest grasses to make nests for us to lie upon; it was really a novel idea.

"This way, beasts and humans will think it is just a log jam," Jaime explained.

Good idea, not so soft bed, I thought. I slept like a rock, or I was one, I'm not certain.

During the night the jungle came alive. The lion roars, the hyena howls, but the snake remains silent. A big anaconda slithered up under our boat and curled up upon my legs for warmth. I just assumed it was one of the other's legs and was too tired to push it away. Its weight, however, held me in my place and I was very uncomfortable.

At daylight, I awakened as the huge snake tried to squeeze between my legs. At first, I thought Ben was acting queerly, but when I looked up and saw him wide-eyed staring at me and motioning for me to remain still, I followed his petrified eyes to my crotch.

I then farted a big one! The sleeping natives moaned disgustedly, and quickly rolled the boat over onto its side to get fresh air. When they saw that gigantic snake, they were more forgiving than before, each frozen stiff with fear. Having no cover for itself, that heavy snake moved quickly up my body, but as he neared my face, he stopped, and I swear that he stared me right in the eye, and then winced, while it shut its nostrils, and slipped past me back into the water…Imagine that?

We all slipped under the waterfall to refresh. That was the only safe place on the river Jaime told us. I noticed the multiple red marks upon my body and Ben quickly said they were just mosquito bites…Hummm, not mistoes? I shall remember that.

We used lye soap, the first I had ever used. It smelled like the medicine chest back at our Nova. I then wondered of the ship's contents. I wondered of my relatives.

In an hour we had successfully transversed the falls with our boats and we were again on our way. Several hours of rowing brought us into an area marked by little hairy images hanging from trees.

"Voodoo, voodoo," whispered the natives.

We continued. Some big crocs swam up and followed us for a while, but then tired of their pursuit and slid up on the muddy bank to grab a dead fish.

"Soon," said Jaime, "we will be at the place my parents and I stayed for a while and spoke to the natives. They are peaceful, because white men have not hurt them."

It was called a 'vey', I think Jaime called it, but the forest opened up and a village appeared before us. The river was shallow and in full use here, as half-nude women bathed openly and washed their families' clothes. The men here manned nets of finely woven vines, trying to catch fish.

The women and their children all ran to greet us from the bank. Here too, were signs of the huge crocs, as one child bore hideous scars on his body, while several older boys hobbled on one good leg, because the other probably had been ripped off in the hungry jaws of a man-eater. Though I felt sorry for the children, it was so common in their lives the natives here learned quickly to accept horrible disaster as the norm. No one was looked down upon, and help was always available to the needy; they were worthy people.

The village was arranged in sort of a large circle from chopped trees. The poles with grasses they made had pointed ends tied closely together with vines. The straw-like thatched door opened and a man dressed in severe plumage came toward us. It was Boombay, their chief, and our host for our stay here.

Our oarsmen greeted the other natives with hugs, almost like we Martians did, but they also rubbed noses and began their own funny little laughter. It seemed that many here were relatives.

It's really a small world, for it was four hundred kilometers from where we first began, I guessed; millions more to Mars. We were now very deep into the continent.

It soon became apparent on the eve that the fat man was going to be trouble, as he asked favor of a man's wife. The husband drew a machete from its scabbard and chased the fat man into our presence. Here the chief reminded the husband that the guests would not be harmed. Jaime immediately got up and delivered a punch to the fat man's jaw, and by its force, knocked him cold stiff upon the mud. This brought satisfaction to the husband and after he kicked the unconscious fat man, he mumbled, I'm certain, foul words and left. Jaime had saved face with our group, and the fat man's life.

When the fat man came to, he sat holding his jaw and collecting his thoughts. His thoughts no longer were of the naked women, but his own welfare. He looked at the young Jaime with a greater respect. When the fat man walked about the camp that night, all the women hissed his presence, a signal that a predator was among them. He stayed his place.

"This is the beginning of the end," Jaime told us. "My memory draws anger from within, so I may hesitate to hold my feelings of rage inside. I keep it for the pygmies. We will now travel across land to the mountains where pygmies murdered my parents. We must travel through their domain, for the river exists with many falls and no boat can travel for any distance. If we get past there, I believe the riches you speak of exist just to the southwest of the big mountain.

"My parents brought no weapons with them in their desire to bring civilization to the pygmies. The medicines were considered voodoo, and the head tribesman issued the death sentence. I was withheld, they told me, sent back free to warn others not to come there. They tied me to a carry pole like an animal. Then they carried me to their border, and cut me loose.

"I struggled for days, till I regained my bearings. When I did, I was chased up a tree by a lion, which camped under my limb for two days. But all was not lost. First, I discovered the moss that my parents had searched for as medicine, for ten long years. It has many cures. I now believe it grew because of monkey droppings that clung to the limb and ripened. But, I am not certain yet. While I sat aloft, I found my avenue of return. I broke off a limb and pointed it towards my destination, as the floor of the jungle is dark and hidden by the canopy of the treetops."

He then came back to this camp, he told us, and received comfort from the natives.

"There was a great sadness among them, and they mourned with me for days. Then the chief took me in his hands and shook me. He told me that I must step into the place of my parents. And I regained my life again."

The story reminded me of my own fate, for I too must step into my parents' place, for them, and continue on. But I did not seek the revenge I knew was in Jaime's heart, a revenge that I suspected would erupt in the presence of the pygmies. Maybe North Star and I could help. I fell asleep on the hut's bare floor.

The morning brought hand waves goodbye, something I did not expect from natives. I guessed it was the learning from Jaime's parents.

The jungle grew darker and the only thing that shown was the fat man's muddy white coat. He hopelessly clung to his funny white hat, as the swinging tropical bush branches continually knocked it off his fat round head.

The chief had given us his best son as a guide, who got us to the border of their little country in four days. When he waved good-bye, he pointed to the direction that we must take and then as fast as he could, he ran from us in an instant. That set the tone of our emotions.

All the chatter of the birds and all the screeches of the monkeys stopped. All the jungle life itself had suddenly disappeared from view. It was like walking into the desert.

"Have you ever had the feeling that someone was watching you, but you couldn't see anyone?" Ben asked.

Suddenly, we approached a standing line of bamboo poles. It was the skulls on top with hair that got our immediate attention and brought us all to a halt. They were fairly fresh. The warning to the front door of the pygmy tribe's nation of man-eaters read, "Keep out!" In words anyone could easily understand.

"Cannibals, that's what they call them in Borneo," whispered Ben. "They were a grisly tribe."

The silence was shattered, first by one, and then by all of the natives who pitched our gear into the bush, and ran screaming back from where we had just come.

"They left us!" screamed the fat man, taking steps back also. But when we stood steadfast, he became confused.

"I came here to get filthy rich," admitted Ben.

That quelled the fears in the fat man, and greed, filthy greed, overtook his filthy soul. But I too had the same desires, though not as open about it as the fat man. I wondered what my nephew would have thought of his uncle right then.

Jaime, however, stood tight-lipped. The gaze in his eyes searched the skulls for his parents' features to no avail. We sat down right there and made a new plan.

The trail became wider, well worn, and the four of us who remained had collected the significants from our packs, hid the rest off the trail, and continued. We decided the fat man should remove his white clothing and dawn darker attire. It was not really because it was white, and the cannibals might spot us, but because he stank.

Our eyes searched hard for a clue to any movement from the bush. Jaime stopped, knelt down, and pointed to a track in the mud. At first I thought it was that of a small animal, but the significant five-toe feature dictated a human. This pygmy's footprint was wide but only about half the length of a hand. It was fresh and had a lot of company.

I embraced my precious North Star with a firm grip, while balancing the powder weapon that Ben had given me with the other. We crept along slowly, ranging our movements from bush to bush. Still, the tropical forest inhabitants whistled, or chattered, or screeched out our positions with each movement. Suddenly a flock of birds lit above us in the tree tops and squawked loudly.

A distant rhythmic beating of drums broke the silence of the jungle, and seemed to be in beat-step with our own, an eerie feeling it was. We sat down again to listen. The forest became alive near us with erupting birds taking flight. They continued with their squawking; the jungle alarm for danger. Jaime motioned and we quickly left the trail into the bushes. We suddenly heard the patter of little feet; first, with their rhythmic poundings of the ground in unison. It became deafening as they ran past us, maybe fifty, and Jaime told us quickly to do as he did and walk backwards upon the trail.

While quietly shuffling backwards Jaime spotted a very large tree that leaned precariously against another.

"Up. Up," he whispered. The bent over trunk offered a runway to the canopy, and we found wild vines that looked like grape foliage to hide in.

"When someone notices our footprints, they will return with a vengeance," Jaime whispered. "Maybe we can confuse them," he continued.

A soft human's grunt froze our bodies to the trunk of the tree and I was afraid the hair upon my neck stood too tall, for those natives were a hideous sight. Peering down at our tracks, they almost silently crept back past us. They possessed small spears, bows and arrows, and poison-tipped darts that they apparently used to shoot their prey. We were now their prey, the hunted, and also their hot pot dinner if we let them catch us.

The grunts from the little human bastards continued, as they seemed to spread out from where we had left the trail. One hollered angrily in disgust, and we could tell that there was confusion. They had walked upon our tracks with their own and had obliterated ours completely. We were afraid that they thought that we had vanished up into the thin air and might look up and see us. But that did not happen. They were short sighted…. pardon the pun, and jumped up and down in anger walking cautiously down the path back to protect their village ahead. Four little people remained, I guess to protect their rear.

After a few moments and several spoken grunts and squeals, the rest left in cadence still grunting, and I realized just then why they must call them "pigmees". We all gave Jaime an embrace for saving our hides from the soup pot, and shimmied down the tree. Jaime smiled and said that he did that same thing to the lion once.

"But that lion, he smelled me!"

We decided to skim the outskirts of their foot trails by walking well away from them.

"Maybe that way we could better avoid being seen," Ben suggested.

"Good idea, Ben," we all agreed in unison.

The trail now was really tough going. Not only was the undergrowth almost impassable, but also the creatures that crawled there were found with each and every cautious step we took. They all slithered upon their vined highway. It was very slow indeed, a snail's pace.

The tall boots that Ben had selected saved us from the snakebites. Ben applauded himself for that good decision, time and again.

On the eve, we found ourselves crossing another pathway. This time we were directly beside their village. It seemed that the pygmy never left his village alone, because they always left in groups. Thus, their arrival was somewhat noticeable, except this time, they were waiting upon our arrival.

A close scan of our surroundings didn't reveal these very small predators. As we attempted to avert capture; one at a time we crept across the trail to the other side. I was last then, and when I completed my stealthy maneuver, I discovered, as did the others, that we had fallen into a hunter's snare. They all stood silently around us, their arrows and spears and blowguns pointed at us. They just stood there quietly awaiting more intruders. Their eyes gleamed with the visions; I'm sure, of white meat under glass.

I was about to fire my powder weapon, when Jaime stopped me. He wanted to go within the walls of the compound and see if his parents possibly remained there alive. That took only a few moments, as their spears goosed us and poked holes in our butts as they grunted us right into the middle of what looked like a big circus ring.

"I sure hope those aren't poison points," Ben whispered.

The screams were joyous, as the little ones really knew how to hoop it up. It seemed as though we were surrounded by a large bunch of naughty kids who were going to chastise their parents for their own inadequate height gene supply. But their mind set was, dog eat dog, and we were the losers.

A sudden hush came upon everyone, as through the crowd walked a taller fellow waddling. He had reddish hair, a pooched belly, and a big pug nose that must have come from an Irishman's blood buried deep in his gene pool, I thought. He slowly looked us up and down. He then stopped in front of Jaime. He had seen his face before, you could tell, as he began to holler insults at him, and stomp the ground.

As if to somehow show Jaime his power of life or death, he flung open a thatched door to a nearby hut and revealed several human heads on sticks, hanging, drying. Two of them were Jaime's parents. It was awfully gruesome.

The big little man laughed a treacherous, vulgar laugh, the kind of snarling laugh that would make a man run directly into the path of death without fear, and grab him up by the throat and squeeze the life out of that little bastard. That's just what Jaime did!

Before we could stop him, Jaime had a death grip upon the chief's throat with both hands. The bizarre scene left the others shocked in their tracks. And when they advanced to kill Jaime, we fired our powder weapons at them. Four or five fell to the ground. The bizarre got worse, as they now collected themselves and charged us full out. Darts narrowly missed us and the arrows penetrated the door of the hut as we jumped behind the door of skulls.

"Now is the time for all good men to come to the aid of their countrymen, huh? I think I learned that on Mars once in a typing class, oops here they come."

I withdrew North Star, and to everyone's amazement, including my own, I fried up into little burnt crispies, one hundred sixty-two pygmies, who didn't move too fast. I let some go, and boy did they! Their little buns were toasted to a crisp. I wonder how they liked it.

"It was colossal!" Ben screamed. "It was simply, colossal! I too must have one of those," he rambled.

Well, I had let that cat out of the bag, so to speak, now what was I going to do? Take them into my confidence as friends, or tell a big fat lie? I wasn't sure. I chose the latter.

"I invented this!" I told them. "Hadn't had an opportunity to test it until now, what do you think?"

"Colossal, my boy, colossal!" repeated a very happy and relieved Ben.

When I finally noticed Jaime still stood there clutching the dead chief by the neck in an insane, sort of feverish state, we rushed to his side to tell him he could quit. We could not break his hold and he couldn't hear us. It was as if his mind was caught up in the revenge that burned inside of him, and I tell you he had a big uncontrollable fire.

The potbellied chief hung suspended by his neck, bulgy-eyed, strangled, and dangling there lifeless, held by Jaime's vicious death grip. It must have been the built-up energies of revenge that sustained Jaime's strength. I think this payback was really worth it to Jaime; his murderous gleam in his eyes meant it was so satisfying to him, and he was really getting his due, I surmised.

Apparently, the fat man had left us somehow. He was nowhere to be found. Just as well, I thought, for he was useless and a vulgar nuisance. We all needed sleep, but what if other little bastards showed up?

Suddenly I wanted to sleep deeply and badly. Someone had to be on guard; Ben could, I thought. He was wide awake and counting the trophies scattered out upon the ground. I think he planned to mount the biggest, maybe it was the chief. When the excitement finally left me too weary, I had no choice but to surrender to my body, so I told Ben to wake me if he needed me then passed out. Ben came over and shook me violently.

"We can't dally around here, boy," Ben pleaded.

I feared the potion had suffered its first setback and I had better save my energy.

"They wouldn't dare come back, but if they do, just point and squeeze. Watch out though, I think it's got a hair-pull trigger!"

I handed my prized North Star to Ben, and shut my eyes. I entered a deep uncontrollable sleep. When I finally awoke, only a night had passed, just eight short hours. But Ben was asleep too.

Looking around, I wondered how we were still alive, for evidently Ben had squeezed the trigger and burned the entire village to the ground. He never told me if he did it intentionally, or not. When he awoke, all that came from his mouth was, "Colossal, simply colossal!"…Imagine that?

It took nearly three days, but when Jaime finally loosened his death grip on the chief, he too fell to the ground very exhausted. To our surprise, in a quiet, sane voice, he told us that he wanted to bury his parents in England and figured they would travel well in their condition. Jaime carefully removed their skulls from the poles upon the door and wrapped them in his clothing. He was headed to the western African coast, he told us, and would return to where we had started.

"Go with the direction of the morning sun from here," Jaime told us. "I hope that you will find your dreams. Thank you for helping me ease away the hate from my heart. I will remember you both."

With that said, he placed his parents' remains in his pack, did an about face and walked briskly into the forest. We never saw Jaime again.

"A strong-willed man," spoke Ben.

We silently left, headed into the morning's sunlight, just Ben and I. Now we thought that we could walk anywhere we pleased with our new little girl-friend, North Star, and we did.

But on two occasions, a very large rhino, and a very mean lion, stood their ground to attack us. Regretfully, I zapped them. "Zap" became the word, instead of shoot.

"That is more explicitly appropriate," admiringly, Ben told me.

I didn't know the true mechanics of the weapon, and after two months walking in the dark forest and occasionally 'zapping' several wildebeests for food along the way, it stopped 'zapping' completely. Each time I had used the weapon, I noticed Ben studied me and North Star closely, up and down. I was afraid we had been together maybe just too long, if you know what I mean. He looked at me hard.

"Now what do you really do?" Ben questioned.

"You're the top hat here, you tell me!" I replied.

He studied for a moment with his hand on his chin, looked me straight in the eye and said suddenly, "You aren't from here, are you?"

"Certainly not," I said.

"I mean, from any place I've been, are you?"

"That depends, Ben, have you ever been to Mars?" I laughed, while pointing to the heavens.

He shrugged his shoulders and his eyebrows arched. He couldn't quite know if I was kidding, or not.

"Here, Jamison, this has served me well on many occasions," Ben spoke to me as he held his pistol powder-weapon out to me for my protection.

"Now this blunderbuss kicks like a mule if you put too much powder down the horn, and I have. It's not very accurate, unless you are very close. Several lead balls can be placed down the horn to accompany the powder, but don't ever get the powder wet."

He then handed me the blunderbuss pistol gun, it looked like a Spanish musician's horn to me. Ben kept his rifle and led the way from then on. We walked and talked to a great extent.

"Save your weapon, if you can, for it is just tired. I think it likes the sun best and this forest canopy thwarts the sun. It needs the sun, so wear it on top of your helmet."

We had begun to travel the plains in a week and viewed a very tall mountain above the tall grasses, many miles away. It appeared much closer than it really was, as we walked a month in that direction. This part of the trip was very pleasant, as the abundance of animals was astonishing to us both. Herds of strange looking animals swarmed like beehives and when they spooked, they all fled, trampling everything in their path. Such was the case this day, luckily!

A breakfast of dik dik, a very small animal that resembled a big dog with a rat's head, was our pleasure. Our fire was dowsed, and white smoke filled the air. We were preparing ourselves to go to the base of the big mountain. While walking slowly through the tall grasses we were suddenly surrounded by the tallest natives that we had ever seen.

"Zulu, two hundred meters…I think they see us," Ben whispered.

Their shields were long and narrow; their spears were shiny and sharp looking. They banged their shields, as if to threaten us. Then they one-stepped toward us, step by step, rattling the shield. It scared the pants off me, and no North Star.

We stood there, probably looking like a sparrow facing a hawk, when a commotion began off to the east. We actually heard a shot fired from a gun. No African, we supposed, had even seen one, or at the very least had one in his possession to fire.

The rumble upon the ground caused panic among these giant hunters, and their eyes shown the whites at fifty meters. They rattled their shields, and hopped up and down, like they had to relieve themselves. Soon, they all scrambled away hollering and that huge skirmish line faded into the east, as their tall figures ran harem-scarem in all directions with fear in their eyes.

"What is it?"

"Stampede!" Ben yelled, as the deafening rumble began to vibrate our innards.

Ben grabbed me and pushed me down near an erosion gully. I peered above the crest just in time to see a million sharp, wild angry horns and hooves headed in our direction, at the speed of a tornado.

Ben fumbled with the powder from his own horn that was used to carry weapon powder. He asked for mine and cursed something when mine was damp and of no use. He quickly spread his powder upon the ground and left a trail to our cover. Then with the pull of his trigger, the flint sparked and ignited his powder weapon.

Pow…Kaaboooom! The tremendous explosion erupted with billowing smoke and dug a hole in the ground that would have challenged North Star's veracity. The smoke plume rose high into the air like a towering warrior. It split the charging wildebeests dead in their tracks, but more importantly, the Zulu could still be seen kicking up dust five kilometers away. What an accomplishment!

I turned to Ben, smiling from ear to ear, I'm sure, and said, "Colossal, simply colossal, Benjamin! We make quite a twosome, don't you think?"

"Only if you remember the next time to keep your powder dry, partner…Ha!"

We sat right down in the erosion to collect ourselves. In about an hour's half we heard a strange shuffling through the grasses, which had now been partially knocked flat.

"Oh, my aching feet!" were the first words we heard.

It was the fat man. He struggled, carrying his boots above his head, waddling as best he could to take a step.

"Boys, boys," he yelled. "Where have you gone? Oh, there you are! I've been following your tracks."

Ka-Boooom!
THE
PWK
STAMPEDE!

He waddled over to us and tried to hug us, but we tried to ignore his coming. When we stepped back away from him, he sheepishly said, "What? What? I had to save myself, didn't I?" He was a big fat coward, although at the time those same thoughts entered all of our minds. Ben and I finally allowed him to rest near us.

He went on to tell us that he ran all the way back to the tree that we all had climbed up before to hide from the natives, and stayed there until he saw a bunch of horrified pygmies run past him lickity-split with their tail feathers burned and smoking.

"I then realized that I couldn't get back down by myself. But during the night, I fell asleep and slid right out of that tree. I didn't feel a thing though, because I was knocked out. When I woke up, I came back, but you all were gone. Where's what's his name?"

Reluctantly, but with a renewed goal, we three headed for the hillside of the big mountain. Its stone was hard granite with very sharp edges. It didn't take long to discover that the stories were untrue. There were no big diamonds here the size of a fist. I never saw a big hunk of gold. But deep in the crevices were large veins of green crystal stones. Ben and I didn't know what they were, but the fat man's eyes gave it away. His double chin shook like a flapper, as he stuttered out his blurted surprise. "Em, em, emeralds!" he finally shouted out madly.

Emeralds were exactly what they were; big green crystalline gems that graced the crowns of kings and queens for centuries.

"Usually found in the Far East," Ben told us, as we really had found our own type of "gold and diamond" mine of massive wealth.

They were there for our taking. Enough for the entire world to be rich!

Greed has a way of causing a man to try to do things far beyond his abilities. Within a week's work, the fat man had collected more than he could possibly tote. He had collected enough riches to last him twenty life times. But his eyes searched for more, and when he spotted a large vein of shiny green, too high to possibly harvest, we couldn't stop him from trying. His wide body twisted and wreathed like a snake, until he had squeezed himself into the crevice that held this gigantic emerald prize, a large fortune by itself. He finally made it to the place, almost forty meters up.

His voice became excitedly high-pitched as he described his view of what must have been the granddaddy of all stones. His hammer pounded rapidly about the perimeter of the stone with an intense fervor. Rocks tumbled to the floor of the caverness hole that he had ascended. But within an instant, the mountain apparently decided not to give up her biggest treasure and collapsed together, sealing the fat man between two gigantic slabs of emerald gems. He had a sealed coffin; his red blood oozed out between the crevice cracks, for there was no way that we could have ever gotten to him. The fat man's tomb would be a greater mausoleum than any known king had ever embraced when he was buried; but the fat man was lost forever, because of his greed.

Without delay, Ben and I stopped our digging, for we too had much too much to carry. We checked the maps and as Jaime had once advised us, we planned our route towards the morning sun.

We had left the fat man's take, all piled up, as his final marker. We had moved away from the easy going of the plain. After hiking a great distance through a mountainous pass, we again found a waterway.

This waterway flowed completely wrong, according to our beliefs. Had we become confused in direction? No, the sun always rises in the east. Had the river simply made a big bend? No, we followed it for some time. But the flow was north. It was then not known, but on each side of the equator the water flows opposite. We had traveled far into Africa's interior, really far…a thousand miles, or more!

"Where in the world have we gone?" barked Ben.

The map was incomplete and of no use. We had only one choice now and that was to follow the river. The muddy lowland clay caked to our boots and we became bogged down. Our packs laden with gems made each step an adventure…in torture. We collapsed within five kilometers and decided to construct a craft that could float us out of this place.

"The large trees that grow near the water don't float at all," said Ben. "I tried that in India. If we want a secure vessel, we must weave the reeds from along the bank."

Ben grabbed up a reed and slit it with his knife. He showed me the chambers inside. There were many hollow sections in each stem, and when packed together, he explained to me, it would float us high upon the water. We would also use them as rope to bind the bundles together.

I quickly agreed, and we both moved into the water to cut the stems. When the reed pile became too large, Ben told me to continue gathering, as he sat himself down and began to weave the stems like I had only seen women do along the Nile in Egypt. Ben worked into the late morning. I managed to sharpen a thick reed to spear some fish in a shallow pool for us to eat.

The craft began to take shape and when Ben tied the long links together.... voila, a fine boat. I started to search for wood to make some oars, but ol' Ben said that we'd pole. This meant that we would use long poles to navigate.

The day heated up as Ben worked feverously without a rest. Ben removed his helmet and left it off when he had to continually wipe his brow of sweat. Bent upon completion, Ben said he could relax plenty while coasting down the river, as I poled. He was beaming brightly and enjoyed looking upon his masterpiece.

When everything was completed, Ben stood up and said, "Outstanding!"

But then, Ben immediately keeled over. The heat had fried his brain, I guess, and though I brought water to cool his body, he fought hard to catch his breath.

"It's not going to do; it's not going to do," Ben repeated.

I took his head in my lap and tried to comfort him more from the sun. His eyes looked up to me and his voice became weak.

"You are one, aren't you?" he spoke softly. "You have more knowledge of this planet than any man I've ever met. You discuss many things that happened in ancient times, as though you were there. You were, weren't you?"

"Yes, Ben, I was," I began. "You are the smartest Earthling I have ever met, certainly the most traveled and now the richest, if you'll just hang on. I have a potion that would save you from death's grip, but it does not work in Earthling's blood."

"What sort of man does it work on, Jamison?" he whispered lowly.

"A Martian, a person from the planet Mars, that's from where I have come."

"I knew it, I knew it!" he struggled to say.

With that burst of energy, Ben slipped into death's grasp and was at peace. He smiled just as he passed.

"I will miss you, Ben, I will miss you, my friend," I whispered as I wiped a tear from my cheek. I had lost a truly great friend, indeed.

"Dargod, if you ever come upon Ben," I spoke out loud, "please give him a special place."

I buried Ben upon a grassy knoll, off the river's way, and planted an orcadia flower there. It seemed the right thing to do.

I placed the packs full of emeralds upon Ben's craft and pushed off with a pole. The craft rode high and the current took me along at a fast pace. I was able to see the interior of Africa as no man had seen before. The big river deposited me in its flow twice, when I failed to watch for low hanging branches. Luckily, the craft remained upright. But each dip was refreshing and a welcomed change from the exhausting heat.

I sometimes fed upon the fish that ate meat. They were easy to catch, as sometimes I just wiggled a stick in the water, until one locked his sharp teeth upon it, and couldn't let go. I was very comfortable upon Ben's craft. He would have bragged on its service, I thought, I would too. "Thanks, Ben," I softly whispered to myself.

I traveled along very slowly for almost two months. I found dik dik animals drinking sometimes at the water's edge and since it had provided nourishment before for Ben and me, I zapped them as needed. Sometimes there were fruits hanging right over the water, easy to get, but I wasn't sure if they were edible or poisonous, so I passed them by.

The river suddenly came to run at a fork quickly, so I poled into the sun and rode that current. I began to notice in a while that this river way narrowed, so much so, that it became shallow, and stagnant. I had to walk from here, I thought. I could not haul two heavy packs. So I searched for a place to hide Ben's pack, if I should someday return. I walked above the river's high bank and noticed an indentation, and rocks of a bluff. Probably, I imagined, it was the high bank of the river long ago. Its rocky crevices surely had some hidden protection for my stash.

As I searched, I found an opening to a cavern. It was damp and cool, and felt so refreshing inside the hole. The opening was protected from sight by many trees, and I only had found it by chance. But I thought that I could someday find it again, since it was near the end of the river and had a pronounced pointed shape above of raw stone. What name was given this river, I did not know. So, affectionately I called it Big Ben.

I lit some wood and started a fire inside. This would be my shelter tonight. I returned to the river and dragged Ben's craft up into the big opening and used it for my bed. When the fire burned brightly, I noticed some important figures of people that had been rock-etched upon the walls. There were many. I took two steps backward when the scratches resembled Dargod's Nova and people with fire.

My heart raced as I hurried to understand their meanings. It was a story, of sorts, about Earth's past. It was an etched-out story of flying ships with big flames coming out of their bottoms. It wasn't hard to understand that this was my people's history; probably a story of their walks upon Earth many centuries before. I was then pleased, for it made me feel at ease and not alone. There surely were survivors.

But where they had all gone, I was uncertain. Where? I sat in the cool staring at the writings and it suddenly dawned upon my mind. They had gone nowhere at all. They were still here! They could be anyone I had met, only their ancestors. It was only our flight group that had the use of the life extending capsules. Therefore, the others must have bred and died in their own time. My feeling that I too belonged on Earth was good. I raised my voice loudly in glorious happiness, "Thank you, oh mighty Dargod! Thank you, again!"

I ventured into the cavern's belly more deeply, and I became startled by some kind of animal birds, so thickly populated that they covered the ceiling completely. They all were clutching the ceiling by their feet and seemed to be upside down. They were sinister looking, and when they all suddenly burst into flight, it scared me enough to fall upon the floor of the cavern. They flew out quickly with a burst of wind. I sat up looking for more.

Then I remembered Ben had told me of vicious birds called vampire bats that clung to a person's throat to suck their hot blood. I hoped it was not those birds; but these creatures were tiny compared to the birds Ben described as enormous bats, I finally surmised. I knew they disliked my fire so I huddled near the flame as best I could. I used a burning stick as light to view more of the cave.

I found other writings upon the walls. This time, it was above a dripping water spring. Below the spring, was a scooped out trough, which held cool, clear liquid. Surely Martians had made it, and I took some. It was very pleasant to the tongue, and I knew my people had taken a drink there. I decided that the water trough was as good as any place to bury Ben's emeralds. I faced the opposite wall and scratched a pointer at the spot where I buried it. A large stone lifted easily, and after I dug out a deep gap, I placed the emeralds inside the hole. I stepped back and found it suitable. I returned to the front of the cave, without going any deeper, but soon I fell asleep peering at the writings on the walls. I wondered who had scribed the messages.

The shadows of daylight struck the entrance to the cave late. But those birds swarmed back inside at the hint of light, and horrified my soul. The wind from their wings beating brought a stench to the air.

It was then, at that exact moment, that the earth's floor shook and a rumble sounded as though it screamed from the bowels of Earth's innards. Rocks began falling upon me and also outside in front of the cavern. Big boulders suddenly sealed off the entrance to my shelter, which was then black as night, in an instant. Dust and large shale rocks whooshed down in billows and covered me. The bird animals fluttered, swarming about with a whistling, batting of their wings. They were confused, struck by the falling walls and each other, and then fell down dead upon me, by the hundreds.

I hugged the floor and heard the rumbling beat of Earth's heart. When it stopped, I was a prisoner of her tomb, held by the falling rocks; I could not get out, until a short time later, another shaking came again and released me enough to slide out free.

Though I immediately felt that I was not seriously injured, the pain started to worsen. I was now a prisoner of a rock hole; I would starve to death, if my injuries didn't do the job. I saw there was still water in the trough, very dirty, but still liquid. It did not fill the emptiness of one's stomach. Could I eat the dead birds, I asked myself? After much deliberation and examination of the tiny creatures, I decided that I'd rather starve.

I felt my way very slowly along the wall of dusty darkness to Ben's craft. It was untouched and in tact. I stirred the logs of the fire that I had made and the small fire came back to life. I knew I had to move back into the cavern quickly while the fire was lit, for the huge rocks here were still unsteady. I picked up a burning log and dragged Ben's craft back, as far as I could. It took some time to do that, because my head caught a low hanging sharp rock and split my skull open deeply. It knocked me stupid, and warm blood ran down my face. It hurt so badly that it made my toes curl. I immediately fell unconscious.

When I finally awoke many hours later, the cave wasn't quite as dark as before, and the dust had settled. Those ugly birds were gone from the roof. Where had they flown? Had they found an escape route?

My head ached and my sight was somewhat blurry. I could see one lone stream of light that flowed from the top of the cavern's roof onto the floor way in the back. There must be an opening, I thought. But I wasn't going anywhere, until I regained my stability. It took an hour, or more, as I tried to wash my face at the dirty pool of liquid. I was at least grateful for that liquid.

When I moved to the back of the cavern, it widened. It also had a very high ceiling; too high for a mortal soul. If I had the wings of a bird, I might be able to escape there. Without them, I was a prisoner. I knew it was hopeless immediately. My time was getting short. My tomb would have the writings of my ancestors on its walls, and my bones upon its floor, I thought. I then planned to write my epitaph upon the walls for future Martians.

But somehow in the dizziness of my thoughts, I found the capsules in my hand. Was this the time to use one, or two, or more? I studied my choices. I reasoned that I would just take one and see if by then the situation had changed. Maybe another great movement would free me from this tomb.

However, because this time I wasn't too tired to go on, but now also slightly injured and trapped, I pondered if I should take a capsule, or search more for an escape, then finally decided maybe I should wait. I was confused.

What about North Star, I suddenly thought? Why, a blast from her and it would clear my exit. But then I looked at the hanging, shaky boulders and feared they surely would crush me instantly, if I dared. I wasn't really sure that they weren't going to fall upon me on their own anyway. Either way, I could never hope to ever escape.

After too much brain usage I was weary, so I slept on it. In the middle of the night though, I was very hungry, deeply chilled, and also feeling very depressed by my helpless situation.

I knew a day of disaster might happen, or a helpless position like this one might occur some day and corner me, but this happened so quickly that my mind was unprepared, after I possibly had become the richest man on Earth. I had to make a life and death decision quickly, for my pains now were throbbing and excruciating.

I tried hard, for a time, to concentrate on this terrible happenstance which I had gotten myself into, and to intelligently solve it quickly. But alone, my injured mind could not. So I finally resorted to the "Martian way" of really difficult decision making.

The procedure had been determined by Martian scientists, named after those same four, to be as accurate as anything known, and this system had been used for ages upon the most important of Mars's borderline decisions. I then used this familiar solution-solver of "Eennie, Meenie, Minie, and Moe". My decision was now final.

I took one capsule, slipped inside Ben's craft, and hoped to witness a better day. The capsule soothed me, and once again, I entered into a wonderful deep sleeping world of my own, free of hunger, free of all my pains.

Life Flows by Quickly
(Chapter 5)

The Earth is a wonderful, beautiful place. In time, hundreds of years passing, even thousands of years passing, bears little scar upon her face and features. Only the inhabitants that dwell here change.

Human life rotates also. The child grows, multiplies itself, ages and then dies. Their begotten children, and their children's children, do the same, on and on, and so on. The process is never ending, unless there is a sudden great catastrophe, or a flood.

While I slept, my dreams viewed the walls of the cavern drawings in my brain, and I could reveal its value. It told this story that was now written on the walls.

Our people were master scientists that arrived here upon Earth. Some had become saddened by the disobeying and wicked children of this Earth, who already lived upon Earth long before Martians arrived. They were an ignorant breed. It spoke of a dispute among our people and one man who was smarter than most. He told the other Martians and the ignorant people to go gather up all the animals upon earth in pairs, male with female, and to place them all upon a craft that he was to build that would be large enough to carry them all. They scorned the thought and became teasers; everyone refused and his words were severely criticized.

When the building was done of the enormous boat, the other Martians and the Earth's ignorant people refused to take their families aboard. Because others threatened this scientist's life, he took only his own family aboard with a selected few wild Earth animals and then closed the door behind him.

Then a great rain fell down upon the lands at length and perished the unclean people from his Earth. Afterwards, the boat returned to settle upon a clean Earth and everything was refreshed.

And so it was that much time had passed before a great flood came back onto this very land. This great flood, though, lifted my body up, lying down asleep inside Ben's craft. The craft floated up to the roof, and out of the top of that cavern's hole above me, I flowed. The current was high and strong, for in my deep sleep, I somehow felt my body twirling in the swirls, but could not awaken to see my path of travel. The ride was rough. But the craft Ben had built was sturdy and rode high as I drifted, and drifted, for decades and decades and still floated high upon the surface following the unknown path Dargod, I assumed, had made for me.

And when the rains stopped and the waters subsided, Ben's craft continued to serve me well, as it came to rest upon a mountainside. When I finally awoke, I was clueless as to where I was. Gone from the cavern that held me, I thought surely Dargod had lifted me out. I was right!

The first thing I noticed was that my head was healed and I was refreshed. My memory was restored this time, as if I had only been asleep overnight. In which case, how did I get from the cavern?

"Now how did that happen?" I spoke to myself. "Everything is still here in Ben's craft. I must be thankful."

I could see for quite some distance from my perch. But it was the sea, not the desert or jungle that filled my eyes. Apparently the boat had brought me completely across the continent of Africa, to a port along the sea. How long this all took, I did not rightly know…. but I had only taken one capsule in my recalling. Ben's craft was gray and faded a color that only weather and much time in the sun could have painted. My mind was searching for many answers.

Below me was a valley of green. Farther in my view was a distant village and I could see the movement of wagons and horses. A ship came into view and it anchored well off the port. Tiny boats came to shore and in an hour, or so, the ship sailed away again. I decided that I would venture there. But this was a new land with different people, I was certain. I'd just have to try to "fit in" some how. I waited until my body regained its balance, as I stood up wobbly-legged. But I was famished and I needed nourishment soon.

The ground was sometimes disturbed and broken, as if big animals had pawed and searched for roots there. I became worried that huge beasts might attack me. So very wearily, I eased on down that mountain, leaving Ben's craft behind, and with my eyes alert to any beasts. On a rocky cliff where my hand engaged a soft, smelly, wet substance, I surmised the blend could have come from only one beast that I was aware; it was a hog. I knew they had sharp tusks that could kill me, but I thought I might strike them with my North Star for dinner, should one get that close. Suddenly, I wondered in disgust of myself, why hadn't I used the weapon on my trapped predicament? I am certain that I could have dissolved the rocks that covered the cave's entrance within an instant to relieve my entrapment…why hadn't I? Then I remembered my dilemma. I had made the right choice. Eennie, Meenie, Minie, Moe had worked.

I continued to descend for several days and my health began to weaken with exhaustion and hunger. Soon, I began wishing that I would meet up with just any vicious hog, straight on; I would devour him raw! But I could only occasionally find a green tuber to munch and draw moisture, until I suddenly came upon a plateau filled with trees. I felt a great relief come over my body, knowing I must soon be near that village and food!

Island of Love
(Chapter 6)

The tropical forest was different here. There was no underbrush, the soil was not gritty sand, and coconuts grew plentiful on the tall trees. But then I found a banana tree. Its laden bunches were two meters length, or more. I searched for a bunch that I could reach, but found little pleasure in the bitter, unripe ones that I was able to gather.

"Here, mon, let me help you!" there suddenly came a deep, gentle voice from behind me.

When I turned around there was a dark brown man standing shirtless with a strange woven hat that had many appendages sprouting from all around its top. He had no shoes and his pants were raggedy shorts. But my attention was brought to just two of his outstanding characteristics, his big white-toothed smile and the long, gleaming machete in his right hand. Somehow I hoped that one fed off the other, for my safety's sake.

His name was Diego, an islander. He pitched me a banana from his bunch and with an inquisitive eye looked me up and down.

"Where do you come from, mon?" he asked shortly.

I pointed up on the mountain's slope, and he was puzzled.

"What did you do up there, mon?"

My mouth was already full of banana, and it was good and ripe. I held my hand out for another, so he just lowered his bunch from his back, took his machete and chopped a bunch from a different tree.

"Here, mon, eat. You must be very hungry today."

"Are you from a shipwreck, mon that you come from the mountain side, on the far side of the island?"

I only needed that for my introduction and I took it from there.

"Yes, out at sea, a big storm. I floated for a long time. Where am I?" I told him between swallowing big chunks of the fruit.

"Jamaica, mon, Jamaica! Ha, ha, ha! You landed in Jamaica! You be safe here, if it don't typhoon. But the boss man doesn't like you gobblin' up all his bananas."

Well, the last map that I remembered looking at, or I thought that I remembered looking at, was a captain's map of the unknown sea of the Atlantic west. Jamaica was an uninhabited island in the new world.

A distant voice rang out calling, "Dayo, dayo!"

"Boss man calls, I should hurry!"

"Can I come along?" I asked.

"Sure, mon, come."

With that he grabbed up his big bunch of bananas, and I hoisted my pack. I walked behind this little man with the big bunch of bananas and a very big voice, into a village. A white man in a wide-brimmed hat noticed me and yelled for me to immediately come to him.

"You, there, come here!" he demanded. He looked just like the fat man, but he had a different hat. He sweated too.

"Who are you and where did you come from?" he then demanded.

Diego immediately spoke up, "Ship wrecked, boss, ship wrecked!" Diego blurted out.

The boss man was an interesting man I found out. His bark was far worse than his bite; a very lonely man, deposited here five years before from Bristol, England. His ship's company grew fruit on the island, and he organized labor to harvest the fruit to be loaded and shipped back to Bristol. He escorted me to his little house and offered me a drink.

"Will you have some rum, sir? It is the drink of the island, the only drink, ha," he laughed hardily as he poured a glass for me.

But I feared I could not partake of any liquor, for it might react with the potion. I was not certain.

"No, thank you, sir, in my condition, I don't think it's wise."

"And what is your condition, sir?"

"Ship wrecked, remember? I haven't eaten for a long time."

"Ha, I thought you might be full of bananas! Ha ha ha!" he laughed.

Then he clapped his hands, and a servant came to him. He told the man that I was hungry.

"Do you like to eat fish? Or, if not, we have fresh caught boar."

"Fish, please, sir."

"Please call me Colonel, everyone else does, that is except for the labor."

"Please call me Jamison, Colonel. And thank you for your kindness," I returned.

Placed before me was an abundance of handsome fish, all dressed out in fruit and cooked in coconut oil.

"Oh, this is excellent, simply excellent!" I raved to the cook and servant.

"Other ship-wrecked people have said the same, but just wait until you have been here five years; fish, fish, fish, if you know what I mean."

"Ummm," was all I could muster.

"There have been other ship-wrecked people?" I asked.

"Well, the live ones that didn't just wash up on the shore, ha!" he mused. "Yes, there's been a few, since I've been here…always the typhoons, you know?"

"Very well I do!" I agreed.

"I have business to do. If you are looking for a ship to return you, where did you say you hailed from?"

"Everywhere," I told him. "Everywhere the wind blows. My own craft got caught up in a big storm and I landed here. The last time I saw land, I was on the eastern coast of Africa, I think. I got sucked up into this storm and I woke up here."

His eyes and brows now grew narrow, and I could see in his eyes the impossibility of that trip was troubling him.

"I guess the sea's currents flowed from there, because here I am!"

"All the way around Hope?" he questioned.

"Yes!" I said simply. "What is the name of this town?" I asked.

"Villa de la Vega, one of the possessions. You know Diego is royalty here. He is the son of the famous explorer Christopher Columbus. He has taken on the island people's tongue and their special ways. I want to leave here before it happens to me…Mon, ha ha ha," as he gestured of Diego's speech.

"If you want to catch a ship anywhere, you're too late. Diego picked the last of the bananas today for the locals, and the pineapples won't harvest for six months. Coconuts will store up and ship with our pineapples. It's not the season," he inserted.

"Season, what is this season?" I asked.

"Why it's the dead of winter here, can't you tell?"

I peeked over his shoulder to see a calendar upon his desk. It was winter all right, December 1512! I had been asleep almost three hundred sixty-five years! I sat right down, and looked again at the calendar. Yes, that was correct.

"Soon we will celebrate Feliz Navidad, the birth of God's son."

"What?" I loudly asked. "You all know of Dargod?"

"No, not any Dargod, God the Father. In Bristol, it's Saint Nicholas, but it snows."

"Oh," I was puzzled.

Maybe, over time, his name was shortened or something. Still I found that superb and wonderful, and I was right there, fifteen hundred twelve years ago…imagine that! But, Dargod was my father, and the baby born was my nephew. But who cares? They still spoke of Him! Jesus had spread the word.

I asked what I was going to do. He told me that there was one of two things to do. Go find a good secluded place along the beach and build a hut, or if I had some money go to town.

"What is the money called here?" I asked.

"Shillings and pounds," he replied.

"Are there any jobs?"

"What is your trade?"

I had to think hard about that. "I can keep books, ehh…."

"What can you do?" he interrupted.

"I can keep the records of business transactions."

"My boy why did you not tell me that, because if you do a good job, you can stay here and be my man, eh, bookkeeper, that is," he spoke out.

"Why thank you, Colonel, I'll consider that. But first I would like to see this island. If it's all right with you, I shall give you my answer in two days."

I bid him good day, and thanked him again, and walked out to see this winter wonderland.

The smell of the ocean and the sound of waves breaking is a combination that always soothes my soul. I walked for as long as I could upon the smooth, white sands while all the time I was meeting people whom I did not know, and were happy to greet you first with their own "Hola", "Hello", or "Buenas tardes". Everyone seemed to be very happy here, and soon I hoped I would be too, if I made my permanent home here.

When the sun eased over the ocean's horizon, the colors there were breathtakingly sublime. The oranges, the blues, the pinks, the grays all swirled into a beautiful pattern that an artist couldn't have collected, for it was gone in minutes.

The night came, but the moon and stars shown so brightly upon the white sands that I could see very well any place I chose. It was my first conscious night there, and I lay down on the beach under a palm tree. I quickly fell asleep upon some of its long fallen leaves, while looking up at the moon and stars. It was the dead of winter!….Imagine that?

It was the cry of a seagull that rudely awakened me so early, but I was glad that he had. The sun coming up on this Jamaican isle was as lovely as when it set. But no one seemed to notice, as the beach was deserted. It was all mine to enjoy, and I was going to make the most of it. I slid out of my clothes and waded into the warm water, as free as any man could be. I swam out to waist deep and continued to enjoy this new place I had found.

"Thank you, Dargod, for leading me on this path that you have chosen for me. I am so grateful!" I shouted. Only Dargod could hear me, and that was just fine.

When first I saw her, I knew that she was special. She too had come to bathe in the deserted bay. Maybe she had done this many times before, before I had arrived, I thought. She slipped from her brightly colored wrap and moved quickly into the water at fifty meters distance, not even glancing to see my gaping mouth, nor my wide eyes.

Her dark smooth, brown skinned body slid beneath the water and she did not return soon. I thought she had succumbed to the surf's outgoing tide, and that she was lost. But she surfaced like a mermaid would have, flowing gracefully above and below the breaks. But she came closer and I saw her face clearly. She was the most exquisite pearl of the sea. Her beauty at this time of day was mine only to behold. I absorbed every movement, every swirl, and her figure left me breathless, wanting more.

She stood up in the break and ran her hands through her hair, as if to dispel the water. Her exposed breasts were firm and pointed, but fortunately, or not, in my direction. When her bright eyes caught mine, she screamed a girlish tiff and retreated beneath the wake. She bobbed her head to look at me clearly and asked me to turn around. I did. She left the surf as quickly as she entered, grabbed her wrap, and ran into the palms. I could not explain the burning desire to have her that erupted inside my body and soul. But she was gone.

I sat in the thought of the image of her beauty, until the shadows of others came into view. Then a seagull above me squirted his night's catch upon my head. "Yikes!" I washed off the mess, a rough thought to awaken from a beautiful dream, and scurried to my clothes heap to dress. I thought that this must be the place to bring in a new dawn. The smile on my face continued as people that I met greeted me with such great sincerity. Life was certainly good here.

I went into the town early where the market people were still setting up their stands. I had to find a place to sell some of the emeralds, but I feared that might be impossible here. There was no business upon the island capable of making any trade. Though the fortune was mine, it was useless here. But I didn't feel too poor, for the beautiful girl that I had seen on the beach must live here somewhere, and the thought of seeing her again was priceless.

The Colonel greeted me with a big smile. "Have you decided to stay on here?" he asked.

"I have."

"Excellent! I've already prepared a place in the storage hut that I think will suit your needs. Is there anything that you require here?" as he showed me the hut.

It was compact, but very livable and clean.

"The servants will be at your call. Get settled, and then come to the house. We can start right away."

JAMISON
SEES
MARIETTA
PWK

The Colonel was a simpleton. His books were unkept and very in arrears. There was no order to his filing systems, so I devised my own. Within a half day, I was completely finished. He no longer needed my service, as I had set everything to his tone, and he understood. But he insisted I remain.

"When the harvest comes, you will understand my concern, because the barter and shipping goes on day and night. I employ fifty workers, who are not happy if I delay their pay, because I have not submitted the proper works to the company. My thinking is that you will be able to spell me from this place, and I will take leave to return to Bristol for a time. You are more needed than you know, Jamison."

The Colonel was a fair man, who advanced me enough money to purchase new clothes. He brought to me a formal suit that he owned, and had a servant tailor it to my size. No more was I able to search for that girl at the dawning.

We received notice of the company's founders sailing to our island prior to harvest time to check the plant stock. Diego was a good foreman and planter. He was the lone employee laborer, besides me, to receive a payment once a month. We became very close, and often we took long walks through the plants, and he taught me his system of cutting down the old plants, and replacing them with cuttings he had grown. The young plants out produced the old, in a short time. He was a proud man. For some reason, he shrugged off questions of his father. But, when he asked me, I had to do the same. Together we did well, and profited for the owners.

The one thing he dreaded most though, was the feral hog that the Spaniards had left behind, before the present occupiers, the British, had chased them off the island, many years ago. The Spaniards left the hogs to multiply themselves, to be hunted for food whenever they returned. They never returned here, so there were many wild boars that rooted up the plants.

"The damage that they do sometimes makes me cry. There is no stopping them, since they quickly run into the hills and hide," Diego began. "Occasionally, a native will catch one or two, in a pit trap. Then the whole village comes out to celebrate. They put the pig on a roasting pole, above a fire pit, and everyone takes their fill of meat and rum. It's a fun time. But the pigs are getting too smart, and only the little ones are stupid enough to get caught. But, it's a fun time when they do."

My suggestion of a happy celebration, during the visit of the owners' arrival, seemed to brighten, both the Colonel and Diego. But how would we get the hogs to cooperate? I knew of a way that they didn't have to…North Star!

I wondered if I could find a way to restore North Star's power. Surely, Dargod would have left instructions somewhere. And then I saw it, a simple logo on the butt of the handle. The sun! She had been idle for almost four hundred years, during my long regeneration. I found her looking well in the stored pack. But I dare not ignite her powers anywhere near an Earthling, so one day I ventured all the way up to where I had landed upon the side of the mountain. I had noticed rooted up ground from when I came down from there, but I didn't exactly know what the cause was. I suspected now it was those feral hogs.

It didn't take long to find the uprooted ground again. It was severe to the land, and the erosion was terrible. I sat alone on a hillside, looking out to the sea. My eyes quickly looked to the long white beach on the west side, wondering if the girl had ever returned there. She was always coming to my thoughts.

I heard a quiet ruffling of the leaves and a soft grunting up higher than my own perch. When I looked up there, the whole countryside revealed a herd of fat pigs.

They were feeding upon the wild fruit that fell to the ground. This sight caused me wonder, as to why they would come from the hill to raid the banana trees? These trees were laden with many tropical sour fruits, unpicked by the residents.

I maneuvered for an hour to view them closely. They hadn't really gotten their snoots up to see me at all. I withdrew North Star from my waist, and pointed her at six porkers that gathered together in greed and began to squeal, in a quarrel of their rightful share. ZAP! North Star amazed me so, that I didn't even look to the kill, as it was a glancing blow off the ground and spewed up rocks and dust. All that I noticed was the other boar's quick exit up higher onto the hillside.

I traveled up after them, as I wanted to destroy as many as I could. They had disappeared from my sight completely, although I could faintly hear them, somewhere. I eased along a narrow rock ledge path, until I saw a large cavern opening. It was precariously hidden at the end of this very narrow trail. The trail was too high and too narrow for any human to travel safely at less than a quarter-meter wide. But a hog could! And sure enough, the snoot of a large boar peeked out from the large cavern, and retreated upon seeing me. The pigs are smart and weary foes, I imagined. They were nothing the size of their hippo brethren, I thought.

I studied the situation. I could see that if I could somehow herd the beasts all together into the cavern, I could partition this narrow path off, and thus keep the pigs penned up, just as the Germans had done in their captive pens, aboard a ship that I once had sailed upon. I would need lots of help.

I retreated back down to where the dead hogs lay. I tied the pigs by their feet, one behind the other, and dragged the hogs all to one level, away from this place. It was an easy task, as their hairy bodies slid easily down the hill upon the gravel, but halted on the level.

I rushed to get Diego. I found him with the Colonel and told them both of my success. They both became excited and wanted to help. Diego and I pulled a large handcart up the path to retrieve the boars; while the Colonel had the servants get their relatives to put out the word of the anticipated great celebration.

By the time Diego and I made two trips to retrieve the carcasses, a large group of family members had created a stir in the community, letting everyone know of the big celebration. I was weary of pushing the cart and asked Diego, "How are we ever going to roast all that meat?"

"Our job is done. The provider doesn't work here. Many men will dig fire pits and roast the hogs, while their women will prepare their special dishes to eat."

Then his face took on a very worried look.

"And much rum will be drunk…men's minds will go wild, fathers will worry for their daughters…and the young girls will get with child…. I will worry this time too," he explained. He really looked disturbed just thinking about his own words.

It was the very first time that Diego spoke of his daughter. He said that he had protected her long after other girls her age had married and had given birth. But he feared that she was ready now, and would no longer abide by her father's wishes.

"She has a mind of her own now," Diego mourned.

The plantation owners' ship anchored inside the bay, and all the people went to greet the big bosses with their paddled canoes. My boss drank very heavily, as the Colonel was very nervous. But when he saw the entire celebration going on as planned, just as his bosses came ashore, he composed himself into a credible plantation manager. He took all the credit for everything, of course, and his bosses were very impressed.

Diego and I sat away from the crowd, along with his small family. But while eating, I did not notice any sight of this daughter that he was so afraid of being here, and had brought him such worries. When I mentioned this to Diego, he quickly replied, "Here comes Marietta now."

Her movement was so light and graceful; you would have sworn that she was a beautiful ballerina dancer of Spain. But I knew her otherwise; she was much more than that! She was the one!

She had occupied every free moment of my mind, day and night. She seemed to have left me forever, but was much closer than I knew. She was Diego's biggest worry. She was his daughter.

I rose to my feet immediately. I felt so weak when Diego introduced us. Her soft hand seemed to pause in mine, as she suddenly stared deeply into my eyes. Did she remember? How could she?

"My father has talked about you many times, as a fine new boy working here. He never mentioned a handsome man."

"I can see I will have my worries begin sooner than I thought," Diego sighed.

"Tell me, Mr. Jamison, do you ever go swimming in the morning?" she giggled as she hauntingly smiled at me. She knew, and she did not care if I knew her well too.

"Yes…I did once."

Just then, the big celebration started, as the ladies began dancing to the loud beat of the drums. I was glad it was that, because I could feel my heart beating so hard, I was certain everyone here could hear it.

The drums began to beat a rhythm that brought Marietta to walk into the arena of women and began to dance also. She received much attention from the young men, and it sickened me. I was already jealous of everyone's eyes that looked upon her longingly, just as I was doing. I turned away.

"She will return, Jamison, I think she has eyes for you," spoke Diego. "She has never danced this way before. I believe it only is now to attract the moth, like her mother had done to me."

I watched this girl dance, and she continually looked to see if I was watching her. It was a combat of sorts, between two new unsure lovers, testing the hold that each had on the other. She danced close to the outreached arms of the young men, who then stood up quickly to be selected by her. But a familiar repel that she gave to their advances, reminded me of Barcelona, and I was not then impressed.

I turned and walked away to the beach by myself, for I could not stand her tormenting way. I sat down on the shore and questioned my feelings, which were causing me such a stir inside.

"I must be crazy," I spoke out loud to the sea.

"I don't believe you are," the soft reply came from behind me.

She then sat down next to me, and took my arm in hers. No more words needed to be said, as I pulled her into my arms, and kissed her long and hard, as she did me. The music on the beach was louder than the celebration, as our hearts found the beat of each other's that night.

It was simple. I knew, and she knew, we had found each other here on this isle of beauty, and we were madly in love.

The wedding was a big celebration for the whole island to share, because that is how it had always been. The bride waited quietly upon the beach in a bride's hut, while the groom came from the sea, upon a boat, built by the bride's father. The ceremony was simple. The bride walked from the hut in her splendid beauty and was presented to the groom by her parents. A large flowered wreath was then tied to their wrists; it was the symbol that held them together forever, as the new Governor himself, Juan DeEsquivel said his praises. Then the drums beat loudly, and the groom swept his bride away upon the boat as he paddled her out of sight to a "honeymoon hut", also built by her father.

There, in the prescribed hidden hide-away they started their lives together, which usually took just a couple of days, until they returned.

We were so in love, that after a week, Diego sheepishly came to see if we had killed ourselves. He was embarrassed to have to come there, but he loved his daughter and his wife made him. The smile on our faces sent him back laughing and shaking his head, as he returned to tell his wife all was well, and that they would probably be grandparents soon.

In the middle of the second week, we heard Diego's voice echo, "Dayo, dayo!" This was the call to the workers to return to the work place; this was the time to be reviewed by the owners. Marietta and I also returned.

An overly anxious Colonel, who then brought Marietta and me into his house for conversation, greeted us.

"You know, Jamison," he started slowly, "you have been like a son to me, and you've helped me manage this plantation well. The owners are very happy with my work, so they are promoting me to a position in Bristol. There will be a new manager here."

"Who will that be?" I immediately questioned.

"It will be you, my good employee, Jamison, you!"

I was very pleased, as it also meant that Marietta and I had a home provided and a payment once a month to draw upon.

"Thank you very much, Colonel. When do you return?"

"Right away, we sail back this very afternoon. You are, as of now the boss man. If you have a problem, Diego will be here to help you. I will write to you when things are settled in Bristol."

We welcomed the good news. And later waved goodbye to all, and set about sharing our new home. After more than fifteen hundred years, I had only just begun to live. The time that Marietta and I spent alone together in our little house, filled all the missing holes ever in my empty soul's heart, which I did not know existed before.

The next news as 'boss', made me very angry. The wild pigs had rooted up our newest plantings and they would have to be replanted. Had they been so intelligent to understand that their actions were revenge towards me?

"Dayo, dayo," I called Diego to my side to summon the workers. With planks of wood for fence and cut tree logs for posts, we all ventured up the mountain to herd the pigs into their cave. We had observed their afternoon wallows and I knew if we could surround them there, while they wasted, they would be easier to herd. In a ploy that I once saw the Zulu of Africa do to me, I had the employees stomp and beat drums in a long skirmish line which covered all of the plantation and beyond, to scare the swine back into their place of hiding. Everyone helped, and soon we ascended towards the small narrow trail that they used to enter the cave. The stench was fresh and I was sure we had done an adequate job, because there were many squeals coming from a very crowded cave. We must have captured hundreds.

The laborers dug holes and constructed a fence to keep the hogs held there. Everyone was happy and when a latecomer hog ventured in from behind, several men chased it down and killed it with their machetes. A triumphant celebration was to begin. And if we ever wanted meat, all that we had to do was come up here and select one or two, for they were ours now. There were one hundred and seventy three hogs caught. I paid a laborer to supply food from forage to feed them, and his payment was a pig. It was a satisfactory pact between us. Problem solved!

When a man moves about countries as much as I had, he tends to collect dialects from his immediate environment. And before long, I too found myself saying "mon", and other dialectical sayings of the island. I had always inadvertently done this, wherever I ventured. I guess it was so that I could find my culture somewhere.

Diego was not only a good friend and father-in-law, but he was my inspiration to speak like a true islander. He spoke so deep. One day he nearly died laughing when I myself hollered, "Dayo, dayo!" in front of him to call the laborers to come to the house. No one came. Diego then gave his version and it brought everyone. Someone mentioned they thought they heard one of the wild pigs again, in the banana plants. Diego smiled and I never tried it again…I let Diego do my beckoning.

A typhoon is a terrible, powerful and a very destructive storm, with high winds that flatten everything, and rain that does not stop, until it floods. We were being trapped upon an island, surrounded by a great storm, from which we had little place to hide. But we found ourselves following the old people of this island, as they always traipsed up the opposite side of the mountain, away from the storm, and waited it out there. It was that very kind of storm that wreaked havoc upon our Jamaican isle.

The dark clouds hung low in the horizon for days, a typical way of a tropical depression's slow movement. But when she came ashore, the winds had killer force, and everything was lost. Everything, that is, but my Marietta's encouragement to pick it all up and build again. But I wasn't that willing, since I still possessed a king's fortune in emeralds and wanted to treat her like a queen…my beloved queen.

All of our plants were gone, the year's harvest was ruined, and no pay came to the workers, until a rich merchant ship from Italia sailed into the bay. I found its captain very interested in the exchange of one large, sparkling green emerald, for more than enough money to support the plantation, and our transportation also on the ship's return to Italia.

"It might take a year, or two," I explained to Diego.

Diego took charge of the money, which was needed to pay the workers who would be rebuilding, and I took Marietta on her first voyage. We sailed aboard a merchant ship that was headed for the east, passed by the big Rock of Gibraltar, and had reached the Mediterranean Sea in just six months…all to the excited wonder of my Marietta.

During all that time aboard ship, alone each night in our cabin, I confided just a little bit more about myself. I first told my lovely wife that I had a married sister who was also named Marietta, and that we had traveled to Earth upon a flying ship from the heavens. I told her of Jesus and my father, Dr. Dargod. She laughed at me and thought that I had spun a great tale to keep her occupied on the trip. But when I assured her that I would prove to her all this was true, she seemed very worried that her husband had surely lost his mind.

We departed the ship in the rich trading port of Tangier. Gems were easily traded here, mainly through clandestine dealers, and usually only with stolen gems. I showed only two, and sold only those to make us terribly rich, and few enough to not draw attention to us and remain outwardly unnoticeable.

From Tangier, we sailed the route to Tunis, left there to Palermo, Sicily, and caught a merchant vessel all the way to Ascalon. Transportation from there was then by camel, and we joined in a caravan that passed near the Sinai.

Marietta now started to believe in her husband's words, and she enjoyed learning of the different cultures. I dressed her in fine silks, bought her oils and perfumes, and when we came to the oasis, I showed her the Sinai in the distance. A day later, she gasped for air in amazement of the tall shiny vessel that stood inside the volcano and the unpleasant incline climb to the top.

I pushed the buttons on the entrance pad and the big door opened. Marietta became very frightened and had to be left outside to watch. I continued to go inside, and found the ship empty. But there was a note from Jesus that bore good tidings.

It read, "I returned to the ship and found Marietta and Josef alive and well. They were sad about learning of all their family passing. So, I am taking them with me on a trip to India, a country where I am held in the highest esteem, but people bow down in the name of Brahman. I am trying to guide them. Some countries named me Mohammed, my name in their language. In other areas I am called Allah. I am happy in the changes I have made in my people's sinful ways. I will return some day, but I know not when, Jesus."

Marietta found the courage to come inside, and felt my great disappointment in the emptiness of the ship. She looked at me, as never before. She touched everything in wonder, and asked many questions. She discovered the large bin of AloevectorP23 capsules, and I had to explain their life-renewing qualities, which my father Dr. Dargod had placed inside them. I then put more capsules inside my pack. She nodded her head in a questionable agreement, but remained confused, and amazed.

When I strapped Marietta into the pilot's chair and lit up the pipe of Nova, she screamed in horror. I felt badly. I took her in my arms, and held her closely; she then understood the power of Dargod, and decided that I must be a Saint, oh my.

"I am only a man who loves you with all my body and soul."

My search was not completed, but it accomplished the fulfillment in my heart to share everything that I knew about Dargod and Mars with my wife. My naive, little Marietta was now facing the new world, wide-eyed and informed. She would then raise our future children in Dargod's word of the "Ten Commitments of Life", who were seeded that very day.

We departed from the Sinai and traveled back to Ascalon. On several transfers of merchant ships, I again found several merchants in Tangier that were willing to "sacrifice" themselves to accommodate the sale of more emeralds. I had to tell them I would return with more, but then quickly boarded our vessel and left, before they could kill me and steal them all. Of course, there was North Star.

After waiting two months in a small Portugal port, we boarded an explorer's vessel. He welcomed the fare that we paid, and we were headed all the way back to our beloved Jamaica. The Captain's name was Juan Ponce de Leon; a Spaniard who had actually been to our Jamaican isle, and a place called Puerto Rico. But Juan, as he liked to be addressed in social contact, told us that he was again trying to locate a beautiful island that he called Cuba. Juan had also discovered a bigger isle that his ship had sailed past which was very nearby Cuba; he dearly wished to explore there, and desperately wanted to name it Terra de Flora, for his Spain. But just when his first attempt was nearing success, he had to return to Spain when his whole crew suffered scurvy, a disease that could have been prevented had he only known of the islands' fruit value in the control of the disease. When I reminded him there would be plenty of fruit from our plantation, I quickly inserted, "If Diego, Marietta's father, had been able to recover from the typhoon's destruction that we left behind."

It had been two years and two days, since we had left Jamaica's shore. Our happy people all came out to greet us in their canoes, in the bay of Spanish Town.

"Welcome home, darling!" I told Marietta. She glowed with excitement. But her enthusiasm was quickly lost when she learned of her mother Victoria's death. Marietta wept for weeks and was despondent that she could not have said goodbye. Diego was also saddened and was indifferent towards me, and hinted his displeasure for our staying away so long. He had lost his position, I learned, when the plants did not yield their quota. There was a stir, and a new "boss man" had replaced me. I was employed no more, and Diego feared his son-in-law would have to move in on him, who himself had drawn upon the pigs until they were depleted, and few still existed on the slopes of the hills.

We went to Victoria's grave. Marietta and I placed a carved stone upon her grave that illustrated her importance in the community. We planted many flowers there and that pleased Diego. Diego's only son left at home departed to become a sailor, after his mother's death.

To Diego's surprise, we moved into the upper financial district, into a wooden built house. I purchased a big house upon a large hill, within the distant view of Victoria's grave. We had seven servants and a boy to help in the garden.

Diego became the Governor, but he always kept time aside to bounce his grandson, Don Diego Dargod, upon his knee. The Governor died ten years later, and we laid him to rest beside Victoria. A larger new stone of imported granite declared their love that we had etched in stone, and Marietta was pleased with my choice.

We lived a normal life of a loving, sharing couple, and when our son married, he married well. His new father-in-law was a shipper from the New World. The people in the Northern Hemisphere had now begun to migrate, and new discoveries of the colonies drew much interest from abroad. Don Diego Dargod, our son, had the wandering desires in his blood; he returned from a voyage and told us that he had decided to start up a trade center in the new colonies. He was a brilliant young man now and pursued his own ideas.

He left us, age nineteen, in fifteen hundred sixty-five. His mother never saw him again, as my Marietta suffered a fever, for which I could not cure. I desperately injected the potion into her dead body, hoping to revive her, or maintain her physical being, but I could not tell if it had any consequence. I knew I had to go to Jesus and find an answer.

The whole town came to Marietta's funeral. We laid her to rest, deep inside a sunken granite tomb, well within the mountainside. It would always be cool there and safe, I hoped. We sealed her tomb, and felt she'd forever be free from any intruders.

Marietta was my all, and I could not stand the emptiness left by her leaving. I remembered her mostly as a young island girl, thrashing in the sea, which had made my heart yearn to be with her forever. That feeling never, ever, had left me, and my sorrow could not be overcome on my own. I became a drunkard and wandered alone upon this lonely man's isle. People often evaded me, as I'd lost my dignity and cursed everyone.

One day, in a deep state of depression, I thought of doing away with myself, and took North Star with me high up onto the hillside near Marietta's tomb, where I first had landed, now seventy-five years ago. I was virtually still in a young man's body, but without my Marietta, I had no will to live any longer. I trekked the path to the hillside, and embraced the death thought for some hours. In the eve, I thought about the cave above me, and thought that would be an appropriate place to end it all, so I climbed to the hilt upon the narrow path.

The trail was still there, and still very narrow. But, somehow my hapless will to die, kept me from losing my balance and falling from the ledge, also a certain death. I finally entered onto the upper flat, and the opening into the cave was before me.

Suddenly, with a burst of great speed, several feral hogs squealed violently past me, and I was brought to my knees. I guess they must have escaped extinction, as I then remembered our adventure penning them up. I was drawn by my death wish to proceed and walked into the mouth of the cave.

It was not unlike the place where Dargod had caused the tremendous rains to fall in Africa, which then floated me out of the top, until I eventually arrived here, I thought. I had come all that way, for what? I took two steps into the cave and I then suddenly knew why. This is the place Dargod had planned for me to land, but I had missed it, I guess. Or, maybe the raft had initially rested there, and the pigs rooted me out of their home, little by little, out into the opening to awaken.

Upon the walls of the cave, were drawings that looked just like a continuation of the ones that were scribed in Africa. It too was from the past, and it showed a ship like Nova, a boat in the rain, and the sun coming up on a mountainside with palm trees. An arrow scratched in, with probably a reddish dye of pomegranates, pointed to a wall and a pile of rocks stacked neatly on a shelf of slate. It was deep into the cave. I went there and undid the stones. A small locked box laid beneath the stones, which was identical in the size of the ledger that I once kept for bookkeeping; the lock had rotted. When I pulled upon it lightly, the lock easily disengaged, and the box's lid opened to reveal a written book.

I took the book to the opening of the cave to gather more light to read. It read like this: "We have come to this beautiful world in search of life. We have all found a different kind of people here, just as upon Mars in her maiden years. There are twelve of us here that bear the blood of our homeland Mars. Mars is our world, but I fear we can never return. Our ship was taken away by a huge storm.

"If some of our Martian people should find this message, please tell Dr. Dargod the potion worked well, as we are now over five hundred years old, and feel no ill affects of aging. Our original flight to Uranus was canceled when the planet moved behind another and froze up right before our eyes with gases, as we approached. We feared to land with the gases around Uranus. We then charted our ship to this planet called Earth.

"We are leaving here to search for a small, red-banded viper, which we learned is poisonous to the people of this world. But, the ringed snake cannot be found here. We have mated with these Earthlings, and they are a kind people; but we have lost them too soon after we married. Other Martians have tested its potential, and it works. If mixed with the Earth snake's venom of a coral snake, the potion can be beneficial to the people of this planet, and extend and restore their lives also.

"Though we are excited about this find, we have not found any coral snakes on this land, and will be leaving on a large ship that is manned by people known as Norsemen. Some are called Vikings with vulgar ways, and we are certain they eventually want to kill us, and they all are warriors from another place on this world. They are afraid of our Zola Ray, which destroys everything that they used to try to kill us.

"The Zola Ray has to have the sun's light to recharge itself. They have now asked for peace and cooperation. Though their minds are infantile, they train well. Tell Dr. Dargod, we thank him for sending us to this wonderful place. There are very beautiful women here!" It was signed by, John Jehovah, Captain elect, of the crew of the Nola Gay.

With a much renewed spirit, I flew down from this mountain, gathered up my finances and the emeralds, told the servants I'd return someday, and headed to the bay's new docks. I was overly anxious however, as there were no outgoing ships, for it was winter, and the crop harvest was over. There would be no new ships, until summer.

But just as well, for I knew not where to find such a snake. My emotions had led me to search, but where should I begin? I dreamed that I would bring its venom home with me, and inject my Marietta with it. I was overjoyed, and ran up to Marietta's tomb, dropped down upon my knees, and told her of our great fortune. I assured her, I would return someday when I found the venom. I would search forever, if I had to. I placed some fresh flowers inside her tomb, and cheerfully told her, "Don't go away, I'll be right back!" I now found a cause for which to live.

That very same night I returned to my home to find the servants all disgruntled about my leaving. I then realized that they could not continue here, if there was no financial support. I drew my most trusted servant Matilda into my confidence, and told her that the money in the safe would support them all, and that she should take good care of my home for as long as I was gone. She thanked me for trusting her and spoke a promise.

Unbelievably, as if it were planned, a big ship sailed into the harbor, with Juan Ponce de Leon as its captain. He was delighted to see me, as I of him, for he was seeking finances that would permit him, and his crew to sail north into the seas along the path of Vespucci, also an explorer.

But Vespucci's voyage was not validated, and Juan was trying to find some of the lands that he had mapped. I offered him a handsome award to transport me there, and as soon as they took the only available fruits upon his ship, we sailed.

Juan showed me his maps, which Vespucci had said were true. I did not know this person that he spoke of, but I pretended that I did. He was particularly interested in the huge lake that seemed to be never ending, and it certainly wasn't fresh water.

"Vespucci must have found a tremendous bay of water, like the Mediterranean," he swore. Then his words brought meaning to my trip.

"At this point of the bay, right about here," he pointed on the map, "Vespucci tried to go ashore and found it to be useless, wet, swamp lands. It was full of dangerous little snakes and crocodiles, and animals from Africa. While they were leaving, a tribe of African-like natives attacked them. The natives fled on the sounding of their blunderbusses. Vespucci also thought there was a big river there, which might lead to the land's interior, or another ocean."

This was the starting point I needed! I grew impatient in the weeks and months ahead, until Juan brought my attention to a big bay that a huge river ran into.

"This must be it, but I can't really tell by the map. It seems closer than it should be."

We went ashore armed, but there were no people anywhere to be seen. The going was slow and the irritating insects caused everyone much havoc. There were all kinds of snakes to be seen though, but no red ones with bands around their bodies. We returned to ship quickly to avoid being devoured by the insects. It was disheartening to me as I knew the going there would be very tough.

"I must search more here, Juan," I told him. "It's only been two weeks, I will need more time."

"I can not stay with you, my friend," he sighed, "for I have thirty men who must continue on to investigate this big bay. I have something for you. It is this scope to view things up closely, from afar. It might help you spot the snake that you seek. That is the best that I can do. I will return to this point just as soon as we chart and map this route completely. If you are not here when I return, I'm sorry, but I will not be able to look for you, as the Trade Winds would be unkind to us on our voyage home."

"I understand. You have fulfilled your commitment, and I thank you now, Juan, in case we never see each other again."

We shook hands before I climbed down off his ship upon a thick rope net and into a waiting skiff. I was then rowed to the western bank by his men to the nearest side of the big river and deposited. I immediately started looking for red snakes with my new long, brass spyglass.

The New World
(Chapter 7)

This place of landing was just a big, muddy, freshwater river, I soon found out. The little red snake could not be seen, though I searched under every log, and in every patch of weeds. I made a lean-to and camped the first eve and listened to the river rippling and strange sounds of animals in the night; they chirped, flopped in the water, or hissed.

One day later, I was eyeball to eyeball with a giant dark snake that was not afraid of my company. His big black eyes seemed to follow my every move, as though he was now the hunter of me. His coil gave no indication of his dimensions, but when he finally struck at me, with a mouth as white as cotton, he was at least two meters long and full of madness. I was just fortunate that he was also lazy fat, and returned to his nest of sticks above the trail where I had walked.

Big fish sucked air along the bank, but they paid no attention to me, until just before I tried to grab one. His splash washed me down. I soon found the river's bank was no place to tread, for it was unlike any mud I had seen. The word that came from my mouth was "gumbo". And I think somehow that was an accurate description. The gumbo sucked me down into its depths, and if I hadn't grabbed a low tree limb, I would have gone under in its gripping. I struggled to get free, only loosing my left boot. Now what was I going to do? This was no place to tread barefooted.

My thoughts ran to poor Marietta, lying in her tomb waiting for me, and her helpless husband that she had married in good faith. I could not leave without my boot, but I had to and then did. I walked north, away from the river. But nothing that looked like a red snake ever appeared. The floor of the forest was dryer and sandy, much better than I imagined.

There was plenty of driftwood for a fire and I slept with one eye open the first weeks. I was all alone, except for those little flying mistoes, like on Mars. I asked Dargod to give me strength enough to cope with my new environment, and give me guidance.

It was easier to walk barefooted upon the gumbo that I often crossed, so I discarded my right boot in disgust. I had no idea where I was, where a red snake lived, or what I was going to do. I just kept walking, for days, for miles, for weeks taking a fruit or tuber to eat as I journeyed.

I strode over a hill and was met by the smell of smoke from a fire. It smelled like there was food, too. I crept up to the fire, until a voice immediately to my rear said something rude that sounded like "Ugh?" just as the point of a knife pierced my backside.

"Ouch!" I screamed out and whirled around in madness. There stood the sorriest excuse for a human being, I'd seen so far. His wet scraggly, black hair looked like a bird's nest, and had a feather in it. His cheeks were high on his face, but sagged on his behind. His nose was long and his lips were thin. His black eyes were crossed, which made him look as though he'd just run full speed into a tree's low limb. I stood my ground, and pointed North Star. But he looked so pitiful that I couldn't stop smiling and then laughed a hardy laugh. I had just been introduced to ol' Crow Foot for the very first time.

From the instant I first looked towards him, I don't think for one minute, that he meant to stick me, nor hurt me. I think his eyesight was so terrible, that he saw two of me, because at the end of his rusty knife hung a cooked fish, which was cleaned so poorly that the guts and half the scales remained. He had cut the tail off, instead of the head! It was his food offering to another being. He stared at me, cocked his head, and then put his hand on my face, I guess to feel my features.

Ugh!
PUNK
"JAMISON MEETS
OL' Crowfoot"

"Ugh?" He took a step back. I suppose that he just realized that I wasn't one of his Earthling brothers.

"Ugh?"

"Hey, Mon," I reeled off in my best Jamaican accent.

"Ugh?" he offered the fish anyway.

I decided it was a definite friendship, for he took me into his camp and offered to feed me without knowing me. Besides, who else could I have conversation?

In his best moment, he pounded his skinny chest, and spoke weakly, "Crow Foot, brave Cheyenne warrior! Ugh? Ugh?" he wanted my name.

"My name is Jamison, Jamison," I repeated.

To my delight, he spoke, "Ugh, Jamison, Jamison, Ugh."

Then he just turned and walked back to the fire, reached in, burned himself, yelled, "Ugh!" and grabbed another hot fish off a stick. I could not help but feel sorry for him. I did not know how old he was, but he looked like he was very near the end. He was blind as a bat in a cave.

After the meal, Crow Foot curled up in his only blanket by the fire and started snoring immediately. No guesswork here, it was bedtime. I had learned by myself to lie down in the sand, wiggle until my body's figure was etched in its groove, and then scrape up some leaves to cover it, while I checked for snakes, and laid my head down on my pack. Crow Foot grunted for me making too much noise, so I quickly finished and joined Crow Foot by his fire.

Prettier mornings had I witnessed, for when I awoke it was raining lightly. But there was ol' Crow Foot, with two wild birds on the fire. He had them impaled upon long sticks, feathers and all. The smell was horrible, and I about puked. So I stood as far from the fire as possible and watched. After some time, the birds were burned pitch black. But the ol' warrior knew just what to do. He quickly pulled upon the burnt carcasses' skins and the mess came right off, feathers and all, exposing their freshly cooked bodies of dark meat. He called it quack-quack. It was my first.

It was I who then said, "Ugh! Good!"

"Ugh!" spoke Crow Foot.

Don't ask me now how he managed to catch those ducks…you wouldn't believe me anyway! Many times afterward, when he snuck up upon a waterway and caught them swimming, he'd somehow capture a couple and we'd both dine on the "quack-quack", as he called them.

We lived the dandiest life, ol' Crow Foot and I. Our day consisted of walk, hunt, and eat, not necessarily in that order. When food presented itself, we hunted. When the other two came, we just barely managed. I still hadn't seen any red snakes at all.

Ol' Crow Foot was a good man. One month after I met him, I guess he thought that I was okay too, for he started talking. His words were always broken, but his first few words were, "Winter comes, leaves fall, quack-quack flies."

I was stunned.

"Soldiers teach Crow Foot to speak good," he started out. "I pony scout…in big war. I get good medicine when I sick, and plenty of firewater…ha, ha, ha," he laughed.

"It was good…then," he sighed.

"Soon, it will be time…for the rabbit. Rabbit skin is…soft. He fills my belly. I run…catch many furs…eat meat…catch buffalo, too, some time. Take furs to post…get firewater…Ha, ha, ha!"

"What is a post?" I asked Crow Foot.

"Post?" he questioned with his hands. "Post…where white man steals from Indian," he frowned.

This was my first indication that there were others and that he referred to himself as an "Indian". I thought I remembered his cousin Indians along the Nile, but they were much different. It made no sense to me. And what were these rabbit and buffalo things? Humm?

We walked for months away from the mouth of the big, muddy river. It seemed that Crow Foot made this trip every year for some reason, I'm not sure he knew why. Maybe since he had no one, it was his way of keeping his mind. Anyway, he was the only human I saw on our trek north.

There was a sudden coolness in the air, and I began to see the foliage turn brown. My clothing was light and insufficient. I began to sit closer to the fire in the dark hours. One morning I felt a rumble. I remembered one just like it once, when it started inside a cave in Africa. Had it begun again? By looking at Crow Foot's face, I could tell that he was excited. He pounced upon the ground with his ear upon the dirt. He listened.

"Buffalo, many buffalo," he said, "Eat big buffalo," as he smiled and rubbed his belly.

Then, as if a clock went off in his mind, Crow Foot grabbed a limb of a tree that had nuts on it, and began to strip the bark. He stood along side of his work of business, and at his middle he chopped off the best piece. He then took the limb and bent it several times above his head.

"Ugh", he grunted. It was a word that meant good, I had learned. He then unwrapped from his waist a long piece of animal strip, and tied it to both ends of the limb. It was a bow! I had seen many in other countries. I watched him gather up more limbs, cut slithers, and peel their bark. He then took bird feathers and stuck them to one end by using a mixture of spit and the juice of a tree. It was a very sticky mess, not very good either. Crow Foot stuck his arrows standing straight up in the mud, and went about searching in a small, shallow waterway. He picked up stones and put them in his mouth. He studied their consistency and spit some back out, always checking their quality. We walked back to camp and he grunted my attention. He sat down by the fire and motioned for me to bring more wood. It was a curious business.

Then the old master went to work making a point for the tips of his arrows. He would throw some in the hot fire to heat up, and then he'd rake them out quickly and dip them in water, which made them crack, leaving sharp edges. When each had cooled, he formed it into a sharp point by using a stone to chip away at it, until it was just right. Sometimes, they would break and he'd get angry, but start all over. He tied them to the end of his arrows; his weapon of war! Ingenious, I thought. But if he knew the power that I possessed in North Star, he could have saved all that time. I was amused by the old warrior's vigor, for arrows I assumed he saw as being straight, were in fact very crooked.

His chest grew large, and he pounded it, I guess to get up his courage. He motioned for me to get low, as we crawled forever on our bellies up onto a grassy hill and peeked over. I could hear grunting, so I assumed these were pigs we were hunting. But when I saw this big hairy animal-thing, grazing right before us, I immediately noticed its big stinky, dirty, behind. It was just ten meters in front of us. I seriously wondered just what Crow Foot was going to do with that tiny bow and arrow.

He placed his little shaft onto the bow and let the arrow fly. He missed the whole animal, but the big wooly thing didn't even notice.

"Ugh!" he shrugged. Again he reloaded, released the missile, and missed. "Ugh!" he repeated. Well, I saw the deep displeasure in his face, as though he was very saddened that he had lost his warrior status skills. He crawled closer and closer. The next event was a real doozy. Crow Foot takes aim and the arrow finds the entrance to the animal's exit hole, and the big wooly creature whirled about to face him.

"Oh, oh!" moaned Crow Foot, when the big monster charged him.

"Ahhhhhhhhh!" yelled Crow Foot, as he began to run away as fast as he could.

When the animal gained ground on him, it whirled and slid to a stop to address me. The beast was wild-eyed and very angry. Snot flew out from his flared nostrils and his angry intentions were then meant for me. He pawed the ground, and then charged full force. So, I just quickly pointed North Star, squeezed the trigger, and brought that charging beast right down to his knees. He died right there with just a short burst. The rest of the herd scattered. The wonderfully astonished look upon Crow Foot's wrinkled, and very sweaty face, gave me all the satisfaction in the world.

He looked at the beast, then looked at me, then looked at North Star.

"Ugh! Mighty warrior chief," as he patted me on the shoulder; which really meant to him that he retired from hunting and I was now the gatherer…Ha!

I learned a lot that afternoon. Crow Foot was a doer, and immediately offered up the liver of the beast as my reward.

"No!" I shook my head, which allowed Crow Foot to gobble most of the organ, before he burped up an awful mess. But he then quickly dispatched the beast with his knife, as I helped him to roll the animal into positions to make strategic cuts that divided the carcass into manageable pieces. He picked up the thick wooly skin and wrapped it around me, as to show me my new winter coat.

During that night, I heard Crow Foot slip out of camp. Some chunks of meat were impaled upon poles, hanging above the flame. It was certainly more than we could ever eat.

At daylight, I heard the grunts of something, and I saw several strange Indians standing at the fire admiring our buffalo meat. Crow Foot had left me to get some of his friends and offered up the food to share with them. Crow Foot herded them before my lying position and told them as he pointed at me, "Great warrior!" They looked as hideously skinny as Crow Foot, and I was glad this would feed them. Maybe we needed more buffalo, I thought.

There was a quiet dinner that afternoon, with lots of munching, and full of "Ughs". I myself added a few words to toast the tasty meal, "Umm, umm good!"

Everyone was happy. The women of the clan immediately repaid the kindness of Crow Foot. They sat down together and with sharp stones began to scrape the buffalo skin clean, then chewed its lining fat with their teeth. Afterwards, they stretched the skin high upon bent poles.

"Big warrior chief...big medicine," Crow Foot again spoke with his one hand on my shoulder, the other touching upon North Star, as to present me to his gathering. They all grunted in wonder when Crow Foot pointed to my little North Star. They stared at it long.

There was an immediate improvement in the physiques of our party. The nourishment of the buffalo was good, and not one part of the big bull was wasted. Even the bones' fragments were used as sewing needles, as one of the women used them. She began walking up to me daily and putting her hands about me, I guessed to measure my parts. Finally about five days later she brought forth and gave me the most handsome, warm winter coat. I greeted her with,"Thank you very much." She could see that I was happy, and she felt proud also by my delighted smile.

I saw how just one beast had brought many, many comforts to the Indians, so I set up a hunting party to get some more. When Crow Foot and the other men returned to camp, they had news of more "katonka", as they called the buffalo. So, during the night, not even considering me using North Star, they went out alone as they had done many times before with their inadequate bows and arrows. They crawled out into the middle of a big buffalo herd, and waited for light to get a shaft deep into the side of a chosen buffalo bull.

Sometimes, I learned, that if a herd spooked, the resulting stampede might trample to death some of the hunters. It happened on their first hunt without me. I had to remain in the camp for they called me their chief. I was supposed to protect them from harm and they would feed me, I learned.

At the deceased warrior's burial ceremony, he was placed in a hole that was hand dug by the women on a hillside and lined with flat rocks. The women sat and wailed over the dead Indian's grave, until they thought he had been raised up and had become a spiritual chief; only then did they bury him. I was not seeking a promotion.

The hunters were very unsuccessful, time and again, while I was there. So finally I went along to discover their methods. When the first arrow flew wide of its target, the herd spooked and started to stampede. I stood up among them with my North Star. She erupted with a blazing light that I had never witnessed in the lighter hours before. All the hunters fell to the ground in fear, and it wasn't until Crow Foot gave a screaming war cry that they all regained their composures and looked at the field of twenty big buffalo all sprawled out, dead upon the ground. They didn't run to the buffalo, but first came to me and praised their new "Warrior Chief".

They then set about examining their biggest buffalo catch of all. Their whole winter's supply of food was now secure. The entire clan came to butcher and carve up the beasts and I realized the group had grown considerably with new faces. I guess others were seeking food also. At the eve, there was only evidence of blood on the ground to betray this massive slaughter as they took everything, piece by piece. I felt very pleased of the good that I had accomplished and what North Star had done.

This small band of wanderers, set up their permanent camp against a high bluff for the coming winter, and since I had no direction, I stayed on. The first snowflakes fell in late November, but the "quack quack" flew in first. That's when I learned how Crow Foot and the others caught quack-quacks and bigger birds they called honk-honks in the wild.

A large noisy flock of birds, flying in a strange pointed shape, set their wings and hovered above a slough, and then they all swooped in at one time. Three men left with Crow Foot and eased into the cold water carrying fresh-cut water reeds in their mouths to breathe through. Going into the water, the hunters eased up to the birds as close as they could, without spooking them and then submerged completely. Seconds later, the birds began to suddenly disappear beneath the water, one by one, as the hunters pulled each one down under.

With a large bird in each hand that was flopping frantically to get free, the successful hunters arose out the water and onto the bank. The proud hunters came back to us and displayed their fat squawking birds. Then they each in unison started twirling the birds by their necks, until the heads actually twisted off in each hunter's hand. The bloody birds, however, went flopping about headless in all directions upon the ground. It was a hideous sight as one slammed into me headless. Soon, they all expired.

It was feather pluckin' time. It certainly was very different than the bachelor Crow Foot's "roast em black, and then skin 'em" method. The women boiled water and dunked the birds. Then they all pulled the birds' feathers, and one woman laid them out to dry. The feather had many uses; mainly to be worn in a feathered bonnet. Again the fire was built and the little band gave praise to their Heavenly spirits for this wonderful feast.

In the morning, we all gathered together around the fire, because the people had found a large cavern and had decided that it would be a great place to sit out the winter, if it wasn't a bear's den. In a short tramp to the hills, we all got to see that there was an opening in a bluff, large enough for everyone. Crow Foot urged me by poking at North Star to go inside first. I knew he was afraid that there might be animals inside that needed to be removed, but I remembered my getting helplessly trapped in one, so I was afraid too. I reluctantly eased inside.

I found nothing of consequence inside its opening, except some small black bats. Then further inside, I saw there were inscriptions upon the walls, just like the ones I had found in other countries. A similar dugout pool of water resembled the others and held fresh water dripping into it from a hidden spring. The water was cool and refreshing.

The writings were very similar and read the same as all the others I'd seen. I was very pleased and came back outside smiling so brightly, that the people wondered why I was so happy and shook me for an answer, which I could not explain to them.

They hurried inside and immediately went to their knees before the wall of etchings. Apparently, their culture had experienced my people here before. Within their own broken up, spoken language, I heard one actually say, "Ah men," somewhere, right in the middle of one's speech. I was simply flabbergasted, but very pleased in their revere of the etchings.

I learned many things about my new relatives, and one lesson was how it hurts to physically become their "blood brother", when you get stuck and your blood is mixed with theirs. They wanted this, and I concurred. I tried to be brave, but I'm certain that my squeamish way was recognized as being a not so brave warrior. We sheltered there in a dreary lifestyle for quite some time, but to venture into the deepening snows would have perished us all. I thanked Dargod many times for the fellowship of my friends.

"a' Crowfoot Goes Duck Divin"
PWK.

Crow Foot Receives a Healing (Chapter 8)

An uneventful winter drew to an end. Besides nearly freezing to death, several women died in childbirth. They were placed in the deep drifts until spring. It was sad, but it brought to my mind that I must not linger here. I must find that red-ringed snake for my Marietta. I knew that she would someday be restored to her life using the snake's venom and mixing it with the capsules. The explorers before me had said it had worked to preserve other Earthlings.

I just woke up on a spring morning and slipped out of camp, I thought unnoticed. I had heard of a trading post, and I tried to find it. But after several days of avoiding buffalo herds and wolves, I heard the grunt of my friend Crow Foot. I stopped and looked back. Way, way back there, was Crow Foot, looking straight down and very hard at my tracks, trying desperately to follow them with his crossed eyes.

It was a cruel trick that I contrived then for laughs, but I walked directly up against a large oak, then I walked backwards in my own footprints, and quietly hopped off the trail behind a rock. I had learned that trick in Africa when we used it on the pygmies. Poor ol' Crow Foot with his head down was desperately trying hard to see my tracks. Donk! Crow Foot knocked himself out when he head-butted that oak. He fell straight back as though he were shot dead. I really felt bad and it was painful to see him so laid out limply like he was.

It was three hours waiting until I could revive him from unconsciousness, but it took two full days of nursing him before his head cleared. But when he lifted himself up from his prone position by the campfire, his eyes were uncrossed. He could see very clearly for the first time, maybe since his birth. My friend Crow Foot forgave me, and then started laughing out loud.

"Ugh. Ugh," he kept saying. He apparently thought I was very ugly. On that day, my friend looked at me in a completely different way…miracles will happen…imagine that?

I explained to Crow Foot that I wanted to go to the big post. He grabbed my arm and turned me to the east, and then spoke, "Ugh!" His arm swung back and forth in that direction, then he patted me on the behind to go. Hummm…watch that!

Three more days passed, and the smell of the river's water entered my nostrils. I got my first sight of the big trading post. It was just a little log cabin house with a big front porch. There were other Indians and white men both, some with furs, some with money. All had a bottle of hard liquor in their hands. They had been back in the hills trapping for furs.

They brought their hides here to a Frenchie named St. Louie, who traded them goods and grubstakes. Then the trappers would drink his squeezins' and drippings, get stupid, play cards, lose their money, and then go back into the hills searching for more furs. This seemed to be repeated every year after year. What else was there to do?

The pounds and shillings that I carried were looked upon suspiciously. Louie questioned where I had gotten them. Apparently there was a disagreement that the French and English were having. In a moment of need, I told him that I had taken the loot off some dead soldiers at the opening to the river to the big lake. Louie wanted to know immediately how many there were. So not wanting to lie any further I said, "None, we killed them all." This brought him much relief, and he shamefully traded traps and grub for half the value of my money.

I asked everyone I met if they knew of the red coral snake, but no one had heard of that kind. They told me to look out for the rattlesnake and the cotton mouthed water moccasin, "They'll make y'all sick, or a biggin' one will kilt ya!"

What was this new language that they addressed me with; it was sort of a slurred report, or a diminished English-French mixture?

Inside my pack was a hefty sum. I was tired of walking, so I bought two horses, two mules, grub, traps, and plenty of "firewater" for Crow Foot. The latter was my biggest mistake.

Crow Foot started hootin' and a hollerin' all the way out to the hills. But when the liquid ran out, he straightened up in a week or two. In the mean time, I had caught no animals in my traps like ol' Louie convinced me I would. I was sure that I was doing exactly like everyone, including Louie, who sold me all ninety-five traps and had explained how to do it. But every morn there was nothing, nothing.

One day, when my anger and desperation came to a head, I pulled out all the traps and brought them back to camp. Crow Foot studied the traps for some time. Then he smelled them and licked them.

"Naaha," meaning they stunk to an animal, I guessed. He immediately set out to gather bark off trees, which smelled wonderful. He took a pot with boiling water, put in the bark, and soaked the traps in the brown bark mixture. This took a day. I was afraid that this would rust the traps. Then Crow Foot taught me how to trap, the Indian way.

Crow Foot set the traps under the waterline, not at the entrances of the dens like Louie had told me. The first check of the trap line the next time resulted in sixty-two catches, mostly beaver and muskrat. There was a beautiful, white ermine in one, so I skinned it and chewed the fat from it myself, and saved it for Marietta. I missed her so.

I'm ashamed to admit it, but being a trapper was the most exciting game I ever played. To trick an animal into the trap was a science, and I was getting pretty good with my partner, ol' Crow Foot's help. But with all of my previously gotten wealth, it was not needed. It was really for the fun of it. I learned to like eating beaver, muskrat, mink and the squirrels that Crow Foot caught by standing under a tree, dead still, and grabbing those little critters as they came down full of nuts. His new sight enabled him to complete this task of waiting then grabbing. Then, Crow Foot cut open the gullets of those squirrels and used the contents to bait the traps. Boy did that work well. Every trap was filled.

Years slid by quickly. Where had the time gone? Louie knew our fine pelts because Crow Foot always chewed the fat off them, and they became really soft. We were a good pair, we were, but ol' Crow Foot was aging and slowed considerably.

One day, ol' Crow Foot and I were just meandering along the Dead Horse Creek, searching for beaver dens and such, in the far west of the Black Hills of South Dakota. We rode our horses up a butte onto this huge, shiny rock pile. The rock pile looked as though it had tumbled down from a bigger chunk, which protruded high upon a ridge. I suspected it must have been a genuine falling star and had landed up there, but since then, it had fallen down. I didn't know exactly what it was then; I didn't recognize it in its raw state. But it looked so pretty that we just grabbed off several big hunks and put them in our saddlebags for posterity, or something.

Our saddlebags couldn't hold much because the rocks sure were heavy, and we needed to have all the room for the furs we were trapping. We were getting plenty of furs for certain. We had already caught two hundred beaver and three hundred muskrats in no time at all. We shot a young bull buffalo for camp meat. We did this all on our way into Sioux Indian country, not after we had been there for awhile. Once in a while I'd take a peek at North Star. She was doin' okay.

Well come to tell ya, five months later we were loaded down below the cinches with fine furs. Just as the quack quacks were flying back north, we brought in all our skins to get their value and to do some bartering for food and supplies. We were surprised to find out that Louie had died, and a new owner took over the big post. I must have looked and smelled ordinary, because he treated me like a real backcountry trapper.

We hadn't tasted some good decent squeezin's since our last visit. The new owner began to count all our furs, all the while saying to me how poor they were and that they would not bring much at all. I knew better than that. He searched them all. But when he saw those big shiny rocks fall from my bags onto the floor, he began to yell something fierce. He became as insane as any person I ever saw. It scared me awful, so I slipped back away, and drew my skinning knife.

He began babbling something, and biting at the rocks like a dog on a bone. He started telling us that we were rich. He told us we could have anything in the store, including the store; just for those darn shiny rocks.

Boy was he a humdinger, I tell ya! Anyway, he began to stare at us funny-like, sort of like when an undertaker looks at you sometimes. Then he beckoned us back into the storeroom, and began asking questions. No trouble for Crow Foot, because he didn't speak anything but Cheyenne and very little other. He just stood there smiling at him. I thought that he was kind of a queer actin' fellow, so I just kept saying to him my piece.

"Those rocks came from Virginia, and I found them in a creek."

"What part?" he says.

"The south, ever been there?"

"No, but I want to go there!"

He wanted us all to pack up right then and head out to Virginia. I told him that we weren't rock searchers; we were trappers. We couldn't just leave. Besides, we could go back anytime and pick up all that we ever needed. His eyes grew wider when I asked what it was.

He began to shake a lot and I thought that he was going to have a body failure. He sure was excited, I'll tell you. So I started talkin' jess like them there other trappers did, with a real country drawl to make him think we were real back woodsy bumpkins. Ha, I guess I really had become one though. I had a long habit of mimicking my environment's inhabitants. My King's English had left me somewhere between the big muddy river and St. Louie. Grunting back and forth to an Indian for years can spoil your vocabulary and your brain. He asked if I had told anyone about the rocks, and I told him, "Heck no, what fer?"

Right then, the devil was in me and I told the most unscrupulous story about where those rocks were. I told him that there was so many that they lay around just to be picked up by anyone. I could see he was really bitin' the bait, so I told him, "Thar's so much of that stuff that it be in the trees too." That nearly ruined everything, but he sat down at his desk and got out his ink and quill and struck us a deal. He quickly gave us everything, lock stock and barrels, for our rocks and a drawn map of how to get there. I drew it.

After handing me the deed to the entire store and its contents, he lit out that back door as fast as he could, and I never saw him since. I sure hoped that he found his way alright, because I had never really ever been to Virginia….."Dargod, please forgive me!"

"Now what the heck are we going to do with this store?" I asked Crow Foot. But it sure was nice of him to do all that trading though, best we ever did! Crow Foot found bunches of cigars in boxes, lit one up and started puffing hard to no end. He loved 'em, and started blowing smoke signals like no Indian I had ever seen.

I had to quickly lock the front door, because people just started walking in to trade. When they banged harder on the door, I had to pull the shades down. We hid in the back of the store. I wanted to just grab up some grub and traps and get out of there quickly, but Crow Foot wouldn't budge. He just kept puffing on those cigars and driving me to no end with all the smoke.

After one night of shuffling around the store's goods, I put together quite a nice stake. I took all the food that we'd need for a year. I grabbed up some bacon, beans, flour, and a few cans of peaches. I even found some bars of lye soap. I handed Crow Foot a few boxes of cigars and pushed him out the door onto the boardwalk. He just stood there like a petrified tree and would not budge. So I told Crow Foot goodbye, I was leaving him behind, hoping he would soon follow me. And then I left him behind to mind the store.

As I rode off to the west though, I glanced back several times hoping to see my friend following, but there was ol' Crow Foot still standing outside the storefront blowin' big smoke rings, one after the other. The final time I looked back, I noticed that a man in a hat had taken some cigars from Crow Foot's box and handed him some paper money. I knew ol' Crow Foot couldn't count, so that fella in the hat wasn't getting any change back…ha…being a little "dumb" might be very lucrative for Crow Foot.

I rode on towards the west. I guess ol' Crow Foot became real famous by just standing out in front of that store selling cigars, because years later, while I was in St. Louie, I saw a statue of ol' Crow Foot, right out front of a store, selling cigars…imagine that!

Trading Post St. Louis
'ol' Crowfoot'
FURS bought Here
5¢ CIGARS

Just Biding My Time
(Chapter 9)

I felt a little sad to have to leave Crow Foot behind, for he had been a sidekick and a true friend. He couldn't go on is my guess, he was all worn out. So, as the time passed, I felt better about it day-by-day. It helped just knowing that he had gotten very old and seemed very happy there. I was in no big hurry, so I just rode along the bank of the ol' Mississippi with my pack animals, about the speed of the current…slow and easy.

It was too early for trapping season, because the weather had to be cold enough to cause the fur to grow thicker on the animal's body to develop a full, valuable, rich-colored winter coat. So, with my pack train just trailing behind, I headed north towards the Dakotas. As I rode, I thought of Marietta and wondered if I would ever find that red coral snake. I was always looking for it, consciously, or not. They say time heals all wounds, but I wasn't buying that, as each moment ached, when thinking about my Marietta in my arms.

It was during that time that I rode up upon two big army colonels camped along the river, pausing as they explored the river. They had a big keel boat with a sail, and a bunch of fellas to help them pole. When I told them that I had been where they were heading, they begged me to join their crew.

One man, Colonel Lewis, was a real nice officer. I traded with him for some powder and balls and a very nice flintlock rifle for some flour and beans. It seems the French in St. Louie wouldn't let them dock to buy any grub to feed his men.

The colonels were undecidedly lost as to just where this big muddy river branched off, so I lead them towards a river that Crow Foot had once called the Missouri. Colonel Clark displayed a map that he was using that was very incomplete, with a lot of bare spots on it. That meant to me that nobody knew where in the heck they were going!

Colonel Clark was kind of crabby and uppity…kind of 'snooty' I'd say. His bellowing orders were always heard, because he ordered everybody around like a real pusher. When Colonel Clark ordered, things got moving very quickly about camp. I think he was such a crank because he didn't want to admit that he was very lost. They told me eventually that they searched for what they called the Northwest Passage, but I'm not sure that's what it was. I think maybe they were so dog gone lost because possibly they had gotten hold of a fictitious 'gold map' and got themselves horns waggled. So, I left Lewis and Clark to search for their dream at the mouth of their chosen river's branching.

Come August, the heat and mosquitoes got so bad that I thought I'd just welt up and die. Smearing on bear grease didn't help one nickel. Then one day, a skinny lookin' fella rode into my camp. He was tall and poor looking; I guess just like me. We hit it off just fine. His handle was Bill Cody, he said, but all his friends called him, and he answered best to, Buffalo Bill. He said that the army nicknamed him that when he used to hunt buffalo for the government. I told him that I was a trapper and had taken a few bulls myself.

Bill was a real shooter…bull shooter that is. We rode together for a few weeks and shared stories of our hunts. Always trying to out tell me, Bill concocted some of the most outrageous tales anyone could tell. When we got to bragging about our rifles one day, we started plinkin' at some driftwood floating down the river. Ol' Bill carried a big long barreled, Sharp's 44/70. Now mind you, I could shoot a gnat off a fly's behind at sixty paces, but Bill, he was much better. Of course, I didn't show off North Star.

One day we were sharing a little too much of my store bought squeezin's. While riding along on the barren prairie flats ol' Bill suddenly stopped his mount, raised his rifle high, fired, and says that he just shot a squirrel. Now there wasn't a tree to be seen within ten miles of us, nowhere.

Later on, many miles down the trail as we began to set up camp along a hackberry grove, Bill picked up this red squirrel off of the ground by its bushy tail below a tree, and says, "Here's dinner!" By gosh, there it was, almost like fresh-killed and it had Bill's ball in its brain…imagine that! An honest to goodness ten-mile shot, I reckoned.

Now, I wasn't overcome by the long shot, I says, "But how in the world did ya see that far?" and bein'a little green with envy, I told him when he offered to skin it, "No thank you, it's a red one, and I only like gray ones."

But Bill recanted, "Twern't no gray squirrels that'd go around a hackberry grove."

I said, "You shoulda' looked a little farther down the road, cause I seen there were two grays eatin' on persimmons."

Bill says, "Ha, you truly must be from Virginny!"

Humm…I guess I'd become a real bona fide hillbilly, as I had almost forgotten my own spoken tongue and had taken on the dialect spoken in the new western frontier.

I again found myself immatatin' the breed I was with, and that it would be just a reoccurring event of my adapting ways in my lifetime of always collecting the current culture around me. Except I never grunted like those pygmies did that I once roasted.

Boom!
Bill says,
"See that RED Squirrel?"
ANK

Making a New Feathery Friend
(Chapter 10)

The days hurried by as Bill and I eventually parted near an Indian settlement called Bismarck. He was steering towards some fort called Pierre Chouteau, as I was heading directly into the Sioux Territory. Along about a week, I began to feel the signs of late fall. My bones ached some and the frost on the early morning ground revealed to me that there was a person wearing moccasins that was sneaking about my camp while I was shut-eyed. An Indian, I reasoned, was snoopin' for food, I thought. I sure didn't mind sharing my grub, but I sure didn't like a fella that would steal from you. Anyway, I decided to set a trap for him because whoever it was kept tagging along and following me everywhere, as I moved from trappin' place to trappin' place.

One day I skinned-out an old possum that I caught in my trap and put him upon a roasting pole above a fire pit. I smeared him up with bear grease and that made him look real tasty. But I bet it was going to give some stealing Indian the runs.

It didn't take very long when I pretended to bed down, that I peeked out of the corner of my eye and saw this Indian tippy-toein' over to my fire from the bushes. He was the scrawniest fella that I had ever seen, skinnier than Crow Foot was, maybe…a real bag of bones; maybe even skinnier than ol' Bill Cody.

Well, he grabbed a hold onto that roasting pole and takes a real big bite out of that possum. I sat up to watch him, thinking that he was going to holler to high heaven from the terrible taste. But, he started going, "Uumm, uumm, uumm!" The uumms that he made got louder and louder, so I walked up behind him and started laughing very hard. He just turned around and kept on chewin' and uumming. He was the hungriest critter that I ever did see. I eased up beside of him and squatted. I could tell that he was a young buck who had probably gotten lost and couldn't catch any varmints to eat.

Well, he decided to stay in camp that night, but along about three, I heard him scurry to the bushes and begin moaning something awful. In the woods, we called that 'green apple quick steppin'…he, he! He had learned not to steal, I reckoned.

I thought this young man was a Cheyenne, or possibly a Pottawatomi, but I learned that he was called Red Cloud, a 'mighty Sioux' he told me. Why was it that every Indian that I'd ever met became a "mighty" somethin? Huh…anyway, he wasn't just your ordinary Indian, he turned out to be something special. He just kinda moved along with me wherever I'd go and kept on following me along to my trap line.

I spoke a little Sioux, so we got along pretty well because he spoke a little "white man's lingo". I showed him how I trapped; he taught me to catch big fish with his spear. He also found time to teach me his Indian game of "stones". I had to hit a stone with a club that he threw at me. Then I'd have to run to another stone that was lying on the ground, which he had placed a good distance away; before he could pick up and "clunk" me with the one that I just hit. Now that hurt! After a few hits on my noggin, I learned to hit that stone before it hit me. I got pretty good at running too, so that he wouldn't get to hit me hard before I reached the other stone. It was a treacherous game, but exciting and fun when we had little to do and had all our skins stretched.

Red Cloud was youthful; his features reminded me of Crow Foot's a lot. Quiet, but kind of interesting in his own way, it all seems that he was a stepson of a powerful Oglala Indian Chieftain named Crazy Horse, and he may have been stolen in an opposing tribal raid. That part, I couldn't quite decipher. Anyways, he really was following me because he was lost.

We became pretty good friends, as by and by I trusted him more, and he trusted me. The darn thing was though; he was a big eater and made my short list of goods, even shorter. So I was saving all the grub that I could to get by. He loved my biscuits and gravy, especially with a little possum stirred in. But flour was as scarce as hen's teeth.

Red Cloud had gotten plum fat, a sign to other Indians that he was a great hunter. I thought he'd be staying with me awhile, until one day we both walked into this big meadow. He acted like he knew the place and immediately got a big smile upon his face.

Red Cloud did recognize the land, he said, for it was near his home in the Black Hills. Just then, a whole band of Lakota Indians came from out of nowhere and surrounded us on their ponies. They were a fierce looking bunch, full of feathers and war paint. I feared my britches were about to fill.

They were screaming bloody murder, and I thought I had drawn my last full breath, when Red Cloud raised his hand and they all became silent. One big Indian slid down from his spotted pony to give Red Cloud a big hug. They exchanged a few words, and then the big one turned my way.

He looked at me and gave me a sign that displayed that I was welcome…for a while anyway. It seemed that he was Red Cloud's step-pappy, Crazy Horse, and he was very glad that I had brought his little boy warrior home.

They took me to their camp where they prepared a big feast. Everyone began to hoot and holler in a big circle. Crazy Horse offered me his captured squaw named Sacajawea as my personal servant. She was very friendly. When I needed something, I just hollered out "Suzy" and here she would come. She sat close to me around the fire and we snuggled closely at nighttime. It was a fun time for certain, but what about my Marietta? I'm afraid my yearnings pointed two different ways. I was a lonely man.

The drums were pounding out loud into the night. There must have been four thousand Indians all dressed up in their Sunday best. As we strolled around, I could see that there was more than just the Sioux tribe here. There were Cheyenne, Chippewa, Comanche, Choctaw, Ute, Blackfoot, Shoshone Snakes, Flathead, Crows, Nez Perces, Kiowa, and a few Apache Pueblo from the Deep South. What the heck were they all doing all bunched up here? I began to worry there was gonna be trouble for some white men.

After a day or two, I began to feel uneasy and decided to move on. Some of those strange Indians were pointing their spears at me and screaming words at me that I didn't feel were polite. I then said goodbye to Red Cloud and all his family. Before I could leave, Chief Crazy Horse led out this pinto pony with the finest blanket I'd ever seen.

On top of that pony's blanket was Suzy, a gift from Crazy Horse for bringing Red Cloud home, which I could not accept. I told them that I already had a squaw, but appreciated the pony and the blanket. I told this to Red Cloud and he explained this to Crazy Horse, so as to not offend him. Crazy Horse was not offended. But instead he then presented me with a necklace that came from his very own neck and told me I was a friend of the Sioux, and it would protect me through his domain. I was so moved that I went to my pack animals and got an old box of cigars and presented it to him.

He then took the long knife from his belt and nicked my wrist to draw blood. I knew what was comin' and I hoped I'd keep that cooked possum down. He did the same cut to Red Cloud. He tied a special cloth around our wrists and chanted special words that brought Red Cloud and me together as blood brothers forever. Simply amazing, I was now another Indian's blood brother. To my surprise, Crazy Horse brothered me too! I half bled to death getting' brothered.

I tied the pinto to my pack string and headed out. There was plenty of hootin' and hollerin' as I passed by all those painted up Indians. They had death in their eyes and I was certain before I could get safely away, some of them might disobey Crazy Horse's wishes and come after me. I just had to look 'em in the eye and remember I had North Star and could take on the whole bunch. I wish I had, I guess.

I heard later that those same Indians got into a real ruckus with the U.S. Seventh Calvary, down along the Little Big Horn. I just couldn't understand why they would do that, but after all that fuss no white man could set foot lawfully in the Black Hills, except for me, of course…I was their blood brother. Anyway, I heard that Red Cloud became a chief and was a peaceful leader. So I guess by him spending that time with me trapping and playing stones I was sort of a good influence upon him.

It Was Infatuation, I Know
(Chapter 11)

Years passed by, and many things changed. The Indians were moving on, and so were the buffalo. I had a considerable stake saved up and decided that I'd just skip this next cold winter on the trap line. The trap line had been real good to me, and fun, but I had seen some pictures of fancy places on the walls at the new trading post in St. Louie. There were pictures of tropical isles, beaches, and palm trees which all brought back the realities of my Marietta and my search for that red coral snake. It was long ago…too long.

St. Louie wasn't just a trappers' hub anymore, as the post had grown into a real big city with lots of buildings and brightly painted signs. As I walked upon the sidewalks, it was awfully funny, as I met those high falootin' big shots with tall hats made from beavers. As they passed by me, I looked upon them and tried to see if I had actually known that beaver when he was alive…ha!

Music filled the air from the show places everywhere I went. The dance hall girls always smelled real pretty-like, and they always caught the eye of some lonesome gents like me. And in a moment of true loneliness, I became stirred inside by Miss Lilly Langtry, the prettiest lady in the entire west. I saw Miss Lilly Langtry on stage at one of the big show places. She sang as pretty as a nightingale. All the men tried to be next to her, but she wouldn't have just any ordinary boys on her arm. They had to be well dressed and had to have a big pocket full of dollars. She became the deciding factor for me to buy my first set of new clothes, for many years, and caused me to visit the barbershop to shave and take a hot bath.

A brand new store started up called Sears and Roebuck. They fitted me up nicely with fancy duds from the east. I thought that the changes I made to my appearance were a dramatic improvement...I looked handsome, I imagined. And guess what...yep, there was a statue out front of Sears of ol' Crow Foot, selling his cigars...imagine that. It brought back good memories.

Then all decked out, I went to Lilly's stage front each and every performance. That's about the time that I locked horns with ol' Bat Masterson. Bat was the marshal and he had the "heart throbs" for Miss Lilly, too. Except, I could see that Miss Lilly noticed my new duds and that they caught her eye. That caught Bat's eyes, too. He began to ask me all kinds of sarcastic questions, to incite me to be insulted. He asked if I was a hillbilly from Virginia. Hummm, I guess he really wanted to fight badly.

This time, ol' Bat went too far, and asked me if I was feeling lovey-dovey for his girl, Miss Lilly. I said, "It's only a jealous fool who would let his big mouth override his brain, and his abilities, and then challenge a man he knows nothing about, don't you think?"

"Who you think you're talking to, you country bumpkin? I'll run you out of town on a rail."

He'd done it! He forced my hand. And when he put his hands on his two shiny, ivory-handled Colt pistols upon his sides, I reached for North Star under my coat. But before we came to brawling inside the show place, Miss Lilly herself stepped between us and had a few words of her own to say.

She told Bat to leave immediately, and to my extreme surprise, he obeyed her like she was his scolding mother. I never saw a man cower so quickly. She had some great controlling powers over that fella. Then she turned to me when Bat left and said, "Buy me a drink, handsome stranger." I could have just farted right then! But I knew it wasn't polite to do that in the presence of a lady. What should I do? What could I do? I'm afraid to admit it, but I was caught up in that moment by surprise. The spirits of the drink affects a person's morals first, then their judgment, as Lilly and I were drawn together, like two hot magnets.

Lilly was a real lady and even though she had chosen to talk to me, I knew she was only doing that to keep the peace. She asked a whole lot of serious questions about me, but all that I could muster was that I was a trapper from the Dakotas. Then she said that she wondered where I had gotten such beautiful brown eyes. I ordered many more rounds of fine wine and whiskey, and she drank them all with me.

Well that starry night was spent with Miss Lilly Langtry, and I never forgot her warm body next to mine. But come morning, I was sick for what I had done; Lilly was gone and so was my infatuated heart. I checked with the hotel clerk and he told me Miss Lilly had gotten onto the morning stage to Kansas City, with Bat Masterson. What a stupid fool I was; I was blue, and hung over, but very glad that I didn't have to again face Bat Masterson's revenge. But, I guess reconsidering the consequences that would have been very interesting when I triggered North Star.

Hang Me, Dang Me!
(Chapter 12)

Before I decided to get into another possible gunfight, I bought a safety deposit box that could hold my pack, most of my money, and North Star. I'd just pick it up when I returned in the spring. I told the banker that I might be gone even a year, depending how things went, so he wanted his deposit money well in advance…lucky me. The banker said it would be very safe with him. Then he handed me the key.

I hopped aboard a paddle-wheeled boat headed down the Mississippi to the gulf port of New Orleans. Riding a big boat is fun, much better than all the times that I maneuvered along the banks on horseback and fought those darn mosquitoes and water moccasin snakes. It was only going to take a few days floating, not two months like a pack mule train. On the second night in my cabin, I got darn lonely, so I ventured into the saloon. After Lilly, my morals had slipped badly and it was a time that I regret deeply. Twas like a real saloon on the ground, with laughing and cussing, and there was pretty music from a frisky Cajun piano player, who kept the room's mood jumpin'.

I spied a table in the corner with a few gents playing cards. Five-card stud, they told me. After standing behind watching those fellas bet lots and lots of dollars, I figured that this game would be lots of fun. They asked me to play, but I told them that I didn't exactly know how. Smiles erupted all over their faces when they saw my stake money, and they sure got friendly. They showed me how to play their game.

I asked a lot of questions about the playing rules. I had a hard time remembering which cards were the best, but that turned out to be a big reward. Money was going back and forth among us. I was catching on quickly, they told me, and they asked me if I was a "ringer"?

I said, "I never rang no ding dong bells before." They chuckled some at my speech, as I watched their eyes. I then began to see these greedy men for what they really were, card sharks, and I resorted to my frontiersman's back woodsy ways to fool them.

My pot hadn't grown, but it didn't shrink much either. I kept getting some real good cards passed to me. I think they called that beginner's luck. Anyway, the dealer sent me over five cards and when I looked at them, I began to murmur to myself.

"There is an ace, king, and a queen lady."

They were staring at me, but they were spades. The other two were red as a berry, a jack and ten. So I says out loud to myself, "Royal?" I pretended that I couldn't figure out if I had a royal flush, or simply an ace-high straight. I was acting very innocently confused.

The dealer's eyes widened and he asked me if I needed any cards, but I said, "No."

Now I really couldn't quite figure out if I had a really good hand, or a weak one. One player, after another, bid higher and higher, and that kept raising the pot fast. I stayed in and raised my share too, all to the suspecting eyes of the dealer, who folded.

I reached deep into my stake to match everyone's raises. I was seriously thinking about how I might pay for my breakfast in the morning, if I lost it all. The money piled high upon the table and they told me that I was "studying" too much. They were getting antsy. So I asked this, "Does a royal beat everything?"

They looked really sick, and everyone there started throwing their cards in, thinking that's what I had. Finally, I was the only one playing. That made me the winner!

Heehaw! I was a thirty thousand, five hundred dollar cash winner. When I reached for the big pile of money, they wanted to see my hand. Now I learned right away that if everybody folds, I didn't have to show anyone my hand. So I just pitched my cards into the pile. No one ever knew if I was just holding worthless cards, or not. They were angry.

I bought drinks for the room and set moving about when they all decided it was too late. The piano player had quit for the night, and the bartender hollered out that the bar was closing. It was near three o'clock. In a bit, I walked away with my money, back to my cabin a very happy man. I didn't really need the petty cash that I won there, but it was a great feeling of self-satisfying comfort to know that I had tricked the tricksters. I was so utterly exhausted, and that pillow felt so soft, that I was asleep almost instantly.

Unbeknownst to me, there was a desperate fella aboard watching my winnings and me. Just before daylight, I heard someone enter my room and saw a man pilfering for my money. I did what any man would do; I plugged him. That brought every man, woman, and servant running to my room to see.

Suddenly the captain of the vessel appeared and called me a murderer. I tried to explain that this fella was robbing my poke, but he wasn't hearing my story. When someone hollered, "I'll get a rope," I got plum mad and grabbed my gun to stop them. Then I grabbed my poke, backed out of my cabin and ran to the side of the boat. I pitched myself right into the deep water and almost drown from the big paddle wheel's wake. I swam a half-mile, or more, to a steep gumbo embankment. There was a loud volley of 'pop, pop, pop, pop', as their bullets' slugs hit that gumbo and splattered everywhere. Lucky for me, those guys weren't shooters like Buffalo Bill…thank Dargod!

I Get Swamped
(Chapter 13)

Well I tell ya; I was on the side of the muddy river that I'd never been on before. I struggled to get up that muddy gumbo bank, and each time I'd almost get to the top, I up-ended and my kiester hit the mud sliding back down with a big splash. I finally got too tired, so I just floated south along with the river's current, looking for an escape, until I luckily spotted a huge alligator gar, before he spotted me. That big fish was longer than me and weighed five times my weight, I'm guessing. He was just floating up near the surface, popping his jaws at minnows and bugs, and he looked really hungry as he swirled beneath a bent over willow. But just as I was about to give up on living, I was able to grab hold of that willow, and somehow flung myself onto its trunk, away from the jaws of that monster. He paddled below me for a while, and when I dropped a hunk of bark on him, he skidaddled. I eased myself off the willow onto the bank, and flopped down exhausted. I was beginning to wonder if it might have been better if one of those bullets had met its mark.

I was deep in the south, someplace, I imagined…maybe Louisiana. I realized that I had committed the ultimate sin…I got my powder wet! So, I had to stomp and wiggle through all that wet swampy land without a shooter.

I came upon gators, lizards, and big giant cotton mouthed water moccasins that were often over seven feet long. I guess I'm just lucky that I'm even here today to speak about all this. After about two days had passed without any food, I remembered Red Cloud teaching me to make a spear from a willow. I cut a sharp point on one and started searching for something to spit. I still knew how to rub two sticks together to make a fire and my stomach was squealing something terrible…I thought. But wait, that's not my stomach, that's a wild boar making those sounds, and he's coming my way.

I shimmied up an old water-dead tree and watched for that pig to come by. Almost two hours had passed. I could hear him softly grunting. My own stomach was gurgling so much and so loudly now, that the big hog thought that I must be his twin brother. Then I spotted his thick, black, hairy, muddy carcass rooting towards me. Now a big boar pig can kill you with his razor sharp tusks…rip your gizzard plum out, and then eat it. But I wasn't too afraid, because I was so hungry for anything to bite down upon, and a hog on a spit is mighty tasty, that I had to take the chance, just had to.

I had to be accurate and stick him deep, if I could. He worked his way right under me, but I wasn't sure when to try to attack. That decision was made for me when the tree I selected let out with a crack. The limb that I was upon broke right off from under me, and I fell right onto that critter's back. I missed my stab, but that made no difference at all. To my fortune the limb had crushed his backbone, and he couldn't run. But he sure was mad! He spun around in a circle, dragging his hind legs and flashing his big ivory. The sound of his squealing was fierce and he smelled like high-hog heaven to boot. I moved around behind him to club him, but just as I raised the club, I heard the creepiest sayings that I ever imagined.

"Who dast? Who dast?" he bellowed. "My mammy was a snapper and my pappy was a croc, and I can break your back with just one chop! Who dast? Who dast?"

I looked up and was horrified, as there stood a huge mountain of a man. He had a size of seven feet tall, his chest and arms were huge like a bear's, and he must have weighed near a half-wagon's weight. His straggly dark beard was pert' near two foot long and black were his eyes. With no powder, all I could do was meditate. But he moved past me, grabbed up that big squealing boar in his bare hands, and slit that hog's throat as quick as a St.Louie butcher.

Then, he picked that big fierce hog up by the hind legs and commences to drinking that hog's warm red blood, as it streamed from inside him, all the while that pig was still squirmin' and a squealin'. I just about puked right there and then. He then bellowed, "Ahhhh, ha, ha, ha!" A big powerful man he was, which I'm sure any devil feared.

After a moment, he turned to me, all bloody-mouthed and says some funny sounding words that I hadn't even heard the strangest Indians speak. I couldn't decipher most of it.

Again, he bellows, "Who dast?" There was this wild fury look in his eyes. His mouth slobbered blood again. I was nauseous.

Then he noticed that I was trembling, and started to laugh much louder and harder. I was very uncertain as what to do when he quickly grabbed me up and then hugged me something terrible; his squeeze just about snuffed me out. He then carried me for a piece and put me back down upon dry ground.

He finally pointed to his chest and says, "I be Mike Fink, king of the river! Who dast?"

He was a real "Coonass Cajun", I reckoned. That's just what he was! I had heard about those strange people who lived off the swamp, part Negro, part Indian, and they seldom came out. I had been told the mixture of cultures had birthed some very beautiful women and handsome men too, but Mike was somehow different.

I once heard of a man called Mike Fink. I remembered jawing with ol' Bill Cody about this biggin' that worked on the ol' Mississippi as a barge tender. Cody said he was a mighty man, and a mighty fine man, if you were the same. Otherwise, he'd just tear you from limb to limb. But mostly he just talked real loud and was kindly towards animals and such.

"I'm Jamison Dargod," I told him. I extended my handshake, but wished I hadn't.

To my surprise, we were just a few feet from his rowboat that he used to get about in the swamp. Together, with the hog laying flat in the dugout skiff, we floated through the vines and trees to a widening of the swamp, which had an island with a shack on it. It stood on stilts and one had to climb up to get inside. Lo and behold, there was a menagerie of crocodile skins, raccoon, and bobcat, fox and rabbit furs aplenty, all neatly tacked up on the walls, on trees, everywhere. He was a mighty good trapper too…I guess you could call us "skin brothers" to the trap.

I helped gather up firewood and he put that pig on a hot fire spit. It roasted up in about four hours just fine. I could hardly keep myself from cutting off a big hunk right then. Mike picked up that pole and flopped that hog down on a big water oak tree stump that he used for a table. You'll have to guess who was the biggest hog, Mike or me. Well believe you me, there was a filling of my stomach that hurt for a week after, as big Mike and I chawed down on that hog. He sliced that boar into bacon and ham, not to mention those two Rocky Mountain oysters that we shared. Mike had six ugly cur dogs chained there to trees that he used to help him hunt. They all shared the carcass of that hog. They yelped to high heaven.

One day, shortly after we ate up that entire hog, Mike showed me a dish I had never tried before. He called it jambalaya. It had little wiggler crawdads in it, that he caught using a net in a real flat slough at the shallow end of a strip in the swamp, which somehow had a rocky bottom.

In that pot was some store-bought grits, boar meat, raccoon and some seasonings…Yikes! It was hot as fire from the devil's own kitchen! A quick drink of swamp water only made it hotter. Mike laughed his Coonass laugh, and finished off the rest of his concoction. Those seasonings were cayenne chili peppers, hotter than Hades and that's what all those Coonasses love to eat…Whoooeee it's hot! Mercy! No taste, just darn hot is what I remember. I guess a fella wasn't troubled by having worms none…he, he! Give me chawin' tabac, or whiskey!

I had to be moving along and ol' Mike said that if I ever adventured along his path again to stop by for some jambalaya. I knew that if jambalaya was his only reason for an invitation, he'd never see me again…ever.

It would be about a half-day's walk, after I'd gotten out of the swamp to the dry road to New Orleans, Mike had told me. But he said that I better had watch out for British soldiers on, "dem dare horses". They had taken over the whole area, but not the swamp. There could be a whole army of marchers and horse soldiers out there, as Mike bellowed, "Dem dare horsymen," he continued, "now dey all caryee' longa lancers to stick ya wid. Dey ain't too par- tic-u-lar' who dey jab in dee assy eder. Owe weee!"

So, as you can foresee, I really kept an eye out as I ventured to find that road to New Orleans.

I ventured along in the swamp a bit, until I heard some splashing. It all sounded just like a whole lot of some bodies with their determined rhythmic slosh…it got louder and louder, like a herd of buffalo. I shimmied up onto an old, rotten, fallen over tree, and saw that I was about to cross paths with a bunch of pirate-looking fellas.They were loaded down with barrels and sacks of guns, heaped high upon pack mules. They were coming directly for me, so I had to just sit tight. That wasn't the best decision though, as it turned out it became nearly fatal, because I got snake-bit by a big ol'cotton mouth water moccasin that was just laying on top of that old tree, sunning himself. I let out a "whoop" and bailed out of that old tree, and landed right in front of this little man with a big pointy-looking sword. I immediately raised my hands high. He looked really amused at my entry, and he stood his place…maybe he was stuck in the muddy-muck.

Now this little man yelled out French words at a rate only a French bartender could decipher, and he appeared to be a real important, uppity fella. He spit out some French words, but I spit back in English; his words I couldn't understand. He regained his composure after I spoke, and then in English, he fluently said, "Let me present myself, I am Jean La Fitte. Are you an A-mer-i-can?"

"Sure, isn't everybody?"

He looked befuddled, but he quickly noticed that I was holding onto my arm and he asked what was wrong with me.

"Snake bit, sir. Right here above my hand!" I pointed.

I knew what I had to do was to get the wound to bleed quickly, and pack it tight with chewing tobacco, the cure for every frontier ailment, as it would help draw out the snake's venom. Jean knew too, as he quickly poked me with that pointy sword and squeezed hard upon my wound. The trouble was I had no chew to put on it. I feared that I might be a goner, because I knew those big moccasins could kill you, or make you so deathly sick that you wish you were. I was just hoping for the latter, since I didn't know how big that snake was. Jean hollered back to his followers, and here came a real honest to goodness doctor of medicines. Imagine that, here in the swamp! The only doctor I'd ever seen on Earth, and here he was in the middle of this big ugly swamp, of all places. My whole world suddenly became upside down and whirled like a twister. Then it went black.

What happened next was real fuzzy-like, because I woke up in the middle of New Orleans with a whole lot of shootin' and fightin' goin' on. It was the cannons booming that shook the ground and my innards that brought me to. There were big clouds of billowing smoke, and men screaming, dying slowly from their wounds that ripped apart their bodies by all the bullets that were being fired.

Then suddenly, there he was! He rode up near me, and looked down on me from his big white horse. I just had awakened from the venom's sickness, so I presumed I'd died and gone to hell. But it was none other than Andy Jackson himself; General Andrew Jackson, to be exact. I was just about to say 'howdy', when he hollered at me to grab up a rifle and to hug the wall. I didn't rightly know what he was thinking, until I saw ol' Jean himself raising his sword. When he dropped that sword, there was a tremendous roar of cannons spitting smoke plumes with hell's own fury. "Ka booom!" They sounded out.

The sound rattled my innards again, and didn't do much for my aching, throbbing head. Without ado, I slid up next to ol' Jean and grabbed a dead man's rifle. It was spent, so I grabbed another. "Click", it was empty too.

"Now what for in heaven's sake am I gonna be shootin' at?" I yelled to Jean. He smiled at me and handed me a possibles bag of balls and powder and then he told me, "I'm glad to see you made it!"

Then I remembered that I was snake bit. My hand was swollen some, and tightly wrapped. It didn't hurt much, so I removed the wrap to study it. It was just a little scratch, cut into an X.

A bullet itself whizzed right past my ear, and that made me real mad. I loaded and fired at some fellas that were shooting at us from across the field. They were sure mad at us for some reason. But I sure could drop them fellas who wore those bright red coats with shiny brass buttons. Must have dropped twenty or more right in their tracks, right where they stood. Nary a one kicked a' tall, cause I put that ball right between their eyes. If ol' Bill Cody had seen me, he'd been very jealous, I think.

It was a furious fight, but in about two hours Ol' Hickory Andy rode up on his horse again and hollered, "Cease fire! Cease fire!"

His horse whirled in circles, as he surveyed and searched the situation. The shooting then stopped. When the smoke had cleared, I peeked up over the wall and there laid those red-coated fellas dismembered, dead, and stacked high upon the field. There wasn't one man standing, not one. I felt bewildered why all those boys had to die. The smell of death was everywhere, on both sides.

As it turned out, Andy himself pinned a medal upon my chest and congratulated us all for our bravery, and for saving America's soul from the English King. We were a genuine bunch of heroes he said that day. But little did he know that the war was already declared over, and none of that killing had to happen at all.

I guess those British fellas didn't know that either. We didn't learn for over two weeks that the war was over…darn, dang, darn!

The Spoils of a Useless Battle
(Chapter 14)

I hung around New Orleans way too long, celebratin', still sinnin' and drinkin' way too much every day. At first, we celebrated being heroes of the fighting, but it continued on and on for weeks, then months. I became a drunkard, but some would say wino. I guess during that time I had sipped every fine wine this world of partying had to offer, one and all, one by one. They all tasted too good.

You had to lie to those Cajun women about who you really were. They'd become too attached to you right away, or maybe it was just your money. They wouldn't let you leave when it was time for you to move on. Why there were three good men I had known that got stabbed to death; their jealous women lovers killed them as they tried to slip out of town unnoticed.

But I was smarter, I told them fillies that I was Mr. Marty Grass, a name that I just plucked out of the air somehow, that used to belong to a crazy storeowner that I met in St. Louie. That away, I'd be safe if they came lookin' for me. And there was plenty that I made love to, and plenty I had to worry about.

But those Cajun women have irresistible ways about them. Each was as pretty as any women that I'd seen anywhere in the world, and they liked to party day and night, night and day. If it wasn't partying, it was parading down the streets, hootin' and hollerin' and pretending to be who they weren't, by dressing up in costumes and fancy ball gowns. All their brothers, fathers, and kinfolk, each played real fine music in the bands, as they marched down the streets. It was the kind of music that you could really hop and skip around to, especially if you were drunk like I always was.

There was a lot of sinnin' goin' on for certain. Those Cajun gals had long, firm, full brown bodies and long, black silky hair with big flashing dark eyes, that were tempting; the sort of women what any man would dream of. And when they looked deep into your eyes, and smiled with them bright white teeth showing ear to ear, there was hardly a man alive that could resist temptation I reckoned…certainly not me.

Now women, I soon found out, are ruled by emotions, so you really have to watch closely when they start gettin' too attached to ya, and want to marry ya. I was spending way too much time with a woman named Rose Marie. She would feed me breakfast, and then we would go drinkin' and partyin' the rest of the day, and late into the night. Other ladies that I knew got real dangerously green-eyed jealous just seeing me walk with her on the streets. Everywhere I'd go, women that I had been with hollered at me that they wanted to see me more. I became sort of a "Don Juan". It was a high ol' time for this country boy, until two girls killed each other, fightin' over me. Shucks, I was good, but not that good! It was a sad affair. That terrible incident brought me back to my senses…thanks Dargod.

One dark night, I just packed up quick and left New Orleans. It's been told that the next morning, Rosie and twelve other women took to the streets lookin' just for me and calling my name, over and over for weeks. So much so, that they tell me today that the name I used to fool all them women in love is a real legend, and you can still hear them speak of ol' "Marty Grass" in the springtime…imagine that!

Which Way Do I Go?
(Chapter 15)

I lit out of New Orleans like a cat on a hot griddle, rode for weeks, swung wide, and came to rest up in a small town named Atlanta, that I discovered was way east of the ol' Mississippi, almost in Virginia territory. My poke was really skinny, but I still had a few gold coins and a dandy filly. I had to get back to St. Louie, somehow; I still had to get my bank-stored pack and North Star back.

Anyway, I got the itchin' to go back to the Dakotas and look for that mountain of gold that I'd found with Crow Foot, because I learned that you'd never go hungry on Earth with a pile of rocks like that. I continued on with the morning's sun at my back.

I was amazed at the large path that had developed by the numbers of travelers who apparently were coming from the east coast, headed to the west coast.

I knew the west side of the big river, which began right from the exact place where I had once jumped off Juan Ponce de Leon's ship had grown also. My trek here, however, first began along the ol' Tennessee riverbed while I was still thinkin' it was the Mississip' and in search of that red-ringed snake. I had searched there many moons before. I guess I was a genuine pathfinder and a frontiersman too. But soon, I was to meet up with a real famous frontiersman who advised me otherwise.

I got sidetracked when I met up with a true Tennessean named David Crockett. Crockett could spin more yarns about the colonies' struggles than most. He told me that while he once was out "bar huntin'", as he called it, he gut-shot a grizzly, and took off after it into a thicket with his unloaded rifle. His knife had accidentally dropped out of its sheath upon the ground near the opening. The bear suddenly rose up from the dead and cornered him inside. He was then trapped and defenseless, as he had stumbled right into that bear's own den by accident. Davy was without his knife and ol' Betsy, which was his affectionate name for his flintlock rifle, sort of like my North Star, I guess. Anyways, he told me he always had good white teeth, and he had to grin his way past that bear to get to his knife, and then stuck him dead when the bear was blinded by the shine off his choppers, hummm.

Anyway, Davy Crockett was a real plain talkin' fella, who other frontiersmen called "king of the wild frontier". His furry coonskin cap reminded me of the wild animal that once bit me at my traps. Ha!

He got plum choked up when he found out that Andy Jackson himself had stuck a shiny medal on me, which I still wore proudly on my chest. He said that he had ridden beside Andy Jackson fightin' Creek Indians.

"Now I once ran into some Creek Indians on the trail near Kentucky," I told Davy to keep our yarns brewin', "and I only escaped with my hair when I lit up North Star. It seems they thought that they had caught me riding one of their ponies that was stolen by the Sioux and given to me as a gift from a Chief Crazy Horse for savin' his step son Red Cloud, and boy did they holler and hoot when I clipped their feather bonnets real short with my North Star. Davy didn't believe me and wanted to see the contraption that I referred to as North Star. I told him I didn't have it with me, it was in a St. Louie bank.

"Why is it in a bank?" he asked.

"It's so precious, I have to keep it hidden," I told him.

Davy said he knew Crazy Horse too, and he was really astounded by the story of North Star. I think I topped all of his spinnin'of tales.

I traveled along with Davy for a little while in the hills of Tennessee, but Davy had his ways and we rubbed the wrong way. He went his way and I went mine.

Three months later, I saw that banker in St. Louie and got back my pack of gold and gems, and more importantly, I got my North Star back. It lay untouched in the very same vaulted lock box where I had left it, so I tipped that banker a nugget as I left his establishment, just for his honesty. He was shocked!

Shanghaied!
(Chapter 16)

I always liked the sea, so when the 'quack quack' started heading south and a chill filled the air; I knew the Dakotas would already be covered by three feet of fresh snow. I didn't think that I could withstand any more cold winters like in the Dakota Territory. Therefore, I headed south, until three months later; I again smelled the salty air in my nostrils. I rode into a shipping port that looked a lot like New Orleans. It was called Galveston. I got to walkin' down to the shipping docks daily, and I saw all those workers loading cotton bales onto big ships that were headed out to the Far East, and some to the western cultures. It was a glorious sight to witness prosperity here in the new world.

My pack and North Star needed a place to hide again, because I thought that I just might get drunk and do something stupid, so I hid them both inside the hollow fork of a big mesquite tree that stood alone, deep inside a scrubby-looking timber. Everywhere, there were plants that either had big sharp thorns, or tiny stickers; it also had rattlesnakes galore, which just jumped out and bit ya. I thought the place was a good choice. I went partying!

After two days, I sobered up enough to remember the Texas State Bank, and I recovered my poke and North Star from the woods and deposited them safely with the fine bank's president, who assured its security and wanted a cash payment. But I guess I was still too inebriated and told him to go jump in the sea, and stomped right back to that old mesquite tree and put everything back…I think…or did I…who knows?

About that time, not wanting to end my holiday spirits, I found a friendly tavern to quench my thirst. I had just eased back into a comfortable chair to finally rest my weary feet and down a brew or two, when some pirate-lookin' fellas strolled into the saloon and quickly started a ruckus.

They were dressed like La Fitte's men, and already loaded to the gills with hard liquor. They started pushin' and shovin' everyone and began throwing chairs. I held my peace, until this greasy fella takes a poke at me. I hit him back and we were tussling to and fro something fierce-like, when suddenly something hit me on top of my noggin. All the lights went out!

When I awoke, it was black as night and smelled horribly like dead fish. The smell was worse than any whorehouse I'd ever woke up in before. I felt poorly, and it was all wet and slippery where I laid, and I couldn't see to get up. When I did, I hit my head on something hard, and it hurt really badly, right down to my toes, it did. I must have gone out because when my eyes opened wide again, I was tied up and strapped to the mast of a whaling schooner. There was this old man standing before me, starin' death into my soul. He was the strangest, ugliest lookin' fella I'd ever run into in my whole livelihood, I reckon; even Mike Fink wasn't as ugly and scary as this man was.

He shouted out that he was the captain, and he was not only addressin' me, but some other beat-half-to-death fellas who were also tied up like goats to the main beam.

"So that you heathens understand me," he shouts, "this is what will happen to you if you fail to do your jobs, steal, or disobey my order."

Then this plank of wood fell across the starboard bow, and some of those men that I saw fightin' in the tavern were leading this poor blindfolded soul out to its end; the man on the board hung right over the deep sea waters, yes he did. If that wasn't bad enough, this captain stuck his sword tip into his leg, and it began to bleed like a spring.

"That will draw them hungry sharks right to ya, Henry Dargod, you disobeying radical! Don't worry none though…you be a dead goner before you drown, eaten alive…Ha, ha, ha," the captain yelled.

"Nobody wants to be a sailor and become drown!" tells another fella, "Cause ya spirit jess floats to the top and drifts forever and a day," he spoke.

"Who? Who did he say he was?" I pleaded. But none dare speak when the captain glanced his cocked, beady eye towards us. I thought he said Dargod. But my head was fuzzy and ached horribly.

Then the poor soul suddenly lost his balance, just as they removed his blindfold and he fell helplessly into the drink. The boson then cut us all loose, and forced us to the rail, so that we had to look upon the poor soul squirmin' to get himself free of the man-eatin' sharks that already were swirling and ripping at his body. But soon as not, he was devoured by this big white that took his whole soul with one gulp. He was gone, and I was sick to death and scared.

I puked up hard over the rail. A sharp pain across my backside shocked me back into reality, and I whirled to kill the man that dare strike me such. But he was the boson, and carried a pistol and his whip, not to mention a long sword that looked like a quarter-moon. Me, I had nothing.

This is the part of my life that I remember as holy hell, but I was certain it was payment for the previous sinful lifestyle that I had lived. Life was now at its lowest, especially when I realized that I had been shanghaied aboard a whaler. The food was cold and moldy tasting. The next few weeks aboard that ship was learning the rigors of a sailor's life. We learned the sails' names, learned to tie knots and scrub the deck, for the salty seawater that came aboard with each breaking wave left behind a slimy scum that would cause a body to slip-slide fore and aft. You had to get down upon your knees and really scrub hard. If you didn't, or if your work wasn't good enough for the boson, you got to meet the 'cat-o-nine tails' across your back and salt rubbed in your wounds to boot. It made many a sailor scream to his death in agony, and if you survived, you never wanted to feel that again, never. So you worked hard. There was no pay to be had; you were slave-like. And they kept an eye out for those who gathered together to whisper mutiny, or escape.

The only good was feeling the warm sun and the wind in your face, and the hollerin' of, "Thar she blows!" That meant that the lookout man in the crow's-nest above us had spotted a whale surfacing, and we'd all hustle to lower the rowboats and paddle after the quarry. If we could catch up alongside one of the beasts, the best man would hurl a long spear-like thing called a harpoon, deep into the flesh of the swimming mammal. He didn't like that none, and you'd be in for the ride of your life, if you still had one. For many a rowboat got quickly taken under into the deep by whales that be smarter than their hunters be, and came they back with a vengeance, and took a swipe at 'em with their tail fin; then it headed straight to the bottom…the tail of a whale is to be respected, sometimes twice the length of the rowboat. One swish, and into the drink you would fly. If the other rowboats near to you were late, you might be swallowed up by the very whale that you hunted, just like Jonah in the Good Book you'd be.

Thar'She Blows!

The wind blew cold and they said we were passin' the Horn. The sea was rough and the ship's timbers creaked, then moaned, and spit water through the cracks. We sat still mostly, waiting for the sound of a whale sounding, which was when the whale would blow water out of his body through a spout that was on the top of his big head to breathe. When the man in the crow's-nest spied a spout, he'd sing out "Thar she blows." Then we'd all scuttle.

I wasn't permitted to go out the first few times that they chased a whale. Only the seasoned sailors that were savvy to the sea left the ship at first. Instead, my job was to help haul aboard the carcasses; up onto the deck in pieces they came, and then we'd pack the parts in piles of salt below deck. Each sailor did his job. The quicker that you got done, and if it was a good sized whale, the captain might share his whiskey. That be our only prize.

As I learned the method, by and by, I slipped out into a boat to chase a whale; sometimes two or even three. For the price of a whale was worth more than a man's life. The fats and oils were like the price of gold, to be had for the taking. It would take about two months of good whaling to fill the hull with whale blubber. I figured thirty, or more whales, had to be caught. One really bad thing was; I began to speak just like the filth that surrounded me, as I usually took on my peers' lingo. I became leaner, stronger, and quicker.

One fine day, I decided to make my way to the topsail, and board the crow's-nest. I shimmied up ropes, and walked along the topsail railing like a squirrel. Oh, what a beautiful sight it was! I could see for many a mile, but the roll of a ship was severe up there, so I had to really hang on tight. I eased over to look inside the nest, expecting to catch ol' Will catnapping, but to my surprise, ol' Will Bennet had died inside the nest and was curled up like a baby. I hollered down to the boson, and he came up to see for himself. We tied some rope around his chest, and we slowly lowered ol' Will to the deck, for he received respect aboard ship. His eyes had been the best aboard, and he could spot a spout many miles away and lead you right to them. Will made whaling better and faster by his spotting.

The boson headed to the deck and told me to stay put. As I watched the mates gather around Will, I thought they looked like little ants crawling, for the mast of that whaler stood very tall, so that you could spot the spouting of a whale far away.

It was then and there, that I got my reputation as a true seaman, for low and behold, I spotted a spoutin' whale far off the starboard bow, and then yelled out, "Thar she blows!"

The seamen crews were so struck to hear me yell, that they yelled back and asked who was sighting a whale.

"Tis'I, Jamison Dargod!" I say. "It's off the starboard!" I yelled again.

Captain Abrams rushed to the starboard with his long brass scope and says, "Sure nuff, steer her starboard!" he yells towards the helmsman. Then the captain looks my way and says, "Keep sight of that whale, boy! Keep sight of that whale!"

"Aye, aye, sir!" I hollered back, as I peered deep out across the sea's white-capped fury. I then spotted three more separate spouts and hollered out, "Three more spouts, sir, three more!"

I suddenly thought about how I had taken on the seaman's call. Where had my frontiersman's "I reckon," gone to? Anyway, I felt useful for the very first time.

Each spout that was sighted meant two boats would be hauled down from their hangers, but four spouts emptied the deck. All the sailors jumped aboard their scow rowboats and took pursuit of the mightiest fish in the sea. I signaled with a flag for which way the men should row when the whales surfaced. It was hard to see, even a big eighty foot whale that was spoutin' in these rough waters, while searching for him from a rowboat that got tossed up and down, and up and down, with each pounding wave.

But the sailors finally closed in on all of the whales, as four harpoons were thrown, and four found their mark. Then the fight began, as the rope peeled off from the rowboat's barreled spool at high speed. Smoke would actually begin to appear when a big whale sounded and took himself deep, and only a fool would grab a hold of it.

"Stand clear!" was the pilot's order, as he drenched the hot running spool with seawater.

Sometimes a boat would run out of rope, and it skimmed across the water as fast as the big whale could swim, and that was pure torture while going against big breaking waves.

All this time, the captain stood looking up at me, then back out across the sea with his scope. I couldn't hear him, as he'd holler at the helmsman for which whale to pursue, as if he himself would fling a harpoon if one ventured too closely. Each time a whale sided-up, the captain would start singing an old sailor's song, and he would get a serious smile on his face, as though he was counting the money already from the whale's value.

During the chase, John Garwood, a seasoned sailor, lost his life to the sea when his legs got tangled in the harpoon's rope and was swept down quickly.

They said that when that monster whale finally succumbed and rolled upon its side, there was John, still wrapped up agin' him, dead, with a big smile upon his face.

As it turned out, the whale John had stuck was a really huge one, twice the size of the others, and deep in fat tallow. It was a prize any sailor could brag upon. We all figured John must have realized that he had caught the biggest whale ever, before he died. To a real sailor it was an honor to die fightin' a whale at sea. Each and every one of them knew that he might be so honored at his end, someday. I wasn't quite so sure about that feeling as yet.

The catch was being hauled aboard; so I climbed down to do my work. To my complete surprise, the captain says I'd done an excellent job and that job was now mine.

But I said, "I'll gladly do my share anyway."

He then reminded me about disobeying his orders.

I snapped to, "Aye, aye, sir!" and headed back up for the nest.

"You may only come down at night," he says. "Or if I tells you to."

"Aye, aye, sir," I was proud; I hoped to be respected and as worthy as Will.

All the hoopla, that usually accompanied a big catch afterwards, was aborted, out of the great respect of our lost seamen, as the captain began his sermon above the bodies of Will and John. They were wrapped in a sheet and slid out onto a plank above the water. After a moment's prayer, the boards were tilted high. They were then quickly committed to the deep. "Kerplunk, kerplunk", and they were gone. They each had shared twenty years sailing the seas. I never knew if they had been shanghaied like me.

It was a grand day for our ship's locker, but deeply saddened by the loss of our fellow sailors. We drank our rewards quietly, and slowly, and waited another day to celebrate. I crawled up and slept inside the nest. Will had always come down from his perch at night and only returned after his morning's nourishment. Therefore, the crew was still asleep at dawn when I spotted a tall spouting and hollered out, "Thar she blows, off the starboard!"

The huge whale was jumping high and looked peculiar, even at such a far distance. When we got up closer, I could see that it was a light skinned whale, very different from any others that I'd seen before, and at least twice as big as the one that got ol' John Garwood. It was a real huge monster.

The crew came out slowly and struggled to get their gear, and I noticed many scowls upon their faces as they all looked my way when the captain hollered, "Hop to!"

I told the captain of the size of this beast, and he saw a prize that he alone must have for himself through his scope. He hurried to the ship's helm and began steering our ship himself, straight towards the whale.

Now it's a real prize to talk in the taverns about that you caught the biggest whale in the world, and this one would top them all. He was too big for a scow to handle alone, so I knew the captain was going to try to poon' him beside the ship by himself.

The captain had a dickens of a time keeping up with that big whale, because the whale knew we were there. The captain would zigzag his course, look up at my flag directions, and curse loudly. Our captain couldn't get his ship around quite as well, like the helmsman could.

Well, soon he was spinning that big wheel so fast and hard, that his belt that was upon his brass scope got tangled among the spokes. It twirled him like a whirlwind, and spit him out onto the deck. It almost choked him to death, before the boson cut the leather strap. Thing was though, his leg caught the sharp edge of a pickle barrel's steel rung and cut him deep. The huge escaping whale then spouted high and disappeared into the deep. Captain Abrams was hurt pretty badly, so the ship's boson steered us to Ocracoke Island, which was just off the coast of South America where there was a real doctor to be had. There was scuttlebutt too, that Black Beard hid all his plunder there.

A week later, the doctor came aboard our ship. He broke out the whiskey and made the captain drunk, but we listened to the captain scream in bloody agony, while he took off the captain's gangrenous leg at the knee. If he lived, he was laid up for some time, pushing six months. The boson had to sell our catch to a passing whaler, before it rotted, for what he could. So, some of us were allowed to take off, and we boarded that inbound whaler headed back home to the mainland.

I never held any grievance against the ones who had kidnapped me. It was a good adventure, and that was my nature. I heard that the old captain eventually regained his health, walked about upon a wooden, pegged leg, and still pursued that big prized, light colored, monster whale most of the rest of his life, until one day that big whale caught him instead…imagine that! What was still more amusing to me personally was the fact that I considered myself, a genuine, seasoned sailor!

Shanghaied...Again?
(Chapter 17)

We dropped ship's anchor in a harbor off Costa Rica, and rowed toward shore. The bay was beautiful there; its sparkling, pale green water and the white sands were shrouded with tall coconut palms, which made a heavenly picture indeed. It reminded me of my duty to my wife, who lay lifeless and waiting for me on an isle just like this one.

Natives, who were sent to greet all sixteen of us weren't Christians, and their women all came to us topless. Having been at sea so long, the sight demented the minds of each of us sailors, and every lady that appeared such before us was a queen. But we dare not start trouble here, for we were advised that taking sexual pleasures with a native girl on this isle, even if she consented, would be a death sentence. They acted more like a Christian than Christians themselves did.

Free spirited, and loving to all they were, but those beautiful ladies walked around all day in the sun bare-breasted; their bosoms bounced freely to and fro with each step; it was maddening. It was just tormenting to sit around and watch all them lonesome women go to the market. A man could just get plum dizzy studying! I was ready to settle down there for a while and rest my soul.

It rained every day. A person learned to move about knowing when the rain would fall. One day a big ship sailed into the bay as I was strolling on the beach pickin' up fancy sea shells and such just to keep as souvenirs, in case I ever got back to the main land. It was so beautiful there; I didn't notice the skull and cross bones flag that the ship flew.

Suddenly, I heard the sound of sabers rattling and looked up just in time to see sixty or seventy pirates swarm onto shore. They soon swooped in on me and I found myself at the pointed end of a very bejeweled dagger. I was forced into a rowboat and held captive there about two hours, until the herd of tyrants returned with all my mates with whom I'd come ashore. Their hands were bound and they too were at the point of a razor sharp sticker. The pirates sang salty songs as they rowed us out to a waiting vessel.

Back to sea, and aboard the awaiting ship named the Adventurer, we immediately set sail. I came face to face with a nightmarish fella named Black Beard. The peculiar thing was that with his name Black Beard, he had a red beard full of tobacco spittin's. He strutted like a cock rooster in front of us with his big-feathered hat, back and forth, back and forth, lookin' us up and down. He waved flints in both hands. He knew we were sailors and told us we were now under his command.

"Or die!" he bellowed.

His captured Portuguese vessel was trim, but a big one, and the whole ship's crew was of riffraff killers and thieves. We had to obey, or die right then and there. We submitted.

I began to regret life in general, but that feeling was quickly reversed. We all were taken below and served one of the most bountiful meals that I had ever eaten. Beef, pork and mutton quarters stacked high to the hilt and served complete with vintage wines, all you could swallow too. We were served on Ming China plates, and we drank our drinks from bejeweled gold and silver goblets that were probably stolen from rich merchant ships, during an earlier plunder. I actually began to envy the scoundrels. Then we all settled back to enjoy a cigar from the Central Americas, places I once saw on a poster in St. Louie. It now seemed like an eternity ago. I thought of ol' Crow Foot just then.

I went to my station upon the floor of the hull and stretched out on the hard oak floor. A fancy, silk covered, horse-haired pillow was tossed to me; one wool blanket, and one silk sheet. The pillow's fragrance was that of a woman's, and I imagined a lovely princess had once placed her head there. Then I thought of Marietta, and how I wish it were hers. That became my reason for sleep that night, as the rolling of the ship rocked my soul into a deep sleep. Marietta became my focus; my dreams of her refreshed me.

The early morning's crispness bit the flesh, but already the captain had begun scoping the horizons for any available merchant's ship with his long telescope. He had an uncanny wit about him as to which ship held the greatest prizes. All ships, coming and going, had to round the Horn, and all were open prey to pirate ships like Black Beard's. The pirates would scuttle the quarry and then head to a port sympathetic to thieves and the like, who had lots of money to spend and gold to swap, pennies on the franc.

Some of the islands were actually owned by sovereign countries. Some would rather buy stolen goods from the pirates at a discounted rate, than sail all the way to the Far East only to have it stolen from them before they returned.

Who were the worst scroungers on the seas, the pirates or the wholesalers? One such country was France, whose simpleton armadas would rather spin a minuet, and curtsy while dancing, than go face to face with the pirates upon the seas. At sea, they always surrendered without a fight, and always the take was a good haul...all Frenchmen were cowards for certain, I was told. But I remembered ol' Jean La Fitte at New Orleans. Jean was no coward. He was a real hero.

Black Beard addressed us below deck and told us that the good life of a pirate was, "Share, share alike."

Any gotten plunder was shared equally among the crew, "Exceptin' I gets a bigger share being the captain and all," he continued.

A holdout meant certain torture and death. No one was permitted near his quarters, which I'm sure overflowed with a king's treasure. Each person had a portion of the floor of the hull as his own, where he slept and stored his share of the plunder. I couldn't believe all the jewels and gold each and every man had at his station. It was just like a vault, except there was nothing at my place of rest but rough oak flooring planks.

If someone ever got caught stealing from another, he'd be strung out on a yardarm to be dragged through the sea, until he'd drown; it was the most embarrassing way to die as a true sailor. Then you'd be cut loose to the big whites for their jaws to clamp down on them. But that didn't happen very often, because there was honor among thieves here. And a strange brotherhood existed like a family, as everyone helped out the other. It turned out that this crew spoke highly of their captain and would die for him...as they very often did! That's when they'd have to raid an island and shanghai replacements. So here I was!

Now I never had any cannon training before, so I had the job of bringing up the cannon balls and powder from below the deck as fast as I could muster. We'd have practice drills that prepared us for combat. At the sound of the captain's whistle there would be a scurry on deck like I never saw before, except for seeing squirrels that scurried when your ball chucked bark beside 'em, instead of their hide. We did this until the captain felt we were ready, boy was I shot…pardon the pun!

Early at the next sunrise, we all sprang up and went right to work scrubbing the deck. But within the hour we sailed upon a rich Dutch schooner that we hoped would be loaded down with silver, gold, pearls, emeralds, and fine silks. They all were being brought back to their king from the Far East. Her bow pitched deep and you could tell that she was laden very heavy.

The captain yelled out, "Cut the mainsail loose, stretch the gibs, raise the flag!" as he fine-tuned the vessel's keel. We were gaining on the slow Dutch ship when a huge plume of smoke belched from its side, and a cannon ball exploded across our bow. They were warning us that they weren't about to allow us to enter their close waters. The helmsman held his course steady and another big smoke plume erupted from the Dutch ship. This time it creased a sail and put a hole the size of a pickle barrel as it tore through.

The captain yelled, "Steady as she goes!"

And we proceeded to close the distance. The captain then drew his big sword, pointed it into the air above him, and hollered, "Make ready on the port side!"

All the side doors opened in unison and the men pushed their cannons forward. We were getting close, too close, as cannon volley from the Dutch ship caught the side of our ship and crashed through our ship's railing. There were screams of pain, but no one moved to help the fallen men who were standing near the blast…it was war! Instead, the captain yelled to the helmsman, "Hard right, full rudder," and our big ship swung violently and presented our broadside view to the Dutch vessel.

"Fire!" yelled the captain.

All sixteen twenty-pounder cannons erupted in a timed succession, which actually made the whole ship spin around in the sea. It was quite a nautical maneuver, for after we had fired off, it only left our stern facing our prey; a small target's view to shoot back, very unlike a terrible volley all at once.

The ship lurched starboard and settled back up right.

"Reload, and prepares to fire on my command!" bellowed Black Beard.

The boson echoed the captain's orders. He then put his hands together as a horn and hollered towards the helmsman.

"And swing'er back around quickly!" added the boson.

Then the first mate grabbed my arm and told me to hurry with the balls and powder. We couldn't keep very much powder on top deck, just in case the ship got hit and the powder that you were holding exploded on deck, killing everyone including yourself. I stacked the balls like a pyramid, and rolled the powder by the keg to each cannon's side. It was a flurry then, and our cannons spit fire as again and again our ship lurched over violently and then up righted itself with each volley. The timing had to be exact if we were going to align the cannons to their targets on the rise and fall of the ship.

Black Beard had lots of experience. It was important not to sink the opposing ship, I learned, because we wanted its cargo. And if you skipped a big ball across the water like a big flat rock into its side, it would sink, or hit the powder hold and explode, losing the whole ship. Either way you lost. Black Beard's theory was to volley so hard and fast, as to completely intimidate the intercepted ship, knocking down its sails, so that its captain couldn't maneuver. He'd have to die, or he would have to give up the ship's treasures for him and his crew's lives. When that occurred they'd usually jump ship.

Black Beard ordered a hard starboard turn, as again the side doors flung open. "Fire!" he hollered, and the cannons belched hot lead balls.

"But don't ya dare sink'er!" he screamed.

This time our volley struck her topside hard, and the Dutch ship just wilted in the water. Black Beard rushed to the side rail with his scope to view the damage that we had just handed out. A big devilish grin he had, as the Dutch ship's men were all jumping overboard into the sea. For it was better to swim for it and fight the big whites, than to stay aboard and die at the hands of the pirates. And that would certainly happen.

"Good job, men!" Black Beard congratulated us all. "She be ours today! Twas easy pickin's. That ol' captain must have Frenchie's blood in his veins…ha, ha, ha!" he bellowed.

"Draw a bead on her helm, and prepares to come alongside 'er," he commanded. "Men, stand ready, be prepared for a fight, if they be trickin' us," he warned.

We then boarded that Dutch ship and surveyed the prize. Everyone had abandoned ship. Then our captain ordered us to quickly cut the Dutchmen's rowboats loose for the struggling, floating Dutchmen in the water, and we did.

"Throw 'em a cask of water and a mutton leg into each boat, so that they can live to come backs to us another day, so we cans rob 'em again ha, ha, ha!" he roared out laughing.

Smart thinking; showing a little mercy to them meant that the next time they'd give up their ship much quicker, knowing that if they did, they could live.

Their bounty was very high. The hull was laden with all the riches of a king. But first, the six men killed by the first Dutch ship's blast had to receive their due rights. And just as our captain of the whaler had done, Black Beard proceeded to read from a book over the sheet-shrouded dead, and the bodies were committed to the salty brine. Except one man we never completely found, we just said "so long" to his right hand. His boots, his pants, and his sword, were the only other things that we found of him; the rest must have been blown overboard. But by the ring on his bloodied finger, they all knew him to be a man called Nate. No sorrow was spent. Men here deserved death many times over for their deeds, and the shares just got bigger without them.

It was just like a marriage here; "Till death do us part!"

All in all, they told me that this was an easy plunder. I was awed. My take in the assault on the Dutch schooner was a bounty that would make any man a rich person on the mainland back home. Home…home…I yearned to return. But I had a long voyage to travel before going back there. And if I survived, I'd be a better man for it, I guessed…a bloody pirate, but at least rich.

My station on the floor got crowded quickly, and I found myself sharing my space with a real treasure. A body couldn't handle much more, I suspected. There was no room. When all the swag was accounted for, we drank and sang songs together in merriment, well into the next dawning, as the captain steered our path into a port to sell our take. I had become a real pirate…imagine that?

It was several weeks into port, while pulling the Dutch schooner in tow behind. In the morning it was back to cleaning the decks. That chore never ceased, even if you were hung over and sick. On the third day, we passed a French vessel headed on its way to the Far East. Everyone laughed as the French ship kept their distance, and said lightheartedly that we'd all be here when they sailed back loaded. But with luck, I wouldn't; I was Christian-like, I presumed, and I never liked stealing, much less killing a body. I had to make a break, before a sinful thing like killing someone in committing murder, for sure.

We dropped anchor in the harbor of Marquese. It was a busy port and I was required to stay aboard to watch the ship, while the others went ashore to sell their plunder to the French merchants.

"In fairness," Black Beard said to me, "for a job well done, mate."

Then Black Beard himself handed me a rather nice sack of gold Dutch coins, in exchange for my take. I was very satisfied.

God Save the Queen and King, but Please, Give Us Something to Eat! (Chapter 18)

With nothing to do but sit, a couple of us stayed behind to guard the ship. Black Beard was going in to sell the Dutch schooner to a French businessman. I watched other ships ease by very closely, as they entered and exited from the port. It was certainly crowded. But when a vessel bearing the name of Resolution, a British ship, eased past so closely, I jumped ship before I could think. I quickly jumped onto the outriggers and hung on for dear life to that outgoing ship. I made it, thank Dargod!

Unfortunately for me, the skipper, Captain James Cook, wasn't too happy when I was found as a stowaway. He was amused at my large coin bag though, and eventually relieved me of some of my take. I was then a high-paying passenger. He and his crew needed the money badly for food. It was hard to carry all those coins anyway, as they were very heavy. The captain was a principled man, who allowed me to continue to ride upon his ship, asking nothing more of me.

The English sailors weren't as I imagined at all. They too had been shanghaied; not by pirates, but by their own navy. Most of the crew was made up of family men who dearly missed their wives and children. I wondered how many of the men were just the same at New Orleans. I remembered them lying dead; killed upon the fields of battle.

Two weeks out from the isle of Marquese, the British ship halted to pick up some weary castaway drifters in rowboats. They were as desperate as anyone could get for food and drink. They were part of the crew of the Dutch vessel that I, as a pirate, had just helped plunder. Of course, they couldn't have recognized me, since they all jumped ship at first volley, long before we closed in. I listened attentively to their brave stories how they had sunk a pirate ship in a fierce battle, only to withdraw in rowboats, when their own ship capsized…imagine that!

Captain Cook was looking for a 'Northwest Passage' trade route. Now didn't I hear that someplace before? His large crew was mostly British, regular sailors. They told me of their hardships that they endured, simply because the good King George III was very frugal with the Crown's money…so sometimes they starved and got scurvy. I couldn't dare tell them of my recent pirate's tour with Black Beard, and how we ate like kings. Never a more dedicated bunch of sailors had I met who served their country.

Strong winds blew and the weather turned warmer, as we entered near the San Francisco Bay in the early spring, and dropped anchor. I was going back onto the mainland and I sure was happy. I was nearly broke, but I was free and walking down the street that was filled with happy Spanish speaking people. I felt like screaming out loud with joy, as I began regaining my landlubber's step back.

Way Up North!
(Chapter 19)

I no sooner had righted my keel and put my feet on terra firma, when a tremendous shaking knocked me smack flat upon my keester. Suddenly, a big building began to crumble all around me, almost. I was pinned by a timber. There were lots of screams to coincide with mine and fires broke out everywhere. I could hear everyone saying their prayers out loud, but I was just hoping for someone to help me from under all this rubble. Some young gents helped to pull me out from under that timber an hour later.

It didn't take me too long to quickstep out of that inner-city for other scenery. Another shaking occurred, which I learned was called an after-shock; it knocked me down again. I got up, dusted myself off and started walking faster straight north.

I decided to find out what territory lay north of this province. I had seen the southern most tips of this new world, why not the northern tip? I met a man named Bruno Heceta. He turned out to be just like me; he was a man who had my same own foolish, always-wondering ways, and we immediately hit it off just fine. Bruno was going my way, so we walked together along a seldom used northern path.

Bruno was Spanish and wanted to go to sea to find simply "what was there", he told me, but had no money. Those too were my feelings many times; just go someplace to discover anything for excitement. He told me of others who he had spoken with and who had gone north. They all had found much beauty in the enormous trees of two hundred meters tall, tall rocky cliffs with high water falls and streams filled with salmon. He said herds of animals called caribou traveled by the millions across age-old paths; slick-backed fury water angels called seals, penguins, and walruses abounded everywhere. The

Indians were friendly and some that were living way up north had you sleep with their wives for your pleasure and friendship.

"However," he told me," I heard they are all homely, smell like fish and sleep on the ice."

I guess in certain lonely times "something" was better than nothing at all, but that didn't sound very inviting to me. It was all the other wonderful things he mentioned, which I knew I wanted to witness on my own.

On the third day, at a small merchant's outpost along the path, which was standing alone in a lovely wooded clearing, I bought our stake. I purchased heavy clothing made of animal skins, a miner's pack, which consisted of a pick, shovel and pots and pans that were neatly packed together for saving space. I purchased a used British-made long gun two possibles bags with two horns full of gun powder for Bruno and me.

I also bought grub to last us for three days. I figured I could hunt along the way, but having a little salt, sugar and flour really helped make the wild meats taste much better. We were set and I now was completely broke. But, it was going to be an adventure worth remembering, I hoped.

The going got tough quickly as we traveled several hundred miles together, just taking our time and enjoying the beautiful scenery. We were constantly going up one hill and down the other. Each exhausting day ended with us camping on a hilltop. That gave us a quick start going down in the morning.

Bruno kept jotting down landmarks for a return map and other information in a ledger. At each eve, he would read to me out loud in his best broken English what he had written, and which we both had seen. He was very alert to his surroundings, much more than I.

At the end of the first month, I had seen so much beauty abounding around us, unspoiled by humans; I wanted to stay for awhile. But when we walked into that big forest, I knew I wasn't the first Martian to tread there.

"Sequoias," Bruno spoke," as we both fell to our butts trying to look to the tops of those gigantic pillars of wood.

But I knew what they were already, for on Mars they stood this tall once before the great explosion. I knew this place must be a reverent place for me, as I knew for certain; these were planted by Martian hands eons ago. The giant trees were as he said and pillared too high for us to see their hilt. I decided that I must climb one, because it might be the adventure of a lifetime looking out among the big birds that nested at some of their tops. But, there were no young trees; all of them were thousands of years old and the smallest one was eighteen paces around. Then I saw it. A lone tree stood in an opening that rose much higher than the rest. Peculiarly, there was a huge hole that I could see ran completely through to the other side. I knew what it was in a moment.

The beautiful gargantuan grew near a lovely babbling brook and its roots received their drink there. But as Bruno scribbled out drawings of the trees and noted points, I ventured there and walked inside. I had learned of a Martian scientist name Garcon who had written about the affects of laser weapons. On Mars, their radiant powers accelerated plant growth and caused mutations in some trees. I immediately suspected that some Martian had been buried there along with his laser. What else could accomplish this huge cavity in the magnificent tree without killing it? I was certain.

I peered inside the opening and it was as if I were the first. There, etched upon a stone, were the words, "Dr.Garcon". That's all it read. I went to the floor and without much effort; I found the handle of a sister to North Star. When I eased it from the dirt, it was as new. I had found a relic, thousands of years old, yet it was like my North Star in every way. How could this be?

I looked around more and jumped across a brook into an open meadow. I found a large flat boulder, sufficient, I imagined, permitting the decent of a rocketed ship. There were gouges in its surface at equally spaced intervals and I knew this was a place Martians landed. But since there was no craft, the Martian ship had flown away. Then Bruno summoned me. I placed the laser in my coat, but let the handle absorb the sun's rays.

Bruno wanted us to measure a tree accurately, so we took a rope and barely got it about its circumference. It was almost twenty meters. Bruno wrote that down and suggested we could find other interesting things ahead, so we left this sacred place.

But as I left, I could always look back and see that tree for many days.

We came upon a waterway and it was a bay of the ocean. There were the seals that others spoke of, which were frolicking on the outlying rocks, and the creek that flowed from it had millions of splashing fish, too many to jump over the water fall. Of course, I had seen this all before, but Bruno hadn't, so I pretended to be excited. However, I always loved the outdoors and each and every animal was my friend, except big bears of course.

On an occasion of searching, we came upon a vicious Indian tribe with their spears and arrows pointed at us who spoke their orders out in a French dialect. They were as fierce as any Indian I had seen, but much taller than most. Their hair was shaved skin bare, except for a bushy outcropping in the center which stood up making them look even taller. They certainly hated us and detested our trespassing. Bruno and I quickly found ourselves trapped, stripped of our packs and clothing and herded down a path to their big camp of wooden wigwams. They bound us tightly, hand and foot.

We were both shoved into a dark hut and tied to poles. They never even questioned us about anything; they were solely bent on killing us by roasting us in a bonfire. Several men in loin clothes poked at us with sharp spears and made us bleed. I guess it felt just a little like my nephew must have felt in his last moments of crucifixion.

I looked at Bruno and he was bleeding more than I was, and then he told me in his weakening voice, "Adios, amigo." He then slumped down unconscious.

But that didn't stop the men from screaming at him and sticking him with their spears. I could see through the large doorway that two large bonfires were being prepared around poles and we were going to be sacrificed at the stake by fire.

That was the most horrible way to expire, I believed, so I pleaded out loud for Dargod's help. Those Indians just sneered at me and poked more holes in me, until I too felt faint from lost of my blood. But just as I was about to give it up for good, I glanced at Bruno who awoke for a moment and tried to say a prayer. I told him to keep the faith and pray for a miracle, and then it came.

A screaming Indian chief walked through the big doorway and came to me with my necklace that had been torn from around my neck in his hand. He dangled it before me and I just smiled at him. With few words he told the others to free me, but not Bruno. He apparently recognized what it was and grabbed up my hands to look at them. The X where Crazy Horse had joined Red Cloud and I as blood brothers was still there and he looked me straight in the eye holding up the necklace and spoke, "Crazy Horse?"

I spoke, "Crazy Horse and Red Cloud."

He wilted away and turned his back on me, for he was dead set on roasting my hide, yet there was honor among Indians and this sign was held with great honor. He quickly came back and took Bruno's lifeless hand and spoke again, "Crazy Horse?"

I said, "Red Cloud."

Again he wilted away, then stomped his moccasins down several hard times as a spoiled child might, before he told the men to cut us loose. They did, and we fell unconscious to the ground.

When I awoke, I had been dragged outside and put inside a cage-like pen with Bruno beside me still unconscious. I wasn't sure how long I'd been out, but Bruno looked dead. When I shook him he aroused some but didn't open his eyes. Apparently, their medicine man had convinced the chief that if they just let us bleed to death, it would not insult the memory of the great chiefs.

I watched Bruno come and go out of unconsciousness and he seemed to be getting more color to his already dark skin, as though his blood was circulating well. We both had stopped bleeding and I was feeling stronger by the minute, but very famished.

At about midnight, I heard a rustle of leaves and saw an Indian girl place a knife between the slats of our prison. Then she scurried back away. I didn't see her face.

I shook Bruno and he finally aroused but wanted to fight me; still thinking he was tied up. But I quelled him and put my hand over his mouth to whisper.

"I have a knife. Can you walk?"

Bruno nodded yes.

"Let's try to get to our packs while they sleep. I saw our packs in a pile by that hut over there. Everyone is sleeping."

"What for? Let's just go now," he whispered.

"I have something precious to me in mine and yours has your map, that's enough reason. Just trust me," I told him.

Again he nodded and showed me he could get up, but he was weak. I told him I would try to get our packs by myself. He waited as I cut the rope and then squeezed through the back side poles. Then, I made a mad dash from hut to hut until a cur dog growled at me. I ignored him and hoped he had smelled my scent before in camp and would not attack. Luck was with me as he just groaned a dog's groan and lay back down.

The packs were still there so I grabbed mine first and found North Star's sister. It was still in my coat jacket and apparently overlooked, because our weapons and powder were gone. I was relieved.

Suddenly I froze in fear as a cold hand touched my back and I whirled in anticipation of a scary face about to stab me. But lo and behold, a beautiful squaw was offering me our weapons and clothing held out to me in her tiny arms. She just stood there. For a moment, I thought she was the ghost of Marietta, but in fact, she was a white English girl who had been kidnapped by pirates and sold to these heathens. She grabbed my arm and led me back to Bruno.

"Go with me, now," she whispered frantically in a trembling voice.

Then she just about pulled my arm off as I helped Bruno walk. We all moved through some bushes away from camp. We stumbled in the dark on an unknown path I'm sure this little girl didn't know, but at least it wasn't going to be easy to follow us, I thought. Wrong!

At daylight, we found ourselves listening to the howls and screams of some belligerent beings that were chasing us in a heated, vicious anger for our escape. However, somehow we had all walked in a big circle and we were squatting in bushes directly on the opposite side of their camp. Soon the warriors left camp pursuing us by the tracks we left through the bushes; their horrible screams made my blood chill.

But then I felt North Star's little sister. I was at ease. If she could be activated like North Star, we had no fears. My trembling partners didn't expect to live. I stood up to let the strongest sunlight cast its rays upon her mechanisms, which I really didn't understand. It received the sun's rays for twenty minutes until we heard the band screaming out and headed our way.

It was now or never, so with a two-handed grip, I released the power of the laser. Nothing happened. Then I gave the relic a firm knock against my thigh and witnessed a great display of limbs being chopped off by countless numbers above me. They fell off upon us. I was darn lucky I hadn't sliced my head off. The weapon was stuck open and when I finally got her under control, I had leveled thirty squares of hardwoods and the huts were flat and burning. All the horrible screaming Indians lay as crispy critters, a scene I had witnessed before. The girl fainted in my arms. It was all over. Whew!

The hours passed and we eventually found out there were also other hostages being held there, but my ray had killed them all with the Indians. I couldn't stand that feeling and only felt better when I realized I had done them a favor from being tortured continuously, as the girl told me so. She didn't know any of them and wasn't allowed to talk to them.

"What is your name?" the young girl asked.

"I am Jamison Dargod. This is Bruno Heceta. Who are you?" I asked.

"I am Victoria Vancouver," she told us, and began to tell us immediately about her plight of horror.

We learned that this little girl was a daughter of George Vancouver, an English explorer who had sailed under my friend Capt. James Cook. Victoria was his kidnapped daughter, taken by pirates who boarded his anchored, but lightly protected ship, just off the western coastline. Her abduction, we learned, had only occurred one month prior.

After Victoria's abduction, she was sold to these Indians. They had tried their way with her, but because she was so frail, but also beautiful, the Indian chief had taken her for his own. She remained untouched under his protection, but feared for her life daily.

We decided to flee west to the sea, just in case I'd missed some hornets in this nest. Our decision was to remain along the shoreline to look for any passing ships.

Three days later, Victoria screamed out that her father's ship was again anchored, but this time he was aboard with his long telescope looking right at us. A cannon's volley sounded, and we saw two long boats drop along the ship and then fill with armed sailors.

George Vancouver hadn't given up hope for finding his daughter and fell ill after he saw his only child safe. The lieutenants took us aboard until Vancouver could address us. But Victoria told him of our heroism and he desperately wanted to reward us. So, I asked him if Bruno could explore with him while I got up in the crow's nest to watch for islands. He laughed and thought it queer, but granted both our wishes.

We sailed with Vancouver as we explored up and down the Pacific west coastal regions for several years, until he died suddenly. I had become a permanent member of his explorations, and Bruno and I both saw the wonderful western coastal ports like no other sailor. After Vancouver's death, Bruno himself discovered the Columbia River and continued on further. I was getting too tired then and had to leave him. I wanted to return to the tall sequoias. We said farewell along the shore of California.

In a reverential moment, I placed the malfunctioning laser back into the ground where I had discovered it under the giant tree with the hole through it, and wondered why I had not thought of my new idea before.

I decided that I should continue to explore; explore though, the science of the capsules that I had carried with me for so long. I felt it was the time, and the hidden shelters of the sequoias were a perfect place to rest for awhile. I had found a loft, high inside among the strong roots.

But I didn't want to remain for five or six centuries, locked in the death-like sleep. So I attempted to partake of just part of a capsule; about one sixth. The affects on me were slower and only occurred two days later, after I had already covered the hole as best I could at both ends with rocks that I placed in stacked walls. I slid up into a root's opening and fell into a deep sleep, and knowing another Martian had been placed below me, I felt at ease. I dreamed again of my Marietta.

The next thing I felt and heard, was the rumbling of an enormous earth moving machine's hot steam exhausts blowing upon my body which cleansed me like a hot spring might as it passed beneath my place of hiding. It was manned by a single human and he was pushing and pulling levers, scraping away my rock walls. Though he looked right at me as he passed, he did not see me. His machine had scarred the sacred ground below me and had then passed completely through. He had made a path for others to follow under the tree.

I felt sluggish, unlike before when arousing. I continued to doze off without the need to get up for some time. Within a month, I figure, men with other machines came through the hollow tree. They did not stop, but passed quickly upon fast horse drawn vehicles.

Eventually, I hopped down from my perch one day and to my surprise a road existed where Bruno and I had tramped upon a path to get here. It was well manicured and I became hungry and searched for food. I found blackberry bushes off the roadway and nourished for quite some time, until unfortunately I developed the "green apple quick step" and sought relief in using only big green leaves to clean myself. That lasted only for awhile, but I never ate blackberries ever again.

There I was, just walking down this wonderful man made road as it skirted through the tall forest. I then walked up upon a little house and a man sitting inside the construction reading a newspaper. There was a chain blocking my leave so I asked him why. I startled him greatly by my appearance and he questioned my being there. I just told him I had been walking from the north and found this place.

"Where did you come from, a stage play?" he laughed, and then straightened up when I frowned.

I then realized my ship's clothes looked out of place. He said no more about it though. Things had really changed.

I bid the gent good-bye and walked for days until I came upon a little opening with a small log cabin that appeared to be the outpost where I had once purchased our grub stake. It was vacant and the sign tacked upon its front entrance read: U S Forestry Service. It also read that the area was a park. That was good, I thought.

Along my way, a man hauling a great load of otter pelts from near the northern areas that I had previously explored, stopped and offered me a ride. He immediately started discussing the fur trade and how his company's new business was dressing the uppity of the world, in tall black hats. He was headed to the San Francisco hatters. I knew if his company was too successful, the poor little sea otters would soon become extinct. I questioned what the restraints were? But he said there was no quota on the numbers of otter's pelts, until the U.S. Forestry Service curtailed them; he cursed.

Since the numbered quota imposed upon his company was lowered, he now entered past the boundary of the U.S. and into the upper coastlines and rivers to catch their otters. I rode all the way to San Francisco listening to him jabber about otters, tall top hats and his tired, poor aching back he developed from the bouncing wagon seat. I felt his pains for I too was seat-sore, but thanked him for the ride. I stood and stretch for awhile.

I found a livery stable on the outskirts of town. Since I had no money, I asked for work with the blacksmith. He hired me to trim horse hooves and maintain his stable, while he forged metal shoes and repaired broken buggy parts. I also kept his ledger up to date.

I endured the winter there, just until I was able to purchase my necessities and a nice little filly horse. She was young and green broke, brought up from the Texas territorial range, but had to be convinced that she was leaving her momma, and her nice stall and oats. She was much too old for the tit, and should have been weaned a long time before now, according to the black-smith.

But I coaxed her along, right out of town, and we shared the trail to the Rocky Mountains. Little Texas was a smart animal and learned my ways, before I learned hers. She grazed upon good grasses all day, as I let her browse at will. Very soon she started to show her good conformation, which I knew she had. She developed very quickly.

I ended up having to head back north just a little, before I could head out to the Colorado Territory, and then east across the Oregon Trail. I passed some people in their wagons coming towards me, but the only thing that they wanted to know from me was, "How far?" The only thing they told me was, "Indians!" I imagined by the tired look upon their sun-scorched faces, that I had a long ride ahead. But the filly and I just kept moving along fine. After several months of meandering here and there, Little Texas became my real friend.

I Had To Grin and "BEAR" It!
(Chapter 20)

The Rocky Mountains were beautiful, simply gorgeous, and also full of big game. There were big elk below the shelf around every turn. It was fall, and the bugling bulls fought over the cows for their share of those that were available to breed. The bulls were huge, a half ton or more, and sported great racks of antlers of twelve to fourteen points. Some points were broken from the battles, others were white tipped crowns, but to win the battle here was everything to them, as the harem of female cows would be theirs. They acted just like some human beings that I knew, who acted really stupid when they "fought for love!"

Often as not, I would discover a freshly killed elk, either by being wounded in a fight, or by being caught off guard by a grizzly or pack of wolves. These carcasses made good roasts upon a spit, and I never hungered much in those mountains. Besides, swimming in those clear running streams were many trout, and sometimes there were big salmon, which I could just scoop right out of the air, as they jumped below a rapid. I had to watch for others doing the same, though…big grizzlies. Little Texas had a nose for any trouble approaching and she'd always whiny to alert me.

I followed the Snake River most of the time, until I did have an encounter with a grizzly bear. Instead of me being the hunter, I was the hunted. The big ol' hungry boar bear followed us, and I bet his hunting range was more than three territories wide, because he had been following us for over a week.

When my filly picked up a stone that split her hoof, I wished I had shod her before we had left California, but I was in too much of a hurry to get away from the madness. I then got off of her and walked, but I still had to stop to rest her, so I picked a high ridge above the river's bed. That night, I slept, but only after I had tied myself high onto a tree's fork; because bears could eat ya while you were sleepin' best; I kept one eye open and let Little Texas graze.

Deep into my sleep, near dawn, the roar of the beast awakened me. I had let my filly graze untied, just fearing this might happen, because bears like horsemeat too. The filly was no fool, and ran away quickly. I watched her as she kept going east at the last that I saw of her.

There I was, though, stuck up in a tree, with only my flintlock, which I'm certain that if I used it on him, wouldn't have hurt him much, and he would only get angry enough to climb up the tree and devour me. I kept it as a last resort if he chose to climb my tree. And, I wasn't about to 'grin him down' like ol' Davy Crockett. Luckily, that bear wasn't smarter than me, because I was high in a fork and that bear was too big and fat to get up here…I hoped!

The grizzly kept sniffing the air and finding my scent…soon he was looking straight up at me. I froze stiff, because a griz sees only movement, or smells its prey. But the smell of my horse's saddle was something he just couldn't ignore, so he tore into that leather like a tender beef steak. I was trapped in that tree for many hours, while that old bear just lay there gnawing all day on that saddle, waiting for me to make a dumb move. I didn't, so he didn't. He had me, and we both knew it; it was just a matter of time. The bear frolicked in the sun as he tore apart my saddle. He grabbed it up and threw it against the tree I was standing in, I guess he thought he could shake me lose. I clung on tighter.

THE
Grizzl

The long day's sun went down on two hungry souls. But worse, into the next night, it began to rain hard. Now I cursed that rain out loud, but it continued. As Dargod would have planned it the river waters rose quickly and that grizzly had to move out. At daylight, I was free to move about.

"Thank you, Dargod," I whispered.

Everything was washed away, except my skillet. I had nothing to cook in it, so I just left it. I walked on down the riverbank and when I could not go any further, I grabbed onto a log that was floating down the river, and hung on the best I could. Now I was getting desperately cold, when I came upon this big Ute Indian encampment. When I suddenly rose up out of the water, those Noochew Utes thought I was a real power. And when they noticed the blue necklace, with many claws from bears attached to it hanging around my neck, they treated me very extra special.

My stomach quickly got replenished with gifts of roasted rabbit meat and fish. They gave me a freshly skinned-out elk hide jacket and pants that I'm sure was meant for the Ute Chief Ouray, made by his main wife Chipeta for some special occasion. They were sort of stiff, but wearing them around would soften them up some he told me. Ouray spoke very good English and I also heard him speak Spanish.

I moved around with the grace of a person with lumbago. These Noochew Ute Indians lived inside huts called wickiups with several wives; they were polygamists. They made their homes from the bark of the trees.

But right then, everyone was dancing around a large bonfire to their ceremonial dance that they called Momaqui Mowat, which meant bear dance, of course. My stay was welcomed here, and that was good. The other Ute people that greeted me spoke mostly Shoshone, so I made out there all right.

Surprisingly, after two weeks of eatin' their grub, they also gave me back Little Texas, who had run into their camp. I was really glad to see the little filly, which they called a magic dog. It was their way of saying, "Here's your hat." I soon learned my directions and said goodbye to the chief, and thanked him.

While I was searching inside my old pants pockets to give the chief something back, I pulled out a huge big bear's jaw tooth that I'd found embedded in my saddle that the ol' grizzly had torn up. He already had plenty, for bears were like gods to them, but he knew what I meant, and he would be soon relieved of me.

As I waved goodbye, I noticed the ladies were whispering among the people, and I suspected that they were just laughing at me because I was a handsome lad. No, not really, it was because the elk pants had come apart at the seams and my derrière was hanging out. Imagine that?

Keep Those Doggies Movin'
(Chapter 21)

We moved along as fast as the wind blew, for the Utes had doctored Little Texas back to complete health by tethering her to an overhanging limb while she stood in the rapids of the river. The water's rush soothed the swelling and they had filed off her split hoof. It was just in time, as winter had started to blow in real cold.

I headed southeast, by my reasoning, towards warmer weather. Soon I was in the prairie flats and knew exactly where I was…the Dakotas. I rode my pony in the direction of that butte's pile of gold that ol' Crow Foot and I once discovered, but it started snowing hard and didn't stop. Before it was over, I was riding in drifts of six feet of snow. I just peeked up every once in a while above the drifts as Little Texas and I veered right, and headed due south for Texas. The gold would have to wait, although I started to realize then I'd have to find income someplace, and that meant work. I was afraid I had gotten Little Texas and myself into a terrible situation, with no escape.

The severe cold will dull the mind and it engulfed me. If Little Texas hadn't continued traveling south on her own, I'd have frozen right there, dead in the saddle, when I fell into an uncontrollable deep sleep. I dreamed of Marietta and her warm body next to mine. Little Texas had stopped behind a large drift. When the pale sun first peeked out behind the gray clouds, it apparently had enough warmth to cause me to regain consciousness. When the big sky had cleared the sun brought the temperature up higher above freezing.

The first thing I must do, I convinced myself, was to head directly south, down to Galveston, Texas to retrieve my North Star and pack. I was apprehensive now as to where exactly I had stored it, but I thought it might have been a bank, I wasn't certain anymore.

The fastest way south was by paddle wheel, if they'd forgotten about me. I sure hoped so! You could take your mount along for six dollars and change. When I boarded the big boat at St. Louie, it was cold and snowy and nobody noticed me at all. I left the boat just north of New Orleans, after paying the captain extra to stop upon the west side of the river. Little Texas and I leaped off together and found a place to climb out onto shore.

I immediately recognized my path. I shed some of my wet, muddy, heavier clothes and pointed my horse in a westerly direction along the route to Galveston. It took twelve days, but I arrived at that Texas State Bank, in Galveston, just at closing time. At first, they thought I might be one of the James gang, but that ol' banker spoke out immediately when he recognized me, and then told me I owed him thirty dollars. His hand was out.

I reluctantly paid him, but he told me it was for slamming the bank's front door so hard when I had left, that I had shattered its glass and sprung the hinges. He should have had me taken to the calaboose, he told me, but no one could find me. And when I headed towards the vault, he quickly reminded me that I refused to leave anything with him. I walked out of that bank very confused. But when I raised my head and saw that familiar saloon, I knew I had stuck my poke inside that mesquite tree.

There it was. My pack was full and North Star was untouched and shiny. Trouble was, there was no sunlight inside that hollow tree and North Star didn't work. But it was working after I left it hang around the horn of my saddle in the hot Texas sun for a week. And just as I tried to cross a little bayou, a big gator leaped up out of the water and tried to grab my horse from under me. When I hit him with the laser, there were little alligator bags all over the place.

Three months later, I found myself in a real cattle town called Houston, Texas. The town was named after Sam Houston, a past president of the republic, and a great patriot, I learned, who had defeated Santa Anna from down in ol' Mexico. I heard about ol' Davy Crockett too and his whole bunch of Tennesseans. They had all got themselves massacred at a place called the Alamo together with a whole bunch of other fine fellas, the local cowpunchers said…darn…imagine that will ya?

Now I decided I'd just have to ride on down there to see what was so special about San Antonio. And dog gone it, when I got down there three weeks later and saw the city, I learned why. It was a real fine place. But I had my druthers if it was worth dying for, being all the way from Tennessee. I learned Sam Houston desperately needed soldiers when he called out for some good men to help him, and Davy and his Tennessee "Volunteers" had come to help him!

Little Texas, a three-year-old now, was in need of some rest. She had become lame in her cannon bone tendon. I needed to move on, so I sold her to a young army colonel who owned a beautiful stud that needed a "girlfriend". That colonel really liked her. His whole regiment of the army was training in San Antonio and they were desperate for horses.

The colonel was going to start a breeding farm, if he could, right there on the pastures near the fort. This colonel said that he'd rest her and turn her out on pasture, until she recovered. I knew he'd take excellent care of the filly and he'd feed and brush her down every day, by the kindly way he hugged her. He was a natural born horse lover. So I hugged her too, but said goodbye. Little Texas had served me well. The way she was getting along with that big black stud, I'm sure she wouldn't miss me at all…ha!

I had gotten only two hundred dollars for her, the normal army allowance, so I hailed a Wells Fargo stagecoach back towards Houston. We ran upon some trouble halfway there, when this desperado kid tried to hold us up for money. He jumped out into our path holding a pistol at the driver, which brought our coach to a sudden halt.

This contrary little dude called himself, "Billy Bonny, from Arizona," he loudly spurted out, just like we were going to start shakin' in our boots. He smirked, as if we were supposed to all be drop-dead scared of him. Now I was aggravated by this delay of his, and I asked him kindly who he thought he was to be stopping us here in the road; he seemed cocky and too young to be holding us up this way. He started actin' real uppity as he advanced towards me. He started pointing that barrel right at me.

He liked to twirl his six-shooter in my face, but he done twirled it a little too much, for he lost his twirling grip; when he dropped that gun that he was twirling in the dust, I stepped on it.

Now he got plum upset without his shooter under my boot heel, because he couldn't bully us none, being skin and bones, he was. When he cursed me, I asked the driver to hold on, I sat down upon a big desert rock and I took that kid over my knee, pulled down his britches and gave him a real whoopin'. I hoped that kid learned his lesson. I took away his gun too, and we left him crying like a baby where we found him. His six-shooter wasn't much; it was a real old booger. It had scratches so deep in its wooden handle it was unsightly, and that ol' barrel was plum shot out. It looked useless to me. That kid Billy was a pistol! I threw his pistol out the stagecoach window just before we entered Houston's city limits.

WELLS FARGO INC.
PWK
"Billy the Kid"
Gets A "Whoopin'"

I was good on horseback, so I hired on with the King Cattle Company, and saddled up with a bunch of real fine wranglers headed up to Kansas, pushin' a big herd of Texas longhorn steers. A dollar a day and found, I got paid, but only after the job was done. It was long hours from sunup to sundown, fightin' those stupid critters till my behind ached in the saddle. When I got off my horse and hit the ground, I walked like a man with his britches full. The grub was always beans and bad coffee. But our stories around the campfire at night were always told and I always was asked to tell more, since I was the worldliest and all.

The whole trip was like the Israelites takin' forty years to travel ten miles. Those critters headed off in all directions, and I had to cut 'em off quick. As a puncher, you had to have a good ride and mine was the best. She was a little filly that I picked out from a string the company offered. She was a liver chestnut with a wide, white blazed face, and four pretty white, matched stockin's. She was flashy and could "whirl on a dime till quittin time", she could. A puncher always took the best of care for his horse, and it would take care of him. My filly always got fed and rubbed down first, before I had my grub.

There wasn't too much else happening for excitement, unless some cowpoke fell asleep on his duty and slid off his pony into some cow poop. Then lots of good ribbin' and laughter around the campfire might lend itself to a little fistfight, but nothin' the ramrod couldn't quell. He'd just make the fella causin' all of the fuss ride along on the night shift with the cowpoke who fell off onto the poop, just to make sure he stayed awake. It was usually real quiet, and to tell you the truth, that suited us all just fine.

But one dark night, while I was ridin' night watch, tryin' to sing those doggies to sleep, a pack of wolves came upon the herd and spooked 'em. The steers lit out in a fever and soon we all were close behind. I guess we traveled a good twenty miles before those stupid critters just up and stopped, for no reason at all. They didn't move for four days and we didn't mind that one bit, because they'd stopped in this real grassy valley with creek water flowing through it, and now they'd need to regain all that weight they'd just run off.

The chuck wagon had lost most of its load, so we needed to go to a town and resupply. The ramrod was a decent fella. He stayed behind to help hold the herd and let most of us go to town to relax some. We slicked-up best we could, and headed for a town called Norman, Oklahoma. It weren't any St. Louie, but it had a dance hall with women there, and that's what we came for. I guess I'd lost my realities of ever finding that red coral snake, and seeing my Marietta…it had been a very long time. I was a changed man, some would say for the worse, because I talked and walked and acted just like these heathen', weathered ol' cowboys, chew and all. I guess you might say I'd lost my reason and direction for everything.

To my amazement, this beautiful lady came out onto a stage twirlin', steppin' and kickin' high. And when she started singin' like a nightingale I swallowed my chaw. Gulp! It was none other than Miss Lilly Langtry. She hadn't aged one bit at all, and still was a big thrill to look upon. By her young looks though and all of the time that had elapsed, I knew she had to be one of us Martians. Though I'd moved quickly to the front of the stage for her to look my way, and she looked me square in the eye, she didn't recognize me at all. I guess I'd aged some too, or maybe it was my clothes…oh well. The boys questioned me why she didn't speak to me, since I had once told a story about my night with her. I asked them if they all didn't notice that ol' feller with the pearl handled pistols sittin' off stage…it be her boyfriend, Bat Masterson. I suspected he had to be a Martian too. They said they couldn't see, so I left it at that. I had retained my campfire tales respect.

We rode into Hutchinson, Kansas one day in the fall. The railway there had a whole bunch of railcars for transportin' our beef to Chicago, Illinois, and New York City, New York. When I thought I'd packed enough of those long horn steers inside one of those cars, a railroad man pushed another dozen in till they couldn't fart or take a breath, either one. He really jammed them in! We had pert' near two thousand head brought in and now we were done. So I got paid. I made one hundred and forty dollars and I got to keep the filly, for all my five months work. I looked at the money and then remembered the entire "take" I shared with Black Beard and his men…but this was honest money.

I hooked up with the train; the filly and I were headed to Chicago. We uncoupled twenty-nine cars there and quickly we were back on the move. We rode the rail for a week more and I had to drop some hay into the top of the cattle cars.

When we arrived in New York City, we were inside a big stockyard. As soon as we'd get them doggies out of those cars, men hit 'em in the head with a hammer and hung 'em high on elevated hooks. There was a lot of bawlin' by those poor steers as they realized they were about to be butchered comin' down the shoots. After they hung the dead carcasses, a man slit 'em open and all their guts came tumblin' out onto the floor. Then two men skinned that carcass so fast you just wouldn't believe it. They saved all those hides for shoes and such, they told me. Another man down the line grabbed a hand saw and cut that beef right down the middle long ways, into two whole sides. As I watched, they pushed all those carcasses into a big freezer to hang.

The fingers of all those butchers, I'm sorry to tell ya, were all scarred up, or had some fingers missin'. When the dinner whistle blew, everyone ate egg sandwiches…I guess they'd had enough lookin' at meat! Anyway, it was so stinky and bloody there that I never looked at a steak quite the same! I moved along into the city's business district end of New York, where all the rich sat on their behinds and made the proletariat work for them.

A Nation Divided
(Chapter 22)

No sooner had I arrived downtown in New York City than the streets began filling with marching people who were carrying signs reading "Free The Slaves", "Emancipation", or "A United Union Forever", among others.

A man from Illinois named Honest Abe Lincoln had just become President of the United States. Where was I when all this happened, I wondered? I became interested and very concerned.

I had heard this Abe fella speak once next to a man named Douglas, while coming back from the Dakotas, at a little town in Illinois called Vandalia, as I passed through. Lincoln was a lawyer and spoke meaningful words and said that the union must stay undivided. Seems the people of the south didn't think much of the people of the north.

Lincoln seemed like a humble man and spoke that "all men were created equal and should have certain inalienable rights" provided in the Constitution and written back after the War of Independence of 1776. Humm…what was this Constitution? Where was I? I was lost. Oh, yes, I remember. It was before I came back from the South Seas pirateering…I think; a time that sure put a black mark on my place in the Good Book.

At first, I guessed that the president was referring to the Indians, from whom the new Americans had stolen all of their property, but it was directed towards the imported brown people from Africa that he was really referring to. What more rights should those brown people have over Red Cloud and his people?

Having been in the south, I thought that the brown people were mostly happy having food to eat and a roof over their heads. Their work was hard sometimes, but they always had a home. They'd get a long rest when the harvest season was over. That's usually when they made their babies, just like the farmers did.

From where they all came in Africa, and I had been there to see them, it seemed they slept on mud floors of their grass-thatched huts and women delivered their beautiful babies in the forest upon big leaves. They really had to work hard there too, just to find something to eat. They often had found themselves hunted down and murdered and then served upon a platter by people-eating pygmies; not to mention being devoured sometimes by wild lions, hyenas or man-eating alligators. No rest for the weary there either.

But, I really loved those people. I guess each man has to do what he wants. The people of the north needed workers in their factories, so when they saw all the plantation owners with all their workers, they sent people into the south to start a fire burning in the minds of the brown people. They told them that they were being mistreated by the plantation owners, and should leave and go "free". Free...no one is really free. You have to work for a living, unless you steal like a pirate does and that's real bad.

I ventured out into the streets of New York City and came upon a man one day named Schellenger. He was building a high fence along a sidewalk that ran past his big garden. The wall was to keep out trespassers. I had nothing much to do, so this kind man paid me to help him build this big, high wall. He really valued his vegetables and such. Years later, I learned, after people started randomly posting sale bills, wanted posters, auction papers and such upon his wall, they named that street "Wall Street"...imagine that!

Meanwhile, there was fighting among most of the states, a civil war, they called it. The Union Army tacked up long lists of killed men who had died while fighting in the conflicts upon Mr. Schellenger's wall. I had to study a lot to figure out just who was responsible for calling this war "civil". There were places called Bull Run, Harper's Ferry, The Wilderness Campaign, Antietam, Jackson's Valley, Fredericksburg, and Gettysburg, which was the deadliest battle in the north. Then there were Shiloh, Vicksburg, Chickamauga Creek, Atlanta and Chattanooga in the south. All were areas that dead bodies numbered into the thousands. Now again I asked myself, was that "civil"?

Anyway, this civil war had me feeling indifferent. I thought I'd never ask anything of a man that he didn't think was right, and this was all wrong. Brother was killing brother, just to get all the brown people to move north...imagine!

During all this time, thousands of men were killed and the American South was ravaged. The great plantations fell into ruin and the dirtiest scourges of them all were called "Carpetbaggers". They flocked into the south with their decrees from the government, making them the new owners. "The spoils of war" they called it.

Now the brown people were free, but from what, I never knew. In their minds they were free, I guess, but with no homes and no one to feed them, they walked "unchained", all that way to New York, Chicago, and other big cities to look for work. They found what was not to their liking, in slums and disease. It was all a big lie. There was no work for the lazy or unskilled, and many resorted to thievery just to survive.

They should have all jumped on a boat and gone back to where they came from while they had their chances, I determined. I would have, if it were me. But that's the way it was and if that's what they wanted, so be it. As I said, I loved those poor people; they had their "rights" to choose.

I Get Ed-U-Ma-Cated!
(Chapter 23)

It turned winter quickly. I rented a room with Mr. Schellenger and he gave me a job helping him in his bookstore. Those folks in New York sure read a lot of books. They'd be better off, I'm thinking, to go out and experience the real world; away from this cooped-up-like-chickens behavior. They couldn't make up their own thoughts, as it was always some other fella's ideas from a book making their decisions for them. I'd always hear people saying, "so and so says this" and "so and so says that". I'd betcha this here guy named "so and so" was a pretty interesting fella, probably one of those Democrats.

Mr. Schellenger was a simple, honest man and spoke his piece freely, whether I wanted to hear it or not. But I always felt his warmth towards me, so it was all right. I carried books, stacked books or swept the floors. I shoveled lots of snow too.

One day at dinner, Mr. Schellenger began telling me about some of the things in his store's books. He wondered and marveled that I told him a man could count to no end and the stars whirled through the heavens at the speed of light. There was no end to the many things that he didn't understand, and when I seemed to have an adequate answer to each, he'd look to the books and find out that I was right.

When I began to answer all his questions, he said I should become a teacher. I vaguely remembered being one, someplace. But I had no credentials here, so I'd have to get a college degree, he said. I really didn't think that was necessary, as I remembered then that I had been a teacher back in the first century in Nazareth. Of course, I couldn't tell him that, besides, I'd forgotten quite a bit. My education came from actual experiences. Ahh…what a refreshing flashback that was!

Soon there after, Mr. Schellenger surprised me with some good news. He had spoken to one of the professors from a college that often came into his store, and had set up some tests for me to take to establish my intelligence quotient. I was amused, because on Mars those kinds of tests were found to be null and void, and very inaccurate in the true fact finding of a man's or woman's capabilities. But I went along with it just for something to do, since it was snowy and bleak, and I was now disenchanted with being just a stock boy and snow shoveler.

One snowy day, we rode out to this college named Harvard University in Cambridge, Massachusetts for me to be brain-tested. That Harvard College was the oldest college in these states, built only ten years after the Pilgrims had arrived in the late 1600s, I learned. Who or what was a Pilgrim? Where was I then? It all puzzled me.

I was afraid to answer all their written questions correctly so as to avoid being thought a cheat. I fabricated on a few…just enough to be considered a genius! They said that they'd pay me to go to school, and be tested now and then, as I progressed. So, with lots of time on my hands, I enrolled. What were two or three months to me anyway? But I had miscalculated some; it took a lot longer than that, as I spent my next six years learning and writing papers about Earth's histories, places and times that I had personally witnessed…and they still thought I was a genius.

I had a roommate. He was a very small individual, who always had a grin on his face. He immediately reminded me of someone I knew of from Mars as a class instructor and who was also a recipient of a lotto seat on another ship that was leaving Mars in its last hours. Little did I know, but this Dick Clarkson was his earthly-born son. Dick Jr. was a real handsome go-getter with the females, but not much for rugby. After a while, and during a full moon as we looked upon the stars of a mid-summer's night, Dick confided in me that he was truly a Martian. I was leery and cautious to unveil my family tree also. So I waited.

He mentioned his father Richard Clarkson Sr., whom I personally knew from the institution of music, but I remained reserved about telling him. Later, Dick and I had a falling out, when I refused to go on a date with his girlfriend's sister and we changed roommates. My heart was far away, so I could not. But much later in my life, I saw a dance program called" Richard Clarkson's Bandstand" on an invention called a TV. He must have really been a Martian, because he had not aged one iota in over one hundred years…imagine that!

My next new roommate was a fidgety soul, who was set upon wagering on anything and everything. But because he usually held the upper hand by his inside information, he'd usually win. Few ever bet anymore with him and he was getting anxious to invent a new game that could be bet on. He showed me his trick games like the shell game, rigged roulette wheels, marked cards and others. But now he couldn't find any new blood that would gamble with him. I knew better than to tangle with Abner.

My roommate, Abner Doubleday, asked if I knew of any game that he could draw a crowd to gamble with him. I believe he was desperate to pay his college tuition to remain in school. At first, I hadn't considered his problem, but one evening, while I sat lonely upon a second story dorm window's sill, I saw some kids near our campus having a regular knock-down fight throwing stones at one another; until one kid was clunked hard beside the head. There was my incentive to create a simple game from the game that I learned from Red Cloud that the Indians called "stones". I only did this for Abner's sake.

I set about reasoning, using my previously taught Harvard business class's ways, thinking first, where I would like to play this new game of stones. It couldn't be played inside; because windows and furniture would be broken…it had to be outside.

Then, I thought about how many people would be able to fit comfortably in the lot across the street from campus, maybe a dozen, or so, so I sat about drawing up a straight line between two points just like Red Cloud and I did, but that seemed too small. Somehow, after much doodling, I made a square and placed a player on each corner.

I decided that the thrower of the rock would stand in the center of the square, halfway in the middle, but if it were square-shaped, which place would the striker go? I moved everything around to become a diamond shaped field, and added a catcher of the rock, behind the main station to retrieve missed and overthrown rocks. That would be a really tough job for someone.

Finally, I decided that if a body hit the rock, he could keep running fast around all the corners, until he got hit in the head with the rock or touched all corners. But he couldn't be hit if he made it to a corner safely and stayed there. Or, if he hit the rock over anyone's head and got to the corner first. It was my first draft and I left it lay there openly.

I was tired and fell asleep, knowing I would have the upcoming weekend to think about improving the game. But along about dark, Abner came into our dorm room mad, packed up everything he had, and told me he was asked to leave for lack of his tuition payment. I shook his hand good-bye, and wished him well, since I didn't have a cent to give him. But he took something more than money from me. He accidentally took along my game plan and didn't say a word later. Oh well, I made it just for him anyway.

I began to hear rumblings around our campus about how one of our past students had succeeded in making up a new fantastic game that was called baseball. The game was drawing many of the area residents to watch its action, and an exhibition game was to be played between two local colleges for the prize of a barrel of beer. Everyone was invited, so with nothing to do, I went to this interestingly sounding amusement game.

The new baseball game was held on a college rugby field, which I found had most of the seats filled before I arrived. To my surprise, a nickel was charged to get inside, and that was half the money I carried. I was curious as to why so many people had flocked to pay to be there. I soon found out, when a campus buddy asked me if in fact Abner Doubleday had once been my roommate?

"Why yes," I replied to the question, "he left because his tuition was over due."

"Well he sure has it now; he's a smart guy to think up such a fascinating game!"

I sat upon the long pine bench and soon found out what had happened to my game invention. There, standing upon a makeshift stage, talking and explaining the rules of the game to the audience through a cheerleader's megaphone, was my old roomy, Abner.

Abner Doubleday had taken my sketches and put together his versions of how the game of "stones" should be played, but he called his game baseball!

I never regretted his fame and actually enjoyed his tweaking of my rules…after all; I got it from the Indians! The wonderful game of baseball grew and eventually became America's pastime.

Mr. Schellenger died two years before I received my degree paper of importance, and I was asked to be one of his pallbearers. I then realized that I had never walked into the House of the Lord before. I hoped that the steeple wouldn't crash down upon me. But Dargod was my father, and Jesus was my nephew, so I figured not.

Mr. Schellenger was of the Catholic faith, and I found the ceremony was a real experience. Everybody threw water upon themselves from a little pot when they walked in the door and walked out. I guess they stunk a little, or wanted to stay awake. Then before they sat down in their seats, they kneeled down to see if there was any chewing gum under the seat to chew, I guess, or to find change on the floor. I never saw such people. Then the choir began singing sad tunes and a tear came to my eye.

Out came these young boys in dresses and holding a big stein of beer, I think it was. It was a glorious bejeweled container though, just like what I drank from on Black Beard's ship. I think Black Beard was a Catholic…nah! But suddenly those crosses that these people wore and then kissed often really represented my nephew Jesus' sacrifice upon the wooden cross. My, how the kid had gotten around! I had even asked for his forgiveness several times out of sheer respect.

The Reverend Father O'Riley then spoke his words like a man singing. One thing though, I could understand every single word that the reverend father said. He spoke in a dead language called Latin, just like Caesar had mumbled. I considered that it was very appropriate, since Mr. Schellenger was dead. So, I guess only the spirit of Mr. Schellenger, and I, were supposed to understand him. But how could anybody who didn't speak anything else but English ever tell what he was talking about? So I stood right up in the middle of his speech, and said a short piece just like Black Beard would have done about how nice Mr. Schellenger was to me. I said it in a nice way; I hoped everybody could understand. Everybody looked at me funny-like, so I sat back down. But I got in what I wanted to say. We carried Mr. Schellenger to his grave out behind the chapel and said goodbye. I had lost a true friend.

I found out later that Harvard University, which is the highest ranking school on this earth, had received special money from the government to continue testing my intelligence quotient, because it seems I was scoring so high on the tests, that one professor wrote about my scores, "He must be from outer space!"…Imagine that!

During my senior year at Harvard, while researching a term paper, I discovered an old, dusty, glass jar, just sitting on a shelf by itself in the biology lab. When I brushed dust off the container's label, it read: "This is the brain of a businessman of unknown descent, who was shot and killed in a bank robbery in Philadelphia, Pennsylvania, on August 10, 1744. Notice the unusually large creases with the depth about the lobes. This may be a good indication of a very unusually high degree of intelligence. This man's family graciously donated his body to the science department of this university. His name was Don Diego Dargod, the Valedictorian graduate of Harvard College, 1700."

I could have died. That man was my own son!

"Oh, Dargod," I felt weak in the knees just then. Don Diego was a part of Marietta, and me I thought. I loved him; however he was always his mother's son and was sometimes distant to me. But he was still my son, who had grown up so fast, that I hardly had time to know him well.

I stared at, and then held the jar, until I realized that he had lived to be over two hundred years old. At least, I had given him something in life…longevity. Something to note: offspring of Martians could possibly live longer with AloevectorP23 injections. But not in my son's condition. I was too late, for they had dissected him in a medical class. The writing didn't explain his being "shot and killed" and I hoped that he wasn't the perpetrator, but the banker.

I polished the jar as best I could and placed it back in a more prominent place, for what it was worth. What greater resting place could one want than an everlasting position at Harvard University! Harvard…the school of two honor graduates named Dargod! I graduated that spring.

DARGOD
HUMAN BRAIN
"HARVARD UNIVERSITY"

Could I Keep a Secret?
(Chapter 24)

I began a new life, with a certificate that everyone called a "sheep's skin" which also renowned that I was a genius. I felt that I now was progressing very well, and I had learned to pronounce words more fluently and correctly, and spoke distinctively more precisely. I had scored well in math, algebra, geometry, science, history, archeology, astronomy, geography, government, four different languages, besides tweaking my own English and economics; not to mention, that I was undefeated in debating class. Yes, I had taken lots of classes, but now I also had to find a job to support myself, though the college offered a professorship to me. I was through with tests, tests, and more tests; my old life had changed forever. I had come full circle in the Earthly world of knowledge, and in Mars's too; so much so, my brain had grown and I needed a larger hat size…Image that!

The U.S. Government contacted me soon after graduation, and I was asked to take a job with the Secret Services Department. I rode a stagecoach all the way down to Washington. But, when I got there, nobody knew why I had shown up. So I guess those people really could keep a secret. The rest of my life, I always was suspect of government offers.

Eventually I joined the Bureau of Indian Affairs. And when I had a chance to right a wrong, I tried. The Indians were being pushed onto reservations, into places that they couldn't survive as before.

I was sent to talk to the tribal chiefs about their settlement in Oklahoma. Seems the government wanted to buy back all their properties at a fair price, to give their lands to the freed slaves. That too seemed reasonable, if the brown people so desired.

But one day in a meeting, I learned that there were people in industry that were influencing the senators to grab up that land. They went right to work with a clandestine plan. I didn't recognize it at first, but I was being used to persuade the Indians into a wrongful deed.

The chiefs met with me in Norman, Oklahoma, a place I'd previously traveled. They all said that they would welcome the sale, since the monies that were promised to their tribes from the U.S. Government, suddenly was too slow in coming, and their people starved.

Now the Indians weren't allowed off their reservation to seek work, so how could they provide for their families? But while I was speaking to the chiefs, the U.S. Government issued papers to push the Indians farther west onto their decreasing lands. The call went out to "land grabbers" who were allowed into our country from all around the world, just to race with their stake and claim a portion for themselves. There were six different land runs.

I decided to tour the western area completely, and tried to find out if there were any alternatives. Maybe they could farm? One day, while I was riding out upon the dusty plains, and all the time thinking that this might be a good swap for the chiefs after all, I came upon some white men with what looked like a water digging apparatus. The substance of raw crude oil blackened it. They were "hush-hush", until they learned that I was from the government. Then, they opened up and were excited to tell me all about the "find" and thought I had better tell Senator So-and-so, that there was oil aplenty flowing under the reservation.

"He'd know what to do," they told me.

We later called these guys "boomers", meaning that they built wildcat oil wells.

Well, I knew exactly what to do too; I told the chiefs. They were smart enough to have the fields tested themselves. Sure enough, there was oil everywhere on the reservation! I was happy for those poor Indians.

I went back to Washington to report that the Indians had rejected the government's offer. The first one to speak out loud was that senator. He said we'd go to war with them, but no others saw it his way. That senator reminded me of that greedy storeowner in St. Louie…probably his relative.

Three years later, I returned to Norman, Oklahoma and there were the chiefs, all four, riding down the street in their shiny new touring car. It was a beaut! Hot-diggity-dog for those Indians! They were very rich now, those poor ol' Indians!

This was also about the very same time that I discovered the first certainty that animals had been deliberately brought to Earth by Martians, or possibly by accidental contamination. While walking in the tall prairie grasses of Oklahoma one afternoon, I discovered an animal phenomenon that I knew existed upon Mars, but didn't even suspect it would be here upon Earth. It was the gray, soft-bodied Dipper! It could infect a whole generation of humans and change the way they perceived themselves. The locals called them "toads" and "frogs", and they said that they were harmless. They were everywhere.

The dipper was a small animal that hopped along the ground on Mars and protected itself from predators by secreting a very small amount of venom through glands upon its head. For those predators that bit upon it, they received a bitterly horrible taste that they couldn't swallow; it could eventually kill them, and certainly they never went back for seconds.

In a human, that same venom didn't kill them. On the contrary, a little secretion upon the skin made a human "love crazy" through an eventual chemical imbalance; the white milky fluid infiltrated the victim's sexual organs through his or her blood stream. Just touching this cute little dipper vertebrate's venom, caused hormonal changes within a human's body that eventually created loss of gender. Soon thereafter, a "he" thought he was a "she", and vice versa. It was relatively slow affecting venom on humans, but could remain in the organs and is transferred to the next generation of breeders.

Dr. Dargod, my father, explained that this was nature's way of stopping over-reproduction, by metamorphosis. The females never came into heat and avoided sexual contact of any male, but herded together with other females. The males actually turned into females, thus there was no breeding success. I guess it worked on Mars. But I was surprised to see it here. Had explorers brought them along, I wondered? I watched my step and cringed when I saw people picking them up and holding them…was "nature" telling them something?

I worked for the Bureau of Indian Affairs for nearly twenty years, passed through a few presidents, but finally quit and returned to New York. Walking down "Wall Street" brought back fond memories for me.

While I was inside a coffee shop one day, I met a nasty old man named Livingston. He claimed to be from England and was studying the people of Africa. He spouted off his multiple qualifications to me, as if I were a peon. I told him that I'd ventured some, and learned that people everywhere were just about the same, except each held their values differently, in comparison to the quality of life their environment provided. His eyes widened and he spoke out, "I say ol' chap, are you an Oxford or Princeton man?"

I replied, "No, ol' chap, I attended Harvard."

"Too bad," he replied sarcastically, "I was about to ask you to accompany me on my most important journey, but a Harvard man couldn't make it alone being away from New York."

I responded curtly, "That's because we've already been there, done that!"

Mr. Livingston…I presume…was perturbed, because he then grabbed up his bagel and retreated to a corner, not to banter anymore…. I hoped that ol' coot got lost in Africa!

Si, Senor, WAR!
(Chapter 25)

WAR! It was July 1st, of 1898, and a big fight between these United States and Spain escalated when the Spanish fought against a company of U.S. soldiers down in Cuba. A real pistol named Lt. Colonel Teddy Roosevelt had gotten confused and charged with only five men up a hill called San Juan. In a fierce and bloody battle that followed, Teddy rallied others to him to defeat the whole Spanish army.

In a newspaper article, one writer said that they called that bunch of fellas "Rough Riders"…I guess it was self explanatory about being a rough ride…huh? But, I heard later that there were "Buffalo Soldiers" there too, and they used mules. But ol' Theodore, he rode a horse that he called "Little Texas". When I saw that picture, sure enough, it looked just like my Little Texas. It probably was a son from a cross between that army colonel's black stallion and my filly. Imagine that? I was so proud.

Anyway, Roosevelt came back to the states as a "hero" when that same journalist published the fighting pictures. Soon after that, ol' Teddy was elected President of the United States. He was an environmentalist person, a real hunter and gun collector type and had the government set aside millions of acres for wildlife. I wondered if he had done that for himself. But that was a foolish thought by me, for he continued to respect animal habitat and supported ventures to replenish the buffalo and elk. I think they even call one species of elk, Roosevelt elk. Now that's my kind of elected official!

Flying High
(Chapter 26)

I left New York in the spring and took a train headed west to warmer weather, and much warmer people. On one of the frequent scheduled depot stops was a small town in Ohio. I found the town very interesting and decided to look around. I saw a little sign on a building that looked unusually intriguing. On that sign was a painting of a new type of bicycle. It still had two wheels, but both were the same size, instead of one big one, and one little wheel, as I had seen on the sidewalks and streets of New York. It was definitely different. I figured that this contraption might be a very cost-saving way for me to travel, and I decided that I would buy one. After all, the stagecoach was very bumpy, usually late, always very dusty; and some of the people that rode upon the rigs were obnoxious, or sometimes very sickly and coughed all over you. I didn't like that at all.

I strolled into this little makeshift garage and was told that the two bicycles that were displayed in the windows there were already sold. Dissatisfied, I wanted to speak to someone in authority. I then met Orville Wright, a bespectacled little guy, whom I immediately became friends with. His soft-spoken words eased my frustration as he showed to me the mechanics of his brother's and his own bicycle. It was a simple contraption that lowered the risk of crashes by having a much lower seat than the old high wheeler. He allowed me to sit on the seat. It was less comfortable than a saddle, as the hard little cloth covered seat ran up the cheeks of my behind when I sat down upon it, and I thought I'd lost my manhood!

"Oh, Dargod," I moaned and I hopped right off.

"We're working on a better idea for a seat," he chuckled. "We're thinking of using oak."

It didn't take me a second to blurt out, "Why not make it like a horse's saddle from leather?"

"Hummm, that's an idea," spoke Orville's busily working brother, Wilbur, who delighted to the thought from his corner work place.

"Not bad, not bad," Wilbur retorted.

It was noontime and their mother yelled out from their kitchen door that their lunch was on the table. It was awkward, but Orville asked me to join them. I was hungry, so I said that I'd gladly join them for a hot cup of coffee, and I did.

Their kitchen was enormous, and so was Momma. She had the rosiest red cheeks from bending over the hot stove cooking. Her gray hair was rolled up upon her head into a bun. Her apron was covered with flour, as she brought freshly baked bread to the table, holding the hot loaf with her apron as mitts.

The aroma smelled so good that I told her she should start up a bakery. Her eyes rolled back and in her cute German accent she lamented, "Auch, du bista boob you, eeeeat now, once!"

She laughed whole-heartedly when I started going, "Uuummm," really loudly. The bread was heavenly, and I told her so.

"Best I ever ate!" I said.

When the fresh-churned butter melted upon it, I could not stop with the"uuummms". The table was just full of German food delights, including the best tasting pork sausages and sauerkraut ever. And that second piece of apple pie was superb! That was my first real taste of German style cooking, but it wouldn't be my last.

"Das est gut," I managed to speak out, as I mangled the German language I had studied in college.

Wilbur was a quiet man, and though I was sitting at his table, he was so engrossed in his eating that he never spoke…he was a listener. He listened while Orville said that he was sorry that he couldn't make a bicycle for me, because it was a very slow process making the parts, and then having to put them all together. They were smothered in orders that would take a year or more to fill.

He said that they had all sorts of ideas about transportation and he discussed that one day he'd make a machine that would fly, only if and when, he could figure out a way to propel it continuously. No more was said about that.

But being a Harvard man, I offered my expertise into solving the production of the bicycles. It became simple!

"Get some help!" I said.

I recommended, "Hire the young boys out of school for the summer to put the 'bikes' together. The boys would work cheap. You could then devote your full time to making the parts more quickly, and the boys could assemble the bikes."

I was interrupted by Wilbur's mumbling, "Bikes? Bikes?" he repeated. "That's a novel name, sir, I like it! I find it annoying to continually repeat writing the word bicycle in the diagram description," as he continued bluntly.

We went back into the garage to survey the area for expansion; it was perfect. And soon I helped move desks and tables around to make stations, where each boy could do one thing. One boy would help Wilbur with his welding of the bike and carry it to the first boy's station, when it was completed. Another boy and he would put on the sprocket wheel and grease it. At the next station, one boy would put on the chain and the front wheel. He would also put on the handlebars, and make certain that the lugs were tight enough, and also that both wheels were aligned correctly.

"Viola, problem solved!" I exclaimed.

I stayed on to setup the assembly area. Soon school was out and four boys were hired to help. They were satisfied with a dollar a day and Momma's great cooking. They worked hard to learn and the business was beginning to boom.

One day, a very tall businessman walked into the shop and observed the boys working at their stations, like a well-oiled machine. He stood scratching his head for a while, writing down notes in a little book. He left after purchasing two bicycles for himself and his wife. When I looked at the receipts for the bikes, I saw that his name was Ford. He drove off with the bikes strapped to the bumper of a shiny new automobile, which was as black as the ace of spades.

Several years later, a man using that very same name of Ford started up a plant that was already building a few cars. He named those cars after himself. In the paper it read where he had invented an "assembly-line" for workers to increase their production of the cars…"modernized the work force" it read. He must have been one of our Harvard men too, to be able to think of that…imagine!

Anyway, I stayed busy with the Wright boys, until one night Orville let me see his drawings of something he called an aireoplane. He had several different types drawn, but said that wasn't all. He then took me behind the garage to a good-sized shed. When he opened the double doors, there was this big bird-looking thing that he said he thought would fly. He and Wilbur had actually flown smaller versions of it, and it floated in the air almost forty steps like a hawk. He said the wind rushing across the wing caused it to lift up. You had to throw the small one from a hill to get it going. The harder you threw it, the farther it flew.

PWK

"Wilber Shows Jamison His Invention"

His problem: How to keep the plane moving and carry a person to boot…hummm. I let my mind study most of the night on that one, and at three o'clock in the morning I suddenly got it and sat up in the bed and yelled out loudly, "I've got it!"

Momma rushed into my room with a frying pan held high, and Orville had his pistol. They both were angry that I blurted out so loudly, but they eventually went back to bed. But when I explained everything to Wilbur who stayed, I showed him that I had figured how to get that contraption off the ground, and with a person aboard. Wilbur listened attentively, until the sun's daylight rays broke through the curtains.

At breakfast, Momma said that she was sorry that she had yelled at me so, and served up the most tasty biscuits and gravy that you could imagine. She too listened, as I told Orville my plan. We all left the kitchen table full, and full of new ideas.

My simple solution was to add a second wing above the first. Use the gears and pedals from a bicycle to turn a fan blade that if turned fast enough, would pull the plane some, while in the air. Immediately, Wilbur says, "Plane? I like that name, sir."

In six weeks, after all our mechanics were done after work, we all put together a bicycle setup on the rebuilt plane with a second wing. Orville knew just where to go to test it. And one moonlit night, we snuck the plane out to a nearby open field, high on a hill. We pushed Wilbur with all our might down a hill and the whole plane lifted off. But Wilbur forgot to pedal fast and the plane didn't go too far before it crashed. Orville was angry and told Wilbur that he would do it next time. It really flew, and that's what was important…imagine that!

The Wright brothers took some of my ideas and changed them before I left. Instead of one prop, they hung two. And so that no more arguments about pedaling fast enough would occur, they mounted a real gas engine. It looked awesome!

To present their invention, they took their plane to Kitty Hawk, North Carolina, where the winds blew steadily. One day, before a large gathering crowd of reporters and onlookers, they got that bird about twelve feet up in the air, from sliding it quickly down a rail, with Orville as the pilot…those two Ohio boys did well!

A Big Hit in Louisville
(Chapter 27)

The world was changing quickly…too quickly for me. Mechanization had put everything in a tizzy, but it also had given me a good job. Construction of big steel plants that heated up the raw ore and belched smoke sky-high, were going up all over in the east. They had to sell their steel. It was the best steel in the entire world.

My job, was working as an "in-between" man. I brought together men and their companies, so that each could help out the other. They in turn, ordered steel from me for their buildings. A commission paid me from the steel companies was my salary.

The world was entertained by the sport called baseball, and I was helping in the development of bringing the woodcutters of Illinois, Missouri, and Georgia together with a company that wanted to make baseball bats in Louisville, Kentucky. My favorite team was the Pittsburgh Pirates, but I always managed to take time off to watch the "locals" play their games too, wherever my job took me.

One day, I met a young man who was literally sobbing outside the ballpark in Louisville. Sixteen, he was then. He had tried to make the local team in Louisville, but was rejected.

Johnny Wagner, from Georgia, was his handle. He would not ever tell a lie, he told me.

"I just ain't good enough, I guess," he sobbed.

OUCH!
CLUNK!
KEEP YOUR
EYE ON THE ball
Eh, ROCK
THE GAME
OF
"STONES"
PWK

He looked strong as a bull, and had "bull-sized" bowed legs to match. Why a pig could get through those legs, if it tried, I imagined. But he was as fast as spit lightning. He had come to Louisville to try to make it onto a ball team called the Colonels. I quickly decided I was going to help him. He was desperate about swinging his bat at the ball. He couldn't hit a lick against those veteran pitchers. He somehow forgot all that he knew about hitting and keeping his eye on the ball. I tried to help him some.

Now I remembered ol' Red Cloud, who had taught me how to play "stones". So I took Johnny out to a rock pile for a couple of days and taught him about the game of stones. He couldn't hit a lick, until I told him that he was holding his left elbow too low. After he got "clunked" a few times in the head, he got real good about keeping his eyes on that ball, eh...rock, and real good about clubbing those rocks back at me; really good!

Now I want to tell you that I can't take much credit, but Johnny went back and made not only that Colonel's team, but also he later made the Detroit Tiger's pro team too.

He must have continued to be an honest boy, because years later he was known as "Honas" Wagner, for short. I saw him one day in twenty-five; he got sixteen total base hits in one game. What a feat! He gave me ten of his new "rookie" gum company sports cards, all signed. He didn't forget me...I put those cards in my suitcase and never touched them since. Today, they say they're worth a bunch...if I can ever find that suitcase! But, I'm getting a little ahead of my story telling. Excuse me please.

Actually, I got acquainted with lots of real good sports personalities. One such person comes to mind that I had actually met the second time I saw him, long before we became close friends. His plight was a doozy.

I was downtown Baltimore one afternoon, at a friendly pub run by a man named Ruth, eh...that was his last name. He tended to the bar while his kid ran wild in the streets as a bully. Herman fought everybody. It wasn't long before this young boy started getting into trouble with the law. He was only seven, but was already nipping at the near-empties that his father asked him to clean off the tables after late-night bar hours. What could you expect? The boy wouldn't listen to his pop and was incorrigible, they said.

One day the boy got into trouble with the local "gendarme". His parents decided to put him in what I call a boys' orphanage, because he'd become just too tough to handle.

I was there. I just happened to be passing through and having a frosty schooner of Griesedieck Brothers' beer, when his father dragged him down the street to St. Mary's Industrial School, and gave a reluctant priest some money to keep Herman.

Herman quickly spit upon the priest, but found a place of refuge in that same priest's arms as protection, when his own father then tried to choke him. At that moment, Herman had found Jesus without as much as a prayer. Ha, I guess my nephew's protective forgiveness had spread around the world, and all the way to Baltimore!

His parents left Herman to simmer and to learn the trade of a tailor. I guess it was the theory of "idle hands cause trouble", so that same priest gave Herman another challenge.

When all the boys went to recess they took turns hitting a ball pitched from the priest's own hand, only few could hit his fastest pitches. Herman didn't want to try, but consented for a bribe from the priest of an extra piece of pie at dinner. When he missed horribly, and the other fellows laughed at him, Herman became furious and refused to allow one more pitch pass the plate. He hit those pitched balls so hard that the rectory's windows looked like an abandoned building from all the glass panes that got knocked out by Herman's fly balls. It was only a beginning of sorts, which you might refer to it as "Genesis".

Years passed by, and the kid grew much larger in stature. His father never once came to see him again, it was stated, but that was good, I think. I didn't get to see Herman for quite some time. He was just a simple, lonely kid then…but years later he began to bully again.

World War I...the First Time Around! (Chapter 28)

WWI had begun when the Archduke of Austria was assassinated in 1914, and eventually 65,000,000 men from almost every country became involved. The Kaiser of Germany declared war on all the surrounding countries. The U.S. entered the conflict in 1917 and our "Dough Boys" were dying on the battle-fields. The bloodiest war of all left 10,000,000 men dead and 20,000,000 injured before it was over in 1918. The fighting men returned, but there were no jobs and the hard times came quickly.

I was in Hollywood, California, looking for a part in the upcoming movie industry. I could see myself playing as a real western hero. Yep, I went across the country, a hobo hopping boxcars or hailing down a ride, when I could. The only work that paid more than a dime an hour was show business. I'd done everything else, so I just thought what the heck...Hollywood here I come.

I wound up in San Francisco, as I traveled along the roadways "hoofing it". I ran into another guy heading in the same direction. He was a tall fellow from Iowa, took big long strides in his steps and walked as if he were very determined to get somewhere. I had a heck of a time keeping up with him. I told him to worry about being hit by passing autos. The only thing he said that he was worried about was that he had to leave his Airedale dog "Duke" behind. But I learned that he could get us both a ride by using his big country smile to influence the few that stopped to pick us up. He had a real gift.

His name was Marion Morrison…"What?" I laughed. "What man is named Marion?" Pow! I then picked myself off the ground, dusted my pride off, and didn't say that ever again. I just called him "sir"!

We arrived in Hollywood in the middle of the night, with no place to sleep, so we parked our carcasses on a park bench. It wasn't two minutes later, before the coppers rousted us. But all wasn't for naught. When Marion slugged the coppers for hitting him across the shoe soles of his tired feet, we both got a chance for beds in the "Hollywood Hilton". That's the county sheriff's slammer!

The Justice of the Peace fined me five dollars, almost all that I had on me, because I was just sleeping on the bench, and didn't cause any trouble. Marion stood up tall and the judge fined him, "Twenty dollars, or twenty days", in the county jail. He didn't have any money, so there went the rest of my dough even though a very principled Marian wanted to refuse and just sit it out. He was now my best friend. I really admired the guy because he got us into dinner places, just using his big smile on the waitresses. We didn't usually have to pay at all. If the manager insisted, the waitresses paid everything for us.

Every single day, we'd search the newspapers that were left behind on the park benches for any kind of jobs, until one day when Marion was out searching for employment, I noticed a little ad for a stage prop on a movie set. I immediately applied and they quickly gave me the job without any bit of previous "movie star" experience.

It turned out to be a real moving experience for me…I moved a prop here; I moved a prop there, then back again…I was getting dizzy with all this movie star business. My paycheck was only fifteen dollars for all that work, but our room rent was only two dollars and we were eating again, and paying our own bills. I found out that they needed another prop man, so I immediately told them I had just the man. I then went back to get Marion, but the big guy was sunning on the beach with some beautiful dolls. They were reluctant to let him go.

You can't guess what happened next. On the very first scene's "take" and the very first set for Marion. This big cowboy movie star ups and hollers something derogatory at Marion when the leading lady looked at Marion, and then sighed. She too thought him handsome.

Pow! He and the big star of the film went at it, while all the time, believe it or not, the director hollered out, "Keep 'em rolling!" and there was the doggonedest fight scene ever made for the screen. The set became strewn all over and I was afraid they were both going to kill one another, when suddenly both men stopped, and just quit.

Each had fought enough and shook hands. There was an outbreak of applause on the set, which totally embarrassed Marion. The big star said he was sorry, and Marion said that he was too. The director came down quickly from his perch upon the raised camera arm excitedly, and said that the fisticuffs between the two were the best fighting scenes that he had ever made.

"You!" he says to Marion, "Go to dress-up and get some western duds on. Boy, I'm going to make you a big star! By the way, what's his name?" he called out to everyone.

I didn't want to see Marion get all upset again if someone there laughed out loud, so I broke in, "Eh, his name is Duke, his friends call him Duke, because he doesn't like it if someone makes fun of his real name," I partially made it up.

"Well, what for heaven's sake is Duke's real name?" the director yelled.

When I said it was, "Marion Morrison", Mr. Ford, the director, chuckled and assured everyone that "Duke" definitely needed a more masculine stage name.

When Marion came out onto the set, decked out in a cowboy's duds, the director simply said, "Your stage name will be…Ahhh, John Wayne," and that was that! Imagine that?

Well, "The Duke" became a stunt-man-actor super star in just one day, and with a little polish, in 1930 he made his first movie, "Men without Women". I never saw that one, but later I saw one called, "Stage Coach", and he did real fine. Marion Morrison was quite the "Duke". I never succeeded in show business, so I moved on with other ideas.

Everybody Gets Depressed!
(Chapter 29)

Suddenly, bodies were leaping out of the high-rise windows in New York, as the big-time stock holders lost their shirts, and their pants, in the stock market crash of twenty-nine. I had lost my movie star, moving job too. Nobody could afford a movie ticket. I had to find some cash so that I could eat. I wouldn't steal.

But I wasn't about ready to drop out of a window; I had my "backups". Bread lines with soup were the "specials" served up at the Salvation Army's Depot. Hundreds, sometimes thousands of desperate, unemployed people came. I had to move on.

I got to St. Louis, Missouri by rail, and rolled off a freight train, just before I got into Union Station. I just happened to be walking down Goode Street, when I met this very cute little brown-eyed boy, who was very ambitious. Now Charles was a very talented young fella, who was singing songs for money, as people walked by. Some real mean tunes came out as he played upon his old four stringed, Hawaiian guitar. He really got everyone's attention. When his long legs gyrated, he'd walk like a duck to his tunes. He was really something! I knew immediately that this kid had it, and he was destined for stardom.

I met his beautiful momma when she came to check on her son, and I could see where he got all his good looks…rhythm too. His mom was a teacher, and she had a wonderfully kind voice. I told her I was willing to pay extra for a ride to South Dakota. His lovely momma then offered to drive me up to South Dakota, about one hundred-twenty miles, for gas, food and thirty dollars. She graciously took my I.O.U., her eyebrows raised, and let me keep the money I had, on a "cross my heart" God's promise. She was a good Christian lady who raised her six babies the best that she could. Charles was a prize!

Charles sang all the way and I really liked his energy. Five hours later, the kind lady dropped me at a lonely place in the country; a place that I figured I knew. I grabbed my pack, waved goodbye, and walked into the Black Hills a determined man.

"I'll be back in a month, or so," I hollered back at them.

Around my neck, was a well-worn bear tooth and turquoise necklace that once I had received as a gift. I camped and walked for two weeks before I spotted that butte's slope in the far distance. That rock, sitting up high, still gave off a twinkle when the morning's sun struck it just right. All this time, and it was still there...our gold! I hurried up the slope and saw that all was nearly in tact, but covered in brush. I looked skyward and saw that the big slab of ore was still protruding high up on that mountain's top. What a glorious sight!

As I dug around, I struck a metal box. I opened it, and found a hand written note scribbled in Cheyenne-Sioux upon an animal hide of some sort. It was ol' Crow Foot's scribbled message telling me, "I waited here as long as I could, until I was headed towards the heavenly spirits in the sky," he wrote. Inside the box also was a long dark cigar...huh...imagine that? A tear came to my eye and I sat for a while.

I filled the pack with all the gold that would fit, but it was so darn heavy to carry for very long, that I nearly ruptured myself. Now in bad times, where was I going to sell raw gold? I guessed I'd picked up a million dollars worth. I was right!

After I convinced a poor farmer to sell his only plow horse for a handful of gold, I was able to pack that gold out of South Dakota, and back to St. Louie in about two weeks.

In a tall building on Market Street, I found a big jeweler who was able to accept my gold for cash. I told him that there was plenty more available and he was anxious to oblige on any amount, as long as he got his thirty percent cut. I felt he was fair, but I later learned that he took plenty extra. But, I had netted nearly seven hundred thousand dollars, and that was plenty. I deposited a cashier's check in the bank, but took out a couple thousand cash. They treated me like a movie star in my raggedy clothes. Imagine that?

Always repay kindness with kindness, I say. So, I went to the big music store on Grand Avenue, near Sportsman's Park, and bought a real nice Gibson flattop guitar for Chuck. But when I arrived at his home, it was October 18th, and his sixth birthday. So I gave that guitar to a relative, I think, who was ashamed he had no gift for him.

Chuck's daddy was a construction man who knew its value and immediately thanked me. Chuck's big handsome smile was all I really needed. He showed his exuberant excitement by first tuning it by ear, then playing and singing to me a real "cute little song"…it was called "My Ding-a-ling" after he had seen my necklace, I guess…ha…and my friend was happy.

Later in life, after singing and playing that guitar really well, ol' Chuck became "Rock and Roll's" greatest ever, and made lots of recordings like "Mabelene", but my favorite Chuck Berry song is still "My Ding-a-ling".

Livin' It Up...Too Much!
(Chapter 30)

I have a hard time remembering this part of my life. I guess it's because I had money to burn and I was on fire, a whiskey-slow-gin-fizz fire. I bought a new Ford and saw a lot of baseball games. I bought some stocks at low buys, like GE, GM, Bell, AT&T and a new one called Shell Oil. I was living high on the hog!

Well, in 1933, at Comenski Park, in Chicago, Illinois I shook hands with this "All-Star" grown up bully and his friend Lou. That duo was none other than Herman "Babe" Ruth and Lou Gehrig, later to be known as the "Iron Horse". I'd say both those guys were considered "incorrigible" to the guys who had to pitch to them! And of course, Babe was now bullying that baseball. I had heard that Babe didn't ever discuss his parents. I didn't ever ask. He was a man on a mission and that was to enjoy his life fully.

Florida, ah Florida! The sun, the water, and the girls on the beaches in their bathing suits! Each spring, I was invited to attend spring practice at a place called Lang Field. Lots of pro baseball teams played there, but the Babe would finish batting practice first, and we'd head out to do some serious drinking and girl watching. He had gotten married and divorced. Babe never liked to be alone.

On one occasion we ventured down to the Keys, as the manager gave the "boys of summer" a short two-day rest. Well, ol' Babe wanted to go deep-sea fishing. He just walked along the docks, until he found a big boat, and offered to pay this guy some big bucks, just for an afternoon's venture. Now the owner of the big yacht wasn't a commercial fishing guide, but a friendly skipper who reminded me a little of an army colonel. I guess he recognized the Babe and didn't want to pass up the chance. Anyway, we all went aboard against this man's wife Pauline's objections.

Now ol' Babe was a lady's man and soon soothed her into a friendly, cheerful person, by using his huge deep-chested tones of voice to captivate her. The skipper just sat back and watched.

We ventured out into the deep, up near Miami's shelf. We had come up the east coast about sixty miles, until we hooked up; Babe sure hooted and hollered like a kid when one of those black marlins took that mackerel bait. But he was certainly up to the match of the catch, and drank two or three beers waiting for that big fish to surrender. He always had this unlit stogie in the corner of his mouth.

After a day's enjoyment, the tropical showers forced us to dock early at a waterfront beach hotel. Babe put us all up for the whole night, including a big steak and martini dinner, all at his expense. Of course, the excitement didn't stop there as Babe partied all night long, as usual. He had infinite energy.

While sitting on a lounge chair near the gulf's incoming tide, I noticed that the yacht was adrift. I could swim like a fish, especially in the salty water; it made a person float high. Anyway, I caught the yacht nearly two hundred yards out, crawled aboard over the side, and realized that I knew nothing about this size of boat. I yelled to see if anyone was aboard, but I was alone. I couldn't raise anyone that far out, so when I noticed a lever that read "anchor" I pushed it. Chains rattled out and the yacht was anchored.

I looked around the ship some, and I noticed a typewriter setting in the bedroom, with words already typed on the paper. It read like a storybook about a war, the First World War. Then I saw the writer's name…Ernest Hemmingway…I guess that was really him, all right…our skipper…imagine that!

I was startled when I heard the skipper summon aboard for a towrope. He had gotten a man to bring him to the yacht and was grateful to me for anchoring it. I kind of stood there in awe as he cranked the engine and we went back to shore. Ernest Hemmingway, a real war hero and writer! I couldn't believe my eyes!

Babe didn't come out until three o'clock in the afternoon, and then, because his stomach felt so queasy, he decided to take a cab back to the ballpark.

It was at this time, that I really got to know Mr. Hemmingway. He was interested in all the stories that I could tell, but when I told him of the whaler I'd once been aboard with Captain Abrams, he listened with utmost attention.

He said that he too loved the sea, as well as the great outdoors. We were two peas in a pod…we were adventurers!

Much later in Hemmingway's life, he authored a book entitled, "The Old Man and the Sea". It was my favorite.

The War to End All Wars!
(Chapter 31)

WWII was a shock! Pearl Harbor was bombed early one Sunday morning on December 7, 1941 and the Japanese joined the Germans ready to conquer the world. I was interviewed as a possible code translator. Uncle Sam pointed his finger at me, and said that he needed me. The army had Apache Indians sending code in their language around the world. Since I had been in the Secret Services, my name popped up on their list as an eligible supervisor.

The interviewer had my government records and seemed very uneasy as he reviewed it before me, then erased and laughed at the date of birth on the application that I had once filled out for the Department of Indian Affairs...February 16, 1720, it read. But I had made that up, because I was older than dirt then already...literally!

"Of course we know it's 1920," he chuckled.

Now I want to tell you that he started staring at me and asked me my age.

"I don't rightly know, maybe two hundred and fifteen," I told him. He thought that I was a kook and rejected me immediately. He had a real dissatisfied look upon his face. He must have suddenly realized that the Bureau of Indian Affairs had closed eighty years before!

I had that patriotic feeling to join up though, so I had to find another way to serve my country, another way; so I walked into a naval recruiting office and told them I wanted to ship out, and they gladly took me into the U.S. Navy!

My knowledge of the sea was outstanding, they said, and they asked me where I had learned everything and where I'd served?

I told them, "Whaling, in the south seas."

They couldn't stop laughing and said, "Good! That's just where you'll be heading too, ha, ha, ha whaling, ha ha, the only fish you'll see are German shark boats, and Japanese junks, ha ha ha!"…Apparently they were amused.

I was sent to basic training in North Carolina, and had to compete with the younger set. I felt young, so why not? After six weeks, I was called to Officers' Candidacy School for testing. To my surprise, I wasn't going right out to war; I was going back to school. I had already spent six years at Harvard. I wanted to go to battle, not to more schooling.

The horrible things that this Third Reich Hitler fella was doing needed to be nipped in the bud right away. My patriotism was burning high. But I didn't want to go back to school. Ever!

So, I deliberately and horribly failed those tests on purpose and soon found myself peeling potatoes in a mess hall. I guess I went too far on messing up on those tests. I was then transferred to a base near Belleville, Illinois, called Scott Field. My life was suddenly about to change…again.

My new assignment was to train to be a naval aircraft mechanic. I really didn't like all that grease, but if that's where Uncle Sam needed me, I was willing. The only thing was grease reminded me of bear grease, and an old Indian I once knew…eh, Red Cloud, how could I forget him? I was getting slower in thought and noticed some gray hairs in my sideburns just before the base's barber skinned me back good again…hummm. Did I need a capsule, I wondered? Not just yet. I had to hold out, til it got bad. I started thinking of how much my life was filled with adventures that just ran on and on, and how it would have been complete if I had found something for my dead wife Marietta. It was something…oh, so very, very long ago…I couldn't recall anymore…huh! I became troubled. It just seemed that I was getting up day after day, doing what I did the day before. I began to think too much, I guess, and finally realized that I was really, really old. I mean really, really, really, really old! But, here I was, living a life of a young man in the same old body, getting three squares a day, plus room and board and pay.

After I thought about it awhile, I perked up and decided to do something good with the rest of my allotted time. But I spent a lot of time with a wrench in my hand trying to remember my past.

"Get back to working'!" the tech sarge bellowed out to me.

I was in a daze thinking…again. We had lots of planes flying overhead, going here, going there; but here I was on a concrete pad in this big old Quonset hut building, learning the insides of a Merlin engine. The only good part was hearing that baby roar when it was tuned correctly. And I was getting pretty good at tuning them up just right.

There were all kinds of flights in and out of the base. But when a new F4U Corsair burnt rubber on the strip, I sat up and took notice…so did everyone else. It was the newest fighter to be employed. It was prettier than Betty Grable's legs…well almost.

There was a schedule for maintenance, but my eye was on that Corsair. I passed up the T-6 trainer and went straight to that F4U. The new plane sported a VFM-224 identification, so I knew some lucky Marine pilot was getting some pretty great wings. I wished it was me. This was the plane nobody knew much about, but they said it could fly over four hundred miles per hour and sported ten, fifty caliber guns that spit hell's fire. It could compete against the German Luftwaffe Messerschmitt, and flew much faster and better than the Japanese Zeros that raided Pearl. I sat in the cockpit and felt its greatness and the deadliness of her designs. I was in awe. The work order noted an engine oil leak, so I quickly repaired it. After all, I was a genuine aircraft mechanic! Imagine that!

When I learned my duty as an aircraft mechanic, I was in and out of all kinds of aircraft each and every day. Though our work was hurried, we never, ever, forgot to double check for safety. I especially liked it when the service called for work inside the cockpit and I imagined myself as an ace. It was great just sitting there behind the stick checking all the gauges and pushing all the pedals. I lived for the times I'd actually crank one over with the shot shell ignition starter exploding loud. Pow! It would pop and then the engine would either sputter a few turns, or kick off loudly, and belch black smoke. But when she caught, the horsepower was simply earth moving. I tuned them so well, that they usually only needed the first shell. I just loved it!

One day, a second-luey walked up to the bulletin board and posted a special notice. We all gathered around it to see its importance. It was important, because the Army Air Corps was soliciting a few men for training as new pilots. A pilot! A pilot! Boy was I excited. But my sarge said I'd never make it, I was too slow thinkin', he told me.

"Have you ever been in the air?" he pointed skyward. "You have to have good reflexes, depth perception, and better than twenty-twenty vision," he explained.

"I can try, can't I?" I replied.

I guess I'd been higher than any other human on Earth. Anyway, as high as Jesus…ha!

I looked around the field and spotted a T-6 trainer sitting between two B-25 Mitchell bombers.

"Now who left that sitting there?" I yelled above a screaming engine.

Here was my chance I thought, go for it! I ran across the tarmac and climbed into a T-6 Texas trainer. I cranked the engine and taxied her down to the hanger. Now I really wasn't supposed to do that and my sarge looked up very amused and frowned. I felt absolutely wonderful! I put my name on the list of potentials.

I was lying under a B-17, our flying fortress, adjusting and repairing a landing gear, when I was told to report to the colonel's office. The colonel was quick to point out my previous scores and how important my job as a mechanic was to the service. But, reluctantly he would sign my request for flight school, if I were so inclined; I was so inclined.

Two weeks later, after they tested me on all my mental and physical abilities, the colonel called me in again and gave me the good news. I was in! But, he was curious as to how I scored so very high, the best at Scott, when my previous scores were unquestionably so low? I smiled and told him it was his influence that encouraged me. He smiled sheepishly, and then gave me my flight school enrollment assignment.

On my very first flight aboard a T-6 Texas trainer, I was sitting up front and feeling all alone, although a real piloting captain had the controls behind me. The long slender canopy glistened in the morning's sun, and the scene below was breathtaking. I wondered if Orville and Wilbur would have believed what they'd done. Hummm.

The captain asked me to try to identify all the controls, and I did. He asked me so many questions about the plane's functions that I didn't have time to notice that I was seven thousand feet up in the air. He told me that I was very good.

Then he calmly said, "Let's see how you handle this bird." He then released the controls to me. I jerked too hard and the plane tilted and then slipped to the right. He said, "Let go!" And the forgiveness of this trainer was unbelievable, as it righted itself without my help. I found the feel of the little plane quickly and began to wait anxiously for my next time to fly. I advanced quickly, and soon found that I was flying faster and more complicated birds that maneuvered in any pattern that I demanded. I buzzed the mechanic's barn real low one day in a Corsair, and I saw ol' sarge shaking his wrench at me…he, he.

On a cool day in May 1941, standing in a line of forty-six men, I was pinned with the wings of a pilot. I considered this to be the most satisfying accomplishment in my entire life. But in reality, I had flown a jet, long before they were invented here on Earth.

Just before I was about to ship out toward the Philippine Islands and Clark Air Base, a new plane flew into our base. It was the Curtiss P-40E Warhawk, better known as the bird of the U.S. Marines' Flying Tigers. It had the painted face of a shark with big terrifying white teeth and had become a work-horse bomb dropper. I had the opportunity to shuttle-fly the bird to Lackland Air Base, in El Paso, Texas.

As I eased back on the throttle to make my approach, because we were stacked up slightly and it was my turn to land there, an enormous bird they called a sand crane, flew up into my path and was devoured by my propeller. Splat!

That new plane not only had a slightly looking red-tinged color, but it had a large dent with feathers. It gave it character, I thought. Ha, before I left, somebody else apparently thought it did too. They had painted the prop's nose cone's spinner bright red! It really looked good, and became the standard…without the dent, of course!

I dropped my wheels and hit the tarmac with a slightest squeal of rubber, then taxied to my directed zone with my guns pointing away from the main office buildings. They told me this was necessary, so if by chance a burst of machine gun fire accidentally erupted from the fifties, it didn't hit the commander's office…I guess it might have happened before, ha.

But, off to my left was an astonishing sight. It was an aircraft made up of just one big wing with engines. No tail, no fuselage, simply futuristic, or was it? I then had a flashback, like I'd been having for some time. I suddenly had visions for a few moments of an upright, wingless rocket, just standing alone upon a deserted sandy field's pad, and again seeing a very similar craft, inside a deep hole of a volcano, but it was smaller and had one rocket engine…now I remember it…think.

This passing vision must have been caused by the changes of altitude I surmised. I dismissed it. The wingless wonder standing alone here turned out to be an experimental Northrop YB-49, with eight gigantic engines.

I presented the plane's transfer orders to the commander there; he in return gave me orders to return to Scott Field. I was getting impatient and wanted to get into the fight. But orders were orders, so I hooked a ride back to Scott with a B-25. It was loud, shook like the dickens, but the B-25 crew told me that it was a lethal adversary. Give me a break, I thought. I liked the thought of a one on one combat. There were five seats in this baby buggy.

I arrived at Scott and hustled aboard a big B-17, combat assigned bird, headed to Midway Island. Now that's what I wanted to hear!

We flew all the way, nonstop, for sixteen hours, and touched down with the grace of a big swan. That whole trip was filled with whirling thoughts and visions of words being spoken to me from a far away world, but only inside my brain. I looked for a speaker, but there was none. I was very intimidated as if a clairvoyant from the past was contacting me. The navigator looked strangely at me and asked if I was having nightmares. I assured him I was not. But I really couldn't say why I behaved that way.

I hastened to the flight commander's office to report. There was reconstruction going on all over, as they were still rebuilding from the attacks of the Japanese back in December.

The commander took my orders and welcomed me to the island. As it turned out, without training, I was assigned to the U.S.S. Hornet, a huge flattop carrier. I was also shanghaied, and assigned to the Marines, who had lost every fighter plane at Ewa, on the Hawaiian chain. Well, I did it. I had been involved with every fighting armed force of the U.S. in less than six months…Imagine that.

Aboard the Hornet, the ship's Captain Mitscher addressed us. He was happy to greet us and he knew that some of us had never been aboard a ship before, and told us, "Even a few of you haven't hit the deck of a carrier with your plane yet, but all that will come easily with practice. You have two full days to get it right!" Everyone laughed. The captain then spoke a serious message that quelled the whole assembly.

"Seriously, gentlemen, our homeland has been attacked," he continued. "And it will be up to you to curb the hostilities of the German and Japanese squadrons that attack our fleets, and you must prevent them from further penetration into our homeland boundaries."

The message lasted for quite some time as he explained our mission and goals. It was simple, kill them Japs and Krauts and let them know that we Americans are not to be trespassed upon! I was fired up! God bless America! Let's go get 'em!

Now it seems all that time that I spent on the rolling deck of that whaler turned out to be very beneficial. Landing my airship on deck was like looking down from that crow's nest and trying to spit on the boson…. it was all in good timing. I did it best.

But sometimes we were waved off and had to "goose it" back into the air. You just prayed that your mechanic had kept your engine in tiptop performance. I had a step up, as a genuine aircraft mechanic; I knew my kitten's purr. I pampered my Merlin engine like my life depended upon it, of course it did. But, I was able to "soup it up". I made adjustments, not written in the manual, which allowed me to stand my bird on end in the air, barrel roll and from near stall speed come down spittin' fire and hell. That was quite a feat in those days. I named my ride Nova. Why, I did not know?

I hoped to see action and wanted to become an ace. An ace was a pilot who verifiably shot down at least fifteen enemy fighters. Upon our ship, was a combination of put-together squadrons replacing several badly hit ones. Within our squadron, we had several veteran pilots who wore the distinction of an ace. Greg "Pappy" Boyington, Charles "Shooter" Kunz, and Robert Murry Hanson, the best of the best, I wanted to be just like them.

The theater heated up and we were called to "scramble alert", but that was practice. We cruised towards the Philippines, which had been annexed by the Japanese now. I got my first real action in a brief "dogfight" with several "Nips" off the coast. They were suspect pilots, as we were able to come in above them for a quick and permanent kill. Four zeros destroyed. I was not fortunate enough to have that Japanese flag emblem put on my plane that day, but my squadron performed well, and most importantly, we all came back.

Each and every night, or each hour of standby, my mind tried to reach back to a time that I could not quite recall. Sometimes I had thoughts of horrible volcanic eruptions, the smell of sulfur, and smoke filled air. I knew not from where those thoughts came. I became troubled and the thoughts began to destroy my thinking apparatus as we went on sorties. And that was dangerous for not only me, but also my fellow pilots.

The F4U and F4F Corsairs that we flew at first, in our FVM-23 squadron, had problems with aircraft carrier duty, so they were returned to duty with the Marine land units and bombing. To our surprise, the next planes in September to land on our deck were revamped Corsairs that were considerably improved in landing performance.

I designed a holster of sorts that could hold my North Star, and kept her "charged" for action, in case I went down in enemy territory. I hadn't used it for a decade or so, I guess. Compared to the issued 45 colt automatic, it was so much lighter, smaller and it looked like a toy. And when one of the men saw her hanging inside the cockpit one day, I told him that it was my "good luck piece", which every guy seemed to have. He laughed and actually picked it up.

I screamed bloody murder at him, afraid he'd pull the trigger and sink our ship; it had that kind of power. I never contemplated using it against the enemy…only if one day I had no choice.

Besides, our birds dominated the airspace above the Philippines, where I got my first zero. I felt sick to my stomach afterwards, even though he, the bringer of death to me, opened fire first and came from a cloud. I choose not to discuss the death of another human, for that was not the way of life on Mars. But, here on Earth, it was necessary to maintain the freedoms that even on Mars would have brought to violence the thought of loosing them. In this case, it was the right thing to do. He was my first emblem flag. But that occurrence became all too familiar as it was repeated too many times. Days became hazy and one ran into the other, as I met myself coming on my way out.

I eventually had my third combat tour and was scheduled to return to the Z.I. for staff duty. I wasn't going. I began to realize that there were times in my long life that I took a hiatus from the conscience living, and entered into a hypnotic state of being. Where I went to, I didn't quite understand? I always returned full of youthful life and exuberance. It was beginning to be clear to me now as my body was speaking to me from afar…rest! I could see the beginning and the end. My whole long life had been a continuous adventure, repeated time and again, as the world that I knew revolved, day by day, year by year, century by century, and I lived through it all.

I was a king that had now moved into "checkmate". It was nothing more, or nothing less. The year of renewal was 1945, and my subscription was used up. A great relief overcame my body, as I slid into the cock- pit for the last time. Part of my body didn't want to go, but my mind told me this was the hour. I was very tired, I felt very old, and I would now be renewed. History had run its course for me, as scheduled, to be born again at a later time.

The deck leader signaled for me to fire my engine. I completed my check, and then did. When the men had pushed me into launch position, all was go. But just as I brought my Merlin to a high pitch, the signalman waved me to shut down. There was a visible oil leak. It happened quite frequently, due to this procedure of revving up the engine with the brakes held. I was shut down and had time to get some java. My whole career was about to change.

A bomber pilot was aboard whom we suspected was here on a top-secret mission. He was in the ship's cafeteria seated, reading a Chicago paper. We were alone, so I asked if I could share the paper that he had already read. His name was Captain Paul Tibbits.

"Hello, Captain, my name is Lieutenant Dargod," I greeted. He shook my hand and there was idle talk of the theater heating up. He was not flying from our deck, but wore many current medals of the war. His face was grim. He seemed to be facing a big decision, as I sensed that he actually withheld his validity here, and wasn't free to tell.

The talk changed to our families and he spoke quickly of his. The war had taken him away from them, as all of us had been, he said, but his life was also held secret from them. It troubled him. He spoke of his mother who lived on every word of his letters, but now he wasn't even permitted to write his family. His mother's name was Nola Gay, a name that hauntingly came to me from the past. That ship that brought twelve men from Mars to Earth. I then remembered…. amazing!

I told him of Marietta and her death from fever. He said that he was sorry, but when I inadvertently said, "That's okay, she'll come back someday," he suspected that I suffered from flying fatigue.

It was the Chicago papers' "Believe It or Not" article that then excited my soul. It seems a man in Miami, Florida had been bitten twenty-seven times by the red coral snake and didn't suffer any complications from the snake's venom at all. People before had all died, almost within the minute, when known to have received the venomous bite. There was a picture. The snake was ringed red, and then black with thin yellow dividing rings.

Its beady eyes were piercingly devilish. Its nose had pits and a flashing forked tongue. It was the prettiest snake I had ever seen! "Yippee!" I yelled.

I had to gather my emotions. I started breathing rapidly, wanting to again scream, but I then swallowed my java down my windpipe, and spit it out upon the Captain. I was horrified! But when Paul looked at my face, he must have known something had excited me so.

As I quickly moved to wipe him off, he said, "That's okay, Lieutenant, that same thing might happen to me soon." I did not know at that time that this man would have the burden placed upon his shoulders of dropping an atomic bomb onto one of Japan's largest cities from his B-29. Millions would die, but it would end the war. It must have weighed very heavily upon his mind that day. But he didn't know that he wasn't quite through with me as yet.

My spirits were suddenly renewed, like a big jolt of adrenaline, as life again with Marietta suddenly took on hope. I feared of the condemnation that would be directed toward me soon from the act that I must now do next.

Reviving my Marietta took precedence even over my sworn duty, and that made my heart ache in my indecision. I longed for my Marietta and she had waited far too long. I believed that now I could fire up the tube to Nova and return to my parents with Marietta by my side. They too were in a state of suspension, as my mind became suddenly more and more restored. It wasn't for selfish greed that I planned my exit, but the thoughts of the Earth's future, and what great deeds my father Dr. Dargod could perform here on Earth. I had a higher calling.

The loud speaker's announcement was for Lieutenant Dargod to report to the flight deck. I was refueled and ready to go again. The deck leader signaled for the men to push me into position. I applied Nova's brakes, and the Merlin pitched her high tone. The flag dropped and when I released the brakes I was off the deck and airborne.

This sortie would be search and destroy whatever I could, since my squad had already left me behind headed near the islands of the Philippines.

My Nova seemed to have it all this day, as I checked my gauges and allowed the drift to send me towards Mid Way, for this gas-guzzler wouldn't take me where my heart now directed me. But, if I shed some heavy ammo aboard, I would extend the flight somewhat, and coming into Mid Way they'd think that I had spent my ammo on combat and I was returning for replenishing. There were so many comings and goings; nobody actually would ever suspect anything; and then a shot at Florida's shore and that red coral snake.

I was headed away from the action, I thought, so I held the fifties down and watched the small explosions of perfectly uniform splatters hit before me upon the water, until Nova rose up from the emptiness in her belly. She was empty. I picked up ten miles per hour in speed from the unloading of my heavy ammunitions.

My mind seemed to be somewhat refreshed, as I began to go over in my mind of what I needed to do. I jerked suddenly, when I thought I might have forgotten the North Star, but upon a quick check, it was in my pack. Whew! I placed it before me inside its homemade holster and hung it in the sunlight to charge.

I guess I was so engrossed in my thoughts of finding that snake that I didn't recognize that I had fallen several thousand feet from the clouds, and into the middle of an entire Japanese air force squadron. There were more zeros here than on the check that the jeweler in St. Louie had given me for the gold. I was surrounded.

Oh, oh, now what? I was so close to this one zero, that I could see the pilot's wide-eyed stare, like he'd just seen the grim reaper in person. I could actually see little American flags on his plane's side that he claimed to have shot down, just as we did for them. He was an ace too. I never looked at it that way before…that I was the enemy…hummm. Behind me was another Zero, whose pilot hesitated to shoot me because he might hit several of his own.

When I noticed him, it was too late. This dumb Jap pilot gave out a distress call that actually came over my own radio.

"Tora, tora, tora!" he screamed out.

Then everyone looked at me. I felt like a coon that had gotten caught in one of my traps, right before I shot him in the head. Oh, Dargod, give me wisdom. As if it was his answer, North Star's brilliance sparkled in my eyes and I knew I was now a match for them all, though my craft was empty of ammunition.

I'd have to get to 'em one on one…nah…too dangerous. I eased the canopy back, felt the strong wind in my face, stood up like the Statue of Liberty, and began a steady Zap! Zap! Zap! Zap! Zap! Zap! Every Zero fell screaming into the sea, most exploded upon contact with North Star's beam, but if I moved too quickly, sometimes I only cut their tails or wings off, and missed the gas tanks and engines. I really learned to shoot that day, but somehow I felt troubled inside afterward.

Well, I choose not to talk about causing the death of another human, but ol' Hero Hereto', or whoever the Emperor of Japan was then, just lost a whole fleet of planes. I gave a good-bye salute to the whole group, did a couple of victorious barrel rolls and continued on to Mid Way. Now I asked myself, how would forty, fifty or even sixty little Japanese flags fit and look on my Nova?…Nah! That would be bragging about taking human lives.

My mind had cleared and so did the clouds, as I caught a glimpse of Mid Way. Were they all going back to attack Mid Way by surprise? Hummm, I wondered.

On my approach, I was waved off, as when there was a signal for being under attack. I caught the frequency to Mid Way and listened to the chatter. When I broke in with my call letters and asked for immediate emergency landing, they asked me if I'd seen a flock of Japs out back where I'd just come from, because the base was on alert and its gunners on standby.

I said, "Yep, up close and personal like. They took one good look at how ugly I am and turned around and high-tailed it back from where they came! Of course, I had to shoot down a couple first!"

"Come on in, report to the commandant."

"Okay, fellas, but get me refueled quickly, cause I can't stay long, I have a hot date with my lady."

All that I could tell the commandant was that I shot them all down by myself and he'd have no more trouble today. And, since I wanted to be called an ace, I asked him where I was going to put all those Jap flags on my plane? He looked at me as if I were nuts. But since I wasn't under his command, he wanted to get rid of me, fast. I went for that. He released me just before reconnaissance had begun calling in massive parts and pieces of Japanese zeros that were scattered, and floating all over in the waters, just fifteen miles off the west of Mid Way. I took off as quickly as I could. I continued toward the states and didn't answer to Mid Way's demand that I immediately return to the base and see the commandant again. I think he finally had figured it out…ha.

I had decided to go AWOL, but I just couldn't do it, I couldn't, it was my country being attacked, and they needed me. I asked Dargod to give me guidance and I quickly thought of my next move.

I swung around and returned to Mid Way's airstrip, and hoped the base commander would embrace my new ideas, as I set my bird back down. Many uniformed people ran to my station to congratulate me for my efforts; I thanked them and headed to the Commandant's office, pronto. And lo' and behold, as if Dargod had conjured up this meeting himself, there was Captain Tibbits awaiting my return. How could anyone have known my secret plans? I knew this was pre-planned by someone I held dear to my heart.

After much ado about my display of awesome pilotry against the Japanese squadrons, Tibbets requested me personally, through proper channels, to be one of his escorts on his secret mission. And as if he had major powers in his decision, I was quickly added to the "unattached secret mission", and advised of our destination.

I wasn't coming back home, they told me, for there wasn't enough fuel to get me home. It was an assignment beyond the call of duty and I would receive the Congressional Medal of Honor, posthumously. I accepted my last assignment willingly for my country.

Just hours before our mission was to begin, I noticed that my plane had been fitted with extra-large, drop-off reserve fuel tanks, capable of getting me to my assignment, but I was informed that it was not enough fuel to get me back home.

What occurred during my sortie towards Japan, while leading the Nola Gay in flight, was top secret. But I can tell you that just off the coast of Nagasaki, when I learned the big doors of Tibbits' plane would not open, and our mission was in dire straights of being scrubbed; I asked permission from Tibbits to perform a feat only my equipment could do and that was to cut the bolts off those big bay doors with careful aim from North Star, which quickly allowed those huge bomb bay doors to fall free of the plane, so that Tibbits could complete his target's mission. I dare not miss, because that bomb was just inches away. I took aim and the rest is history.

North Star helped to complete our mission's assignment, and I was released from duty, and bid farewell for a "job well done", just before the Nola Gay slowly banked away to begin her run. Even though I was many miles away, that sudden burst of energy, which was emitted from that blast, sent cold chills down my spine. I was advised not to look at the resulting plume, because I might be blinded, but I did anyway; it reminded me of the moments before I had left Mars. I rode out the air turbulence and continued back west feeling sick to my stomach. It was a horrible sight.

I never knew how far this ride would take me, but I would seek out my way, wherever my plane would run out of fuel, as I now had completed my duty to my country with honor. All I could think of then was how I was going to capture the venom of that red coral snake.

This was the beginning of an all-new adventure, and I was prepared to make the trip, for if there was a need and the opportunity, I would take a capsule and rest, wherever I might become marooned. Eventually, I knew that I could regain my position and renew my search, for nothing on this Earth could stop the powers of Dargod. I must succeed.

I smiled, only to my own audition, as I thought of my Marietta awakening to once again kiss me and hold me closely. That was all I needed to sustain my desire to live on.

I hesitated to guess my previous fate. What if I had gotten off the east side of that big muddy river, which would have lead me straight to Florida's swamp, the snake's home? I had experienced many adventures, and many faces I had met, simply because of this quirk of fate. This world was now my world, and I wanted even more for her. I wanted to give this Earth my own wonderful father, who could give them hope eternal.

My father would be very impressed with my knowledge of this planet, and most of all, I suppose, he would be very proud that his son had graduated from Harvard…. imagine all that! THE END OF THE BEGINNING.

ZAP!
PWK
'NORTH STAR'

The Power of Dargod
(Final Chapter)

It was August 6th, 1945, early in the morning, when that sudden flash of bright-white heat blinded me, as it lit up the heavens in every imaginable direction; the lift I demanded and desperately needed to escape from it all, strained the big Merlin engine, which was pulling my escort fighter plane up, up and away. It was powerful, but so was the turbulence and lift from the aftershock of that enormous mushrooming explosion, which resulted into one huge, billowing and towering, gigantic plume of Earth's matter, which was now being spewed up high into the heavens and refused to descend peacefully back down upon Nagasaki. Our sorte mission was done.

One quick glance and I saw everything that my father, Dr. Dargod had said was unacceptable in human life; the death of anyone, much less the horrible roasting of the multitudes below was sufficient to make me puke; I soiled my cockpit. But I knew this act was meant to save millions more who were the very same people that had become his followers. Surely, Dargod would understand, I hoped.

I immediately noticed that all of my plane's electronics had suddenly quit working, including my compass, radio, and most importantly, the altimeter and fuel gauges. I was flying blind, relying on my own natural abilities in this bird, in an unknown direction without a designated destination, for there really were no plans for my return. All that I could do to control her was to brace my knees against the stick and hold on tight!

The actual warmth that was building up inside my cockpit had developed from the expended heat of that explosion and now surrounded me in my place; it actually dried the mess I had spewed out inside against the closed port window of my airship. The heat made me uncomfortable, but may have served another purpose.

North Star was dangling in a leather holster, attached above the firewall and may have gotten an overload, if that was possible, from that radiation emitted from the blast that might have simulated the sun's light bursts of a thousand years. I was worried she may have suffered irreversible damage, as did my plane's instruments. Upon touching its handle, North Star was very warm, but I couldn't ignite her inside this cockpit to check her, for that certainly would be my last day on Earth.

I was stupid enough to have looked upon that blast I told myself after I had been warned, for my eyes were showing white blotches and tainted the center of my vision. I couldn't focus well now and the horizon was reaching out as far as the human eye could see upon an empty sea. I just had to hope Dargod had not left me for my deed and was with me still. Was it His doing that the big doors jammed? He controlled all, I believed, so it must have been in His plan for me to remove the bolts with North Star to allow the horrible to happen.

I sat back in my seat, unbuckled my restraints and eased the canopy rearward to get some fresh air inside. My eyes immediately began to burn and I quickly closed it back. It didn't matter, I thought, this surely was the beginning of my demise and it must have been in the design of my father's plans. I sat listening to myself ponder my next move.

The sudden appearance of small clouds below me, and how high I must be above them now, caused me to think I was well above my ten thousand feet limit. I should have begun to breathe desperately for oxygen, but that didn't happen. I blinked my eyes a hundred times to clear the tainted obstruction, but could not. Though those clouds were sporadic, the clouds seemed to be getting smaller and smaller, and without the altimeter's assistance, I thought I was flying way too high. I eased my throttle back some and felt the immediate descent.

When my engine sputtered, I switched the reserve fuel tanks that had been attached to the outer wing surfaces to give me added flying distance, and dropped the empty one. Before I had assisted the Nola Gay, I had noticed that my gauges read that I had three quarters of a tank, plus one reserve left. The motor used the spares up first.

I was suddenly amazed that my blurry eyes saw the empty tank's splash into the ocean. Had my fuzzy eyesight deceived me with damaged depth perception? I sent some fifty-caliber rounds out into the open and saw the hits that simultaneously splashed up before me on the horizon of the water's surface below, not very far out. I then realized that those clouds weren't clouds at all, but they were tiny islands, which filled the Pacific Ocean's wide span; most of them were un-chartered and very few were occupied.

I eased back the stick to rise up, just in time to miss colliding with the tall greenery of mountaintop trees, which I hadn't even noticed before me. It was then that my fear began, as I assumed I was about to crash…somewhere. Suddenly before me was a high plateau opening that I thought would offer a place to land, even haphazardly, if I could just judge the distances. So, I quickly slid back the canopy to get a better vision than through that stained, puke-hardened port side.

I swooped in, and landed in tall green grasses that appeared to be as thick as a small bamboo forest. I was shocked to discover as I entered the field that it really was a bamboo forest; I was skimming the tops of trees and I was doomed to crash.

I pulled back hard upon the stick, but the Merlin's propeller already was sputtering as it began chopping off the upper limbs. I didn't have enough lift, so I just held on and closed my eyes, until I felt a sudden jolt. Then everything quickly turned upside down, including my derriere. I had forgotten to rebuckle my restraints and I was catapulted up high, flying head-over-heels out from my open cockpit and above the wooded forest at a landing plane's fast pace. The treetops slapped my rear like I was getting a real whoopin'.

It all happened in an instant; my body's flight was terrifying, especially when I saw the plateaus' end nearing and I was flying right over its top, clawing at the air frantically to hold my upright position. Suddenly, I was in mid-air, hundreds of feet out above the surface of the blue Pacific again, and falling. I thankfully had jerked my parachute cord, which didn't open fully until it landed on top of me, but it had slowed me up enough to stay firm and upright when I hit that water. Splash!

I struggled to unharness, and finally shook it lose. The wet silks had bubbled up upon the surf and I found air in its opening, as I hadn't gone below the surface very far and bopped up quickly with my vest's buoyancy. Oh, what a ride! Thank you, Dargod, because I realized many intricate things had to have happened to allow me to go through this nightmarish happening without so much as a scratch on my behind. Not!

A gash upon my leg was tainting the water around me with a pinkish hue of blood. I had never encountered a shark before, but suddenly there was a hard smack across my back. I struggled to grab up the entire wet parachute into my arms to get between it and the shark. I was completely surprised when that big shark suddenly succumbed and lay still. He was now floating aimlessly upon the top of the surf. Maybe the potion's mixture in my bloodstream killed that shark, or had he hit me so hard that he knocked himself out? My eyes were still blurry and burned from the salt water. I barely could see the isle on which I had crashed; it was just two hundred yards away.

Without further complications, or sharks, the surf's surges shoved me quickly onto the beach and I lay there exhausted, and very thankful. Soon, that shark's body slid up onto shore near me and he looked untouched, but very dead. I couldn't understand it at all.

I rose up from the sand and crawled over to the shark. He looked healthy and I had been advised in training that he might be good to eat as my next meal, so I slid the hundred pounds, six foot fish up farther onto the beach and sat back down to get my bearings. It was then that I saw the tall precipice from which I had fallen, and its height. It must have been over five hundred feet high, or higher, I just couldn't tell.

The drone of a B-29 is hard to disguise and I knew the sound. As I rolled over upon the sand and looked skyward, I could barely see what I knew was the Nola Gay. She had made it and was pointed towards home, Midway Island, I imagined, for I never knew her return route. I raised up to wave my arms, but it was useless for she was over ten thousand feet high; even my North Star might not have summoned her attention that high.

I then realized North Star was missing, possibly still where I tied it firmly to my plane's canopy brace, if it hadn't perished in a fire or lodged up in a tree. I hadn't stuck around long enough to see anything happen. I only had my forty-five with one clip of seven rounds that was still strapped firmly upon my belt. I flopped back down, glad for the airmen on the Nola Gay and closed my eyes. I was strictly on my own.

Peculiar things happen in the Pacific. Voodoo, weird cults and pygmies occupy the most unattainable, uncharted isles, but still are alive with inhabitants. I learned about that from Benjamin of Tudela back in the seventeen hundreds, I think it was.

So, I wasn't prepared to welcome some frantically waving inhabitants who were making noises like little grunts and now advancing toward me; my eyes again deceived me. These were the same type pygmies that dwelled in Africa's dark jungles. Those weren't arms that they were waving; it was their spears with small shrunken heads atop them...I was their prey now, I guess.

The horde swooped in upon me quickly; I didn't have time to defend myself. I suddenly was raised three feet into the air, still in my prone position and being carried by at least ten little men. They gibbered and jabbered in a language of grunts, but they never stuck me with anything sharp.

After a short horizontal ride into the bush, I was laid softly down upon some palm leaves and several bare breasted women surrounded me and placed flowers in my hair. One woman had removed my leather pilot's cap and was admiring it closely, then replaced it backwards upon my head with flowers attached.

They seemed friendly, but I didn't know if they were sincere, or if they were just decorating me up for their big pot. I watched them as they raised their arms, I guess, to illustrate how tall I was. I became confused, as my eyes were still cloudy, but better.

The decorations of large plumed feathers around his head suggested that he was their chief; everyone bowed before him and remained until he passed. He was slightly taller than the rest, and his smile was something more than I expected, but when he spoke out to me by using my name, I was unavoidably shocked…it was my old roommate from Harvard, Dick Clarkson!

"Well, Mr. Dargod, fancy meeting you here!"

He raised me up and placed his hand upon my head and squealed out some gibberish, which sounded quite like his followers used.

"Now kneel down and pretend you understand," he instructed.

"Gimbo, gambo, gumbo, bulla bulla bango!" He then tapped me lightly upon my noggin with his long stick he used for a scepter.

He then gibberished to his apparent followers and they exploded in delight.

"I told them you're my big brother," he whispered.

Dick took my arm and led me to a hut that was braced up upon palm tree stilts, high above similar others, and we ascended the wooden stairway arm-in-arm, until he closed the thatched door behind us. The gathering behind us was jumping and hooting and their grunts became little giggles.

"Well, ol' buddy, it's good to see another white man…how'd you end up here like me?" He didn't stop there.

"I was the unfortunate recipient of the U.S. government's 'greetings' to draft me into the First World War. You know that's against everything Dr. Dargod taught us, so I had to have a way to skedaddle. I boarded a ship to Australia, but a U-boat's torpedo hit it. When the ship sank, I nearly died while trying to hang onto little debris and floated for weeks, until I finally washed up ashore here. Luckily, I had my laser to zap fish…it cooked them right where they swam. Where's yours?"

"I hope it's still up top on that mountain, I crashed my fighter up there. I was in the Second World War…I was a pilot that escorted Paul Tibbits."

"Who's he?"

"He's the pilot that just dropped the atomic bomb on Japan. They attacked us at Pearl Harbor."

"You mean there was killing and you took part in that?"

"Unfortunately, yes, I was partly responsible for thousands dying in a terrible blast; the first big bomb of its kind."

Then a pleasant looking little woman came into the hut and Dick said it was his maid. She stared at me, and then spoke.

"Mobo holly bamma!" she spoke.

"Dolly com, dolly com," Dick told her and she then bowed down before me and stepped back outside keeping her head very low. It was kind of a power surge thing.

"What did she say?"

"She said that you fell from the sky."

"Oh, she had that right; right over the cliff and into the deep blue sea."

"That's perfect! Everything here, of any value that is, or of great importance, comes from the sea, including me. They accidentally caught me up in their fishing nets and they still believe I'm someone special; a god maybe. So don't do anything stupid to ruin this gig, it's a real swell to be treated like their king, okay, ol' buddy? You'll find out very quickly because as there are always lots of things floating up here on shore. Make sure it isn't you."

With a clap of Dick's hands several little people came into the hut bearing baskets of fresh fruit, raw fish and fruity alcoholic drinks. I didn't realize at the time how unusual alcoholic beverages being served here was, until later. I just took only a banana and then suddenly thought of Jamaica and Marietta, my dead wife. I asked Dick to tell me all that he knew about during his walk upon this Earth, but after many hours, when I asked him, he said he had never run into a red coral snake.

"I think it's supposed to live in Florida, inside the swamps. It's the key to eternal life in Earthlings and can actually raise the dead to living. Alone, its venom kills almost instantly; I don't know about us Martians. Its venom is the ingredient necessary, when combined with AlovectorP23 and injected. Gosh, I'm glad to see you again," I suddenly added.

"Well, the last time I saw you, you were too stuck up to date my former wife."

"Your wife," I asked? "I thought you wanted me to date her roommate, or friend."

"Yeah, big guy, if you had taken that date, that woman might have been your misery, instead of mine. She took me for all I had in divorce court."

"I was already married and I couldn't tell you then. My Marietta died a beautiful, kind, and wonderful woman. I buried her inside a mountain vault in Jamaica, just until I can find that red coral snake venom cure for death. I found the answer, inscribed by one of our own in a cave, deep in the jungle of darkest Africa, but not the red coral snake."

"Sounds like you've been around."

The hours passed by and we told our own happenings throughout the past two thousand years.

"By the way, do you know what Martian year it is exactly? Our onboard clock short-circuited and stopped before we landed," I explained.

"No, I hate to keep track of time. I take one of those capsules and within hours I'm rejuvenated."

"A couple of hours?" I questioned him.

"Yes, is that so different than you taking yours?"

"I have been in the sleep mode sometimes hundreds of years."

"Hummm...do you just take one AloevectorP25?"

"No, it's marked AloevectorP23."

"Dr. Dargod must have issued several different varieties, amazing...hundreds of years, you say?" He was theorizing to himself.

"Didn't it ever dawn on you that Dr. Dargod was my own father?"

He just stood there dumbfounded and somewhat upset at himself.

Then he said, "Yeah, sort of..." and he lingered at the thought. "Do you have the power?"

I wasn't certain which power he meant, the power of the mind, or the power of North Star. I shook my head no, and left it at that.

While discussing my father's accomplishments as a scientist elect, I discovered that my father had given me many more capsules than Clarkson's ship had gotten, and apparently, each had its own benefits. I believe mine lasted longer, but required a longer rest, while Clarkson's lasted just a century, or so, but revived him in only hours...amazing.

Life on this isle reminded me every day of missing Marietta. The yearning in my heart for Marietta was growing deeper, as the island constantly reminded me of her every waking morn, and somehow, I had to find a way back to civilization.

Here, the little people were kind and respectful, but always delaying me wherever I roamed and followed me like children. Finally one afternoon, I asked Dick how to get to the top of the mountain. He said that he had never tried, nor liked heights; therefore I'd have to search for myself. The tropical foliage was very tangled and thick and probably held many unknown animals waiting to take a bite out of us, he added.

After many months of just lying around being waited upon hand and foot by the female natives, and enjoying it all, my eyesight had become fully restored. I could see the little people well then, and they weren't exactly like the little African people that wanted to kill me. Dick looked remarkably different too; younger looking than I first thought and he wore his long brown hair in a ponytail with a freshly picked flower in it every day.

We had our daily discussions about our gained Earth's knowledge. Time passed by quickly, as one would expect with everything we needed brought to us on trays and there wasn't a care in the world lying around upon the warm sands of this treasured isle for almost a full year.

Sometimes we found ourselves divulging the secrets we discovered about Earthling women. When it got steamy hot one afternoon, Dick asked if I wanted to walk in the surf to cool off. I had told him of my beautiful Marietta and her beautiful figure, her warm smile and loving ways; the kind of woman most men could only dream about, but had been mine and would be again, someday. I wanted that someday to be soon.

That cooling surf sounded like a winner and we found ourselves enjoying the pleasant dip, until I noticed debris floating almost a mile out in the ocean. I remembered the shark that hit me when I first arrived and decided to see if the little people had boats…yes, they had very little boats, too little for me, I guessed.

Dick pointed out to them the floating debris, "Gobo, gobo!"

They immediately brought out their little boats from under palm leaves that were hidden from view and began to dance a little ritual upon the beach, before they got into their boats and paddled out after the targeted debris with a singing, chanting rhythm, which sounded very good to Dick and me too.

"You know," Dick began. "I really like the way those little happy fellas dance and sing…it makes me very happy, especially when the whole tribe gets together to dance after I take the laser with me out into the edge of the forest by myself…that's my biggest power to them…and come back with a pig to roast. It's not hard to get one and I only have to go a little ways. But, I think I depleted too much of the stock, because there aren't as many as twenty years ago. It all gives me ideas for running a night club or something, in maybe New York…or if I ever get back to the states, Boston." He began to dream.

"They've got it, but I don't think they can pull it in…it must be too big, cause here comes a boat back now," Dick advised.

I struggled to keep upright, but I just borrowed their boat anyway and used it as one would a small kayak. I zipped through the water quickly, as the waves that crashed over me didn't matter much to this tiny vessel, and it was really fun. I was doing super.

I didn't know what the thing was from afar, but as I got closer that "thing" bobbing around in the water was a huge wooden crate, wrapped in a green canvas, and was being shipped from California, USA, and marked for delivery in Europe, or somewhere; the labels were all wet and faded. It must have fallen off a ship, or something.

There was a rope tied around the whole thing, and after I was able to untie the knots, I linked them together. But, there wasn't a place to tie the rope onto, until one smart little guy sunk his spear deep into the wood and quickly tied the rope to it. Smart thinking!

It took six hours of cannibalistic grunting and rowing together to get it close enough so that the island's undertow could draw the big wooden crate into its surge, and suddenly it started moving on its own and came crashing upon the shore. The big crate itself would make an excellent home for one of the tribesmen, but we didn't have the slightest idea what those painted-up, pointed boards were good for, "Do you, Dick?" I asked.

"No, but they'd make a dandy fence around our hut by just sticking them all up on end together in the sand, or maybe a roof…but look…they float, and look what that little guy is doing out there with that blue one!"

There on the water was this little guy standing with his spear looking remarkably impressive as he stood floating upon the board, balancing himself with his weapon, and then he suddenly speared a fish for his lunch. Then he quickly did it again, and again.

The people saw him and soon all hundred and sixty-two boards were being paddled out into the surf and everyone was spearing their dinner…it was a beautiful sight with all those colors bouncing up and down on top of the waves, and everyone was having lots of fun as I could hear their little giggles.

"Now, they're going to think you had something 'powerful' to do with this, remember I told you about how everything good comes from the sea, so what should I tell them you brought them from the sea gods to make you their true friend?"

"I don't know…they're boards that float in the surf, I guess."

Just then, some of the women came to us and asked that very question.

"Sooba, sooba," Dick told them.

They turned around and ran quickly to the breaking surf and hollered out to their mates, "Sooba, sooba!"

They called out to their mates because they wanted a ride too.

"I told them they were 'surf boards', in case someone asks," Dick grinned.

Anyway, after hours of fun, one little guy finally caught a wave and found out he didn't have to paddle back, but could come charging in atop a wave's crest and though he tumbled several times head over heels when the board hit the sandy beach, he got up and did it all over again. Then everyone was doing it. I think Dick had really started something; he was always such a people-person. But I got an idea too.

"Dick, can I borrow your laser? I want to go up into the hills and get on top of that mountain to see what's left of my airship."

"Well, if you really have to do it, I'll just tag along. You go first and the rest of us will follow you, okay?" he laughed.

I knew he had really wanted to see this island, after nearly twenty-five years, but alone, and being the only edible 'white meat' available, he thought the little cannibal people might have found him very nourishing, if you know what I mean. Here in his hut, which they made for him, he was treated like their king and safe. Why push his luck?

Dick jabbered with some little men and they all seemed very scared to follow us up the mountainside. But when Dick shouted very loudly, "Pussies! Pussies!" they seemed to cower down and obeyed him.

"Is that word listed inside the little cannibal people's dictionary?" I asked Dick.

"Well, no, I made that up, but ol' Roger Benedict back at Harvard used to holler that out at our soccer opponent's team members and it always worked for him."

I just shook my head and laughed with him. Dick certainly had a fun side to him; I guess that's why his smile was so captivating to everyone.

The trek was slow, but the next morning those little guys had whacked a path with their machetes into the tropical forest's floor before us, and we had come at least a mile or more on the first day. Tired, we decided to camp out right where our bodies fell to the ground on some soft tropical leaves.

"I think we should all sleep in the trees tonight. I don't know, but some-time back I thought I heard a lion, or leopard's roar…me thinks?"

"Sleep in the trees? You got to be nuts! I am not movin' an inch. I'm all scratched up from the vines and my muscles ache. No, you sleep in the trees, we'll sleep right here."

Then he looked around us and saw many of the natives had already called it a day and had tied themselves up onto a tree's limb, and were snoring their little people snores.

Soon, we were the only ones on the ground. Dick and I both quickly shimmied up a tree and I knotted him in real tight with vines, because I remembered how in college he used to roll around in his bed at night and wake me up; I knew he'd fall out otherwise.

A kookaburra's call awakened us all, as he was excited that we had taken his resting place. We both got down, somehow, stiff as a board and hungry. The little people brought us some wild fruit and honey. I hadn't eaten honey since being with ol' Crow Foot back along the muddy Mississippi; that's when he got stung while stealing some honey from a hollow tree. That taste brought back fond memories.

We ate, then searched and found a rocky slope to ascend to the top. It wasn't hard at all to find my plane; it hung high in the trees and scared the little people half to death. Their fears of the unknown overtook them and some lit out as fast as their little tootsies could go. Dick stood fast, shocked at the advancements made since the First World War.

"Pussies, pussies!" Dick yelled out loudly. He summoned them all back and made his superiority known again to them. I laughed very hardily and embarrassed myself, for it was always shameful to critique another's courage.

The airship was upside-down; its rigid landing gear, made strong enough to repeatedly land upon an aircraft carrier's hard deck, was entwined in several treetops. With a little imagination, I visualized that if we could cut a few trees down, one at a time, the plane's weight would slowly bend the trees over, until the plane came down softly onto the ground. Not!

With the first blows of their tiny axes, the plane broke loose of its position and came clambering down. Dick and I scurried to get out of its way, as we had stupidly been standing on the wrong side, nearly right where it was headed to fall.

Several weak, shrill little voices chanted out from the people, "Pussies!" Giggles erupted and we got our touché. I think that's the last time Dick used those foul words.

The fighter plane had bounced up high off the ground upon its rubber tires, and then back onto the ground. It had flipped completely over while tumbling from the treetops and finally came to rest upright. There was visible damage to the one wing tank, which allowed the fuel to leak out upon the ground; the foliage was dead looking beneath the trees where the fuel had dripped. I quickly hopped up and peeked into the cockpit. There, on the brace where I had tied her, North Star gleamed; she wasn't warm at all this time and appeared to be fully charged.

"Thanks, Dargod," I spoke, and I put North Star back on my belt.

With a little banging around on some minor dents, here and there, my plane's structure was still airworthy and I imagined if there was still some fuel that I could possibly crank her over. Dick rubbed his hands upon the fuselage and asked what it was made of, certainly not the silks of 1900. I told him it was plywood and a sheet metal.

I showed Dick how to crank the prop, without his fear of it backfiring and slicing him in half. But he was too short to spin the prop quickly, so I showed him the ignition switch and the throttle, put him in the cockpit, and hoped he could nurse the Merlin into running by choking it…he was always a good follower of directions.

After several turns of the prop and no response from the engine, I got up into the cockpit to see if there were any old shot shell igniters…there were none, until one little person found them all, as he searched the crash landing area. He chose to barter for them as "finders were definitely keepers" here. I gave him my leather pilot's cap and he was very satisfied, but he looked as goofy as I felt that I always did.

The loud pop from the igniter shot shell sent all the little people to scattering, but the Merlin just sputtered. I had no fuel gauge, so I opened the gas cap, which was located behind the cockpit and then stuck a long stick in there to see if there was still enough fuel in it to run her.

I was surprised to hear Dick yell out so gallantly that he could get it to start, because he used to nurse his Model T's engine when it was wintertime in New York.

By gosh, the next time he tried, he got it running; but the timing had been thrown off and it was difficult to keep it running. I reached in and turned off the ignition, and when the noisy engine stopped, I told Dick I'd have to make adjustments on the carburetor and timing chain.

I reached into the cockpit's tool compartment and found the tools I needed. When I again spun the prop, it fired right up, and Dick had the engine whining at nearly half throttle. The plane started to lurch forward in the tall weeds. The little people were not afraid by then, and sat amused.

It was nice to tinker around with the Merlin again, I remembered Scott Field and my earlier days as an aircraft mechanic, but I also knew it was all for naught because there wasn't enough fuel in the main tank to get me ninety miles, or less. It was just a hopeful wish.

"What's wrong, Jamison?" Dick could read my face.

"Well, no matter how good it runs, there's only enough fuel to fly, maybe a hundred miles or less, that's provided we can even launch her off the cliff."

"Now exactly what kind of fuel does it take?"

"High octane airplane fuel," I reluctantly told him.

"Does that mean almost pure alcohol?"

"Well, a little oil would have to be mixed in for cylinder anti-friction and it might run, but not very well, I'm afraid. I'd have to readjust the carburetor to use it."

"You never came to any of my college parties, did you? I can make a dry martini with the best of them."

"I'm afraid there isn't that type of alcohol around for a thousand miles," I asserted.

"Where do you suppose my wonderful subjects get those fruity drinks they serve us?"

"Where?" I questioned.

"From my still, ol' buddy, my still," Clarkson told me.

Dick told me that he used fresh spring water, which the native women brought back from the interior every day inside their homemade clay jars, and then they put fresh crushed-up, mixed fruit inside and stopped it up with bamboo sticks to allow the gases to rise out. After a certain time, maybe a month, viola! Pure alcohol; after he drained away the squeezins' through a women's silk stocking he just happened to find one day in his pocket…that was Dick for you!

I didn't have a clue if it would work or not, but it was something to do and it offered us hope of getting off this isle and back to civilization.

I closed up the cockpit and placed a block under one wheel made from bamboo; but it really wasn't necessary.

Our trek back down the mountain was much easier. When I heard the faint grunts of wild hogs, I suggested to Dick I try out my seldom-used North Star; he said to go for it. So, motioning for the little people to sit tight, Dick and I eased through tropical bushes and found several pigs gnawing on old bananas.

I raised North Star and fired; her power had grown so much from the big radiation blast that there was nothing much left of the pigs, but lots of tiny curlicues. Dick walked over to where the sizzling porkers lie and examined the burnt crispy critters. He started sniffing around.

I was shocked when Dick actually picked up some pieces and put some pork crisps in his mouth to eat, "Crunchy, tasty, little bits of heaven," he said gleefully. "Try some! They're well done, no use to waste the effort." So I did.

"Yah, ummm, they are good! Needs some salt! See if our guests like them," I told him.

Then Dick summoned the little people. The little people quickly came forward and took a chunk each, which ignited their little delightful giggles. They really liked it and didn't stop at the skins, but inhaled the innards too, and the ears, and the snoots, tails, everything. Like piranhas, there was nothing left but the bones, a tribute to their cannibalistic way of life...I imagined then, what if they did that to me.

"You know, if I ever get back to the states, I might try to manufacture some of these crispy things. I bet with some seasonings they'd go good with the 'in crowd', if not, they'd make good fill for packaging material...think?" He was again thinking business.

"Let's go home. I can't wait," I told him.

Dick's small still only knocked out five gallons of brisk, fiery wine liquor, almost vinegar-like, and by its taste I knew it wasn't high-octane quality, but it sure gave us a buzz trying to experiment. I thought of trying to use the already made brew and refining it by an old Kentucky drip copper-coil-type still, which dripped out its condensation of pure white lightin', 120% proof alcohol, good enough to use as high-octane anything. Mixed with coconut oil, or fish oil, or both, it just might work!

Using the eighty-gallon damaged gas tank off the plane as a still pot and its fuel line coiled up, we knew it wasn't copper but when heated up, the wine condensed into about eighty gallons of pure alcohol. After about four months of watching and waiting, and collecting every drop, Dick said, "We've got enough."

I poured the first few gallons of our homemade fuel, mixed with about two cups of coconut and fish oils into the main tank to top it off. Then we reattached the one auxiliary tank back onto its hanger upon the wing, in which we had used a shark's cartilage to plug up the small hole.

There was an imbalance of wing weight when I filled it up completely, but I didn't mention that to Dick. I cranked the Merlin and she purred like a kitten...everything was go.

We all pushed the plane back as far as we could away from that cliff, four hundred long paces, and tied down the rear wheel to a tree. I was going to try and launch my ship by holding her down, then cutting her loose like upon an aircraft carrier deck.

Seventy-five gallons of white lightning-like fuel, mixed with coconut and fish oils were good enough, I calculated, for six hundred miles. We ended up with slightly more than that. I surmised that if our plane was stripped of the damaged gauges that were of no use, and I put in an old whiskey barrel we had found that was small enough to be inserted inside the fuselage with a fuel line attached to gravity-siphon it into the main tanks; we could add another two hundred miles, or more.

That's exactly what we did. I systematically removed the gauges, and levers, which gave us at least sixty pounds and plenty of extra room. The dash was a skeleton. I taped an old glass bottle vertically to the dash, so that I could establish a somewhat level flight.

Two months later, after I used North Star and Dick lit up his laser in a glorious blasting of the plateau's top, we etched out a six hundred feet runway to the edge of the cliff. If the engine stalled, over the top and down we'd go.

Having to tell his long time followers he was leaving them caused panic in the village. There was much ado, until Dick placed his hand upon a nice little fellow and said, "E pluribus Unum!" which he said, meant that this guy was their new leader. Only then did I realize Dick hadn't learned their language whatsoever, but made up every word along the way…it worked!

When it was time to crank the Merlin, which I was waiting until the very last minute to save fuel, I advised Dick of the predicament that we were in.

"Now gasoline weighs about ten pounds per gallon," I told him, "and the eighty-gallon wing tank has to be offset somehow before we leap off this high cliff, hell bent for leather." I needed him!

"Heck no, darn it, I won't do that! Forget it, buster! Why didn't you tell me this before I got all my hopes up?"

Needless to say, Dick was furious that I hadn't told him of my plan that I was going to tie him securely to the tip of the wing; out far enough to help counter-balance the auxiliary tank. I had traded back my goggles and pilot's cap for some white lightning to the little fellow who found my shot shells.

I forcibly placed my pilot's cap and goggles on Dick and promised him as soon as we were airborne and some fuel burned off that he could come into the cockpit. He still didn't want to do it and absolutely refused. It wasn't until I told him I would send someone back for him, if they could discover the longitude and latitude, because I had no clue where this isle lay in the vast Pacific, but I was leaving. He then reluctantly agreed to do it.

"I've been here for nearly twenty-five years, and no one but you ever showed up…I can't wait another twenty-five. Get all my stuff together, get me good and drunk and tie me down really well, for Dargod's sake!"

I secured him tightly, but we had used up all the spirits; he'd have to fly sober.

The new chief had the privilege of cutting us loose. I gave him a brand new 1945 buffalo nickel that I'd gotten before I left for my un-returnable last sorte to Nagasaki for luck; it was now almost three years old.

When the Merlin roared and it wasn't safe for her to be held back any longer, I signaled to the new chief and he cut the rope. My plane zoomed down the makeshift runway and then leaped off the cliff without as much as a sputter. Everything was good to go, even Dick, when he screamed out a long "Geronimoooooo" going over that cliff, just like we use to do when diving steeply upon a target. Though we were successfully launched, Dick lost hold of his laser and it was lost. It tumbled off the wing into the sea. Dick didn't even notice.

The morning sun was coming up and I flew east into the sun. Dick, however, was now scared stiff of the height and never looked up from his position for several hours. I had tied a rope to him and to the end of my canopy, so that he could scoot inch by inch over to me when he was ready. He finally lifted his head and looked at me. I motioned for him to begin to come to me, "ol' buddy!" If eyes could kill, I was a dead man.

It took an hour or more for the Merlin to burn off enough equalizing fuel weight, and then brave Dick scooted along the rope, inch by inch bless his heart, and finally reached up for my hand. I grabbed hold of him and pulled him inside. The wind nearly sent him sailing, but I held onto him tightly.

There wasn't enough room right there inside the cockpit, I told him, and he'd have to scoot down and lay under the empty dash, so he curled up his small frame and eased inside. It was cramped-up quarters to say the least, but we were homeward bound, Dargod willing.

It was nearing the noon hour and I figured we had flown over five hundred miles. I had noticed several barren isles, but nothing with the sign of civilization. I was flying by the seat of my pants and I prayed my direction was correct. We continued east.

More dauntless hours passed, but I really began to worry that we were going to fail, as there couldn't be much fuel left. We had come over seven hundred miles, maybe not far enough. My eyes searched the horizon to no avail…we just kept flying east.

The sudden miss in the engine's hum alerted me that the end was near. "Oh, Dargod, give me guidance," I spoke out loudly.

"There's something, there's something!" Dick hollered from his hidden position.

I searched the horizon but couldn't spot a thing that resembled an island. It wasn't. Dick was peeping through an emptied screw hole from removing a lever and he saw the surface of one of the tires. I asked him to hold on as we might be going down shortly.

Then, deep into that dusk-fading horizon, I saw it. It was just a tiny speck, but I had seen it many times before. It was good 'ol' home away from home, the USS Hornet, our aircraft carrier was in my sights and I hoped I could make her. She must have been returning to Pearl, I wasn't sure, but "thank you, Dargod!"

I rose up above the canopy to see if she was going or coming my way. But when the Merlin's prop clanked to a stop, I had no choice…I was headed in dead stick.

No one was there to wave me in, but I soon heard the top deck siren's scramble-alert repeated sounding of that familiar "Whooop-whooop-whooop", as I neared the deck's marked runway. I had been here before many times, it would be a piece of cake, but when I realized Dick was shoved against the landing gear lever and I couldn't possibly shove him down any farther to use it; I again prayed. I had attempted a belly landing once before on Scott Field's dirt strip, which I immediately learned then that it was not a very good idea; it tore up my plane. If I skidded onto the Hornet's deck wheels up, it probably wouldn't explode because the fuel was spent, but if I skidded over the top, with no stop-wires laid out, I'd be eaten alive by a churning ship's prop as the ship crossed on top of me…no, icy water felt better. So I tried to ease up off the port bow of the ship's travel direction, and told Dick we were about to take a cold dip in the sea.

"We're what!" Dick screamed out to me in terror.

I pulled him up from his curled up position and he was very stiff, but he was going to have to swim anyway, very quickly now. I knew that the ship was calling me on the radio, but they didn't know it wasn't working, because of that radiation blast. I could only hope they were telling me that they recognized my troubles and ol' Betsy, the ship's recovery helicopter, was heating up and would be ready to snatch us up out of the sea. I knew the captain had his field glasses on me from the helm's tower.

"Hold on tight, ol' buddy!"

My fighter skipped across the water like a thrown stone, and held its own against the white caps, but Dick suddenly bounced up and out of that cockpit like a Jack-in- the-box and he was gone. I peered back quickly at him and he was upside down, trying to right himself when almost two hundred yards away, I unharnessed, and then rode her out. She was sinking so fast that I quickly walked out onto the wing and slipped into the cold water unnoticed, I guess.

I saw Betsy hovering above the waterline behind me, the diver had already hooked up Dick, and Betsy had him dangling and squirming around helplessly on the cable, just like a caught fish…Betsy was a very good fisherman!

Apparently, the copter pilot thought Dick was the downed pilot as he hauled up the diver too and banked back towards the ship. When the copter landed, I saw Dick being carried onto the ship's deck and Dick was being smothered by personnel who attended to the downed pilots. But that ship just sailed on by me, without so much as a toot good-bye.

It was fifteen minutes, while my body chilled in that freezing water. I began to imagine Dick was unconscious and with my pilot's cap and goggles on they didn't know I was out there. Dick apparently hadn't told anyone about me, and since my airship had already sunk, I don't think they suspected there was another dumb fool fighting for his life to stay afloat. But, "my ol' buddy" must have finally realized I wasn't with him and then told my fellow warriors about me, because Betsy lifted off her high perch and headed my way, finally.

Hot java! Boy it smelled great and so did that aroma coming from the food in the mess kitchen. I ate with Dick at the very same table that I had sat with Tibbits when I discussed my Marietta's fate. After reading a Chicago newspaper's article about a man in Florida having gotten bitten twenty-one times by a red coral snake and lived, I became excited and almost went AWOL to get to that ringed snake to save my wife, I told Dick.

"Dick, now that we're alone, could we trade off some capsules? I think it could benefit us both, because there were times I needed a lengthy hiatus to rest away from my environment, just so I could continue at a much later date. But there also were times I wished to be restored more quickly. Do you agree?"

He opened his little pack and we traded off five capsules; that was enough.

The officer's voice on the intercom suddenly requested our appearances with the captain, and I knew it meant pronto, for me. Dick however was chilled to the bone and couldn't speak, so I asked Cookie to see to it he was taken care of, and suddenly delighted in myself knowing that we had done it!

A new skipper sat in the chair, as I removed my hat and stood at attention before him.

"At ease, Lieutenant, sit down. I'm sure you're exhausted; have one of my cigars and tell me how in the hell you made it back, three years later after your sorte?"

He listened amused to my lengthy report. He was dramatized by my efforts to fly off a cliff, and my courageous desire to return to my ship; he certainly was impressed to say the least.

"There will be a ceremony this afternoon on deck. Dwight Eisenhower is flying in to decorate you. Withdraw your new uniform and credentials from our PX, Colonel Dargod." I guess I had been posthumously greatly upgraded in rank.

There I was, at attention out on deck with the whole crew, adorned in my new Marine colonel's attire, standing tall, white gloves and all, representing the courage of my country, here on Earth.

Ike told me that I was a Medal of Honor recipient, as he placed the bright medallion around my neck in all its glory. Then the general thanked me for helping to save fellow American lives and to quickly end the war. It was the proudest moment of my life, and a returned salute from General Dwight David Eisenhower, followed by his handshake, made my heart flutter.

Then Ike bent closer to me and then whispered, "Off the cuff, tell me now, what the hell did you use to shoot off those steel bombay door's bolts, all the way from your fighter? Tibbits wants to know. He said the stream of bright light was spectacular."

Little did I know he was bound for great political things, for within the decade he became President of the United States. He showed his valor also. What the General failed to advise me though, was that I had been granted a post-service, honorable discharge, and really was now a civilian. I had served my country with distinction.

With little ado, the Hornet docked in Miami, Florida. We exited onto the platform, and finally I was in the venue of my prey. It had taken me almost four hundred years of searching and now I was punished in my mind by the thought that my Marietta was still waiting for my return after all this time.

Dick bid farewell, and boarded an east coast train to New York and told me he was in a hurry to patent his thoughts. Dick still had it and looked his teen-ager boyish self, still going, going, going, until he was gone. I guess he was another Martian genius really. I never saw him again personally, except on national TV several years later. He had become the master of the new music industry and was doing very well.

I began my immediate search of the poisonous red coral snake, by enlisting information from the local Miccosukee Indians. Indians were always honest with me and I felt close to each and every one I ever met, so I trusted their word…it meant something to them when they gave it.

John True Blood was a scholar and a chief. He knew of the deadly red coral snake and advised me if I wanted to die quickly, "Just go poking around in the Okeechobee swamp. I'm sure you'll find them there." He told me that it wasn't far away.

However, there was also a local man, he said, who had a sideshow along the great road and he had alligators, and snakes and possibly he had one. The name that John gave me sounded like the guy in the Chicago newspaper, but I couldn't remember who I had read that was bitten twenty-one times by the snake and lived. I immediately sought him out, and when I saw the great road was actually named Ponce de Leon Blvd., I knew I was headed in the right direction, for it was ol' Ponce who had brought me to the mouth of the Mississippi, many years prior…imagine that?

David Castillo was an avid collector of Florida's wildlife and he was licensed to harbor dangerous animals such as the alligator and the red coral snake for his exhibition's display. I found him one morning at his highway exhibit where he was showing a small group of people a very large alligator, which he claimed was a vicious man-eater. It lay there motionless like an enormous twenty foot log; a position he said was natural for its wanting some unknowing swamp animal, or an overzealous soul who wanted to pet him, to get near enough for him to leap up to devour them whole.

Then he poked the monster with what appeared to be a pointed bamboo stick and it lurched up quickly to scare the heck out of everyone, including me. He delighted in our retreat.

"The alligator, unless he's famished, won't eat you right away. Once he has you in his powerful crushing jaws, he usually pulls his victim into the deepest waters where he rolls over and over, until his victim succumbs. Then, he neatly tucks his meal under a drift or logjam, where it will decay, soften up and tenderize, until again, maybe a month later, he returns to devour the carrion." He made it sound so ghastly and fear-provoking.

He included, that throwing coins at the alligator's thick hide didn't affect him most of the time, but he may move. Then some pitched their pennies and nickels at the alligator in its large concrete pool home. There were lots of coins showing in the pool's bottom, but these onlookers were satisfied just looking. Then Castillo added.

"It has also been said that if he moves, the thrower will receive great luck."

Many reached into their pockets to toss more of their change, but the huge alligator just lay motionless as their coppers and silvers bounced off his rough hide. They had been fooled and they knew it.

But they all seemed to be happy vacationers, and just wanted an easy access to see just what the swamp creatures really looked like up close and personal, for a mere fee of three dollars each. There were twenty-three viewers here, not bad for twenty minutes work.

Though he looked and dressed his part as being on a safari, he also appeared to be too adolescent-looking for such a knowledgeable exhibitor. Mr. Castillo was quite extensive and very informative with his tour as we each passed by his displays. Always seeking questions, he now asked if there were any, so I asked, "Why did you not die when you were bitten by the red coral snake? Were they defanged like some cobra snake charmers I've witnessed have done to fool passersby?"

He glanced up quickly to see who asked that question and his eyes found me.

"I really don't know why, sir, maybe I became immune somehow or the bites were not that venomous, but believe you me, the first time that I was bitten, I just about peed my pants! I thought for certain that I was a goner. The snake was inside an alligator's nest of twisted up sticks, mud, and cattails in the Okeechobee Swamp. I was there searching for creatures to capture for this exhibition many years ago. As I removed some alligator babies from their freshly cracked-open shells, the snake was feeding there, and struck me on my hand. When I saw its colored bands, I really said a quick prayer!"

His eyes showed his frightful experience's look, and quickly the crowd laughed.

"Whom did you pray to?" I inquired.

He hesitated, then said, "Why, my dear God, of course." He looked insulted.

"What do you call your God?" I continued to distract him.

"I call him Jesus. He protects me."

I suspected he was somehow different; he had familiar ways about his looks that I just couldn't grasp. Was it the slope of his forehead, or the eyes that seemed too wide for his head being separated by the hooked nose? Was it his long firm jawbone or his long pointed ears? I don't know, but he sure reminded me a lot of Josef.

Josef had come from a huge family on Mars and some of their genes surely were found in a strange looking man like this. It had been so long though since then, and I wanted, no I prayed, that he was the key to my Marietta's return and mingled to see if he might be one of us; but I wasn't sure, so I challenged him more directly.

"Could it be you're from another world, since the bite left you with no ill affects?"

Now he became perturbed by my badgering and ignored my question, but stared hard at me as we moved in before that ringed red coral snake's exhibit.

"Here is your answer."

He opened a large glass display case containing many venomous snakes, which suddenly slithered up onto the glass as he placed his hand inside where he carefully grasped one of the red and black ringed snakes. The crowd stepped back quickly as he offered a chance for me to disprove him.

"Here, sir, feel his warmth for yourself. See if your God protects you too."

He was now taunting me for my questioning and my disbeliefs. When he squeezed the pit viper just enough to make it bite his arm, the crowd gasped in unison, but some also screamed in horror when it viciously struck him again. Visible marks showed and blood arose from two pricks of his skin. It truly had used its venomous fangs upon him.

"The poisonous venom of a red coral snake takes only seven seconds to kill a human," he eerily spoke.

He held out his wristwatch on one arm and the squirming snake in the other; and then he noted it was a minute, then two, before he kissed the viper on its flashing tongue's mouth and returned it to its glass case. Then, he went to a mechanical counter attached to an old wooden shed's wall and flipped the numbers that he said represented the number of times he had been bitten by the red coral snake; it read 542. He assured everyone that this was a special demonstration, for he seldom allowed himself to get bitten in his audience's presence.

I remembered seeing the "believe it or not" article that I read in the Chicago paper while aboard the Hornet only three years prior, and it had mentioned that he was bitten twenty-one times. He had either duped us, the number machine malfunctioned, or he was awfully busy here…maybe a little of all three.

"Thank you, ladies and gentlemen for visiting my exhibition. I hope it was as enjoyable for you, as it always is for me…good day, my exhibit's show is finished."

Everyone seemed to be thrilled as they exited his exhibits, but I stayed, to his dismay.

"Sir, my exhibition has been completed, if you want to remain in this dangerous environment, you'll have to join the others who are waiting for the noon tour, please leave now."

"Sir, I came here for another purpose, but I found you so intriguing that I developed other thoughts which haunt me. I once knew a man who resembled your fine features; his name was Josef Dargod, of Nazareth."

He stood there motionless, his steely eyes looked deep into mine, then he turned away saying, "So, one of you has found me."

The chill that spread up my spine almost made my knees buckle. Then this man turned back around and said, "Josef Dargod is my father."

"I am Jamison Dargod, your uncle. Marietta is my sister."

He immediately opened his arms and hugged me, just the way Martians always did and it felt wonderful. Then without anymore talk, he took my arm and we entered his home. There, seated on a large leather couch was Josef and my sister Marietta and some others…I was dumbfounded and speechless. They arose and we hurriedly embraced one another long, for it had been many years since our eyes had focused upon the other. Tears came freely and we sobbed, our eyes searched for untold questions, while looking upon one another's face and we could not begin to speak, except to raise up our eyes and say, "Oh, Dargod, thank you."

After a long enough time to regain our composures, we suddenly were refocused when David welcomed his new noon flock of visitors to his exhibit. They passed by the outside lanai and seemed spellbound by David's displays, and we could often hear the words, "Oh, looky here!" There were twenty, or so, inquisitive tourist visitors.

"Whew," she sighed in relief. "I think I need a capsule from this!" Marietta suddenly exclaimed, but then she quickly introduced her other children, all unbeknownst to me. They were beautiful, I told her.

"I, too, my wonderful sister and brother-in-law feel the stress, because for many years I have sought out this place, or the home of the red coral snake, but couldn't find it. To find you all here, somewhat depresses me…if only I had known…for there is someone who has my heart and still beckons me to restore her; my own deceased wife named also Marietta. She lies in a vault on the isle of Jamaica, awaiting my return for over four hundred years." The very thought of her choked me into tears, but I continued.

"But relatives, I'm delighted you all are safe and I am refreshed by my sister's retained magnificent beauty; and I am happy for that."

Like any woman would, Marietta primped her hair, realigned her dress and looked into a wall mirror. She had come the distance unscathed by time.

"We have followed your words when you wrote to Josef about the life-restoring affects upon Earthlings, which the red coral snake's venom provides. There were many relatives we hoped to have helped to be reborn, by including it in the mixture. It has worked well, except some have not responded to its injection. Their bodies don't decay; they just stay in an indeterminate state," Marietta told me.

"What about our life ship?" I asked.

"The Nova may have suffered, for an explosion upon the Sinai Mountain sent the Earth skyward and down flowed red hot lava in river quantities. We dare not trod there before we left," Josef advised.

"But how did you get here?" I wanted to know.

"It was a long journey. After the crucifixion, we left the desert searching for more compassionate people and to the Mediterranean we ventured, until one day a merchant's vessel took us to a land of light-skinned dwellers in a place called Eurasia. There we stayed in comfort until the war. We fled the country by ship to this fine land and found your goal by chance. Josef was bitten by the red coral snake and actually felt better than he had for many years. His aching body immediately rejuvenated, and he has not used a capsule since then. So, we surmised it was good to be near the snake."

"I must think, is Jesus around?"

"You just spoke with him, could you not recognize his father's good looks?" Josef chuckled. "He calls himself David for his disguise, named after one of his many true followers, and his Castillo name was the name on the mailbox when we purchased this home and business. It was a Laundromat and it fit the area's people's names. But it is Him," Josef assured me.

I looked out into the yard and saw a different man. He was very affluent looking in his garb, but very temperamental, as I remembered. He was scolding an obviously inebriated young person who had cursed him as a con artist for all the coins he'd thrown without the alligator moving just once, or even batting its eye.

So, I immediately arose and assisted in the matter. Hiding behind the wooden shed, I poked the gator with a long stick and he lurched high up against its retainer wall to almost capture the young intoxicated man's extended arm after he reared back and threw his coin as hard as he could to justify his claim.

The nearness of his escape and the alcoholic content of his brain caused him to run screaming around blindly and then finally out through the exit gate. He stumbled once, but found security in his new flat-head '49 Ford, and then took off squealing its tires as he accelerated the car until he was well out of sight. It was a new phenomenon for Jesus, but an ordinary occurrence to the drunken souls that I had met along my way.

"Great thanks to you, my dear uncle. I remember when you were in need of my help, now you have repaid me, for I had lost my wits with him and was about to strike the ignorant fool." Jesus had made his journey well also.

"Well anyway, I'll count many of his tossed silver coins to help me build a church to my liking. This place is very demanding, but offers much reward during the main tourist season."

There was almost fifty dollars in change at the bottom of the clear alligator pool.

When the last crowd left, Jesus and I spent hours discussing his travels. He liked what he had accomplished, because far and wide, in good faith, or in vain, his name was repeated throughout the world.

"Nephew, I need some of your intelligent expertise."

He cocked his suspecting head and squinted.

"I have a wife, a beautiful, mortal Earthling wife, but she died almost four hundred years ago on the Isle of Jamaica. I gave her the AlovectorP23 by injecting it into her dead body and placed her in a sealed tomb's vault upon a mountainside. I hoped to restore her to the living with the use of the red coral snake's venom. How do you suppose I could take a snake all the way there and have it bite her?"

"You can not. You need not, for I myself can give you my blood, which is sufficient to restore any lost soul to the living. I am the way, my father told me so."

"Don't be so undignified and conceded with me, my good nephew, for if you have forgotten, my father is Dr. Dargod; he's not yours."

A sudden stir in his mind came to him and he was very angry, but speechless. I placed my arm around him and reminded him that I too had made that journey.

"You were placed in a deep hypnotic state and couldn't be held accountable for the feelings you have of yourself, for my father had implanted them in your mind and you served my father well. Through you, with your enthusiastic obedience to Him and teachings, Dr. Dargod's name is remembered always. People on this planet are for the better because you have spread his words of peace." He seemed at ease.

"Is it possible, that you have the venom already embodied heavily in your bloodstream by the bites and that is the power you possess?" I asked.

He pondered, and then said, "Maybe you have discovered my true powers, for I have been bitten fifty times."

"Your sign reads you have experienced well over five hundred bites."

"Look closely, I inadvertently tacked my first sign right next to this home's address and somehow it blended right in with the sign that I tacked up and became a big number…Dargod forgive me for my continuing to use it for mortal gains."

"Well then, what if I myself feel the warmth of that coral snake's fangs; fill my own veins with his venom?"

"That, my uncle, I can not tell you for certain. It might work, and it might not, or you might suffer unknown difficulties that haven't affected me."

"Tell me about your first encounter, was it a big snake and was the bite long and deep?"

"All the red coral snakes that I have seen are about the same length; some are just fatter and older."

"I have to get to my Marietta; I promised her before I left her, I must."

"One thing I am certain, my uncle, you must love the woman to risk your being."

"Was it not you, my nephew, who did the same for your followers, nailed to a cross?"

I planned my feat early the next morning. We celebrated our togetherness during the eve. The stares we gave each other were the same we had given once when we were catapulted into the atmosphere from Mars for the first time in space. We were worried never to see one another again then and it now came back into our thoughts, should the experiment fail; I was ready.

The hiss of a startled snake can give one other desires, such as running away. I had hugged my sister and Josef, and then hugged my nephew before he opened the glass door. There, lying curled up before me, were several red coral snakes ready to strike my extended hand. Before me was life and death all combined into one.

"Ouch! Ouch! Ouch!"

Several serpents attacked in unison as my arm showed traces of pricks and blood oozed; it was done. My heart was racing, though their strikes hardly could be felt; it really was less painful than I imagined. Five minutes expired before I did, thankfully!

"You have survived my uncle; you may breathe easier," Jesus spoke with admiration. Then we hugged again, the Martian way.

Moments later, I felt stronger, younger, and full of strength. The serpent's venom was working quickly, almost instantaneously. My first response was, "Thank you, Father!" Then I looked at Jesus to see his manner. He was accepting my words well.

"Now is the time I must go to Marietta. I will use my blood transferred into hers and we will be one again. I must bid you all ado, without so much as a second's delay; for my urge is stronger than anything I have ever felt for hundreds of years." Needless to say, I felt very virile, like a stag in rutting season. I immediately took my leave.

The plane rose suddenly from the turbulences and I wished I had listened to the airport's weather advisory that a tropical depression was forming in the Caribbean and flights may be changed or cancelled due to severe weather. The Air Corps Marines flew in all weather, but their planes had 900 horsepower engines, and if we couldn't get away from the storm, we'd go over or around it, but never through it like the "ishcabibbles" who were flying this plane did.

The sign read "fasten your seatbelts" and I already had, because the shaking of the frame told me we were going for the ride of our lifetimes, or demise. The sudden up, then down motions made me queasy and I was certain I needed the barf bag. Then the dive started. The eye of the hurricane was sucking our plane into its downward funnel. The cold air from above was falling into a tropical depression and onto the hot waters of the Caribbean which drew moisture from above. I wish the Jamaican Sunshine Airline had just turned around. I became angry at the thought as why this was happening to me.

I unbuckled my seat belt and went forward without the usual resistance from the lone stewardess; she was clinging on to her mike, yelling to be calm in Spanish, but her trembling voice sounded unconvincing to her frightened passengers.

I looked into the cockpit, just as the pilot and copilot were putting on parachutes and were about to leave the cabin via their escape door. I had no idea that they thought they would be safer inside a hundred and fifty miles per hour twister than trying to fly that plane, but they did, and did jump out when I hollered for them to halt!

Here I go again. "Oh, Dargod, guide me through this peril!"

I immediately removed the autopilot, not that it helped at all and hoped the plane's frame could withstand what I had planned for her. The eye of a hurricane is nearly quiet in the middle and I fought tooth and nail to head directly for it. My speed had doubled and I strained to know the altimeter's reading on a straight downward dive. With my Merlin I could have penetrated the weakest wall, but this crate needed more speed and now I had it.

When the altimeter read twelve hundred feet from a ten thousand foot fall, I jerked back upon the wheel for the ailerons and elevator with everything I had. At almost seven hundred miles per hour, aided by the fall and the twister's winds, I barely skimmed over the surface of the floor and headed into the weak side wall with all she could muster. It sounded as though the crate was coming apart with its corrugated tin rattling outside, but somehow, some way, I steered that baby a hundred feet above the sea waters and zipped through the weakest sidewall unscathed.

Suddenly, it was clear and the tropical sun was beaming and the hurricane was behind us. I realized I had no clue where the airport was. The stewardess had regained her composure and came to the cockpit to tell the pilots that almost everyone had literally lost their lunch and she couldn't handle it. Then she walked in on me behind the wheel.

Her eyes grew wide when I tried to explain "no hablo Espanol" and that I was a real pilot and was flying that thing, because her friends had jumped out to save their own lives…"Compadres…pilotos…vamoosed! Aeropuerto, air…port? Por favor!"

I hadn't spoken Spanish for four hundred years and my vocabulary was virtually nil.

She was a smart little senorita cookie as she picked up the mike and sent out an SOS to the airport. Then she asked them for an English translator to help me.

"This is Kingston, Jamaica tower calling Jamaican Sunshine flight 222, come in."

I told the fellow that we had been through a hurricane and the pilots jumped ship. I told them my instrument's position and that I needed bearings for the Kingston Air International, and then regave them my bearings.

"Set your course to 245, that's 2, 4, 5, you're twenty minutes away…good luck."

When I set that bird down on the tarmac, the wheels didn't even burn or squeal one bit, before the DC-8, two-engine airship smoothly came to a stop in front of the airport terminal. I was immediately smothered in kisses and hugs from the passengers.

When the airport personnel came forth wide-eyed pointing randomly, I ignored their excitement. I guessed they were anxious to see who had saved their airship as their happy passengers surrounded me. But after one put his hand over his mouth in a look of horror, I turned around to see that the plane's corrugated metal sheets covering had been completely ripped away to bare fuselage and there was no tail, as it had fallen completely off upon touchdown and lay spewed out in a long trail of pieces upon the runway from the point of touchdown. I was then really sick to my stomach…"Thank you, Father!"

The airline eventually gave me an award, a free lifetime pass, which I promised myself I would never use. But I, Jamison Dargod, had received a very warm and much appreciated "welcome home greeting" on my return after four hundred years. Of course, they didn't know anything at all about that. I looked toward that mountain.

The first thing I did was to find bus transportation to the old plantation where I had once been employed as its "big boss mon". When I finally stepped from the bus, I immediately saw that the banana plantation had remained the same, almost, all of this time; whoever was doing the work here was doing a fine job. When suddenly I heard the old familiar call being sung out, "Dayo, dayo!" I knew I was really home and upon my home's isle of Jamaica of almost three quarters of a century. The familiar call sounded just like Diego's call and it brought back many memories of my wife, my father-in-law Diego and his family, and also of my illusive son Diego. It made me feel wonderful inside. I stepped forward with an enlightened mind's foot speed.

All the workers in the banana tree forest came up quickly to the main building, which now was much larger and surrounded by storage sheds, cooled by refrigeration. It all was certainly a big improvement to the operation. I went to the call and stood away while the "big boss man" told his employees that the passing hurricane had damaged all the banana crops on the other isles. Because of this, and since it had missed them this time, bananas would bring much more money in the market, so if they all worked harder they would all share more money. It looked like a very profitable crop. There was much happiness and it brought tears to my eyes remembering the past.

Then I saw it, it was the opening among the trees that led through the forest and up onto the mountainside. Up there, in a sealed tomb, lay the body of my wife, still waiting for my return. I slowly was drawn to the path.

I suddenly felt a hand upon my shoulder and turned to see who had halted me.

"Yo, mon, where do you think you are going, mon?"

His voice was stern, but pleasant. I expected to suddenly see Diego standing there behind me. The Jamaican "mon" stood taller than I immediately imagined. I looked up into his brown eyes and by the big white-toothed smile on his face and I just hoped the machete he held wasn't meant for me.

"Hello, mon, I am Jamison Dargod, mon…who might you be, mon?"

He stood there amused and smiling brightly; looked me up and down, and then to my surprise he hugged me tightly. I was shocked.

"Welcome home, my father," he told me.

But I did not recognize his face and thought at first it was a terrible mistake.

"Who are you?" I asked weakly.

"I am your first born Diego, named after my mother's father. I also am the big boss mon here; what took you so long?"

I actually thought I was having heart failure, for the only son I knew that had been born to Marietta and I had his brain on exhibit inside a jar that was upon a shelf at Harvard University.

"How can this be?" I asked of him.

"What do you mean, you are still here, are you not?"

"I mean, I saw your brain, the label read it was you, killed in a bank robbery, and it was stored in a jar of formaldehyde…how?"

"Oh, that," he laughed. "It was a bad joke gone wrong, I guess. I placed a cow's brain in the jar as a joke, that's all. Why, is it still there?"

"Yes, it is! Finding it gave me sickness and cold chills. I read the label, but, but…"

"No buts about it, mon…it was sick, and I'm sorry, Father…well how do I look now?"

I stood there with very mixed emotions, and as a father might, I wanted to spank this child of mine for wrongful deed, but also wanted to hold him tightly and never let go again…I did the latter.

"I came back for your mother."

His eyes told me that he didn't know of my power to restore her. So I hugged him again, and he took me inside his home. I guess he thought I had come to visit her tomb.

Diego was a bachelor; his family had died of small pox in the new world and though he had survived, he wanted no other love, and soon left the colonies to return to his mother; but she was dead already. There would be no more Dargods being born to our family in its future, I immediately thought.

I couldn't help wanting to stay next to him, for I was now looking upon his mother's nose, ears and her eyes; and he certainly also had her chin. We had not been very close in my younger, earlier years, and I remembered that well, and how now I might rectify that, so I hugged him again, this time the Martian way.

There was so much to tell him and I learned so much from him also, as we sat for hours explaining; he didn't pause but for a moment to give orders to his foreman who came and asked for help in the business. Then we went right back to learning.

First of all, he told me that his mother Marietta's vault was still maintained and had become sort of a point of interest for vacationing travelers who were interested in the isle's history; how nice that was. But he arose from his seated position with joy when I explained my venture here was to restore her life by Martian means. Again we hugged in much happiness.

He had learned of his Martian family's being and their plight from Marietta when he was very young, but was told to keep it secret; and again from a voyager who was looking for Jamison Dargod here on the island, and took Diego into his confidence. The man's name was Clarkson, Diego recalled. Diego told him I had left the isle troubled, but never knew why, unless it was his mother's death, and he ached also.

Since I had recently left Dick in Miami, it must have been one of his Martian relatives. But that Clarkson had left long ago and hadn't returned since.

I asked Diego of a hospital or doctor with whom he was knowledgeable. He then asked if I was ill, but I explained I needed the paraphernalia of a blood transfer kit to place my venom-laden blood into Marietta's veins to begin her resurrection.

A new foundation called the Red Cross had begun, he told me, taking blood donations on the isle to restock the hospital supplies at Kingston. The voluntary organization had been established during the earlier world wars for wounded soldiers, but only recently had found their way to Jamaica to help victims of hurricane disasters. They now helped everyone during trying times with their physical help to restore populations with disasters.

"I do know one nurse who may offer us some assistance. I'll call her now, she's off work," Diego delighted.

A telephone call to Marabeth and we were in business, and as a matter of fact, she said she'd perform the service free for Diego. But she wanted too much information and too much of Diego's attentions and affection, so Diego just got her to donate the bags, tubes and needles; I supplied the blood.

It was with great hope, and much pain from an unskilled hand that finally found the vein in my arm from which to draw my blood; it was my own. Diego suddenly became ill when he tried to sink the needle. But after releasing the band and squeezing my hand several times as Marabeth had showed Diego, life flowed quickly into the storage blood bag. I drew four, two more than the usual and felt light-headed and dizzy. I lay down on Diego's couch and elevated my feet upon some pillows and allowed the emptiness of my brain to drink again…I resumed normalcy in an hour or so.

Now I was ready to make the trek to the mountainside's vault and bring back my wife Marietta. From my recall, I remembered how well I had secured the vault's construction and I thought North Star might just come in handy, so I put her in my pack. Unlike so many of the other times I had laboriously hiked up the steep slope, Diego summoned me to his Willy's Jeep, the leftover variety from the war, which was still the mule of my fellow Marine and Army infantrymen. We rode up together on a new macadam road that was built for tourists to drive up there.

I felt like a colonel who was being chauffeured by the first class private…well, I was a colonel once, if only for a day. The grind that took most of the day in the past, took only twenty minutes on a winding hardtop roadway. I primped my hair in the passenger side rearview mirror expecting to see my Marietta very shortly looking back upon me with her beautiful brown eyes; I could hardly wait. But with one thought, and that was if I didn't succeed, I became lame and scared and afraid to look upon the tomb.

A slow loitering tourist was the last among many tour bus visitors to get back aboard. We waited impatiently to be alone, and then Diego closed the gate at the road's opening to stop further traffic. I looked upon the tomb where I had hidden the lifeless body of my wife and became horrified something might go wrong. But it was Diego's mother's teachings that he should always venture into the unknown, because by passing it up only left many yearnings and doubts.

"Father, if we don't try, Mother will be angry, for you promised her you'd try; it's the chance we have to take. We'll do it together for I too can not wait to greet her…we can do it!"

Diego gave me the strength and determination to succeed. I surveyed the vault that was built by crafted masons and tried to visualize what North Star could do to reconstruct an opening that was designed to be permanently sealed. I pictured her coffin inside and where it must be and withdrew North Star.

"What the heck is that thing?"

I suddenly realized that I hadn't told Diego about the power of North Star.

"This, my son, is a Martian weapon given to we travelers who last left Mars. My father advised to use it only in dire need and otherwise it should remain dormant and hidden from view. It has the power of a magnum blast like an atomic bomb, or the slicing ability of a surgeon's scalpel that can draw a picture onto solid rock if necessary. Let me now show you the power of North Star. I brought North Star to the rise and aimed her brilliant red beam upon the top of the tomb's side and drew her powers with the pull.

Zap! Zap! Zap! North Star tumbled tons of solid granite stone, the exact place I had chosen for Marietta to lay in state. Diego was awestruck and speechless. When the dust had settled, I had neatly carved a huge slice from the tomb's edge, exposing a cave. A sudden whoosh of stale air filled our nostrils and I knew we had succeeded.

The coffin where Marietta lay was now before us, but I couldn't get the courage to open its seal. Diego stepped forward and released the locks that held my Marietta's body and lifted the lid slowly.

"Your husband is home," I whispered to my lovely Marietta. She lay exactly as I remembered, still beautiful, still unharmed by her time in limbo; the AloevectorP23 had served her well. I began to tremble as I bent down and kissed her cold lips once more and looked upon the face that had launched me on a four hundred year search for that red coral snake. She was all that I remembered, even after all the illness, she looked like she was twenty. I continued to look upon her, as did Diego, but he was more rational.

"Let's do it now, Father, Mother is waiting. The time is now," he encouraged me.

I took one last long look and searched for a vein to place the needle, but her thin arms showed no sign of a possible place.

"Father, I learned at Harvard in my anatomy classes and remember the carotid artery, which lies vertically along the side of the neck is the main flow to the heart and brain; here let me find it on her neck."

He placed his hand lightly upon his mother's neck and felt the path of the carotid, and then he pointed to the place where I should insert the needle. I took a deep breath, but stopped short.

"Dear Father, please give me the guidance to restore my Marietta, for she is my chosen one as your Tara."

I felt eased then and without delay inserted the needle and secured its position with tape, just as Marabeth had instructed Diego. The blood traveled down the clear tube but found resistance at the point, so Diego massaged the neck there and the flow began slowly into my love.

It took an hour until the first pint bag was empty, and there was no noticeable improvement in Marietta. The second took the same, without results.

"Maybe it will take some time," Diego said.

I had waited many years and I suspected now my venomous coral snake bites may not have been as potent as I'd hoped, so with the two more completed transfers of blood, I finally withdrew the needle. We just had to wait.

The hours became days and Diego advised the community that his great, great, great, grandmother's tomb was now closed to the public for renovation. They concurred with his wishes and didn't suspect anything. We still waited for a sign, any sign that would show us the venomous mixture was sufficient; I began to doubt.

A week passed, then two, and on the third week the community was questioning what was taking so long, so they sent a tourism employee who came through the locked gate to ask personally what the problems were we had encountered. When he saw no workers, he came inside through the opening and surprised us.

"Perverts, just what do you think you are doing opening that casket?" he screamed at us.

The little man was an American and he was losing money on his tickets to show interesting sights to his bus tourists. He wanted accountability.

"You, sir, are trespassing upon our sacred ground. This land, this whole mountain is deeded to the Dargod family, of which I am one. We came to investigate the story that my dear relative was actually lost at sea and didn't lie in state as your commercial advertisements claimed. I believe we will close this place forever and stop the tourist trade, for we must do the costly upkeep of this park-like setting and you get the rewards." Then Diego turned his back on the man.

"Oh, please don't be upset now. I can see you have already verified there is a body, I suspect soon everything will resume…please forgive my intrusion." He then left without further threats.

"Diego," I asked, "where did you learn to tell such a quick, false tale?"

"I thought you told me you also graduated from Harvard!" That was that!

When the weeks became a month, a month became six, I thought all hope was lost and I became as depressed as when Marietta first passed. I had lived a good life, strange but often rewarding and Diego was my last prized possession.

I discussed with Diego that I was getting very tired now; the tense-filled waiting for my Marietta to return to the living had put a strain on us both. I also told him that I had received new capsules from Dick Clarkson that he said had restored him in only hours, AloevectorP25, a different mixture than the ones I had received from my father. I was about to tell him that I was going to give him those capsules, along with all of mine, and also the possession of North Star. He looked angry, but held his peace; until I told him I no longer wished to be alone without his mother.

"Damn you, your pity is self-serving, for I must mean nothing to you, I your own blood! Wait, sir, I'll just join you in this demise and we both can fill a coffin."

He took North Star from my holster and put it to his head.

Trying not to further his anger, afraid he might carry out his threat, I asked, "Then tell me, my son, just what I must do?" His answer was simple.

"Why don't you just try one of those quick-acting capsules from your friend Dick, maybe they might work, but for Jesus' sake, don't give up on Mother, or me!" Tears then flowed from his eyes and he handed back over my North Star.

"Okay, maybe I'll take one," I told him.

Then I asked him to please stay with me as I journeyed quickly away into the state of rest from the pill, and when I awoke relieved of my burdens, I would work to fulfill my promise to her, even if it were eternity. He agreed.

Then Diego handed me my pack with my stored capsules. My disturbed wits caused me to be careless and unknowingly I reached inside and withdrew out one of my own capsules and swallowed it.

"Father, the capsules you showed me were in this case," as he pulled out a smaller case of bluish color and mine were inside a red case.

I had taken the capsule that extended my sleep long, and although it was accidental, my psyche might have made me do so because I was depressed. I asked him to put me by Marietta when he could and hoped he'd forgive me.

"I love you, my son. Keep me in your thoughts and I shall again return one day. Then, you and I will seek out the ship that brought me here and I will take you to meet my parents; it will be a most exciting adventure I assure you…good-bye."

The capsule began its relaxing hold upon my body like a gentle blanket being placed upon me. I last saw Diego standing over me and he was reaching out for me; then deep sleep enveloped me and I was gone for four hundred years.

Nothing is forever, life, riches, pain, and death, nothing. It was 2350, by my calculations, the immediate world that I had left behind in my mind had vanished, and I suddenly awakened to a cold chill embracing my skin and I was lying on a concrete slab. When I knew I was alive in my mind, I opened my eyes. I was outside in the cold weather lying beside a tall spaceship. It was Nova, no the USA Saturn, it read; bigger than Nova it stood. I had miraculously awakened back on Mars, somehow, some way. How could this be?

I was stiff, my body had lain for four hundred years motionless, and now I was asking my legs to climb the steep ramp up into the doorway of this strange spaceship. I rose up cautiously and pointed my toes in the ramp's direction, expecting the lack of gravity to help me arise. But the weight of my being felt no such relief and I was wobbly and slow, but I grabbed onto the rail and made it to the top, then slowly peered inside.

There, in neatly arranged airtight capsules, not unlike the ones on Nova, were my family; wife Marietta, son Diego, Josef and sister Marietta, nephew Jesus and twelve others whom I didn't immediately recognize. They were all in a sleeping state of limbo, probably from the capsules I had possessed. They all looked peaceful and undisturbed, so I made my way to the dash and examined the calendar of electrical flashing seconds, which kept repeating themselves in ten second intervals.

"Hello, my son Jamison, how do you feel now?" a voice spoke out behind me.

I whirled around quickly to discover Dr. Dargod, my own father. He was standing there elegantly attired in a golden space suit. Behind him in a co-pilot's seat was my lovely mother, Tara. Both had been restored and I was thrilled.

We all quickly embraced the Martian way, and I felt the soft touch of my mother's arms once again, a thought that lingered in my mind always. It was a joyous moment, which I had waited for many lifetimes to enjoy. Finally I was appeased in my soul.

"But how, how?" was all I could ask.

"First, sit down next to your mother and buckle your lifebelt," and I did.

He then began, "We're going on a long journey, my wonderful son, and I'm afraid you aroused before I could place you inside your own capsule for travel, so I thought it best to put on delay our taking off, so that I could update you about your past life and the future life that you may encounter; for again this is just an experiment for us.

"Most important of all, thank you for helping to return your mother and I to life, by providing the way for your son and wife to travel to Mars. They alone took it upon themselves to fly up and get us and inject the anti-venom, which I had planned for someone to do. It took over twenty-five hundred years, but my mixture proved its worth, for here we are as new."

"Are we preparing to go back to Earth? I think you'll both really like it there. It's a beautiful world with many countries and many different peoples. I knew many wonderful, important people there, and I will be proud to introduce you both when we arrive." His eyes would not meet mine then.

"You have been under a long time and before I tell you everything, I best tell you first that Marietta awakened from her death and is alive and well. You kept your promise to her and your wife loves you; she told me so herself. That was her message to you before I placed her in the capsule. Son, she is a beautiful Earthling and now possesses eternal life too.

"Diego, your fine intelligent son, but only one of my grandsons, is a very intelligent man who orchestrated everything and flew the Nova untrained with the help of my written instructions and Marietta's assistance; but only after he successfully blasted Nova free from its own tomb inside the exploded Sinai volcano, which I had mapped out and planned for your first place of landing. His stress caused me to have him ingest a capsule of long length, because he needs the rest.

"Earth, like Mars, has become a political pawn of chemical disasters, like the blasts that ruined Mars; their results have hastened the death of the planet by unsealing the environmental covering surrounding the whole planet. Thus, the Earth has lost its protective shield and she warms quickly."

"Maybe, if you use your great knowledge you can save her," I pleaded. "Her seas are the bluest to match her skies, just as Mars once was, and just like Mars had been, her trees are many and wave in the clean air breezes. There's heat at its equator and even snow which covers the planet's top and bottom like Mars, with fresh ice water reserves almost a mile thick at the top and bottom...I think Earth is worthy of your expertise, I pray you at least attempt something to save her."

He turned his back to me and pulled a lever that closed the big door and I began to feel uneasy, for I had just awakened from a long rest of four hundred years and didn't expect to return to that state again of being unconscious for centuries.

Then Father pushed a button, which opened a sliding porthole and summoned me over to his side to see its panoramic view. I released my harness and went to him. There, I saw the barren burnt plain of the Martian wasteland, the Martian mountains of black soot, which rose into the blackening acid-rain clouds that billowed high into the sky. There were orange bursts of light cloud plumes coming from distant volcanoes that were exploding. Mars was still a scary and depleted land.

"Look hard, my son, for your last time. Remember this always in your mind."

I'd seen this all before, I told him, when we had left Mars upon our maiden flight to Earth, I said, and now I wondered what was so amusing to him for showing me this small porthole's view and this display of an ugly sight.

Mars hadn't changed at all. It was still very depressing to me, for the whole Martian environment had been suddenly destroyed before me back then, and it all had deeply etched its memory into my youthful mind; so strongly that sometimes I dreamt of it being a true hell.

"Do you want Earth to end up like this?" I begged. "Jesus has spread your words of peace on Earth; you are considered the Earth's supreme Savior."

My father smiled at me, placed his arms around me, hugged me and he told me that it all was for naught. I immediately became upset for I too had believed in His words and tried to follow only his "Ten Commitments", which had been driven into my brain a thousand, repeated times aboard Nova, and also upon Earth. I had used them exactly as I could, without question, and sometimes was ridiculed for being a religious fool. I then told him so.

Dr. Dargod had become complacent, I then thought; a liar, a hypocrite, I suspected. My own father was letting Earth down by his unwillingness to use his vast knowledge to make that world a better place for us; again I told him so.

"I should have immediately told you, I guess, before I became your bitter target of dissention. I did use my knowledge upon Earth, but no one listened, except the travelers who are with us now. The others have expired because of their refusal to find peace among the multitudes and segregated into separate beliefs and ways. I shared my knowledge with Jesus and Diego to help build this life ship and each is equally responsible for its superiority to Nova, your first conveyance."

Suddenly this terrible thought began to stir upon my mind, and he knew it by my eyes and led me to my place. Then he buckled my lifebelt harness and told me that he loved me, and then he said to me, "My son, oh, my son, you poor soul, you all tried so hard, but this is your Earth, there is her final view through that open porthole," he pointed. "She has succumbed, as Mars had, that's why we are removing ourselves to a different planet of another solar system."

I was devastated by his words. He then turned and left me in my place as he went to the multi-instrument dash panel and flipped many switches and pushed several buttons in a special sequence.

"This is the galaxy map which will take us there; it is the autopilot's given directions of destination for this ship." He slid a disc into a slot and turned it on at the panel.

I saw the red flickering numbers suddenly stop at ten, then it descended in numbers until it read zero. A mighty surge upward kept me spellbound inside my position, and that tremendous force held me in my place. So, I could barely breathe, much less speak back to him.

I could see through the porthole the last views of my Earth leaving below us as we were launched and ascending quickly into the darkened atmosphere. We had now begun another long journey through space; this time I was awake. I eventually began to feel the weightlessness of space and the feeling of the freedoms of movement.

Then, away from our presence, many light years later into our travel, the Earth erupted into nothingness; a cold, solid ball of dust and iron, just as all the galaxy stars had done for zillions of years before her and continue to do to this date.

We had again begun travel afar to another developing, uninhabited sphere to amplify our species; it was part of that repetitive sequence. Father began telling me of his own thoughts, and I listened intently while we rode into space together for a first, as father and son.

For it definitely is someone, or something else of higher being, I learned, far greater than my scientist father, Dr. Dargod; who himself had used a dropper and a mixture of substances, which he stirred and let mingle before he placed it all in several different capsules to watch its affects upon us.

"So does this someone or something watch over us?" I questioned.

"Yes," was his answer.

"There is a uniquely diagrammed puzzle within us all. Each of us are being made individually, born of many variables with only our own learned weak knowledge, combined with our strong self-survival-seeking desires to guide us through the heavens of this immense galaxy as we move and search from place to place. This master wonder watches us from many views and has much interest in how we perform, how we populate, how we respond to each other in trying times, and how we gather together to quarrel after we have satisfied ourselves and have become fat with our own designs; and especially after we had set and won our fortunes and refuse to share. These are his interests. If we falter, he tweaks the mixture to help us continue along our way to achieve our goals, and his.

"His, maybe theirs, or even hers, or its eyes are always upon their creations, each one of us; each Earth-like ball planet that whomever suspends it twirling in its planned vacuumed environment, watches over it all," Father explained.

"It sounds like we are just experiments, like in the big jars of a science class at Harvard, which held minute algae, mold, germs and amoebas. Are we only an experiment?" I questioned.

"Nothing more, nothing less."

A HUG
"THE MARTIAN WAY"

978-0-595-82655-1
0-595-82655-5

Lightning Source UK Ltd.
Milton Keynes UK
UKHW040627081221
395271UK00002B/13/J